"Does your fiancée know you make a habit of kissing other women?"

"Not other women." He folded his arms. The material of his shirt strained across the expanse of his chest. "Just you."

"And what does that mean? I don't count?" Silence answered her question. The realization cut her to the quick. "You don't think I'm worth much, do you?"

"Abigail's a woman of breeding. Hell, her uncle owns—"

"Your integrity?" Kit unleashed her own anger. "Just because you think my lineage isn't rich enough doesn't give you the right to maul me and walk away with a clean conscience."

"You don't understand." Garret spoke through clenched teeth. "Abigail's name carries a lot of respect."

"Well, it's a good thing it does. 'Cause you haven't any." Kit felt tears sting her eyes. He considered her good enough to seduce but not good enough to be seen with in public...!

Dear Reader,

Autumn is such a romantic season—fall colors, rustling leaves, big sweaters and, for many of you, the kids are back in school! So, as the leaves fall, snuggle up in a cozy chair and let us sweep you away to the romantic past!

We are delighted with the return of Diana Hall with *Branded Hearts,* a terrific Western chock-full of juicy surprises! Here, a privileged young woman is on a quest to find the man who attacked her family. When she goes undercover as a cowgirl, she soon must fight her feelings for her boss, a stern cattle rancher, and eventually choose between love and vengeance....

Jacqueline Navin returns with *Strathmere's Bride,* an evocative Regency-style historical novel about a darling duke who suddenly finds himself the single father of his two orphaned nieces, and in dire need of a wife! *Briana* by bestselling author Ruth Langan is the final book of THE O'NEIL SAGA. Here, a feisty Irish noblewoman falls in love with a lonely, tormented landowner, who first saves her life—and then succumbs to her charms! In *The Doctor's Wife* by the popular Cheryl St.John, scandalous secrets are revealed but love triumphs when a waitress "from the other side of the tracks" marries a young doctor in need of a mother for his baby girl.

Enjoy. And come back again next month for four more choices of the best in historical romance.

Sincerely,

Tracy Farrell
Senior Editor

P.S. We'd love to hear what you think about Harlequin Historicals! Drop us a line at:

> Harlequin Historicals
> 300 E. 42nd Street, 6th Floor
> New York, NY 10017

BRANDED HEARTS

DIANA HALL

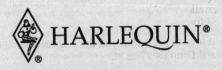

HARLEQUIN®

TORONTO • NEW YORK • LONDON
AMSTERDAM • PARIS • SYDNEY • HAMBURG
STOCKHOLM • ATHENS • TOKYO • MILAN • MADRID
PRAGUE • WARSAW • BUDAPEST • AUCKLAND

ISBN 0-373-29082-9

BRANDED HEARTS

Copyright © 1999 by Diane H. Holloway

Visit us at www.romance.net

Printed in U.S.A.

DIANA HALL

If experience feeds a writer's soul, then I must be stuffed.

I've worked as a pickle packer, a ticket taker at a drive-in movie, a waitress, a bartender, a factory worker, a truck driver cementing oil wells in south Texas, a geological technician with oil companies, a teacher, a part-time ecological travel agent and now an author. The only job I've kept longer than five years is wife and mother.

A geographical accident, I was meant to live in the South. After high school I left rural Ohio and attended college in Mobile, Alabama. There I fell in love with balmy nights and the beaches of the Gulf. I lived in Texas, but now live in the Lehigh Valley of Pennsylvania with my understanding husband, a beautiful daughter, a sedate, overweight collie and a hyperactive dalmatian.

To Mom and Dad:
Thanks for all the love and support through the years,
especially this past one.
Thanks for being there when I needed you most.

Love,
Your daughter Diana

Prologue

Denver, Colorado, 1865

Katherine Benton's hands shook as she ran them down the soft silk of her mourning dress. She had to remain firm, no matter how Father tried to manipulate or frighten her. This time, her will would prevail over her father's. Her mother's last wish would be granted.

Taking a deep breath, she demanded, "Mama asked me—no, begged me with her dying breath—to find my brother. And I will, just as soon as you tell me why I never knew he existed."

Sam Benton rested his elbows on his mahogany desk. An angry flush of red tinged his neck and cheeks. Gritting a smile, he cajoled, "Kathleen was delirious in fever before she died. Forget those ramblings." He pointed to the stack of papers surrounding him. "Now, kitten, I have work to do."

Katherine gathered her fortitude and patience. She wasn't one of her father's lackeys, and she refused to be dismissed as one. "I'm almost sixteen, Father, not six. You don't need to protect me from the truth."

The gentleness left Sam Benton's face, replaced with the ire of a man used to getting his own way. "It's a cruel world out there, daughter. Be glad I'm here to run interference."

"Mama may have allowed you to keep her in a gilded cage, but not me. I'm tired of you telling me what I can and cannot do. You won't even allow me to see your own brother and his family."

"Eli's a wastrel, riding on my coattails. That daughter of his is no better. They would only use you."

"Well, maybe I'll use them—to help me find my brother. I'm stronger than Mama," Katherine stated. "I'm not afraid."

"Well, you sure as hell should be," her father roared. "Perhaps I've protected you too much. A little fear is a good thing."

Drawing a cigar from his desk humidor, he let his dark gaze search her face. "Hearing about your mother's life might make you understand."

He lit the stogie and inhaled deeply. As the smoke left his lungs, he released his story. "Kathleen's family was well off back east. When she was about your age, she ran away and married a ne'er-do-well by the name of Stoker. Her husband then blackmailed the family. If they wanted to be sure their precious daughter was safe, send more money. Her family hired me to find Kathleen and bring her home."

"I never knew anything of this." Katherine slowly sank into the leather-bound chair, stunned by the revelations of her mother's past. Mama had always been so quiet, so afraid.

Sam's face and tone hardened. "Before I could find her, the bastard had taken the family's last dollar and abandoned Kathleen in the wilderness. Alone, hungry and nearly dead from exposure.''

"Is that when you found her?'' Katherine wrapped her arms around her shoulders, feeling her mother's misery. How could her delicate mama have survived such hardship?

The stern lines of Sam Benton's face deepened with anguish. "I didn't save her, a Cheyenne brave did. Eagle Talon nursed her back to health. Got her with child.''

"My brother?'' Elation bloomed in Katherine's heart. Her mother had not been just rambling with fever. She had a brother to find, and her mother's last wish to fulfill.

Her father nodded. "I never stopped looking for her. After three years, the government made a treaty with the Cheyenne. All white captives had to be returned or the villages would be burned. Kathleen left, but decided that the boy should stay with his father. Better to grow up a Cheyenne warrior than cursed as a half-breed.''

Katherine's own heart broke at the thought of abandoning a child. The act must have haunted Mama all this time. "She must have been brokenhearted to lose a child and the man she loved.''

"Loved?'' Sam roared. He jumped from his seat, sending ash over the Persian rug. "I'm the only man your mother ever loved. Kathleen had a schoolgirl infatuation with Stoker and felt only gratitude for that Indian buck.''

Sam ran his fingers through his gray hair, his voice cracking. "I found her when she came back to the fort, confused, weak and nearly broken with sorrow. I married her and vowed to erase those horrible memories from her mind. So we moved west, where no one knew us or her story. I built an empire of beef, mining and stocks. I bought Kathleen everything she wanted and kept her safe.

Kathleen loved me, and only me, because I protected her.''

Her father came to Katherine's side. ''And when you were born, I swore no one would ever hurt you like that.''

Now Katherine understood her father's anger. This lost child represented a living reminder of Father's inability to protect and find his wife. And a rival for her love.

Pretending submission, she asked, ''But what happened to the boy?''

''He's an uncivilized savage on a Cheyenne reservation. Leave Winterhawk be.'' The last came out a command. ''He belongs to your mother's past, not your future.''

Sam pulled her from her seat. ''And to ensure that, you are to stay in your room. Tomorrow, you are going back to Boston and finish your schooling, not searching the Colorado Territory for some Indian.''

This time, Katherine could not fight her father's will. Sam propelled her up the stairs and into her room. Closing the door, he spoke as the key locked her in. ''You'll thank me for this someday.''

''No, I won't,'' Katherine fumed. ''And I will find my brother.'' How hard could it be to find one half-Cheyenne young man named Winterhawk on a reservation? How hard would it be to convince him they were brother and sister?

Opening the silver filigree box on the vanity, she removed her mother's jewels. These pearls, ruby pendants and diamond pins would finance Katherine's search for her brother, for her mother's son.

Her blue traveling gown lay across a trunk marked for Boston. Pulling out her sewing kit, Katherine began to sew the jewels into the full hem. Tomorrow, when Father thought she was on her way to Boston, she would get off

the train, pawn a few gems and set off in search of her
brother. From this moment on, Katherine promised, she
would no longer be her father's daughter. Instead, she
would become her brother's keeper.

Chapter One

Front Range, Colorado, 1868

Garret Blaine rode straight into a ranch yard full of commotion. Cowhands crowded the corral, yelling out bids. Dollars spilled from their lifted fists.

"What the hell's going on here?" He gave each of the Rockin' G wranglers a calculated glare. Hellfire! First the news from town of rustlers in the area, and now this.

Cracker, the cook, ambled over, the afternoon sun shining off his bald head. His porcupine whiskers bristled as he spoke. "I told Cade you weren't gonna like this."

Cade! Garret should have known his brother would be at the center of any fracas. The rocker on their brand stood for his younger brother; a deck of cards would suit him better. Garret dismounted and threw his reins at the ranch tenderfoot, Davidson. With long, skinny limbs, big feet and sad eyes, the boy looked like a hound puppy as he scrambled to retrieve the leather reins.

Garret used his height and the width of his shoulders to cut a wedge through the crowd. Guilty looks flickered over the faces of the cowhands. Standing with his feet wide, his arms crossed, Garret faced his brother.

It was like looking in a mirror—ten years ago. Cade's hair was a shade lighter than Garret's sandy color, and his eyes more blue than green, but the attitude was the same—cocky and arrogant.

Leaning against the corral post, Cade tipped back his new Stetson and appraised his brother with a mildly curious stare. "Howdy, Garret. Good time in town?"

Garret ignored the question, his attention riveted on the tall man standing next to his brother. He was bare-chested except for a buckskin vest, and his tree-trunklike arms were corded with power. Scars crisscrossed a chest so wide that if he sighed, a man would feel the draft. His dark hair hung in two thick braids. Skin the color of burnished copper and eyes as blue as the Texas sky heralded the man's heritage. Half-breed.

Power radiated from the big Indian. And Garret detected a carefully controlled savagery in the man's stare. Garret asked, "What's he doing here?"

Cade's lips tightened, then his aggravating grin returned. "I hired him to break the black."

Inside the corral, the wild mustang bellowed a challenge. He shook his coal-black mane, then reared back, his deadly hooves shaking the ground.

"I told *you* to break that horse." Prickles of impatience skimmed down Garret's spine. While he broke his back working, Cade wasted time gambling. But what should he expect? Growing up in a saloon wasn't the best schoolroom to teach responsibility.

The half-breed straightened. His voice rumbled like thunder. "We seek work. Not trouble."

"Them's cowboys." Cracker gave Garret a nod and spit out a long stream of tobacco juice onto the ground.

"They rode in with hackamores." More than a little awe colored the old-timer's comment. Only the best riders guided their horses with just a rope bridle.

They? Garret scanned the crowd. Standing a few paces from the tall Indian, a slight figure held the reins of two horses. Despite the thick shirt and fringed leather jacket, the boy couldn't hide his age. There wasn't even a trace of peach fuzz on his chin! Just a scrap of dark hair could be seen beneath the slouched brim of the youngster's hat.

The boy looked up. A gaze, the identical shade of the Indian's, contemplated Garret. The two must be brothers. That shade of ice-blue was too rare for happenstance.

Suspicion pricked his reasoning. Two drifters arrive on the same day as news of rustlers. "I'm not hiring."

Cade traced the outline of the brand burned into the corral fence post. Letting his finger rest on the rocker, he said, "I thought this rocker on our brand *C* stood for me. Guess not."

For a year, Garret had lectured, threatened and scolded Cade about taking more responsibility. "The ranch's half yours."

"Then I figure I can do some hiring since the ranch is half mine," Cade said.

The government contract to supply the army forts with horses and beef came up for bid this summer. The Rockin' G rode a tightrope between poverty and prosperity. That contract would guarantee enough income that Garret could start to make improvements on the ranch and generate some savings.

But Sam Benton held the most influence as to who would get the cavalry deal. In the last few years, the only thing of Benton's that had grown faster than his bank account was his dislike of Indians. And then there was Abigail Benton, the old man's niece. Garret had been courting the girl for six months, and she shared the same views as her prestigious uncle.

Hellfire! Cade couldn't have chosen a worse time to hang Garret over the coals. He could feel the men's gaze glued to him. Waiting. Ready to judge Cade's position. Half owner or just a tolerated little brother? If Garret ever hoped to have his brother as a full partner, he couldn't afford to embarrass him in front of the wranglers. And the Indian did look hard as a whetstone and tough as jerky—two traits that would help Garret protect the herd. "How do you know he can break a horse?"

Cade smiled and pointed to the churned ground in the corral. "I think we can test just how good a cowboy he is."

The stallion raced along the fence, his mane flying, his tail high, pausing to trample some imaginary foe.

Garret barked, "The stallion's a killer. Can you handle him?"

"If we do, will you give us a job?" the smaller Indian questioned as he pushed his way forward. His gaze fixed on the lathered sides of the stallion. He tucked a few loose hairs under his black felt hat.

"Break the stallion, and he'll give you the ranch." Cade chuckled.

"Don't need a ranch, just a job." The boy's cold stare met Garret's. For a youngster, the lad showed merit. His gaze didn't falter as it drilled into Garret.

The two Indians were drifters. Trail dust layered their clothes and bedrolls. They'd move on after a few months, and the army would be none the wiser.

Garret knew what it was like to be spit on and insulted. Being the son of a saloon gal wasn't much different from being half-Indian. "If the stallion is broken, Cade'll hire your brother."

"What about me?"

"I'll give you a job for as long as you want it," Garret promised.

The big half-breed gave the younger one a long, silent look. Without a word passing between them, a decision was made. Both moved toward the corral.

"Two bits says he lasts longer than any of us did." Cade gave Garret a devilish wink.

"I'll take that bet." Cracker joined several other cowhands clamoring for a piece of the deal. Fists rose again, money exchanged hands.

Wranglers leaned against the top rail of the corral, eager to see exactly what the powerful Indian was capable of. The cowhands looked like a poorly constructed Navajo blanket. Their shirts wove an uneven line of desert reds and browns while their jeans formed a uniform lower border.

Both Indians walked into the corral. Pine needles littered the ground, soaking up the moisture from last night's summer rain.

The big Indian carried an old flour sack, the boy lugged a dally saddle. The stallion paced, whirled, then raced toward the youth. While the small Indian plowed through the mud toward the fence rail, still toting the saddle, the older one whipped out the sack and covered the black's eyes. Blinded, the animal halted, his nostrils flaring.

"Kit?" The big Indian faced his smaller brother as he held on to the stallion's halter.

"I'm fine." Kit's breath came out in short bursts. He slapped on the saddle and tightened the girth. The stallion pranced sideways.

Cracker, the ranch doomsayer, muttered, "Pshaw! They done got the black madder than a cornered polecat. Ain't that right, Candus?"

The old Buffalo soldier's black face creased into deep furrows of worry. "Ain't no one a-ridin' that animal now."

While the stronger Indian held the stallion's halter, the boy eased up to the animal's side. He held out his hands and cupped the horse's velvety nose. Laughter and taunts from the sidelines melted away as the cowboys watched.

Nostrils flared, the stallion possessed a lot of fight. The boy lowered his head and let out a long, slow, even breath. The stallion stilled. Then the half-breed youth inhaled as the animal exhaled, stealing the stallion's breath.

Silence settled on the scene, the cowhands and Garret mystified by the action. Again, the two adversaries exchanged breaths, as though they were exchanging souls. The stallion's fidgeting quieted to an alert twitch of his ears.

The tall Indian removed the flour sack. In one fluid motion, Kit pulled himself up onto the stallion's back and his brother released his hold on the halter.

Surprise flickered across the stallion's expressive face. Uncertainty tensed his muscles. Pawing the ground, the horse took a few steps forward.

Kit straightened in the saddle. Garret heard him utter a few Indian commands he couldn't understand, but the black did. The horse moved away from the rail toward the center of the ring, shivering, but held in check by the steady hands of his rider.

Indian magic? Garret doubted it, but there was something about the thin boy and the powerful horse that bristled the hair along his neck, made him feel he was seeing something unique and special.

"He ain't done nothin' yet." Traynor stood, his belly dipping over his belt buckle. The best bronc rider on the ranch, he had been thrown twice by the black. Traynor's hurt pride snarled his face into a mask of hatred. "Listen here, Cade, that don't count none on the bettin' time. He ain't a ridin' 'im."

Cade gave the angry man a crooked smile. "Bet was the Indian would last longer on the black than any of us. Nothing was said about which Indian or about just sitting."

"Well, let's see some ridin' then." Traynor tossed his high-crowned hat into the ring. The stiff brim struck the stallion in the corner of the eye.

Outrage and raw power broke Kit's mystical control of the stallion. Stopping short, changing direction and bucking, the black fought to throw his rider. Mud flew into the air. The smell of crushed pine burned Garret's nose. The fear of a crushed boy quickened his pulse.

Riding like a veteran cowhand, the slim boy clung to the horse's back. With each lunge of the horse, Kit leaned back, one arm flying into the air to keep himself balanced. Shouts of encouragement for the rider and disapproval for Traynor created a noisy din.

The stallion twisted and gyrated. Foam spilled from his mouth and lathered the bit. The acrid scent of sweat and horses heated the air. Each time the animal's crushing hooves pummeled the ground, Garret expected to see the Indian boy fall and the stallion trample the life from him. Yet Kit outthought and outmaneuvered the horse. Perhaps they truly had exchanged souls along with their breath.

His most ingenious tactics a failure, the stallion gave a few halfhearted kicks. Sweat dripped from the girth. The horse sucked in deep breaths of air. Surrender loomed just ahead.

A calm settled over the corral. Cracker stopped in mid-chew, watching the boy and the horse. "If I live to be a hunerd, I'll never see a ride like that again."

One look at the older Indian, and the calm shattered. Anger blazed across the red man's face and his stare centered on Traynor. With his brother back in control of the horse, he headed toward Traynor, his tight fists flagging a warning. The cowboy made a beeline for the barn.

The half-breed was loaded to the muzzle with rage, ready to kill. Garret jerked his thumb toward the barn. Cade slipped away from the fence and headed for Traynor. A fight, with fists or guns, could always draw Cade's attention. Garret cut off the Indian and faced down the taller man. "Traynor'll get what he deserves."

Fists the size of cannonballs slowly unclenched. The Indian took a step back, a look of sarcastic disbelief on his face. "Then I will see your judgment. But if I do not agree, I will see the man pays a harsher price."

With the Indian at his heels, Garret strode into the barn. Irritation, with the Indian and Traynor, made Garret's lips twitch into their usual scowl.

"I came to collect my winnings." Cade blocked Traynor into a stall.

"I ain't a-paying you squat." Traynor lowered his head and charged. Stepping aside at the last minute, Cade watched the muscle-bound cowboy run by and crash against the opposite stall gate.

Military discipline checked Garret's urge to give the cowboy a mind-numbing blow. He jerked his chin toward the horizon. "Collect your wages and ride out."

"You're firin' me and a-keepin' them Injuns?" Traynor snorted, and puffed out his chest. Pointing toward the breed, he added, "That kind ain't no good unless they's dead."

The breed's fist shot out like a lightning bolt and landed square on the wrangler's nose. Blood spurted over Traynor's face. He fell back, wiped his face with his hand and shook off the blood. "Goddamn breed." He reached for his gun.

Cade's gun snaked out of the holster with the speed of a rattler's strike. Traynor halted, his hand inches from the butt of his pistol. Despite the tense moment, Cade drawled out, "You don't want to wind up dead as well as fired. You'll have to spend all your wages on a casket."

"Listen to him." Garret tugged on Traynor's belt and collar, bringing the stunned cowboy to his feet. A pulpy mass, bleeding and skewed to the left, marked where his nose used to be. "Cade, pay Traynor his wages from your winnings. Then see he gets his horse and rides out."

"Dammit, Cap'n," Traynor protested. "He didn't win that money fair and square. You know he chea—"

Cade blocked his gun barrel with Traynor's chin. "I'm thinking you oughta be buried at sunset. Right peaceful then."

Traynor took the hint, shut his mouth and pulled his face away from the gun.

From behind Garret, the breed growled, "It will do for the injury to Kit."

"It wasn't for you or your kin," Garret snapped as he laid the truth out bare for the Indian. "Traynor's actions could have damaged a valuable piece of my property."

The hooded look returned to the breed's eyes. Turning to leave, he replied, "Indian lives are worth less than horses. This I have heard."

Let the Bluebellies starve. They ain't worth feeding. The prison guard's taunt echoed in Garret's head. He knew the value of human life and how it could be cheapened. Hell, the Indian took it all wrong. Mexican, Black, Indian, it didn't matter. Even after surviving Andersonville prison, he had hired on Johnny Rebs.

That stallion could guarantee Garret a visit with Sam

Benton. The word in town was the rich man appreciated good horseflesh, and that appreciation might manifest itself in the army contract.

"*Señor,* come quick." Vega, the ranch foreman, waved both hands in the air. His handlebar mustache bounced as he added, "The rider fell...."

Aggravation threatened to break what was left of Garret's iron-willed control. Running to the corral, followed by the breed, he pushed past the silent ring of cowboys. "Someone help him out of there..." His voice dried in his throat like grass in a summer drought. Kit's slouchy hat blew across the chewed-up ground.

"Damn you to hell." Garret shouted at the half-breed and slipped between the rails. The black, all fight out of him, rested at the opposite rail, far from the figure sprawled on the ground.

"Are you crazy?" Garret demanded. He reached out and jerked Kit up.

Kit stumbled to remain upright, then pushed his arm off with a strength that surprised him. "The black's broken. I rode him longer than you. Now, keep your word."

"No way in hell am I giving you or your brother a job." Garret pushed Kit toward the corral gate.

Long ebony hair, released from the confines of the hat, whipped into the air. The scent of mountain columbines and pine surrounded him. An icy blast of anger stabbed him from the fallen rider's stare. "You gave your word to hire me."

"That was before I knew the truth." His jaw clenched into a vise of outrage, Garret could hardly speak. Emotions corralled for years threatened to break free.

The gaudy posters advertising his mother's saloon extravaganza flashed in his mind along with heartache. Why was fate sending him this blatant reminder of a time he

wanted to forget? As a punishment for his youthful intol-
erance or as a reminder of his mother's last wish? *Make
Blaine a name to be respected.*

To hide his turmoil, he made his voice harsh and grating. "The Rockin' G is no place for your kind."

"My kind?" Kit's eyes opened wide.

Garret felt himself drawn to the deep azure pools. He
fought to swim free of their crystal-like depths and answered hoarsely, "Yeah, a woman."

Chapter Two

Kit yanked her misshapen hat from the outstretched hands of a bug-eyed cowpoke. She stuffed her hair back into the crumpled crown, curbing her desire to rub her pulsating backside. Her legs trembled and her joints ached, but now was not the time to show weakness.

Inside, rampant emotions screamed at her to back down and run away. She set her features into a mask of calm, buried the fear and confronted the scowling face of Garret Blaine. "Where do you want us to livery our horses?"

The rancher's green stare ripped into her with the fury of a dust devil. Just above his left eyebrow, a starburst scar whitened. A warning of his anger. He pushed up his shirtsleeves. "I don't know what you're trying to pull—"

"My brother and I want the jobs we earned." Kit waylaid the rancher's argument. Two years of searching had worn her patience thin and callused her determination. There would be no backing down. The ranch was perfect for their needs. Quiet. Out of the way. With a sizable head of prime livestock.

"You and I both know I'd never hire a woman." He spit out her gender like an insult. "Ride out."

Garret Blaine didn't have the foggiest idea of who he

was dealing with. There would be no retreat. She looped a rope through the exhausted black's halter.

"What the hell are you doing?" Garret's deep baritone voice reverberated against the barn wall and echoed in the shocked silence of the ranch. A three-legged dog hopped toward her, his teeth bared.

"Getting my pay."

The old dog growled at her. Kit growled right back, baring her teeth and wrinkling her nose. The dog cocked his head to the side, raised one tan eyebrow, then the other, and tried another growl. Kit answered, her growl deeper and a shade more menacing. The dog backed off.

Her brother edged closer. She pretended not to see his signal for retreat.

"Do you really think I'm going to let you steal my horse?" Garret widened his stance, his lip curled into a one-sided smile. He crossed his arms across his broad chest, just under where his shirt fell open. The timbre of his full voice deepened. "We hang horse thieves."

His threat rolled off her like water down oilcloth. All her emotions froze into a thick icicle of stubbornness. Narrowing her eyes, she dripped sticky-sweet sarcasm. "You promised us a job if one of us rode the black. Now you're welching on the deal. I'm taking the stallion as payment."

Cade cracked a wide grin. "The black did get ridden. And it'd be cheating to back out of a deal." The younger, less intense Blaine snickered as he faced his brother.

"Shut up, Cade." Garret's tone shifted from furious to logical. "There's no place to keep her."

His objections made her sound more like a flea-riddled cur than a person. Keep her! The gall of that man. In Boston, a snap of her fingers and men would line up to escort her to the opera or symphony.

But Garret was far removed from those eastern gentle-men. Not a spare ounce of fat on his body. Lines etched the corners of his eyes, created from hours of riding into the hot western sun. Rugged muscles bulged along his upper arms, built from wrestling steers and creating his homestead. His gaze penetrated her, sapping her strength with its intensity. Garret Blaine was a desert. Bleak, for-midable, relentless.

Her brother remained silent, but Cade gave her a wicked grin. Amusement twinkled in the cowboy's eyes. "There's the tack room in the barn."

Kit pressed her point. "A job or the horse, it's your call." It was an empty ultimatum. One word from Garret, and she and Hawk would be facing down a half-dozen guns. Her challenge lay in the code of the West, where a man proved his worth by the strength of his word.

Flecks of green serpentine sparked in the ranch owner's eyes. "You want a job? You got a job. For as long as you can stand it."

"Whoo-ee!" Cade slapped his hat against his leg and danced a little two-step, creating dusty whirlwinds to coat his jeans. "The little lady got the best of Garret Blaine."

Nervous laughter snared the cowhands as they gave the boss a sidelong glance. Garret's sudden acceptance of the situation threw Kit off kilter. A man didn't survive the harshness of the West by giving in. No, Garret Blaine didn't strike Kit as a person who would concede defeat easily, but then, neither would she.

"You can livery in there." Garret directed her toward the long, peaked stable.

A trickle of warning snaked down her spine and settled in the small of her back. The glacial tone in her new employer's voice did not bode well. She could almost smell the man's intense disgust with her and her brother.

Unhooking the lead, she freed the black. The horse nuzzled her hand and gave her a sympathetic look before trotting to the far corner of the corral. Kit squared her shoulders and followed the shadow of the tall cowboy.

Garret slid the hinged door to the right. New wood and fresh straw perfumed the barn. Horses whinnied and a challenging neigh came from the stalls as Hawk led his buckskin and her Appaloosa mare down the narrow aisle. Half of the twenty stalls were filled with horses and mustangs.

In the last one, a fine-boned mare paced, her belly distended from pregnancy. A tight collar of sheepskin circled her throat to keep the fidgeting horse from cribbing. Catching the scent of the strange horses, the mare kicked at her stall and neighed.

Kit heard the agitation in the mare's call. High-strung and nervous, not a good combination. When it came time for her to drop her foal, that mare was bound for trouble. "Best build yourself a stanchion for this one." She pointed toward the pregnant mare.

"Leave the mare to me," Garret barked. He pointed to the empty stalls. "Bed your horses here."

Kit led her mare into the narrow space and unsaddled her mount. *Too stubborn to take good advice,* she thought. *Let him learn the hard way.*

Heaving her saddle onto the wooden shelf, she grabbed a handful of straw and gave her horse a rubdown. The time gave her the opportunity to study the sulking ranch owner.

He folded his arms, constructing a thick wall of sinew and muscle across his chest. The top button of his faded cotton shirt was missing, exposing a sleek V of tanned skin. Worn jeans strained at the seams near his thighs.

Blunt-tipped cowboy boots completed his attire. Typical cowhand. But Garret Blaine didn't strike her as typical.

The past had made her wary of men, except for her brother. Panic knotted her stomach when a man ventured too near. Only Hawk knew the tremendous effort it took for her to face down the rancher. But now, since she knew he would honor his promise, her stomach relaxed, and she didn't have to concentrate on governing her alarm.

Grabbing her saddlebags, she asked, ''Where do we bed down?''

Garret steered her to a small room. The leather-hinged door swung open. Squaring her shoulders, she entered.

She sneezed. She sneezed again. Dust tickled her nose. An overpowering smell of horses and oiled leather clogged the air. One curtainless window allowed light into the narrow room. It was hardly larger than one of the saddles, and saddles and tack blocked most of the free space. A cot with a straw mattress lined the far corner.

Fur brushed her leg. The ranch dog rushed past and jumped on the bed, nesting the few blankets before lying down. Obviously staking out his territory.

Not the Revere House in Boston, but at least it would keep out the snow and be warmer than the cold ground. The door would have to stay open for any kind of air circulation, but she wasn't worried. Her brother possessed the light sleep of a hunter and the long months on the trail had taught her the same. The dog would have to go.

She dropped her saddlebags. Her aching shoulders thanked her. The ride on the black and the argument with Garret had consumed her stamina. ''Come, brother, we can move these boxes and—''

''This is where you bunk.'' The scowl on Garret's face deepened. ''Your brother sleeps in the bunkhouse.''

Through the open window he pointed to the building on the opposite side of the house.

Hawk pounced forward like his namesake. "I will not leave my sister." His eyes blistered with anger.

Despite her brother's murderous look and powerful build, the ranch owner remained cool. "If you don't like the arrangement, you're both welcome to leave."

"I'll be fine. Really." She placed a gentle, restraining hand on her brother's arm. "We're staying."

Whispers and snickers sounded behind her. The Rockin' G cowboys gossiped with the enthusiasm of old women, but with the intentions of lecherous cronies. A woman alone sounded like easy prey for a cowhand eager to relieve the thickness in his jeans.

From her hip, she pulled out a long Indian knife. She held the blade in the sunlight. A rainbow of color appeared along the tip and across the silver steel.

"I'm no prairie dove. See your cowhands are aware of that or they might find themselves nursing an injury." Burning hatred heated her voice, her message loud and clear. If attacked, she knew how to protect herself.

The knife slid into the butter-soft sheath. Moisture filmed her eyes as her fingers traced the intricate beadwork on her belt. Hawk's wife had labored hours over this gift. Hours filled with love and laughter. Hours that would never be again. Kit drew strength from the rising pain in her soul. There would be no surrender, no running home to hide with her father.

"Don't worry about my wranglers." Garret eyed his men. "No woman, no matter who or *what* she is, comes to harm on the Rockin' G." Bitterness sliced through his tone.

The tight circle of cowhands widened, as though the

rancher's words had constructed a fort between Kit and them. A sense of safety comforted her.

"If you two are working for me, then get a move on. We're wasting daylight." Challenge rang in Garret's tone.

He wanted to hear her complain, to whine. When pigs fly. It didn't matter that her muscles screamed with every movement. That her knees had the consistency of hot molasses. That the lumpy bed with the fleabag dog looked inviting. Kit slapped an overeager smile on her face and met Garret's daring stare. "We're ready."

"I'm not paying you men to stand around," Garret shouted as he marched from the barn.

Cowhands grabbed tools and spread out to complete the day's tasks. Cade sauntered over to the hitching post and watched the working men from beneath his lowered brim. Blaine also noticed his brother and made a beeline for him. Kit hesitated, then followed with Hawk at her side.

The younger man looked up, ignored his older brother's get-out-of-here stare and reached out his hand. He pumped first her hand, then, without hesitation, Hawk's. That one unconscious motion made her warm to the handsome cowboy. Many men would never consider shaking the hand of a half-breed.

"Kit O'Shane." A genuine smile tugged at her lips. The man's good humor lessened the tension. "And you've already met my brother, Winterhawk."

Cade slapped her brother on the back. "You two won me a sizeable grubstake for my next poker game. You play cards?" A gambler's joy lit his soft blue-green eyes.

"No." Hawk dashed the cowboy's hope as he hefted his saddle and bags onto his shoulder. He headed off toward the bunkhouse. Kit started to follow.

"No, you don't." Garret's firm hand clamped down on her shoulder and held her in place. A shiver of protest and abject fear shook her tired muscles and made her groan.

Her brother dropped his bags. His lion-claw necklace clinked a warning. The look of savagery on his face took Kit's breath away.

"Hawk, don't," she pleaded. It took all her concentration to dominate her erupting panic.

Unperturbed by Hawk's threatening glare, her new boss lightened his grip. His fingers tangled in her hair, then moved across the sensitive skin beneath her ear.

He's not out to hurt you. Not after that warning in the barn. The knowledge deadened her fear and opened the door to a different emotion. His touch caused a strange tingling sensation down her neck and across her throat, erasing the cold terror. Warmth smoldered in her like an old campfire.

Garret's voice sounded hoarse as he issued orders to her brother. "You and Cade can round up the herd from the east pasture."

Turning to her, he fixed his gaze on her face. "The tack needs to be completely cleaned, every bridle, saddle and halter taken apart, oiled and put back."

"Come on, Garret," Cade complained. "Kit deserves a rest after that ride."

"Hope not, because she needs to muck out the stables and start cutting a cord of wood."

"Kit's a horse trainer, not a stable hand." Hawk's sharp voice added to the tension.

"She's what I make her," Garret shot back. "If she doesn't like the work, she can quit." A crafty smile slanted across his lips as he disclosed his plan. "You're free to leave when you want. I expect it'll be soon."

Compressing all her fear and her anger into a tight lump

in her heart, Kit met his gaze without flinching. "Only time will tell, Mr. Blaine, which of us lasts the longest."

Annoyance hovered in his eyes. The scar on his temple blazed. Kit thought a lightning bolt might come from his head like the Greek god Zeus. "A week. And you'll be lucky to last that long."

Smugness she had learned at her father's knee. Haughtiness at her Boston finishing school. Kit drew herself to her full height, dismissed the fact that Garret still stood a head taller and gave her chin a regal lift. "Then we'll be discussing this issue again, Mr. Blaine. At the end of the week."

Garret swore, pivoted on his heel and entered the cedar-sided cabin. The plank door jumped the hinges from the force of his slam.

Cade stamped the ground with one foot.

"What are you doing?" Hawk asked.

"Putting out sparks." Cade gave her a saucy wink. "I figure the lady here and Garret done kindled enough to start a range fire."

Amazement hit her full force when Hawk bit his lip to keep from smiling. Her brother hadn't found life amusing in a long time.

Kit combed a loose strand of hair behind her ear. "He's got Blacks, Mexicans, Johnny Rebs and Bluecoats all working here. Why not us?"

"He's got this bur in his bonnet about getting a contract with the army. And there's this big-mouthed sonofa... Excuse me, ma'am." Cade gave a two-fingered salute to the brim of his cowboy hat. "I mean a big-mouthed know-it-all that calls the shots here. And if there's one thing Sam Benton don't like, it's Indians."

"Sam Benton," Hawk growled. "This name I know."

As do I. Kit rested her hand on her brother's arm.

Heaven help them if they ran across Benton. Her father would make sure Kit never saw her brother again, and if Sam Benton discovered the truth about Kit's time in the Indian village, he would use his power to destroy Hawk and lock Kit away in a protected shell for the rest of her life.

"Garret's counting on Benton to help him with the contract. But it's those pants of yours that've really set him off." The laughter melted from the man's eyes. Every muscle tensed in the handsome young cowboy's face. "Our ma was a whore." He waited to see if the news shocked her. It didn't. Hardship forced women into many roles. She had only to look at herself for proof.

"We don't hide it under a rock," Cade went on, leaning against the hitching post. "Don't paste it on a billboard. She wore pants and cracked a bullwhip. Ma was pretty well known in the cow towns. Wichita, Dodge City, Abilene. Spent her last years salooning in Colorado City. Garret don't cotton to being reminded of that time."

Kit knew the pain of rejecting a parent. Garret resented his mother, whose life-style had forced him to face the unpleasantness of the world. Kit, a father who had tried to shield her from life. "Does he hate his mother so much?"

"Hate?" Cade rubbed his face as though to wash away the memories. "At one time, I'd say that was the only thing that drove Garret. He was a wild one. Full of spit."

"What happened?" She wrinkled a brow in bewilderment.

Taking a deep breath, Cade seemed to evaluate whether she was searching for gossip or really cared. He must have found her worthy because he answered. "The war. Garret turned as somber as a preacher at the Pearly Gates." Cade tapped the edge of her nose with his index finger. "Don't you worry none over Garret. I got me a feeling you're about as hard as some of Cracker's week-old biscuits.''

He turned to her brother. ''Hawk, I'll be waiting for you to saddle up.'' Cade adopted Kit's nickname for her brother with the ease of a trusted friend. ''Take one of the ranch horses and let that buckskin rest a spell.''

Waiting until Cade ambled over to the bunkhouse, Hawk shook his head, the blue feather in his braid rustling against the stiff leather of his vest. ''This man, Garret Blaine, he is like the mountain above the treeline, cold, hard, never to thaw. We must find another ranch to take us on.''

She faced the rising peaks. In the distance, sunlight glistened on the snowy tops. Glaciers plucked the rock and, after centuries, carved jagged ridges and horns: Garret Blaine had a will harder than granite, and it would take more than ice and snow to dent it.

''The desert,'' Kit corrected her brother. ''Every bit of softness has blown clear of that man. He's got a heart of stone and he's as relentless as the desert sun.''

Closing her eyes, she concentrated on the tiny spots of brilliant light behind her eyelids. ''But we will stay. The Rockin' G is perfect for us.'' Her soul cried for peace, for an end to the quest that had kept her on the trail for two years.

Just a few more days and her long search would be over. At last, she would be able to sleep without having to tire her body to the limits of endurance. The thought gave her a much needed boost of morale. She opened her eyes, ready to fight.

Hawk had lost so much. To the bitter end, Kit would stand with her brother and see this mission to its bloody conclusion. Then perhaps she and Hawk could start again.

Someplace where the nightmares of the past could no longer haunt them.

"Garret Blaine will have to make do with our company for a while. His ranch is remote, understaffed, and has some prime livestock." Lowering her voice, she added, "The place is perfect for rustlers."

Hawk's icy stare heated. He clenched his fists into boulders capable of crushing the life from his enemy. "If Jando is here, I will find him. And kill him."

He left Kit to wonder how long she would have to endure Garret Blaine before they could make a move. She prayed it wouldn't be long. Both she and her brother needed a rest from their pursuit.

"Let this be the last time," Kit whispered to the slight breeze. Only the sound of the evergreens and the sharp perfume of the cedars replied.

Chapter Three

As soon as Cade stepped out the bunkhouse door, Garret hauled him around the corner. "In town, I heard news about rustlers. Nearly two hundred head of cattle are missing."

He paused as he faced the barn where Hawk waited with two mounts, ready to ride out. "The last spread they hit was McVery's, and he's just north of town."

Cade's gaze followed Garret's stare. "Kit and Hawk ain't lassoed up with thieves."

"We don't know that." Garret had to be positive Cade realized the danger to the ranch and to himself. Those two Indians could be tracking the Rockin' G's livestock and defenses. Both were scarce. "I've got nothing to go on except those Indians showing up at the same time as the rustlers. That's nothing to condemn a man for."

"Or a woman."

Garret chose to ignore his little brother's baiting remark. "You keep an eye on that Indian. Remember, he's your responsibility."

A roguish smile stretched Cade's lips. "I'll do that. But you be sure to do the same."

"What's that supposed to mean?" Garret felt as if his brother were luring him into a box canyon.

"Kit's your hire." Cade gave him a wink. "You make sure you keep an eye on her. A real close eye." He gave Garret a jaunty salute then whistled as he strolled over to the barn. Slapping the big Indian on the back like an old friend, Cade saddled up and the two rode out.

Striding to the cabin, Garret threw open the door and entered the cool interior. He peeked out the curtainless window and spied Kit toting out saddles, her shoulders draped with bridles. She settled down in the shade near the pump and started scrubbing the leather.

What was he going to do with the likes of her? Garret rubbed his hand down his face. He paced between the cookstove and table until he reached the flour sacks that marked off Cade's room. A quick pivot, ten paces, and he had reached the ragged quilt that sectioned off his room.

Memories tugged at his heart. He found himself lifting the curtain and walking over to his bed. At the foot, he stared at the trunk. Rubbing his hands down his jeans, he worked the stiff straps free then unlocked the trunk and swung the lid open, releasing the scent of cedar.

With reverence, he pulled out a quilt. Evenly spaced stitches held a kaleidoscope of patches. The red square came from Pa's shirt. A faded triangle of blue had long ago been Garret's coveralls, then Cade's, then finally a part of his mother's creation.

Time slipped away, and Garret returned to the homestead of his childhood. He could hear the sound of his pa's fiddle and Ma's clear voice calling her family to supper. Cade, just a baby swinging in a hammock in the dugout, giggled and sucked a sugar-water rag.

Why had he even saved the quilt? The bits of cloth no

longer represented his life. They belonged to a family that existed fifteen years ago. Before his pa was bushwacked and his ma turned to whoring for money.

Despite the weight in his heart, he placed the quilt back in the trunk and picked up a leather satchel. His fingers shook as he flipped back the cover.

Brown, wrinkled papers, the ink faded with age, crackled as he shuffled through them. His mother's fine script pleaded with him from the pages. The shame of his desertion stirred up a guilt so strong, so overpowering that it threatened to choke out the tears locked in his heart.

That trunk had remained unopened for five years, since the start of the ranch. He knew why the desire to hold that quilt came over him. Crossing over to the open window, he watched Kit working under the shade of the pines.

Deceitful, conniving, ice water for blood. He knew the type. Wasn't surprised Cade took a liking to her. Every saloon packed the bar with them. There was nothing demure or soft about Kit. Except for her hair. Like dark cornsilk. His fingers had slid through the strands with a mind of their own, reluctant to leave the satiny touch.

Heat flamed in his groin. Lust didn't play a part in his plans for the future. A good year, some expansion, then he could propose to Abigail.

Abigail—she'd jump to the wrong conclusion about Kit faster than a jackrabbit headed for the brush. And then there was Sam Benton. Slighting his niece and hiring two half-breeds would not win Garret an introduction and a chance at the cavalry contract.

But if he threw the two off the Rockin' G, he'd be saving his ranch and losing his brother. He'd deserted his ma. Garret wouldn't make the same mistake with Cade. The ranch represented Cade's best hope of amounting to something besides a cardsharp. And to secure the ranch's future, Garret needed that army deal.

Solving this quandary was about as easy as tying down a bobcat with a piece of string. Near impossible. But not completely out of the question. All Garret needed to do was drive Kit away. Her brother would follow. He would be rid of the Indians without overruling Cade.

Kit O'Shane would leave and leave soon. He made the vow and left the cabin. As he slammed the door, he wished he could shut away the memories sewn into the quilt and his heart as easily.

Chapter Four

Kit's eyelids flew open. Her heart pounded in her chest. A quivery weakness raked her body as she lay on her rickety cot. Another night, the same recurring nightmare.

As she sat upright, her feet collided with the sleeping ranch cur. After nearly a week of sharing quarters, she and Chili had reached an uneasy compromise. She got the bed. The dog retained ownership of the moth-eaten blankets. On the floor.

"Kit?" Hawk paused from coiling his lariat near the window. "I thought you had fallen asleep."

Each evening, her brother lagged at the barn until all the cowhands had bedded down. A formidable wall of protection against living, breathing men, Hawk couldn't ward off the horror in her dreams.

For a second, she wished Hawk could take her dreams from her, make her forget the terror she had lived through. But the nightmares helped her focus on her goal. A man's death. The annihilation of Jando's evil. She closed her eyes and asked, "Did you find anything today?"

Her brother's silence answered her question. No. Five days without a sign of the rustlers.

She dislodged her boots from under Chili's warm body,

slipped them on and wove her way through the tack to stand next to her brother. "There's a few hours before sunset. I think I'll take a walk down near the river."

Her brother rose, tight-lipped and scowling, seeing through her white lie. "You walk when the spirits speak. I will go with you."

"No." Kit shook her head. "I know you mean well. But I have to learn to not be afraid."

Her brother's lips tightened into a firm line. "I failed you in the village and fail you here. Garret Blaine works you like a slave." Frustration seethed in her brother's voice. "And I allow it."

"*I* allow it," Kit corrected. "And every chore is worth it if it helps us find Jando." Shrugging her shoulders, she gave her brother a wry smile. "The Rockin' G's not so bad. Food's good. Accommodations livable. And then there's Cade." Humor brought a smile to her lips. "I think he could charm the rattle off a snake if he set his mind to it."

"He cannot charm his brother."

"No, he can't." She bit her lower lip. If Garret was hard on her, he was twice as severe with Cade. Not once had she heard the older brother praise the younger, or offer a word of encouragement. Then again, Kit had stumbled onto more than one work-time poker game, with the younger Blaine scraping in the ante. "I suppose Cade enjoys our presence. It gives Garret someone else to criticize."

"You do more than your fair share of work."

"I get a great deal of satisfaction provoking the elder Blaine." So far, Kit was the winner in the battle of wills between herself and the rancher. The heady thrill of victory lifted some of her dread.

"This I have noticed." A mild tone of censure tempered Hawk's voice. He cuffed her chin with his fist. "Go take your walk. But do not go far."

"Only to that rock." She pointed toward a dark finger of granite at the river's edge. "I'll be back at sundown."

Hawk handed her a wool serape as she passed. "Sundown, then I will come for you." Finality carved his words.

Kit accepted the terms—a solitary constitutional timed by her protective brother. There had been a time when she would have chafed at the limits on her freedom. Now she understood the necessity. Father had been right—the world could be incredibly cruel.

The door creaked as she opened it. Chili pulled himself to his feet and rushed out ahead of her. The old dog took every opportunity to put her in her place. Second. Master and hound had a lot in common. She glimpsed the dog's tail as he rounded the cabin.

Outside, pale shades of amethyst and turquoise tinted the sky. She rested her elbows on the corral fence and whistled low. The stallion lifted his regal head, sniffed the air and trotted over to her. He nosed her shirt pocket, aware of the sugar cube hidden inside.

"Here you go, big fella." Kit dug the cube out and held it flat on her palm. While the horse munched contentedly, she admitted, "You know I don't bring you treats just to drive Garret crazy."

The horse snorted, not fooled by her entreaty. All right, getting under Garret's skin was her foremost enjoyment.

He had expected her gone after the first night. One look at her hard at work before sunrise, and the swagger had left his step. And this morning! Oh, if only she could have preserved the rancher's shocked face. It was worth every aching muscle to see his cocksure grin melt and his eyes glitter with surprise.

Garret Blaine might not be a man to push, but she wasn't a woman to easily succumb to pressure. She and Hawk would remain on the ranch until they no longer needed a cover. Then she would gladly wave farewell to the scowling rancher.

A refreshing soak while she reveled in her remarkable tenacity with Garret would ease her nerves. She headed for the river, knowing that after a bath she'd sleep well, especially knowing Garret wouldn't.

Enjoying the coming sunset, Garret watched Chili wind himself into a comfortable position on the porch. A faint line of smoke rose from the bunkhouse chimney. The tinny sound of Vega's guitar floated in the air along with Cracker's off-key singing. His wranglers were fixing to bed down, worn out from an honest day's labor.

A few solitary minutes to collect his thoughts and he'd be ready for some shut-eye himself. If he could get any. Peaceful sleep was a memory. The sound of Kit's ax chopping wood until the late hours had kept him awake last night. Along with his conscience. A woman, no matter if she dressed in pants and wore a knife the size of his forearm, could take only so much.

An irritated neigh called from the corral. Garret shifted from his seat and craned his neck around the corner. Kit with the stallion again. And not another soul around.

Where the hell was that brother of hers? Come quitting time, Hawk usually stood sentry over Kit, an imposing barrier to any cowboy that tried to saddle up to the girl. A barrier Garret was mighty glad to let stand. He wanted Kit gone, but he didn't want her hurt.

He watched her as she ambled toward the water, glistening with the late-day sunlight. She walked with a natural grace, unafraid of the night sounds. The setting sun and long shadows chilled the air but she carried a poncho instead of wearing it. Her hair cascaded down her back, swaying gently as she moved, giving him a glimpse of her jean-clad legs and backside.

A primitive beauty in a primal land. His blood stirred. Barbaric urges roused in his loin. He had lived too long in a brothel not to recognize pure, unadulterated lust. The intensity shook him. Downright frightened him.

If she tempted him, there was no telling what fire burned in the jeans of his wranglers. And Kit wasn't helping matters. What was she doing walking alone this close to night? Was she hoping some lonely cowboy would wander down to the river?

There was just one thing to do. Go down to the river and, in calm, simple language, lay it on the line. He had a ranch to think of. A woman of upstanding reputation he was courting. She and her brother could take an honest wage for their work and ride on. Cade would never be the wiser.

He'd mind his temper and strive for a civil conversation. If he talked to her, it would be man-to-man—or rather, man-to-woman. The thought carried an unwelcome sensation to his blood, sending heat branching through his torso.

Andersonville had starved the wildness from him. Or so he thought. Each time he looked at Kit, a fresh rain fed those urges. He felt them taking root, pushing forward and growing stronger.

Kit had to go. But he needed a few moments to brace himself for the confrontation and calm the fire in his gut.

For centuries, the block of dark granite had battled the river, forcing the water to divert around its immovable mass. Unable to wash away the obstruction, the river pounded into the unyielding rock, until it gouged a U-shaped indentation. A perfect pool for a sheltered bath.

Kit swam through the cool mountain water. She let her worries and concerns float away. Tension and weariness seeped from her bones but an undercurrent of caution remained. Would always remain until Jando died.

Standing in waist-deep water, she watched the current tumble stones along the stream bottom. The rock and the river, neither willing to give up the battle. She and Garret, neither about to accept defeat. But nature had reached a compromise in forming the pool. There could be no such concession between herself and the rancher. To the bitter end, she would fight to stay, and give Hawk time to track down Jando.

She emerged from the water, her hair plastered to her neck and back, and shivered as a breeze skipped across her skin. Her flannel shirt served as a towel first, then a robe. Lifting her mass of hair, she untangled it from her shirt collar to let it dry.

Covered to her knees, she retrieved her pants from the scraggly branches of a juniper and wiggled into them. The cotton material clung to her still-damp body. She hopped up and down to work the jeans up her legs.

Clean and refreshed, Kit slipped on her boots, then wrapped herself in the thick warmth of the serape. Leaning against the rough granite, she listened to the prairie.

Crickets chirped. Fish splashed in the stream. Sweet grass whispered to the wind. The sharp, pungent smell of sage and juniper scented the breeze. Serenity floated away the last vestiges of her nightmare. She had to give Garret credit for choosing this spot to place his ranch. The Rockin' G was an Eden.

Like a mother tucking in her child, evening enveloped the rolling hills. The sun balanced on the mountain horizon. Stars dusted the sky, the twinkling lights pale in the twilight. Three radiant stars lined up low in the sky. Orion's belt.

Lightning bugs winked in the tall grass, and she heard the swish of prairie grass being stepped on. By habit, she placed a hand on the hilt of her knife. Steady footsteps thudded the ground, drawing nearer. She kept her voice smooth and unaffected by the approaching stranger. "Do you share an interest in astronomy or are you spying?"

Garret Blaine rounded the tip of the boulder and stopped short. A small cowlick danced in the slight breeze. His full lips were pressed into a scowl, ready for an argument. "I want to talk with you."

"About astronomy?" Kit gave him a delightfully obtuse smile, meant to throw him off balance and give her time to regain hers. The fluttering in her heart started. Fingernails of fear dug into her soul. Swallowing hard, she refused to allow anything more than a casual facade to show. Words rambled from her mouth. "I prefer the myths that correlate with the constellations to the actual science."

The old dog sat on the rancher's heels, his growl like the sound of a distant tornado.

"What are you talking about?" Garret shook his head. He had been working the girl too hard, she was talking loco.

"The stars." She looped a strand of wet hair behind her ear and pointed toward the sky. "There's so many, how could you miss them?"

"I've seen stars." Garret brushed away her comment while his gaze riveted on her appearance. Droplets of water hung like dew on her walnut-colored skin and glistened at the hollow of her throat. Ebony hair lay sleek and wet against the nape of her neck.

Bathing! Out here. Alone. Didn't the girl have a bit of sense? A timber wolf could have crept up on her. Or a lust-frenzied cowhand. Then what would she have done?

As though reading his mind, she rubbed the hilt of her knife with her thumb.

"I got a ranch to run," Garret reminded her and himself. "I don't have time to waste looking at the sky. Now, I want to talk to you—"

"Never just a few spare minutes to enjoy your surroundings?" She taunted him with her clear azure gaze. "Come now, Mr. Blaine, a man doesn't choose to build his home in this location without appreciating the beauty of it."

She didn't waste kindling getting a fire started in the pit of Garret's stomach. "Best place to put the cabin, there by the pines," he said.

"Oh, I agree." That little half smile came back, along with his own longings. "Those evergreens make a tremendous windbreak, plus the scent is heavenly. And the river's close enough to draw water from."

"I got a well, so come winter I don't have to break river ice." These few hundred acres were his life, his future. "I plan to keep building."

"Another corral? A smokehouse?"

That thorn of discomfort stabbed deeper. Kit seemed to know what he was going to say before he did. Caution and surprise made him answer slowly, "Thinking about those and adding on to the cabin."

"The cabin?" Kit wrinkled her brow. "That seems rather extraneous. There's only Cade and you. The bunkhouse is sufficient, even if you increase your employees."

Garret wasn't quite sure what *extraneous* meant, but he could guess. "For right now. But with a good drive, I might be thinking of taking a wife."

Her eyebrows unfurled, one arched in a delicate dark line. "Taking a wife? Interesting choice of words, Mr. Blaine. And do you have an intended hostage selected?" Her tone implied she extended her deepest sympathy to his betrothed.

"Abigail Benton."

"Ah, so you intend to marry for money."

"I do not. I can take care of my woman. If given the chance."

"So, you're marrying her uncle, Sam Benton."

"Benton can open doors that are usually shut to the son of a saloon girl."

"And love?" Kit leaned back against the boulder. The action accentuated the graceful arch of her neck.

"It'll come," Garret assured Kit. Abigail expected a man who would honor his vows and supply her with a fine home. In return, she would present him with a social standing in the community. Business, pure and simple. No cumbersome emotions to tangle up between them. "Abigail's a fine woman."

"For a parlor room. She'll make sure all your china matches, your silver is polished, and your household staff doesn't cheat you." Cocking her head toward his one-room cabin, Kit snorted. "I can see now why you'll need to add on, at least a wing for the kitchen staff."

"Now hold on." Garret didn't like the condescending tone Kit was using. "You got no call talking about Miss Benton that way."

"I can talk about Miss Benton any way I choose." Kit emphasized Abigail's title. "And everything I said was the truth."

"You know, you could learn a few things from a lady like her."

He expected anger. A sharp, witty retort. She laughed.

Nothing like Abigail's titter behind her lace fan. Kit released a gut-busting, side-splitting caterwaul. She licked her lips then pressed them together, composing herself. "There might be a few things Abigail Benton could learn from me."

"Like what? How to wear pants and throw a knife?"

"Yes." A distant look came over Kit's eyes, like looking at the far shore of a mountain lake. "The West is untamed, Mr. Blaine. Your Miss Benton wouldn't be able to protect herself very well with a silver spoon."

"I said, I can take care of my woman."

"Yes, I'm sure you will. But no one can guard a loved one twenty-four hours a day." She puckered her lower lip and gave him a heavy-lidded glance. The spark left her eyes, replaced with sadness. Then, like a summer storm, it was over. A sly smile crossed her lips. "I would think Cade would be more to Abigail's taste than you. He's quite the ladies' man."

"My brother wouldn't know a lady if she bit him on the nose."

"Well, if she did bite him on the nose, she wouldn't be much of a lady, now would she?" Kit's smile deepened. A dimple formed on her left cheek. "Cade is quite witty, and very handsome."

Hellfire! This whole conversation had drifted into the badlands. A horrible suspicion congealed in Garret's mind. Was that little hellcat thinking of sinking her claws into Cade? She might be about the same age as Cade, but Garret would guess she was years more experienced. His brother was just fool enough to fall for her.

"Cade is off-limits to you," he warned.

"Off-limits?" The smile disappeared. Its absence sent a strange sense of disappointment filtering through Garret. Animosity blistered across her face.

"Don't think you're going to worm your way into Cade's affections."

"Worm?" she huffed. The dark blue of her eyes frosted.

"You think you can get a piece of my ranch by latching onto my kin."

"I don't know which is more pathetic, your overinflated pride or the way you treat your brother."

"What the hell is that supposed to mean?" Garret's voice rose. He lost all hope for a calm and logical conversation. The woman was beyond it. Chili's growl grew louder; he bared his teeth.

She faced him and poked him in the shoulder with her index finger, "It means you have a poor opinion of Cade if you think the only woman that would marry him would be after your ranch. Your brother is kind, generous, delightfully amusing and extremely attractive." Her voice rose, also, not shrill, but forceful and direct.

Kit's list of Cade's attributes stung. Garret didn't want to hear her thoughts about him. "I know exactly what kind of man my brother is."

"You certainly don't express it."

"I've had it with this." Garret swatted his hand at the air between them, brushing away her comments as if they were an annoying gnat. "You've lectured me on the woman I plan to marry and the way I treat my brother."

"There hasn't been time to address any other issues." She clipped each word with a back-east accent.

Chili picked up the lull in the conversation by snapping at Kit then sitting back, a deep rumble in his chest. Undaunted, Kit snapped right back and growled lower. The old dog looked at Garret, surprise and confusion in his dark brown eyes. Chili didn't know what to make of Kit any more than Garret did.

"And I want you to stop that. Quit picking on my dog."

"He started it." Kit turned her attention from Chili to Garret. Her glacial stare pierced him. Two icicles of sapphire blue.

The woman was impossible and always had to have the last word. "You'd argue about anything, wouldn't you? You'd even butt heads with a three-legged dog."

"Why not?" she called over her shoulder as she marched past him. "I argue with the two-legged variety." Rounding the boulder, she disappeared from Garret's sight. He detected the exchange of whispers, then the soft thud of feet retreating back toward the ranch. Looking around the boulder, he spied Hawk standing near Kit, his arm protectively around her shoulder. So where was Cade? Obviously not following the Indian.

Kit O'Shane had more prickles than a cactus. And Garret felt as if he had walked right over every thorn. He watched her ramrod-stiff back melt into the darkness. That woman was cantankerous. Ill-tempered. Hardheaded. And she had succeeded in keeping him from discussing her departure. He added "crafty" to her list of faults.

Pompous. Extraneous. Address the issues. Astronomy and constellations. Kit threw out three-dollar words as if she had a vault full of them. Hawk didn't tote around a vocabulary like his sister's.

Something didn't sit just right about that girl. How'd a half-breed learn words like that? Missionary schools taught more Bible learning than reading and writing. Kit didn't learn to speak with that tone or with that accent growing up on a reservation. The mystery surrounding the two Indians muddied like a river after a downpour. How much of Kit and Hawk's story was true, and how much of it was just a tall tale?

Garret walked back toward the cabin, a twister of thoughts and speculations blowing through his mind. And the warning of rustlers whirling in his heart.

Chapter Five

Scrape! Kit's file gouged into the grease coating on the bunkhouse stove. The sound of metal grating against metal sent spine-tingling pain up Garret's backbone. The needlelike ache lodged at the base of his neck.

Resting his elbows on the plank table, he rubbed his temples. The pain in his head continued to throb. He took a sip of his coffee. Cold. Lord, how long had he been watching her work? Too long.

After a morning of scrubbing, she ought to look like hell. So why did she look so damn beautiful? She knelt near the old stove, a bucket of ashes and dirt at her feet. The red dye of her cotton shirt had faded to the color of dry desert rock. Her cut-off shirtsleeves left threads hanging down her arms. Soot dusted the tip of her nose. Perspiration curled the fine wisps of hair around her face and neck.

Kit's translucent blue stare never wavered. Standing, she swept the ashes into her bucket with the broom. "I'm finished as soon as I dump this into the ash bin."

"Good." Garret racked his brains for another tedious chore. Hell, she had already cleaned tack, shoveled horse manure and now the stove gleamed like new. But he wasn't beat yet. "There's hay to stack in the barn loft." A sweltering afternoon of breathing chaff and lifting heavy bales would do her in. Maybe.

"Anything else you need done before dinner?" Insolence darkened her eyes.

I want you and your brother gone. Garret didn't need to voice his desire. She knew he didn't want her around. He resented the position he found himself in—stuck between kowtowing to a prig like Sam Benton and obliging Cade's sudden interest in the ranch.

Garret had to admit his brother had finally found the blister end of a shovel since Hawk's arrival. Following the Indian forced Cade to work side by side with him. And Hawk had turned out to be a hell of a wrangler.

But the promise of the cavalry agreement made Garret wince. Sam Benton and his lackey brother, Eli, unofficially governed its control.

A look at Kit's full lips, slightly pouting from her effort, and a traitorous longing threatened to weaken Garret's will. He fought down the hot licks of passion and ordered, "Tomorrow, you and your brother ride brush."

A full day of riding in the hot sun through thorns and dry brush for longhorns would finish off her stubborn streak. By this time tomorrow, Kit would be long gone. Just a bad memory. One he wasn't likely to forget.

"We'll leave at first light." She spoke with quiet authority then went back to sweeping ashes into the bucket.

Dark circles shadowed her eyes, and slowness dogged her steps. A thick blanket of guilt nearly smothered him. She was wearing down. Finally. He should be exhilarated. He wasn't. A snake with two bellies couldn't crawl as low as he felt.

The urge to explain himself, to make her understand his predicament forced Garret to make a stab at conversation. "Kit, there's this contract with the army coming up."

She puffed back a strand of loose hair and kept working. "That's a lucrative proposition."

"One I aim to make come true." He paused, wet his lips, considering how to be tactful but truthful. "There are powerful people in Colorado that feel Indians and cavalry don't mix. 'Specially Cheyenne."

The wire file stopped in midstroke. Straightening, she lifted her chin and gave him a glacial stare. "If you plan on firing me, then I'm taking the black. I rode him. I broke him. I'll own him."

A wagonload of nitro on a bumpy road couldn't be as ignitable as that woman. "Now wait just a minute." The hairs on Garret's neck bristled with her high-handed attitude. "I give the orders around here."

"Really? Sounds to me like the 'powerful people' run the Rockin' G."

"Sam Benton can make a helluva enemy."

Her fingers clenched the wire brush until they turned white. A flicker of indignation and pain flashed across her face. Garret wasn't surprised. Benton had an intense dislike of the Cheyenne. He had men combing the reservations, drumming up reasons to search their homes and stirring up trouble.

The depths of Kit's eyes heated to the color of an inner flame. "Perhaps I should just wait for Sam Benton to give me my work on the Rockin' G."

Every blade of grass on his ranch, every drop of water in the stream, every cool mountain breeze laced with the scent of pines were a part of Garret. A swell of ownership and pride swept over him.

Poking himself in the chest, he laid down the law. "This is Blaine land and no one else's. I give the orders around here." The declaration lifted a weight from his heart and his conscience.

A secretive smile played on her full lips. "I see. Then, Mr. Blaine, if you'll excuse me, I've got work to do." She headed for the door.

Frustration made him mutter, "I oughta save myself the headache and run you and your brother off."

Her whole body stilled. She lowered the bucket and pivoted to face him. "So why don't you? You could have us gone if you really wanted it."

"When a Blaine makes a promise, it'll be kept." The angry steam boiled out of him, and he dropped the huffiness from his voice. "And I've gotten more work out of Cade in the week you've been here than the whole time he's been on the ranch. I'm willing to put up with anything that can draw my brother away from the poker table long enough for him to see his future lies here, on the Rockin' G, and not in some saloon."

The thunder left her stormy eyes. A half smile curved her lips. "Even when it comes between you and the army contract."

"I stand by my word and my brother."

Her tone softened. "Mr. Blaine, I think there's hope for you yet." Picking up the bucket, she left, leaving Garret exactly where he started. Stuck with her and her brother.

"Cap'n." Davidson burst through the bunkhouse door and skidded to a stop, nearly tripping over his overgrown feet. "There's a fancy buggy headin' this way. Cracker's thinkin' it's yore Miss Abigail."

"Argh." Garret ran his fingers through his hair, wishing he could rake the trouble from his life as easily. Abigail didn't venture far from the comforts of Colorado Springs without a good reason. Traynor must have spread the word in town about Kit and Hawk. Thank goodness the cowhand had ridden out before discovering the Indian youth was in reality a woman. Abigail was a sensitive woman. She couldn't handle too many surprises at a time.

Garret slammed his hat on and threw open the door. He spotted Kit heading toward the barn, ready to tackle his latest chore. How could two women be so different? Abigail's delicate form would collapse under the weight of the heavy feed. And if he didn't handle the next few minutes just right, his relationship with her would collapse just as quickly.

Dust from the hay and barn chafed Kit's neck. After only a few minutes of work in the stuffy loft, her clothes hung heavy on her body and sweat drenched her skin. A breeze traveled through the window, cooling her but stirring the dirt and her irritation. The whole barn could ignite from one spark of her anger.

Garret Blaine had her perplexed. He seemed a man tearing himself in two. On the one hand, he was so like her father. Ambitious, thirsty for power, trying to control his family.

On the other, Garret labored from sunup to sundown to build this ranch. And he carried out a promise no matter the consequences. A soft lump rose in her throat. That she could take to heart. Fulfilling a promise was the center of Hawk's and her world. The reason she was willing to endure the herculean labors.

Honest, stubborn, strong, money-hungry, dependable, trustworthy. Garret Blaine was a strange mixture of all the traits she abhorred and admired. With each confrontation, her panic decreased and new emotions grew. He fired her temper and a strange hunger in the pit of her stomach.

The smothering heat intensified. Kit pulled her shirttails free and fanned herself, but the warmth that traipsed through her blood didn't lessen. Moving to the window, she dangled a leg over the ledge, opened the collar of her shirt and prayed for a chilling breeze.

The creak of wagon wheels drew her attention. A fancy surrey rolled into the yard, its red tassels swaying from the canopy. Two dapple mares trotted in front, their heads forced into a fashionable arch with a tight martingale.

A short, stocky man kept a heavy hand on the reins. His high top hat shaded little of his face. Sun exposure reddened his ample cheeks. On his spotless white shirt, rows of ruffles hid his chin.

Next to him sat a young woman whose blond hair was caught up in an impractical hat the size of a currycomb. Pastel flowers bloomed across the top and anchored a swath of black netting across her face. Her frock coat covered her gown from neck to ankle, protecting her dress and the velvet cushion seat from trail dust.

Kit chewed on a hay straw and watched the driver halt the buggy in front of the lodgepole cabin. "Blaine, I want a word with you," he commanded.

Her gaze shifted to Garret. Rotating his shoulders, he took his time crossing the yard. Curls at the nape of his neck coiled in several directions. A too long lock of hair draped over his eyes, giving him a roguish look.

Kit let her fingers slip through the loose hay on the loft floor. A remote attempt to brush back Garret's wayward strands. Surprised at her response, she pinned her fingers under crossed arms. A fluttering sensation swept across her chest and nestled just below her heart.

Touching his finger to his hat, Garret nodded toward the woman. "Miss Abigail." He didn't look at the driver as he added, "Fredrick."

Abigail Benton! Kit grabbed the pulley rope and leaned out the window. So this was what her cousin looked like.

When Garret had mentioned he was courting her, Kit's stomach had flip-flopped. She had made some discreet inquiries about Abigail and her father, Eli, hoping to gain their help in her search. Both turned out to be self-centered wastrels, living off Sam Benton. Kit had avoided any contact.

A sour taste puckered her mouth as the dainty young woman leaned over the driver and clasped Garret's hand. "I've been so worried about you. Rumors are flying."

Worried? The only thing Abigail Benton ever concerned herself with was Abigail. Kit fumed as the young woman stepped down, lifted her hem and displayed small, delicate ankles.

Ensconced between the buggy and Garret's tall frame, Abigail slowly withdrew her lace-covered hand from his loose hold. Lifting the netting from her face, she displayed clear alabaster skin and a cameo profile. "Garret's going to clear this whole thing up."

She's batting her eyelashes! Kit retreated into the loft and pulled the crown of her water-stained hat down to her eyebrows. *How can Garret be so naive? Can't he see he deserves better than a simpering tease?*

Disappointment sliced through Kit's heart along with a nasty emotion she was afraid to identify. It felt too close to jealousy. She shouldn't care what the lean rancher did or whom he married. But she did. Somehow, Garret had become more than a convenient hideout.

"You hired anyone lately?" Fredrick issued the question like a command.

"What business is it of yours?" Garret stiffened. What happened on the Rockin' G was none of Marvin Fredrick's concern.

Fredrick's heavy jowls looked as though they'd been sandpapered. He gave Garret a nasty smile, baring white even teeth. "Word has it two Indians tricked you and that brother of yours into hiring them."

Garret looked past the buggy to the barn. Kit sat in the loft window, eavesdropping along with the other men.

Abigail fluttered her hand like a fan. "Don't take Fredrick's comments the wrong way."

"Don't worry, Miss Abigail." Garret constrained the anger from his voice. "I wouldn't stoop to a fight with you here. I'm sure Fredrick realized that when he suggested you come with him." Garret watched the man's face contort in a grimace of anger and outrage at the intended insult.

Behind him, Vega and Cracker snickered as they inspected a saddle Kit had already cleaned and repaired. Candus stooped to examine the hoof of a mule tied to the hitching post. His deep chortle could be easily heard. Bug-eyed and with a wide grin, Davidson sat on the porch and shouted, "Good one, Cap'n."

At least Garret didn't have to deal with Cade's biting wit and Hawk's imposing presence. They were bringing in cattle from the valley pastures.

"Cade hired a man. Goes by the name of Hawk. And I took on Kit." Now was not the time to tell Abigail that his new employee was a woman. Not with Fredrick after him like a snapping turtle. Garret'd ride into town in a few days and explain everything to her. After she had some time to digest his next bit of news.

Abigail patted her elaborately coiffed hair. "All of this was just a silly mistake."

"Kit and Hawk are half-Cheyenne." Garret's voice dropped in timbre, but he made the statement without apology.

"Garret!" Beauty could hide many flaws, but Abigail's china-doll face magnified the prejudice in her soul. Her eyes narrowed to slits and the Cupid's bow of her lips thinned to a stiff, tight line.

"Indians are nothing but filthy animals." Abigail's whine pained his ears. She clutched the throat of her frock coat. "Really, I had thought you better than your upbringing."

The verbal slap rubbed salt into the wound of his childhood. Garret tried to reason with her. "There's no cause for this."

"Of course there's cause." Abigail's voice turned shrill with indignation. "I cannot believe you would put all the women in the area in danger like this. My uncle Samuel says—"

"Your uncle Sam talks a lot." Garret could have bit his tongue after he spoke. Hell, where had that come from? It sounded like something Cade would say. Looking toward the barn, Garret spotted Kit still leaning dangerously out of the window. She gave him a nod of approval. His lips twitched. He almost found himself smiling.

"Sam Benton knows what this territory needs to become a state." Fredrick reached out his hand and helped Abigail return to the carriage. "And he knows exactly what should be done with every murdering redskin."

This kind of talk could only lead to trouble for Kit, Hawk and the Rockin' G. Wild talk and a liquored-up crowd were a recipe for a hanging party. Garret replied staunchly, "Those Indians haven't murdered anyone."

Fredrick pointed his finger at Garret. "Four nights ago, rustlers hit Ben Harris. He lost twenty head of cattle, a string of prime horses and three men. The outlaws took scalps."

Four nights ago! While Garret had been arguing with Kit by the pool, rustlers had attacked. She had an alibi, but what of Hawk? He hadn't shown up until sundown. Where had he been for those few hours? As soon as Cade rode in, Garret had some questions to ask.

He wasn't about to let Fredrick see the lash of doubt. "If I catch any of my men tossing a loose rope, I'll be the first to turn them in."

Abigail sat primly in the carriage, staring straight ahead. "Garret, you have the potential to make something of yourself, despite your mother. Are you going to throw that all away for a couple of savages?"

A whore's son. He couldn't escape it. Every cowboy that had ridden the range in the last ten years knew about his ma. His fingernails dug angrily into the soft leather binding of the surrey. "Leave my mother out of this," he rasped warningly.

Startled, Abigail pulled an immaculate handkerchief from her drawstring pocket and waited, the clear expectation of an apology on her face. Garret didn't oblige.

Abigail bit her lip and let a fine line of hardness into her voice. "I am well aware you are sorely lacking in education and breeding. I'm willing to overlook that, but if you expect to ever court me again, then you had best get rid of those creatures."

Her gaze flickered over his face then lingered on his mouth. Her voice turned husky. "I don't hold a grudge. Unlike my uncle Samuel. Get rid of those Indians, and everything can be just like it was."

It didn't matter that the words came from a pretty package and that Abigail's voice sounded sweet as sugar, Garret detected the threat. Fire the Indians or have Sam Benton as an enemy. Garret fingered his collar. It felt tight and restrictive, as did Abigail's attempt to bring him in line.

Thundering hooves pounded into the yard, bringing a

groan to Garret's lips. Cade and Hawk trotted toward the
corral. Dark sweat lined their mounts and Cade's shirt.
Dressed in fringed leggings and a vest, Hawk looked like
a marauding warrior instead of a cowhand.

"I'll be watching you, Blaine." Lifting his whip, Fredrick flicked it in the direction of Hawk. "And that heathen." He smacked the rump of his matched grays with
the whip. The carriage rumbled past. Dirt and sod rooster-
tailed from the wheel, spattering Garret's jeans and shirt.

Hawk didn't give the surrey a glance, just untacked his
horse and started rubbing the animal down. Cade moseyed
over to Garret, a slight smile tugging at his lips. "Something I said?"

"I gotta talk with you." Garret propelled his brother
toward the cabin. Pushing the door open, he dragged Cade
inside then spied out the window. Davidson was walking
toward the outhouse. Near the barn, Vega and Cracker
were actually repairing the supply wagon. Candus hoof-
picked a mule near the corral. No busy ears to overhear
his conversation.

"I want to know if you've been keeping an eye on
Hawk."

Displaying his palms, Cade lamented, "'Course I have.
See these blisters? I got just as many on my backside."

"You know where he's been every minute?"

"Mostly. We can't herd in longhorns tied to each
other's hip. But he's never come up missing on the
range."

"And the evenings, here at the ranch?" Garret asked.

Cade twisted his lower jaw, as if he were having the
barber remove a bad tooth. "He just goes over to the barn
and sits with Kit. Ain't no reason to follow him—"

"Four nights ago—" Garret glanced at the window,
then lowered his voice "—where was he?"

Cade removed his hat and ran the brim through his hands. "Four nights ago? Let me recollect. I seen him at supper. Then just after sunset with Kit down by the river."

"Two hours unaccounted for." Garret slapped his hand on his thigh. "Hawk could have ridden to the Harris spread and made it back by sundown."

"Why would Hawk want to ride over to the Lazy Bar T?"

"Rustling. Harris lost cattle, horses and three men." Garret dipped himself a mug of cold water from the crock. He sipped the liquid and contemplated the evidence. Hawk had no alibi. The Indian hated being parted from his sister, so why let her stroll, alone, in a secluded spot?

And what of Kit? If Hawk was involved with the outlaws, what was her part? An innocent sister, or a luring temptress? Was her bath a ploy to keep Garret occupied while Hawk sneaked away? Her nightly walks an attempt to keep his mind on her and not on the ranch's defenses?

Cade stood, determination hardening his features. "I ain't firing Hawk just 'cause Abigail Benton says so. He's worked harder than any man we've got."

Garret examined his little brother. Cade had his dander up. And not about a card game. "You like this Indian, don't you?"

"I like them both."

"Why?"

A casual shrug and a shuffling of his boots accompanied Cade's response. "They sorta remind me of us. Got the world telling them they ain't no good 'cause of their blood." Sincerity strengthened Cade's voice and made him sound older than his eighteen years.

Garret released a long, slow sigh. He should just fire those two and be done with it. If Cade wasn't involved so seriously… If this wasn't the first time his little brother had shown some responsibility…

Scratching his eyebrow, Garret made up his mind. There was just too much at stake to leave it to Cade and his history of recklessness. If Hawk was involved with the outlaws, Cade could get hurt. "From now on, you stay clear of Hawk."

"But, Garret—"

"No buts." Garret would brook no arguments. "These outlaws are desperate men. They've already killed."

"You think Kit and Hawk are guilty," Cade accused.

"If I believed that, those two would be riding off this ranch now. And I'd be talking to the sheriff. I got questions. And I want answers."

"I can get them."

"And wind up shot." Garret sucked in a breath. "Cade, just do as I say. I'll be watching them from now on."

Cade stared at a knot in the floorboard. His jaw worked like a gristmill, grinding his teeth together. "I'm sure you won't ever need it, big brother, but if you want some help, you can count on me." Stuffing his Stetson back on, he took three long strides and left the cabin.

Help was exactly what Garret required, but none that Cade could give. He'd need a flour sifter to sort out the medley of emotions in his heart. Passion and desire tempted Garret to lay aside his suspicions. The anguish of his youth cried for him to be lenient. His sharp-edged instincts, honed in Andersonville, commanded him to think first of himself, his brother and his ranch.

Indecisiveness was a new emotion for Garret. He didn't like it. If Hawk and Kit were rustling, Cade was going to need indisputable proof. And Garret wasn't prepared to even hint to the authorities his concern unless he had the same type of evidence. One way or the other, he would find out the truth about the two Indians.

Kit studied the furrowed brows and tight line of her brother's lips as he climbed the ladder to the loft. "You found something?"

White streaks of anger tunneled across Hawk's neck. "I found an old campfire. And these." He pulled a dark leathery circle from the pouch on his belt. Long dark hair hung in a snarl from it.

Brilliant sparkles formed in front of her eyes and she gripped her brother's arm to keep from fainting dead away. "Did Cade see this?"

"No. Cade talks too much. He is easy to lose on the trail. Jando could walk in front of him and he would not notice." Hawk replaced the scalp in the leather pouch and tugged the leather ties closed. The look on her brother's face made Kit fight back the raging waves of horror.

"This time, my brother, we'll get our revenge."

Chapter Six

Garret's eyes adjusted to the starlit darkness. The North Star twinkled high to the left, pointing the way toward Denver. Just above the mountains, three stars lined up along the western horizon. Kit had called them Orion's belt. He would never be able to look at them again without visualizing her at the pool, her hair sleek and wet, her lips full and red, his body primed for the taste of her.

The cabin door opened and a sliver of firelight sliced the night. Cade stuck his head out, exposing his bare chest. "She go to bed yet?"

Clearing his throat, Garret tried to cover up his confusion. "I always sit a spell about now."

A devilish smile crossed his brother's lips. "Yeah, but you usually take a seat facing the bunkhouse, not the barn." Cade walked out, propped his bare feet on the porch rail and clasped his hands behind his neck. "She's a woman to ride the river with. Got grit. I like that."

"You mean she's hardheaded and stubborn as a mule." Garret forced his voice to remain unaffected by his brother's ribbing. Cade's praise also caused Garret to fret.

At eighteen, it didn't take much for a pretty girl to turn his head. And Kit was more than beautiful. Kit was breathtaking. And not just in her looks, but in the way she moved and blended with the frontier, as though she were a part of it.

Garret could understand Cade's admiration, but he couldn't tolerate it. Not if it might hurt Cade in the long run. What if the two Indians were really more than they seemed? Cade couldn't afford another run-in with the law. In a cool tone, Garret reminded, "Stay away from those two."

Cade used both hands to scratch his head. His blond hair stood up on end. "Those two ain't cut out for rustling any more than I'm cut out for ranching."

"But the Rockin' G's half yours, Cade."

"A piece of paper don't change who I am."

Cade couldn't be more wrong. Two years in Andersonville and a piece of paper had changed Garret. Ma's will. That one sheet of dry, crinkled paper carved a wound in his heart that would never heal. Made him pray he could turn back time and put to rights all the wrongs he had done his mother.

"You're thinking about Ma again." Cade wrapped his arms around his bare waist. The cool night air caused gooseflesh to prickle up his arms.

"What makes you say that?"

"That ugly scowl on your face, like you owe the world." Cade stood and walked over to the door. "Big brother, you don't owe no one nothing. Not the past, not me and 'specially not Ma. Start living in the here and now and stop looking for trouble where it ain't. Give Kit and Hawk the benefit of the doubt. It's what we woulda hoped for." Opening the door, he slipped back inside the cabin. Except for the soft glow of the lantern in the cabin window, blackness prevailed.

The benefit of the doubt. A fair chance to show his

mettle. It had taken the worst hellhole in the Confederacy
to give Garret his opportunity to grow to manhood. To
show other men and himself just what he would do and,
more important, what he wouldn't do to survive. Was the
Rockin' G Kit's chance? Could Garret turn his back on
her and still live with himself?

He entered the cabin. Cade had already hit the sack.
His deep, regular breathing brought a twinge of envy and
regret to Garret. His brother had no worries. He could
sleep easy.

Garret peeled off his clothes and lay on his straw mattress. Restless, he was tempted to get out his mother's
quilt and wrap himself in the memories of his early years.
But he didn't. That life was long ago, best forgotten, along
with the desire that flared each time Kit O'Shane looked
at him with her icy blue eyes. He fell asleep haunted by
images of her full lips and soft body.

A knock hammered through Garret's dream.

"Mr. Blaine? Wake up, Mr. Blaine." Kit's voice
pleaded from behind the door. Garret fought off sleep as
he shook his head. He wrapped a Navajo blanket around
his waist and trudged across the room.

He threw open the door. The lantern in her hand
blinded him for a moment. His eyes adjusted to the light,
and Kit materialized from the glow. Fine, thick strands of
ebony hair blended into the night, streamed down her
shoulders and framed her oval face. The first few buttons
of her shirt were undone, exposing a hint of the fullness
beneath. Blood rushed to his brain and he came instantly
awake, aware of the pulsing energy in his loins. "What
the hell's going on?"

"It's the mare." Kit's gaze flickered over his face, his
naked chest, then hid behind a thick fringe of dark lashes.

Her voice sounded hoarse. "She's going to drop the foal. I thought—"

"I'd want to know." Finishing her sentence was like sharing an intimacy. "Let me get my pants on."

"I'll meet you over at the barn." Her eyelashes fluttered, and she bolted off before he could stop her. The swinging light marked her progress across the yard.

Garret grabbed his frayed jeans from the wall peg. From behind his curtain, Cade mumbled. His rope bed creaked as he turned over, then his even breathing returned. Garret thought about waking Cade then changed his mind. He didn't want to throw those two together any more than necessary. Sitting down on the bed, he pulled on his pants and boots, then headed for the barn.

Kit alone, with her hair unbound, could be a helluva temptation. A temptation even he might not be able to resist. Eve in the Garden hadn't been able to resist the serpent's apple. Garret only hoped he could do better against Kit's native beauty.

Heat radiated across Kit's cheeks as she returned to the barn. She hadn't expected Garret to answer the door with only a blanket around his waist. The hard lines of his chest had stirred a deep yearning in the core of her body.

The intensity of the emotion bewildered her. After the destruction of the village, a part of her had died, but Garret's tousled hair and contoured arms and shoulders rekindled life into her dormant woman's soul. Made her dream of his lips on hers. She pushed open the door and wished she could leave her quivering knees and pounding heart outside.

Chili danced outside the mare's stall, following the horse's restless movements. Hanging the lantern on an iron hook, Kit leaned on the stall gate. Lines of sweat darkened the sorrel's brown hide. A trickle of blood snaked down the horse's fetlock. The mare kicked the gate, sending vibrations through Kit's fingers.

The barn door opened, and Garret strode in. With his shirt open, she could see the corded muscles along his ribs and abdomen. Panic tore at her. Kit fought and controlled the fear. *He's not going to hurt you. He doesn't want you.* The wave diminished to a ripple of apprehension. Along with regret. Deep inside her, a part of her longed for Garret's touch. Fear forced her to bury the hot emotion.

She stared at the door expectantly. "Cade coming?"

"No. Didn't figure we needed him." Garret's eyes became flat and unreadable.

He's too close. Survival instincts screamed at Kit to back away. The scent of soap clung to his clothes, beguiling her. With little effort, she quieted the warnings in her head. "We should be able to handle this."

An undercurrent of tension evaporated from his voice. "Yes, we should." Kit didn't understand if he was referring to the mare or to something else.

The mare kicked the stall as her extended stomach quivered. "She could break a leg or cut a tendon," Kit worried out loud.

Garret pondered for a moment then suggested, "We can pad the gate with blankets, but we don't have enough to line the walls."

We. The word left his lips and lodged in Kit's heart. Garret made her dream of a man who could permanently destroy the fear Jando had instilled in her.

One day, maybe, she would be able to dream. But not while Jando lived. She turned her mind to the task at hand. Yesterday's chores gave her an idea. "We could use the bales in the loft to build a wall."

Approval warmed his eyes. He smiled, and Kit found herself lost in the curve of his lips and in the hint of a dimple in his left cheek. "You get the blankets. I'll throw down the bales."

He lit another lantern on the shelf, then climbed the ladder. The wood floor creaked under his weight as he moved to the far side of the barn. She could hear him grunt softly, then his heavy steps back. A bale fell to the floor in front of her. Then he retreated for another.

The steady beat of his feet reassured Kit. Each step told her of his presence, but she didn't have to deal with the strange conflicting emotions his closeness caused. Searching the barn for blankets and flour sacks, she let the task command her thoughts.

"Move aside." Garret puffed behind Kit. He lugged a hay bale over his head. With controlled strength, he dropped it inside the stall, next to the wall. The mare pranced to the opposite side.

"Let me help." Kit turned to grab a bale.

A callused palm checked her motion. Garret's thumb massaged her arm, and heat radiated through the thin cloth of her shirt. "Those bales are too heavy for you to lift." The hard line of his jaw softened, and his eyes melted into a gentle moss-green.

Confusion with her own smoldering emotions made her blurt out, "You didn't seem to think so yesterday."

"I said lift, not shove." Garret tossed the gentle reprimand aside as he released her. Her arm felt cold, as though she needed the warmth of his touch. He returned to the pile of bales at the foot of the ladder.

Kit had to compose herself. Garret Blaine had actually been considerate. He had teased her. She glanced toward him, his back straining to lift the heavy bale. Lantern light turned his hair golden, and without his Stetson, a cowlick sprang free. For once he didn't look dry, hard and unforgiving. His broad shoulders seemed ready to support her, his strong arms ready to protect her.

Three more bales and he effectively boxed the mare into the center of the stall. When he had finished, he paused, standing so close she could study the swirls of his ear, the way the hair around his neck curled, and see the rays of the starburst scar on his temple. His shirt smelled of crushed hay and a musky masculine scent from his labors.

Kit tore her gaze away from him and concentrated on the mare. "I don't know what else we can do." She used that word, too. *We.* And she was without fear. Instead, she felt an anticipation that offered both promise and danger.

Kit and Garret spoke to the horse, their voices intertwining, alternating from one to the other. Their comforting tones and gentle pats soothed the animal. Only when her sides quivered, the signal of a labor pain, did the mare toss off their hands and roll her eyes.

"This could go on for hours." Garret leaned on the gate, his shoulder brushing hers. "Why don't you turn in?" Chili whined as he looked eagerly at the dark tack room.

Shaking her head, Kit combed her fingers through her hair. "No. I wouldn't be able to sleep anyway." The dog slumped to the floor, clearly disappointed.

An awkward silence dominated the barn. Garret rubbed his temple, his fingers tracing the rays of his scar.

"You get that in the war?" Kit's gaze centered on his temple.

Self-conscious, Garret withdrew his hand. "In a manner of speaking."

One dark brow arched. Her exquisite mouth crooked to the side. "What does that mean?"

He shifted his weight from one foot to the other, clasped his hands together and stared at the spot where his thumbs interlaced. "I was in Andersonville for two years."

"I've heard stories about the place—"

"None of them could be as bad as the truth." He unclasped his hands and stepped away from the stall, turning his back on her. "Twenty thousand men stuffed into a prison built to hold a few thousand. Disease, starvation, abuse were everywhere."

"Did one of the guards do that?" The concern in her voice made him face her. Garret found himself hypnotized by the play of lantern light across the planes of her face and the shimmer in her hair.

"No." He fought to find his voice. "A Union officer. He threw a rock, hit me in the head."

Long, slender fingers lay over his hand, then withdrew, trembling. Kit bit her lower lip. "It must have been horrible."

He stood with her in the glow of the lanterns, surrounded by darkness, and felt they were the only two people on Earth. Nervousness made him try to make light of his situation. "I came in with about twenty other Blues. Nineteen years old, brash, tough and cocksure."

"Sort of like Cade."

"Worse than Cade." He smiled at her exaggerated shocked expression. Then the smile faded as he remembered the rest. "That lasted all of ten minutes. That's when the rocks started flying. The prisoners were trying to stone us. Kill us for our boots, uniforms and share of food. I saw a captain aim for me and then everything went black."

Memories dredged from the darkest days of his life haunted him. Made him remember the depravity of men. How little it took for some to revert to killers, how much it took others to recall their humanity.

Garret's throat constricted as he spoke. "I woke up without my boots, blood dripping down my face, and Cracker and Candus complaining about who would get my jacket. When they saw I was still breathing, they nursed me back to health and dubbed me 'Cap'n,' since that's who almost took me out." Emotion made his voice stick in his throat. "As men died all around us, I vowed I'd get us out of there."

"And you did." A melancholy softened her voice. "You live and wonder why you and not the others."

"Because we worked at it." Garret ground his teeth together. "We slept in shifts. Hoarded food. Raided corpses." Ferocity stiffened his body and lowered his voice to a growl. "I found out the difference between being a man and an animal. And when those gates finally came open, I walked out looking men in the eye."

Lifting her face, she studied him from beneath her thick lashes. "No one goes through hell like that without losing something of themselves. What did you lose?"

"An attitude," Garret spit back. "And the belief that I would never amount to anything. Prison was a great equalizer. Rich or poor, old blood or new, it tested us all the same. Andersonville freed me from the shame of being a whore's son." The anger in his voice caused Chili to lift his head.

"And you plan to do the same with Cade." She spoke with a hint of accusation.

Garret studied the shadows the lantern cast on the high barn roof. "I know what he needs to drive out the shame. Something to fight for. Something to work at."

"The Rockin' G?"

"It's all I've got." Garret pushed past the lump of guilt in his throat.

"But why here, where everyone knows your past? Why not California or Oregon?"

He stabbed the air with his finger, nailing each word to an imaginary tombstone. "When my pa was alive, Ma walked down the street with her head high. The townfolks talked to her, invited her to quiltings and socials." He lowered his hand, but anger still burned in his chest and leaked into his voice. "When Pa died, we lost our ranch. Ma turned to the only job offered. Salooning and selling herself.

"I ran out on her and Cade when I was sixteen because I was ashamed of her. Of how men treated me and Cade because of her. It wasn't until after the war that I found out about this place. Fifteen years of working the back-room of a saloon bought my mother an early grave and her children this ranch. Ma died a few days after I came back, but she made me promise to look after Cade. Made me promise to make Blaine a name to be proud of again." Staring into Kit's dark blue gaze, he finished, "I got Cade out of a Louisiana jail and came here to start the Rockin' G. I let my ma down when she was alive. I'm not going to let her down again."

"A promise to the dead." Kit looked away from him, her voice small and sad. "There is no greater vow." She turned back toward him, her eyes glistened, and her gaze seemed to focus on a spot far away from the barn and him.

The mare suddenly stretched her neck and bared hard, powerful teeth. A tremor rippled down her sides, and a dark shape began to emerge from her womb.

Kit closed her eyes and shook her head. As though breaking a trance, she said, "The foal's dropping."

Trapped by the bales, the mare was forced to stand and endure. Wet and shivering, the newborn tumbled off a bale then landed in a heap on the floor.

"Damn, I wish I had started that stanchion earlier." Garret scratched the nape of his neck. The mare's labor had been far easier than he'd expected. But the real question was if the mare would allow her young to nurse.

The foal blinked its long eyelashes and gasped for breath. Its frail rib cage fluttered like a hummingbird's wing, slowed, then evened out.

"A colt." Kit identified the male foal. The colt raised his head and pondered her. Then, with nature's gentle urging, he wobbled to his feet.

Like a pale beam of sunlight, the colt wavered as he stood. His skinny legs splayed out, but he held his balance. Trapped in the narrow confines, the mare shifted from side to side.

On trembling legs, the colt lifted his head to nurse. The mare gave a terrified neigh and kicked. The colt fell in the straw, its sides heaving from the exhaustion.

"Garret, we've got to do something." Worry lines furrowed Kit's forehead, and he fought back the impulse to massage them away. Garret picked up a flour sack. "What if we blindfold the mare with this? That oughta make her docile enough to allow the colt to nurse."

The sadness left Kit's eyes, replaced with hope and expectation. "I'll draw her attention, you slip on the sack."

Garret climbed and balanced on the rail behind the horse. Kit crooned to the mare as she motioned him closer. He laid the sack over the horse's head, smothering out all distractions.

"I'll hold the sack, you help the colt." Garret took her place at the mare's head. Kit gave him a triumphant smile before ducking under the mare's belly.

By looking under his arm, he could watch Kit with the foal. She gently aided the animal to his feet.

"Keep at it. You can do it." Garret offered what help he could. He let his weight drag on the halter, keeping the mare in position and the cloth across her eyes.

"It's working." Her hushed words lilted with pure joy. "He's nursing."

The loud smacks and slurps made Garret smile. "He sounds like a whole mess of cowboys getting grub."

"He's hungry." Kit defended the colt's rude sounds.

The mare fidgeted, her foot coming down on Garret's toes. He held on to her halter with one hand and pushed the heavy hoof off with the other. His toes pulsated, but he felt prouder than a dog with two bones.

When the colt's overeager suckling slowed, Garret called a halt. "That's enough for tonight. Hold the little feller back while I lead the mare out."

"I've…" she grunted, "got him." The colt strained against her arms, attempting to follow his mother. "No, you don't." Kit sat on the floor and tightened her grip on the colt's neck. The milk-covered nose sniffed her neck. Warm, sticky liquid dripped down her shirt.

She could hear Garret's low voice coaxing the mare forward. There was a squeak of a gate opening, then closing. A few minutes later, he reappeared, swinging the stall gate shut. With relief, Kit released the colt.

The foal tripped forward, nuzzled Garret's leg, then walked stiff-legged around the stall. With his belly full, the newborn lay in the fresh hay and closed his eyes.

"We did it." Kit couldn't contain her happiness. The colt would live. The feeling of accomplishment made her a trifle giddy. She giggled. The colt didn't seem to mind the noise she made. Neither did Garret. He stared at her, his eyes shining, just as happy as she with their night's work.

She started to rise. Garret extended his hand. Without thinking, she took it. A gentle tug, and she was on her feet, standing just a breath away from him.

His gaze lingered on her lips. The gentle shine in his eyes heated, turning them to the shade of evergreens. He did not release her, but combed the fingers of his other hand through her hair, freeing a piece of straw. Panic whirled in the pit of her stomach. She could feel the rising tide within her, threatening to make her lose control. Like a frightened rabbit, she stood frozen, too terrified to move.

Garret had grabbed her before he could think what touching her would do to him. Being near her, working with her and sharing his past had been exquisite torture. He liberated her hand, letting his fingertips caress the inside of her arm. His thumb rested on the fullness of her breast.

Passion erupted through his body. Hunger, so long denied, craved the taste of her lips. He pulled her to him, crushed her chest to his and covered her mouth with his lips. Tasted her wild-honey nectar. Simmered his desire in the essence of her hair and the perfume of her body. He felt starved for her. Craved her. Could only be sustained by Kit's touch and taste.

The heat of his wanting dulled his instincts and made him slow to comprehend the terrible change that took place in her. She stiffened in his arms, and her lips quivered beneath his. Raising his head, he stared into her glassy eyes. She seemed in a daze, or a nightmare. "Kit." He relaxed his hold and life shot into her.

As she scrambled away, her shirt twisted, exposing one

breast and a long, thin scar just above it. Her hand clutched at her hip. "Where's my knife?" She dropped to all fours searching the hay for the nonexistent weapon.

"Kit, you weren't wearing it." Garret knelt on one knee. She was lost in her search, digging her fingers into the hay, scraping the hard board underneath, frantic to find her weapon. A pitchfork rested in the neighboring stall. A shovel leaned in the corner. She didn't seem to notice the weapons within easy reach. Her dark hair draped over her face. He reached to pull it back and offer comfort.

"Don't touch me." She scooted across the hay-littered floor and stared at him with eyes wide and frightened. No, more than frightened. Terrified. Her hand kept feeling her hip. Her gaze darted from him to her room. "Stay away."

Garret found he didn't know what to do with his hands. He folded them, unfolded them, patted his thighs. Anything to keep them from doing what they really wanted. Wrapping around Kit's waist. Weaving through her silky mane. Whispering words to ease her panic. From outside the stall, Chili whined.

Standing, he opened the gate, took the lantern and entered her room. The feeble light cast the narrow room in an amber glow. Under her pillow, the beaded sheath and belt protruded. Garret carried the knife to the stall.

Kit lay limp as a rag doll. He threw the covered knife at her fingertips. Her shaking hand curled around the bone handle and the trembling stopped. Withdrawing the blade, she clutched it to her breast like an amulet. Her quick breaths steadied. The unfocused stare left her eyes.

Pulling herself to her feet, Kit lifted her head. Her limbs felt so heavy. Brilliant sparkles danced in her vision. "Go away," she croaked. "Go away. And never touch me again." She stared into darkness. The barn door creaked open then closed.

Reality seeped into her terror. Kit realized she was alone. And feared she always would be.

Chapter Seven

The morning crew sat sleepy-eyed over their breakfast of eggs and hominy. A crock of butter, a jar of persimmon jam and a basket of golden-brown biscuits moved from hand to hand down the table. Garret counted heads as he accepted his plate. Two missing. Kit and Hawk.

Kit deserved to sleep in. The mare had kept her up till past midnight. After his kiss, she deserved to walk in here and slap him in the face. How could he have lost control like that? And how could a kiss turn a spitfire like Kit into a petrified woman?

He dropped his plate on the table. His fried eggs slid over and broke apart, mixing with the butter-coated grits. "Candus, the mare dropped her foal last night."

The man's ebony face creased into wrinkles. "I had my worries about that mare."

Garret sipped his coffee and answered without thinking, "Kit and I managed to pull her through."

The sound of utensils scraping granite plates stopped. Garret felt the stare of his cowhands boring into his back. He brazened his way out of the silence. "We blindfolded her and let the little guy get a bellyful. But he'll be hungry this morning. The mare needs that stanchion."

The old Buffalo soldier stood, shoved his hands into his loose pockets and gave Garret a wink. "I'll just mosey over and take a peak at that mare and foal."

Cade munched his biscuit, a pleased smile on his face. "Why didn't you get me up?"

"No use waking up everybody. Kit and I handled it."

And I manhandled her. Garret tasted his eggs and discovered his appetite had left him. He couldn't forget the way her lips had tasted. The softness of her body. The silkiness of her hair as it caressed his face. Or the glassy-eyed fear that had possessed her.

It had taken every ounce of control he had to leave her last night. He had wanted to wrap his arms around her and take away the fright, but the fear of what he might do once he touched her held him in check. That would only add to her terror, not abate it. Damn! He was acting like a greenhorn in a brothel. Why did Kit rile emotions in him that should be callused with scorn?

His youth had been filled with half-naked saloon girls advertising their charms. He should be immune to a woman's wiles. But it wasn't Kit's body that fueled his obsession, although he craved to caress each curve and delicate plane.

Her spirit beckoned to him like a mirage of water to a thirsty man. She embodied the frontier and was as untamed as a winter blizzard. Comforting as a summer breeze. A woman to ride the river with. A woman to build a future with. Dropping his fork, he pushed his plate away.

"You want them eggs?" Davidson asked, his bony arm already reaching for the abandoned plate.

Nervous energy made Garret restless. He walked over to the door, leaned one arm high on the frame and watched Chili lapping up a mixture of eggs and grits. The black trotting in the corral. The knotholes in the wood floor. The sky. Anything but the barn. Anything but Kit's window.

"Bah!" Garret told himself he didn't care. But where the hell was Kit? It was getting late. The sun shone low on the eastern horizon, the sky a blend of pastels. Yellows like rich cream. Pinks like a woman's blush. Blues the shade of Kit's eyes when she smiled.

There he went again, thinking of her. Was she avoiding him? He found himself back at the door, staring at the barn. Waiting.

Kit couldn't have told her brother about their kiss. If she had, the big Indian would be using those sledgehammer fists on Garret's face. His feet started moving. Pacing.

"Where's Hawk? He should be up by now."

Cade gave him a sidelong look. "Kit and Hawk already ate and rode out. Said you told them to ride brush on the west side of the ranch."

Hot coffee streamed down Garret's throat and left a burning trail. "It's barely daylight!" He wiped his mouth with the sleeve of his shirt. All that worrying and Kit wasn't even here. Like nothing happened.

A horrible thought occurred to him. Had she pretended fear so that he would feel like a louse and leave her alone? Of course, that would explain her rapid change. Her masquerade as a boy should have sweat the fat off his brain. Kit lied as easily as she took a breath.

Anger lashed every gentle, foolish emotion from him. With a snap of his fingers, Garret was back in control, of himself, his emotions and the Rockin' G. He threw his mug in the sink and spoke to his brother. "You should have gone with them."

"Me? You told me to steer clear."

Garret raked his fingers through his hair and gave his

heart the same advice. Steer clear of her. The dull pang in his chest told him otherwise.

Kit reined in her mare and slid from the saddle. Mud squished under her boots. Water danced along the shore and splashed across the smooth rocks in the wide, narrow stream. A raccoon washed its food at the water's edge, spotted her, then scurried away.

Her brother knelt at the creek bank, impervious to the delightful sound of the water or the shocked look on the raccoon's face. She didn't have to ask what he'd found. The tight line of his jaw told her all she needed.

"Three men, ten cows." Hawk traced the hoofprint in the mud then pointed toward the mountains. "They went upstream. One, maybe two days ago."

Cottonwoods trimmed the banks of the creek, casting shadows on the cool water, but Kit felt feverish. Her anxiety built as Hawk crouched near the tracks. The pounding in her heart caused her to gasp, "Is it Jando?"

Hawk lifted his head, and hate lit the depths of his eyes. "It would be his way. Hide in the canyons. Wait for the roundup and get away with as many heads as he can."

"And kill anyone who gets in his way." Kit choked out what they already knew. Fatigue settled in pockets under her eyes. She rubbed one corner and wiped away a tear.

"The spirits came to you last night?" Hawk stood and smoothed her tears away with the pads of his thumbs.

"Yes." Kit released her breath slowly. "I stayed up most of the night." She did dream last night. Of the village. Of Jando. And of Garret. Her lips burned as she remembered his mouth covering hers. The bold statement of his lust bulging his jeans. Why had he kissed her? What must he think of her reaction to him? Why had he found her knife for her?

Completely oblivious to her turbulent thoughts, Hawk let his hands rest on her shoulders. Their weight helped Kit to concentrate on her brother and not the remembered feel of Blaine's lips or her response. She must never let Hawk know of Garret's transgression. Her brother would kill the rancher and then a posse would do the same to Hawk. Only her silence could protect them both.

"Soon, you and the spirits of our friends will rest." Hawk dropped his hands and scanned the hip-high grass-lands, then swept the forest with a critical gaze. "It is strange Cade did not ride with us."

"Perhaps he trusts us."

A subtle grin flickered across Hawk's lips. "Cade speaks to me as though we have ridden together for years instead of days. And he talks and talks. This man will never be a good Indian. He cannot be quiet." The smile disappeared. "It is the other one that wishes us gone."

Is that why Garret kissed me? Kit tugged her lower lip. Was last night just another attempt to make her leave?

Hawk's gaze darted from the creek to the denseness of the upper forest and on to the rolling vista of the prairie. "I would follow these tracks but would not leave you."

"Then I'll go with you."

Older-brother authority echoed in his voice. "You will return to the safety of the ranch." Hawk vaulted into the saddle.

"How could I explain not being out on the range with you? Garret already suspects our motives," she argued. "At least let me stay here until you return. If you don't come back by supper, I'll round up those strays we spot-ted downstream and head back to the Rockin' G. I can tell Garret you rode after a cow that broke away."

Her brother scanned the countryside again. Kit pressed her point. "Jando never uses the same trail twice. His men won't be this way again. Let me stay."

"Why could you not be an obedient Indian woman?" He gave her an affectionate pat on the head. "I tell you to wait at the mission, I will find Jando on my own. You follow me on the trail. I tell you to wait in the hills, you play the part of a boy to be near. If I tell you not to follow me now, you will do it anyway. I should tie you—"

"To a tree." Kit smiled. "But you won't." And he wouldn't. Hawk's idle threat meant she had won. Pulling her rifle from the scabbard, she cracked the barrel and showed Hawk the filled chamber. "See, I'll be fine."

Unimpressed, Hawk gave her a no-nonsense stare.

"Kit, the only way you could hit a barn is if you were trying to miss it." His turn of phrase hinted of Cade's influence.

The truth hurt. So she couldn't shoot, but she wasn't defenseless. "I also have my knife."

"With an Indian weapon, you are lethal." Hawk looked at the trail, then at her. "You stay here." He pointed downward, straight at her. "Supper—" he pointed in the direction of the ranch "—you leave."

"I promise." Before he could trot off, Kit was determined to get a vow of her own. "Don't take on Jando without me. I need to see his death as much as you do."

A shudder traveled down Hawk's leg. Kit knew it wasn't from fear. Loathing consumed Hawk's soul and refused him rest. "I do not wish Jando a quick death. He will suffer and know a Cheyenne hand spills his blood. I will wait."

Kit watched her brother ride upstream along the grassy banks, his gaze deciphering the markings along the water's edge. Just a few more days and, with luck, Hawk would find which of the canyons hide Jando's raiders. Then her brother would serve up his own brand of justice. Cheyenne justice.

They could turn Jando in for the stolen cattle and watch a trial. See him hang for beef. But how many cattle equaled the terror of a child? The rape of a woman? The death of an entire village?

Indian lives came cheap to white men. Their law would have no reason to try Jando for his killing spree. And that was important to her brother and to her. Jando had to die for the Cheyenne deaths, not for rustling cattle.

Kit leaned against the side of her mare and fought down the deep despair inside. When she had set off in search of her half brother, she had forsaken her father, her friends and society along with all the luxuries of that life. She never regretted it. Her time in Hawk's camp was the happiest of her life. And the most heartbreaking. It made the bond between them unbreakable.

She reached for her canteen and prepared to wait for her brother's return. "Let him come back to me," she prayed.

Afternoon light filtered into the thick stand of firs and pines that hid Garret from Hawk and Kit's view. Mockingbirds screeched at him for disturbing the sanctity of the forest.

It had taken him the entire morning to track down the two. Along the trail, he had spotted cattle marks. Tracks Kit and Hawk had ignored. What was down at the creek bed that interested them so much?

He dropped his spyglass into his vest pocket and walked back to a clearing. Mounting his horse, he studied the thick forest on the mountainside. He could follow

Hawk and see what the Indian was tracking. Or stay with Kit.

Both had heard Fredrick's warning of outlaws. So why would Hawk leave Kit alone unless he was sure she wouldn't be molested by the rustlers? The Indian was sharp. He would be able to detect Garret's presence easily. Nor was Hawk likely to answer any questions. Garret reined his mount toward the lowlands and Kit.

Regardless of her guilt or innocence, she didn't belong out here in the wilderness alone. He'd find his answers and get her home to the Rockin' G.

Summer heat vapors rose from the grasslands, blurring the line of trees downstream. Kit swished her bandanna in the cool water and washed the grime from her face and down the deep V of her shirt.

Shading her eyes with her hand, she located the sun straight overhead. Hours remained before Hawk returned from tracking the rustlers' trail. Hours to think of nothing but him being captured or hurt.

She uncapped her canteen and filled it from the foaming water of a stair-step waterfall. The refreshing liquid quenched her thirst. A few drops dripped from the corner of her mouth, and she licked them off. The action reminded her of Garret's kiss. The way his tongue had teased her mouth. Suddenly, it wasn't water her lips desired. It was Garret. Her mind and body were at odds. While her arms ached to touch the rancher, her mind reeled at the thought.

Kit twirled a loose strand of hair around her finger, her thoughts tangled in questions about Garret's actions. Most of their conversations were arguments. And he had flatly told her he planned to marry Abigail Benton. So he must be after what so many men wanted. A woman. Any woman.

Kit felt torn between unextinguishable rage and unbearable despair. Anger that Garret would use her so. Despair that she had allowed her fear to make her vulnerable. Not again. Never again.

The endless prairie unfolded in front of her. In the distance, a herd of pronghorns leaped across the miles of golden grass. Her Appaloosa grazed on tender shoots as she swatted flies in the heat with her tail. The trees along the water's edge served as orchestra seats for a multitude of birds and small animals.

Nature offered a wide assortment of company, but Kit felt isolated. Separate from the fabric of life around her. Alone. Her fingers tightened around the tough leather canteen strap as she hung it on her saddle. *Be strong,* she ordered herself. *Hawk needs you. Get control.*

Her Appaloosa stopped grazing, lifted her head and twitched her alert ears. Kit recognized the warning of a herd animal. Something was coming. Through the heat waves rising on the hills, she saw a dark spot heading down the incline. Slowly, but straight toward her.

Whoever it was, she must guide him away from Hawk. A bumbling cowhand could endanger her brother and their mission. She cradled her rifle, but her real confidence rested on her hip. In the hard steel of her knife.

A few stray wisps of hair hung near her face, the heat twisting them into curls. She tucked them behind her ears, planted her feet wide and aimed her rifle at the approaching rider.

Ten yards away, the rider halted and Kit's heart slammed against her chest. The wide brim of his hat shadowed part of her employer's face, but she knew it by heart now. Hard green eyes and a mouth that scowled more often than smiled.

"You aim to shoot me?" Garret Blaine leaned an arm lazily on his saddle horn. With the other, he thumbed back his dark brown Stetson.

"I didn't know it was you." She took her eye from the rifle sight.

"Now you do." He leaned back in his saddle, the leather creaking from his weight. "Be careful with that." He nodded at her weapon. "It might go off."

"Yes." She lowered her aim slowly. "It might. You looking for something?"

"Nope." He dismounted, hesitated before facing her, then turned, a sarcastic smile on his face. "Just enjoying the scenery." Sun-carved lines near his eyes crinkled. His gaze wandered over the contours of her body. Lingered at her lips and the swell of her breasts.

Like a distant storm, Kit's panic rumbled in her soul, warning her of its approach. Heat burned her neck and cheeks. His smile deepened but never warmed.

Kit refused to surrender to her fear. She schooled her features in a cold mask of disdain. Garret wasn't the type for a casual ride. Either he was spying on her and Hawk or he had deliberately sought her out. And Kit could think of only one reason why he would want her company, to pick up where he left off in the barn.

"I don't see your brother."

"He's out looking for cows." Kit kept her finger on the trigger of the rifle. Fear leaked into her control, and she fought to restrain it. Hawk needed her to cover his trail if he was to find the outlaw's lair. She would not let him down. "My mare picked up a rock. I rested her so she wouldn't come up lame."

He dismounted and wrapped his reins around a twisted

cottonwood branch. "And Hawk just left you out here alone?"

"Not alone." She patted the butt of her rifle. Pointing the barrel at the river, she pretended Hawk rode the opposite direction. "He rode downstream."

Ducking under a low branch at the river's edge, Garret leaned one arm on the branch. He kicked over a rock and a few scattered leaves. "So we have some time," he drawled.

Kit found her gaze following the line of his parted lips. "Time for what?" she croaked.

"To make our peace about what happened in the barn last night." He slipped his thumb under his waistband. His fingers splayed along the denim material, drawing attention to the area just under his belt buckle.

Strange, exotic feelings shot through her body. Temptation begged her to release her control and give in to her desire to feel Garret's lips on hers. To lead his hands to where his stare had lingered. At the same time, her mind flashed images of Jando's lecherous face peering down at her.

Garret's smile faded, and a flinty hardness sliced his eyes. "When we kissed—"

"We kissed?" she squeaked. "I seem to remember it as being one-sided." Anger flattened her weaker desires. She built her irritation to a powerful flame and used it to stoke her control. She had to concentrate on leading Garret away from the river and the tracks.

His emerald eyes narrowed. "That was a good act you put on. Pretending to be afraid." His stare tore into hers, probing into her soul. "First you play a boy, then you play a frightened schoolgirl. I'm just disgusted I keep falling for the same trick."

Kit's heart skipped. He thought her panic a ruse.

Thanking God for delivering her, she glued a sly smile on her face. "Don't worry about it, Blaine. Better men than you have fallen for it. Just remember, I only use it once." She rested the heel of her palm on her knife handle.

"It won't happen again."

"You got that right."

He leaned over and touched the ground. Kit's heart stuck in her throat. Had he seen the cattle and horse tracks? Would he recognize the signs were from the rustlers? When Garret lifted a stone and threw it in the river, her heart plopped back into place.

Resting one hand on his hip, he pointed at her with the other. "I aim to marry Abigail after roundup."

"My condolences—to her," Kit shot back. A sliver of jealousy snaked up her spine, and she tried to shake it off. "Does your fiancée know you make a habit of kissing other women?"

"Not other women." He folded his arms. The material of his shirt strained across the expanse of his chest. "Just you."

"And what does that mean? I don't count?"

Silence answered her question. He dropped his gaze and let it sweep over the horizon. The realization cut her to the quick. "You don't think I'm worth much, do you?"

"Abigail's a woman of breeding. She's refined and civilized. Hell, her uncle owns—"

"Your integrity?" Kit unleashed her own anger. "Just because you think my lineage isn't rich enough doesn't give you the right to maul me and walk away with a clean conscience."

"You don't understand." Garret spoke through clenched teeth. "Abigail's name carries a lot of respect."

"Well, it's a good thing it does. 'Cause you haven't

any." Kit felt tears sting her eyes. He considered her good enough to seduce but not good enough to be seen with in public. A pulsating hurt throbbed in her soul. How right her father had been all those years ago. The world was full of cruel men. But she wouldn't hide like her mother. No, Kit intended to fight back. Garret would never see how his words hurt, and Jando would taste her knife.

"Don't worry, Mr. Blaine." Kit draped her words in false sympathy. "I have no intention of mentioning your indiscretion. I have my pride."

That was plain enough. Garret lowered his hat to shade his eyes from her azure stare. Dark circles fringed her eyes, accentuating the angry sparks in their blue depths.

The rifle in her hands drooped so that he could wrench it from her at will. Burs clung to her leather chaps. A scratch ran along her temple. Her shirt had a rip in the shoulder, exposing a tiny bit of skin to the sun. And to him.

Dawn-to-dusk chores were whittling down her hickory backbone. Kit needed to be home, to get some rest. Garret was determined to see she got it. Whether she wanted it or not.

"Mount up." He hauled himself into the saddle and away from his dismal past.

"I'm not going anywhere." Kit was running on stubbornness. Garret could see it written all over her face. In the tilt of her chin. In the whiplike way she stiffened her back. He rubbed his fingers over his mouth to hide a smile. This time he would win the argument.

"I want to ride upstream and look for steers."

She replaced her rifle and tacked up. Reaching for the saddle horn, one foot in the stirrup, she commented, "We'd be more likely to find strays downstream. Better grazing."

"Isn't Hawk already there?"

"Yes." She mounted up. "But he planned to swing wide. There's a good chance we'll miss him." A northern wind carried more warmth than her gaze. Looking at the sun, now on its western track, she added, "Hawk will catch up." A click of her teeth and she cantered off downstream.

Pushing his sorrel to a matching gait, Garret rode by her side. He stole a glance at her profile. Nothing about Kit O'Shane should be attractive. She wore men's clothes, broke wild horses and had the disposition of a rattlesnake.

But her hair...it was like silk threads of darkness. Threads that could bind a man's heart, sew a seam that was soft to the touch but strong enough not to break.

Admiration sneaked into his heart as he watched her ride. Reminiscent of a mythical creature, the woman and horse were like one beautiful animal. Kit sat tall and straight in the saddle, her dark hair whipping out from beneath her hat, creating a moving dance of wind and motion. The desire to become a part of the magical picture teased at his sensibilities. Warned him that more than the release of his body's wants colored the dream.

There was no denying the attraction he felt, but he cursed his weakness. Falling in love with Kit O'Shane meant forsaking his ma's last wish, to "make Blaine a name to be respected." Garret had abandoned his ma and Cade before, but not again. His family had to come first.

Forcing himself to study the landscape instead of her, he coerced his passion to a cell in his heart. Still present, but imprisoned. With his ardor contained, logical thinking resumed.

Apprehension took root at the base of his neck. At the river, he had spotted shoed-horse prints surrounding cattle marks. All heading toward the high timber, and in the same direction Hawk had ridden. Why hadn't Kit mentioned the signs to Garret? Or that Hawk had followed? Could Hawk and the rustlers be meeting in secret?

The puzzle pieces about the Indian and his sister fell into place, forming an ugly picture in Garret's mind. Maybe the two were shells sent to keep the rest of the gang informed on what ranches to hit. That would explain their insistence on staying.

Innocent or guilty?

Cade wasn't going to buy a few coincidences as evidence Hawk was rustling, no matter how much Garret argued with him. Firing the two, without any proof, would drive Cade away and add to the gossip in town. The two Indians might find themselves the main guests at a lynching party. Garret was going to have to stick close and watch. Hope that the sheriff found the rustlers and cleared Hawk and Kit, or that they made a mistake. One Garret could use to show Cade how misplaced his allegiance was.

The base of his neck twitched in a spasm. Headache and a pain in the neck. Good analogies for Kit and her brother. Riding alongside her, Garret cursed the unexpected pleasure and dismay that churned in his heart. He had to start roundup and, like it or not, Kit was going to be a part of it. Long hours working side by side, and nights alone in camp. It was turning out to be a hell of a season.

Chapter Eight

Soft pinks and blues tinged the sky as Garret trotted into the ranch yard and cast the water pump an eager glance. He smelled of old cows, bull chips and sweat. A long, cool draw of water would wash the dirt from his body and the thirst from his throat. But water couldn't quench the thirst in his heart.

Kit, riding next to him, shifted in her saddle. Pasted to her chest and shoulders, her chambray shirt hung like a wet rag on her trim frame. Raven wisps of hair escaped her slouch hat. He caught the essence of her perfume. Mountain laurel and lavender. And the hint of betrayal.

Chili bounded across the yard, scattering the hens and sending the fowl squawking. Garret felt about as useful as wings on a chicken. He still had no surefire answers about Kit or her brother. As he dismounted, the saddle creaked and so did he. He gave the old dog a scratch then filled his hat with water and drenched his face. Hell, he felt old and tired.

Sweeping one leg over the horn of her saddle, Kit eased to the ground. She kneaded her thighs as she walked slightly bowlegged to the hitching post. Her jeans stuck to her legs, outlining shapely calves and thighs. The only part of her body not covered in dust was her backside. Suddenly, Garret felt very much alive and well.

"The next beef I see had better be sizzling on a plate." Kit wrapped her rein around the post. Chili snarled at her. She didn't even give the dog a low bark. Herding in the longhorns they had found on the way home must have shaved the last splinter off her stamina. They hadn't seen a sign of Hawk.

Garret's stomach gurgled a loud complaint. A knowing smile tugged Kit's full lips while a hint of amusement lit the depths of her eyes.

Hunger flared in him, but not for the cook's chow. This ache dug deeper than his gut, deeper than his soul. He loosened his girth and pulled the saddle from the gelding's back. "I could eat a whole pot of Cracker's stew."

"And a tin full of biscuits," Kit agreed as she untacked her mount.

"With a crock of fresh churned butter." Garret fell into the game. He tugged his saddle forward, slipping his arms underneath.

"Don't forget the honey," Kit added as she balanced her saddle on her forearms.

"No. I don't think I could ever forget that." Or her. Two saddles separated them but a bond joined them. He knew her fatigue, she knew his hunger. Working side by side made her a part of the Rockin' G. A part of him.

More than anything, he wanted to take her hand and lead her into the cabin. Sit down to a meal over the cherry-wood table and talk about the day's chores. Turn in with her warm and giving body at his side. He hefted his saddle onto his shoulder and welcomed the pinch of the leather. The pain deadened his wasted dreams and desires. "Davidson can give our horses a rubdown. If I don't give him something to do, that boy will lick the stew pot clean."

"He's growing." Kit laid her saddle on the hitching rail and looked at her sweat-caked mount. Garret could see her fighting between a sense of duty to her animal and the weariness in her body.

"The boy'll take good care of your horse. Trust me."

She stiffened as if he had struck her. The color drained from her face. Her eyes darkened to sapphire orbs lined by dark lashes. "Very well. I'll see to my supper." She folded her arms across her chest, rubbing her elbows in the waning daylight.

Garret led the way to the bunkhouse. One step on the cedar porch and he sensed trouble. Mud tracked over the white boards. And blood. He flicked the iron latch on the door with more force than he needed. The bar clanged like a bell clapper. He pushed Kit forward. The smell of cowboy feet and coffee peppered the room.

"That cow had horns as wide as a canyon and a belly full of mean." Cade sat on a flour keg, his arms spread wide, covered with grime. Mud lined his boots, and his usually spotless gray Stetson sat on the table spattered with dirt.

When trouble hit the Rockin' G, his little brother was usually at the heart of it. Garret fixed a hard stare on Cade and ordered, "Start explaining, and make it fast." He crossed the room in three strides.

"That's what I was doing." Cade flashed Kit a smile. "Just passing the time while Cracker doctors up Hawk."

Near the potbellied stove, the old cook squeezed one eye closed as he patiently stabbed dark thread into a gold needle. His face gleamed from the steam rising from a kettle on the stove. Standing beside him, the Indian held a cotton bandage to his bare forearm. A bright red stain soaked the cloth.

"Hawk!" Kit rushed forward, pushing past Garret.

Cracker removed the bandage, exposing an ugly gash. He spilled a few drops of whiskey over the cut. "A couple of stitches and he'll be right as rain."

"Do not worry." Hawk brushed a strand of hair from Kit's face.

Eager to be a part of the gossip, Davidson spilled information. "Hawk saved Cade from a rampaging longhorn. He nearly got skewered a-doing it."

Kit crumpled backward. Her hat fell, and a stream of ebony hair cascaded free. Garret rushed to her side. Cade leaped from his seat. Hawk disengaged himself from Cracker's hold and wrapped his uninjured arm around her waist. His icy blue gaze centered on where Garret's arm held Kit. Garret gave the big Indian a cool stare of his own and helped her sit on the vacated keg.

"Get her a drink of water." Garret pointed to Davidson. "Then get out in the yard and see to our horses." The boy poured a tin of water from the clay pitcher and spilled most of it as he handed it over.

"I'm fine. Really." Kit sipped the water, her eyes closed. "Hawk, please see to your arm."

"And somebody tell me what happened," Garret demanded. Davidson opened his mouth. "I told you to see to our horses." The boy closed his jaw and skulked from the room.

Taking hold of Hawk's arm, Cracker looked down his nose at the gash and proceeded to tend the wound.

"I was riding on the west side, just minding my own business." Cade handed Kit a full bowl of stew.

"I told you to ride east." Garret bit out each word, letting his anger escape like steam from a teakettle. He slit open a biscuit and layered it with butter and honey. Wrapping it in a cotton napkin, he passed it to Kit.

Cade opened his eyes wide with childlike innocence.

"I must have clean forgot." Cracker "tsked" under his breath as he continued to sew Hawk's arm. Kit's brother quirked his lips, whether from pain or humor Garret couldn't tell.

"As I was saying—" Cade grabbed a ladder-back chair and straddled it "—I was riding just where the timberline starts, and I heard this terrible bawling." He wrinkled up his nose and made a low honking noise. "Naturally, I just had to see what was making the commotion. And what do you think I found?"

"Hawk?" Kit licked the brown gravy from the back of her spoon.

"Nope, he didn't start bellering till later." Cade laughed as Hawk started to protest.

"Kit said Hawk rode downstream." Garret pressed his point, hoping Cade would pick up on the discrepancy. "How'd he wind up in the timber?"

"I also told you he might swing wide." Kit flashed Hawk a cautious glance. The Indian gave a single nod in agreement. His blue eyes froze to a wintry gray as he contemplated Garret.

Cade fell back into his story with gusto. "What was a-making that noise was a calf bogged down in a mud hole. So I waded in hip-deep, tied my lasso 'round him and commenced to hauling his hind end out of that muck. And I woulda done it except for his mama."

"Finished." Cracker peered at his stitches with a gleam of approval. Hawk stepped away to hover near his sister and glare at Garret.

"How can I finish telling this story if you're gonna keep talking?" Cade threw up his arms in despair.

"You talk too much," Hawk countered. He turned slightly toward Kit, his lips twisted in a wry smile. "That is how I found him. Trying to talk that longhorn into leaving.''

''And I just about had her convinced before you showed up and scared her into charging.''

The friendly exchange worried Garret. Cade and Hawk were getting thicker than feathers in a pillow. Like partners. It had been a mistake to tag his brother to the Indian's side. It was going to be twice as hard now to convince Cade that Hawk might be rustling.

Wiping the crumbs from her mouth, Kit nudged her brother with one shoulder. ''So just what did you do to get rid of the longhorn?''

Cade answered for him. ''Oh, Miss Kit, he was a sight. He came riding down on that big ole buckskin screaming a war whoop that would scare the devil himself into going to church. Well, that mama cow just near died a fright right there until she remembered just how big she was.''

Using his fingers, he imitated the longhorn. ''That old she-cow commenced to waving her horns this way and that. And Hawk rode circles around her. And while he was a-dancing with that longhorn, I got the calf out.''

A sly grin creased Cade's mouth. ''Once Hawk seen I was clear, he tried to dance away. I'm thinking that old cow didn't appreciate him cutting their waltz short. She nicked him with her horn on his last do-si-do. It's either that or Hawk here ain't the cowboy he thought he was.''

''I make a better cowboy than you would an Indian.''

''You're on.'' Cade stood and slapped Hawk on the shoulder. ''Bet stands I can out-Indian you before you out-cowboy me.''

''Enough,'' Garret commanded. ''Cade, you nearly got yourself and Hawk killed because you didn't take the time to use some common sense.''

The mischievous light in his brother's eyes snapped off.

An oppressive silence cloaked the room. The kettle on the stove released a high, shrill whistle. In the quiet, it sounded like a train blast.

Pointing his finger under Cade's nose, Garret rammed the truth down his brother's gullet. "You were damn lucky Hawk came around when he did or we'd be burying you. When are you going to start thinking first?"

Cade stood, a halo of fine dust in the air around him. Slapping on his hat, he drifted toward the door with lazy steps. "I don't reckon I ever need to." He opened the door and spoke over his shoulder. "Not with you doing all my thinking for me." A few steps and he disappeared off the porch and into the dimming daylight.

Kit walked to the limestone sink. Her boot heels clicked on the wood floor, a Morse code of her displeasure.

"He nearly got your brother killed." Garret threw up his arms as she silently washed and dried her supper dish. She slammed the bowl onto the tilted stack near the washbasin and wrung out the dishcloth. Again and again. She probably wished it was his neck.

Garret could sooner talk a polecat out of spraying than talk Kit out of one of her simmering spells. Might as well let her stew while he acknowledged his obligations. Slipping his thumbs into his belt loops, he braced his fingers on his hips and faced Hawk. "I'm obliged to you for saving Cade's skin."

The Indian stood, his lips taut as a telegraph line. He crossed his arms, causing the jagged tooth necklace around his neck to clatter. "I gave my aid to Cade, not to you." He turned to his sister. "I will walk you to the barn."

Kit shifted her weight from one foot to the other, the hankering to get her two bits into the conversation plain as day on her face. Her arched brows wrinkled. The line of her lips swayed from left to right. A slight hand signal from Hawk and Kit took a deep breath, then, like a meek lamb, followed her brother to the door. She shot Garret one final angry glance from over her shoulder before she left.

"That Indian's got a chip on his shoulder the size of a two-by-four." Garret kicked at a dirt clump on the floor as he watched Kit's midnight-colored hair blend into the shadows.

From behind him, over the clanging of tin plates and cups, he overheard Cracker mutter, "He's not the only one."

Kit marched ahead of her brother and threw open the door of her room. Her anger fueled her tired body with outrage. "Garret is impossible. It was reprehensible the way he admonished Cade this evening."

Her brother trailed into the room. And the dog. Hawk lit the kerosene lantern. Instantly, insects bombarded the glow. Chili placed his two front feet on the bed. "Harrumph!" Kit cleared her throat. The dog sank to the floor with a grumble.

"Blaine give you trouble?" Hawk's question threw Kit off-kilter.

All the time. In a variety of ways. She felt like wringing his neck for the way he treated Cade. Garret wanted to bond Cade to the land, but instead he was pushing him away. One day, Garret would wake up and find himself alone, with nothing but the Rockin' G to keep him company. The thought caused a twinge of regret. He didn't have to be so hard-nosed. He didn't have to be so lonely.

There were times when Garret could be…what? She sighed. Tarnation, he could be an attractive man when he wanted. Earlier today, when the herd finally moved, she had looked to him for confirmation of a job well-done. And he had delivered. Removing his hat, he had wiped the sweat from his brow and his eyes mellowed to deep forest green, lit by admiration and pride, for her. Warmth had crept into her cheeks, not from the hot noonday sun but from his gaze.

When he asked her to trust him, she had been torn. A part of her cried to share the horror of her past and have him stroke her hair, giving comfort. But the cold center of her soul refused to melt. The part that Jando had frozen. Garret had asked for the one thing she could never do. He was more than troublesome, he was dangerous to her and to her quest.

"Kit?" Faint lines near Hawk's mouth deepened as he interrupted her thoughts. "I lost the trail in the canyon, but it's Jando."

A fist grabbed her gut and twisted. Shivers of pain and fear threatened to choke the breath from her. Fighting down the panic, she forced herself to meet her brother's eyes. "You're certain?"

Grimness robbed the gentleness from his face. From his vest pocket, he pulled a small amulet. Colorful beads formed a complex geometric pattern, the same symbol as on his own leather vest. A Cheyenne design.

Hawk clasped the amulet. "This is from our village. Jando is hiding in the high country on the Rockin' G."

Kit sat down on her narrow cot, bracing her weight with her arms. The dog gave a disgruntled snort.

"Why here? And why hasn't he hit Garret yet?"

Her brother glanced toward the soft light in the cabin window. "Jando wants Blaine's cattle. All of them."

Air squeezed from her lungs. "No. It will destroy him." She'd bet there wasn't a spare penny in Garret's bank account. The outhouse was the only luxury on the whole spread. The theft of his cattle would drive Garret into bankruptcy and steal away his reason for living.

"Jando is no fool. He has thought this out." Hawk interpreted her words as questioning Jando instead of concern for Garret. Squatting on his heels, her brother scratched a line in the dusty floor, then used small pebbles to form a rocky barrier.

Pushing herself off the cot, Kit commanded her lungs to work, her mind to clear and her heart to regain a normal beat. She peered over her brother's shoulder.

"Here is the river." Hawk pointed to the dirt line. "Jando uses the water to cover his tracks. Upriver, he herds the cattle out of water and toward the mountains." Hawk's hand swept over the stones representing the foothills of the Rockies. "A dry riverbed would make him hard to track. And explain why he steals only a few cows at a time. Easier to drive and keep on the rocks.

"Many cattle and horses die on a hard drive. Jando must have a large herd, or he makes no money. This man is evil, but he is crafty. He would not make his camp on the Rockin' G without reason." Taking slow, deliberate steps, he stopped at the barn entrance.

Following, Kit centered herself in the opening. Nodding toward the heavy black outline of Pike's Peak, she spoke to the night wind. "Jando sits in those mountains and sees Garret's cattle being herded into the prairie."

"And counts Blaine's men," Hawk added. "Seven now. How many more can he hire?"

"One or two." The conclusion of her conversation unfolded like a bad dream. "How many men does Jando have?"

"Fifteen, probably more."

"All Jando has to do is ride down and take what he wants."

A finality settled on her shoulders, crushing her with its enormity. How could she warn Garret of the danger without exposing her own reason for staying on the Rockin' G? "How long until the rustlers strike?"

Her brother's words shook her. "Just before the drive. The men will be tired. Jando will hit Blaine last and hard."

She held a man's future in her hands. Garret's future. The responsibility blistered her need for vengeance.

Her brother's gaze swept over her face, his penetrating stare observed the tremble in her fingers. "You would tell Blaine the truth? Can you trust him?"

Trust Garret? Could she tell him about Jando and expect him to stand back while Hawk hunted the elusive criminal on his own? Would Garret allow her brother to exact his own deserved revenge without interference from the law or the other ranchers?

"No." She toyed with her lower lip. "Garret isn't the type of man to give anyone leeway. Look at how he treats his own brother." Standing tall and proud, she cocked her chin to fortify her own lagging spirits and show Hawk she felt confident in her decision. "Blaine would notify the sheriff and the local ranchers. A posse of loud-riding cowboys is only going to muddle the trail and warn Jando someone's looking for him." She hesitated then asked, "But what about Cade?"

The night breeze ruffled the fringe on Hawk's vest. His bare torso didn't seem to register the cool temperatures. "Cade has no love of this land. He is here to please his brother. Leaving will cause no grief."

"Garret isn't going to give up the herd without a fight. Jando could kill them all." Kit shuddered as she faced the full impact of her silence. The wake of the rustlers had always been bloody. Her hands would be tainted with the deaths of the Rockin' G crew.

"Men die."

"But we know these men. Cracker tended your wound. Garret gave us work—"

"Blaine gives us nothing." Hawk's voice rose then softened. In a harsh whisper, he scoffed at her concern. "Garret Blaine has no heart except for what he owns. Land. Cattle. And I think he would own you, also, my sister." At her gasp, Hawk fingered his necklace. "I failed you before. I will not do so again. Garret Blaine will not touch you."

He already has. Kit lowered her gaze. Hawk and Garret were a lot alike, emotions tight as a bowstring. If Hawk realized Garret had already kissed her, her brother would gleefully release a quiver of arrows into the rancher's heart. What would Hawk do if he realized that Garret might have done more than just touch his lips to hers?

Kit rubbed her brother's arm. "We can't just let Jando kill these men. Will Jando wait until the cattle are completely rounded up?"

"Yes. He will let Blaine do the work, then steal."

"Then we'll stay silent until after the roundup is finished. If we haven't found Jando's lair by then, we tell Garret our suspicions." Relief saturated her pores.

"I will find Jando and kill him before the trail drive." Hatred dripped from her brother's tongue.

Roundup would take a month at the most. This time, there would be no mistakes. No seeking help from the blundering law. No warning to local ranchers, only to see bounty-hunting posses warn Jando off. This time, just Hawk, herself and the added drive of a time limit.

Four weeks and Jando would be dead by Hawk's hand. Four weeks and the Cheyenne spirits that haunted her dreams would quiet. Four weeks and she would leave the Rockin' G. Ride off. Never see Garret again.

Chapter Nine

Kit lay on her cot, her hands interlaced behind her head, and watched the sky change to prelight gray, no longer night but not yet morning. The heavens lay in limbo. As did she. Revenge or friendship? Hawk or Garret? Jando's death or Garret's future?

This should not be so difficult, she scolded herself silently. Her brother deserved her undivided loyalty. There should be no question in her mind about what to do. And there wasn't one in her logic, just in her heart.

In many ways, Garret was a seeker of his own type of revenge. Instead of a man's death, he sought to kill the shame of his mother's past. He would never deviate from his path. Neither would Hawk. Neither could she.

A tightness encircled her chest, squeezing at her heart. *I will not be weak. Hawk will have his revenge. No matter what the cost. No matter who gets hurt.* She pulled on her jeans and whispered, "Even if it's me."

A shaft of morning light cut the darkness of the cabin. Outside, the old banty rooster crowed, shattering the quiet of the new day. From across the room, Cade's breathing never broke the regular rhythm of sleep. Garret rubbed the stiffness from his neck and rotated his shoulders. He used to sleep like a wintering bear. Now he felt like a grizzly—cranky, stiff and mean.

And who the hell was responsible for that? A dark-haired siren. He had lain awake for hours thinking about the taste of their kiss. The honey scent of her skin. The possibility that she was a thief.

Doubt wallowed in the pit of his stomach. Sitting on the edge of the bed, he was tempted to lie back down and throw the covers over his head.

Sunbeams continued to invade the cabin and nagged of wasted daylight. He pulled on his jeans and padded over to the cast-iron cookstove. Filling the coffeepot with water and grounds, he waited for the morning elixir to heat and beat off the chill.

Cool air sifted through the cracks in the doorjamb and flickered across his face like a woman's caress. How would it be to have his woman lying in his bed, the sheets warm from their bodies. Scented from their lovemaking. And the woman he daydreamed of wasn't blond and fair like Abigail.

No, she was wild and untamed, with raven hair that felt like silk in his fingers. The dream seemed so real that he took a step back toward his bed, half-expecting to see Kit beneath the covers. The rattle of the boiling water and the reviving aroma of coffee stripped away the melancholy.

Cade finally started to rustle about behind his curtained-off room, the smell of fresh coffee a better wake-up call than the rooster. Garret poured himself a cup of the muddy liquid then shoved his feet into his dusty boots. Stepping outside onto the covered porch, he let the sun warm his face while the mountain air chilled his bare torso.

The land unfolded like a golden carpet before him,

stretching for miles. A scrap of paper said he owned this valley, but in reality, the land owned him.

A willing hostage, Garret watched the wisps of fog lift from the stream and reveal the cottonwood trees on each of its banks. Leaves, dark green with summer's color, would soon turn bright orange and amber announcing fall's arrival. A cowboy marked time by hard work, and autumn brought the hardest—roundup and the drive to Kansas.

Like the circus for a little boy, roundup inspired a sense of wonder and passion in a cowboy. Backbreaking, dust-eating work lay in front of him. And Garret couldn't wait. The last vestiges of unease fled in the wake of roundup thrill.

A multitude of duties had to be completed in the next few days. Cracker could make up the supply list to take to town. No need to even look at the tack. Kit had repaired, cleaned and oiled every strap of leather on the ranch. The thought of Kit and Hawk made Garret pause. What to do with those two?

He wrestled with all the possible choices. Keep them on the ranch while the rest of the crew rode into town? But if Kit and Hawk were rustlers, Garret would be giving them the perfect opportunity to steal.

Let them ride into Colorado Springs? Luckily, Traynor had skedaddled before finding out Kit was female. By now, the fired cowhand must have flapped his jaw about the two half-breeds in every saloon. The news would be a hot topic in the little town.

Just being a half-breed was a hanging offense to many of the miners and cowboys. If he let those two go into town, he'd need to send a watchdog. And that meant Cade. His little brother not only could talk his way out of trouble, but had enough of a reputation as a fast gun to make a man think twice before crossing him.

Cade in Colorado Springs caused problems. One, it threw the Indian and his brother together again, and two, the town lay just a short ride from what was left of Colorado City. Filled with working gals, saloons and gambling, the county seat had decayed into a den of vice. Every two-bit saloon and dance hall would be a magnet to Cade's bad habits.

So, he'd send Cracker, Kit and Hawk to help with the supplies. Cade to watch over them. And...? Garret scratched the back of his head. And he'd ride shotgun over the whole shooting match. At least he could count on Vega to ramrod the rest of the cowhands until he got back.

Garret slammed open the door. "Cade." His brother stood near the stove in his red long johns, pouring a cup of coffee. "We're riding into town for supplies."

"Town?" Cade cocked one eyebrow in pleasant surprise. Then a frown creased his lips. "We?" His eyes turned hound dog, pleading for a bone of hope.

"Yeah." Garret wagged his finger back and forth between his brother's chest and his own. "We ride in, get supplies and ride out. The faster, the better."

Squinting his eyes, Cade asked, "Not even one drink?"

"You're gonna be too busy scouting for trouble. I'm sending the two new hands in to help Cracker."

A cagey awareness glimmered in his brother's aquagreen eyes. Gunfighter savvy narrowed them into slits. "Why don't you want Kit and Hawk here at the ranch?"

Garret swung a chair free from the table and propped his boot on the seat. Resting his elbow on his bent knee, he didn't mince words. "I saw Hawk and Kit down by the river. Hawk rode upstream following tracks. Looks to me those signs belonged to rustlers. Neither Hawk nor Kit said a word about them.''

Cade sipped his coffee. His boyish good looks hardened. *He looks like me.* Garret found the comparison uncomfortable. When was the last time he had looked like Cade? Carefree and smiling.

''So leave them here. I can watch out after them.'' Cade's fingers tightened on his coffee mug.

''Better if they come with us.'' Garret swished the last swallow of coffee in his mug. *Don't push it, Cade. It'll only lead to another argument.*

''You don't think I can handle them.''

''It's not that.'' But it was. The Indian was just too much for Cade. Bigger, meaner and craftier. In town, Hawk wouldn't dare try anything. If they kept to Garret's plan, stayed near the store and kept their heads low, there should be no trouble. And Cade would be safe.

All of Garret's work to build the Rockin' G wouldn't mean a thing if his brother wound up dead. Cade was all the kin he had; if he lost him, then Garret truly would be alone. ''You're too close to them.''

''Hawk saved my life.'' Cade's gaze shifted to his holster hanging on the hook. ''I stand with him. Hell, the man works twice as hard as any cowhand we have.''

''He could be just trying to throw us off.''

''Hawk ain't like that.'' Cade slammed his mug on the table, adding another dent to its surface. ''And neither is Kit.''

''You don't know anything about her.'' Her name conjured up dreams in Garret. Images he wanted to forget.

Cade's defense heightened. ''I know she's a damn fine woman. Just look at her. That smile, her hair—''

''Don't talk to me about her hair.'' Garret sliced his hand through the air. He knew about the midnight tresses with their heady perfume of wildflowers that could make a man drunk. "Kit is off-limits to you."

"Why?" Cade demanded. "'Cause you want her yourself?"

"No!" Garret roared his denial at the same time that his heart leaped at the truth. "Ma whored to buy us this spread. I'm not about to forget that or let you."

"I watched her fade away same as you."

"Not the same as me. I up and left."

"'Cause you had to." The hinge on Cade's jaw clamped shut like a bear trap. "She understood. Ma just wanted us to be happy."

"She wanted to make Blaine a name to be proud of." Garret felt the full weight of his shame. How could he have left his whiskey-addicted mother and wild younger brother to fend for themselves? He had been too full of himself when he should have been thinking of his family.

"Ma only wrote that in her will 'cause that's what she thought you wanted." Cade released a slow, measured breath.

Garret knew how the ostracism of the townswomen had hurt Ma. She had wanted the blot erased as much as Garret. "Carrying on with a woman like Kit isn't going to wipe the shame from our name. She wears pants. Works like a man."

"I bet she'd love like a woman," Cade shot back.

Those words drove deep into Garret's heart. He couldn't help himself. The image of Kit, naked but for her ebony cape of hair, pirouetted in his mind. She reached out, and he stepped inside his daydream eagerly. Lips, full and yielding, met his. Her fingers nimbly unbuttoned his shirt. He could feel the hardness straining in his jeans as she wrapped her arms around him. Asked him to make her his.

Cade pulled him from his trance. "It ain't been that long since you were walking in their boots. Or has spending time with Abigail Benton washed the saloon out of you?"

"Abigail didn't. Andersonville did." Garret could feel the heat of his anger coalesce in the star-shaped scar on his temple. Why couldn't Cade understand he had to be suspicious? Trust was something earned, not given out like a politician's promises.

Cade studied the grounds in the bottom of his enamel cup. "I know you lived through hell, and a man can't go through something like that without changing. You say you're a better man, maybe so. But you don't trust nobody, not even me."

"Cade, you're my partner."

"I'm your little brother. And always will be in your eyes." Sadness darkened Cade's eyes, and resignation lowered his voice. "When are you gonna see a man?"

This was a side of his brother Garret had never seen. Maturity stiffened Cade's spine instead of obstinance. Lines of sorrow deepened near his eyes and mouth. Again, his charming younger brother reminded him of himself. Garret found he didn't like it.

"I didn't say they were burning brands, only that they might be." The words sounded halfhearted. One part of him had already found the two guilty. The other half flinched at the image of Kit's body hanging from a gallows.

"Get your pants on, Cade, then tell Cracker to get the wagon hitched." Bitterness and guilt made Garret's voice harsh.

Cade shoved back the curtain to his room then turned. "You want to know if Kit's rustling?"

"Of course I do."

"Then ask her." Cade slipped inside his partition. The burlap bags swayed as he dressed.

Ask her? Deep inside, Garret knew she was already guilty. Maybe not of stealing his cattle, but definitely his thoughts and reason. Kit O'Shane was dangerously close to rustling his heart.

Kit bounced alongside her brother in the buckboard. The boy, Davidson, had kept up an endless chatter of insults since they had left for town. These insults were a small price to pay for a chance to get a message to San Antonio.

In each town she and Hawk stayed in, she telegraphed the mission friars at the San Antonio school. And in each town she hoped there would be a reply from Hawk's son, Raven. The five-year-old had not spoken since his young eyes witnessed the destruction of the village. In two years, Raven had not spoken or asked to see his father. Kit prayed this telegram would have an answer. And her brother would have some small reprieve from his guilt.

"Cade," Kit addressed the cowboy riding alongside the wagon. "While we're in town, I need to run an errand." She glanced at Hawk. The light amusement left his eyes.

"Garret'd sorta like us all to stay together." Cade's eyes hardened as he reined his mare to a slow walk. "I vouched for you but that don't hold no sway with Garret."

Her heart reached out to the young man. Hurt lingered in his gaze and resentment echoed in his voice. She didn't want to wedge the two further apart but she and Hawk had been eager to get to town for one reason. "I need to send a telegram to—"

"An old employer." Hawk finished for her. "He came up short on the payroll. Promised to wire us the money."

Kit kept silent, registering her brother's lie in case Cade interrogated her further.

"Now, money I understand." A grin tugged at Cade's lips. "I'll see what I can do."

"Whoa." Cracker gave the reins a steady tug. The wagon slowed to a halt. "Gotta water the mules."

Peering over the cook's shoulder, Kit spotted Garret waiting under a stand of cottonwoods. The collar of his deerskin jacket had flipped up, the color matching the long strands of hair at the nape of his neck. Just a shadow of stubble darkened his jaw, a sign he had shaved too fast or with a dull razor.

Dismounting, he spoke to Cracker and Davidson. His gaze never wandered back to her. "Water the mules and stretch a bit." His lips twitched almost into a smile.

Kit vaulted over the side of the buckboard, grateful and confused by Garret's consideration. "I'll be back in a minute," she assured her brother, then scrambled uphill to the juniper and piñon trees. Time enough for her to stretch her legs and do some exploring.

The wind and time had carved the red rocks around her into marvelous shapes. Thin needles of sandstone sliced the sky like bloody fingers. A breeze channeled down through the gullies and brushed her face.

Allowing the breath of the canyon to support her body, she closed her eyes. She wanted to fly away, not to another place but another time. Before the massacre, when she was a young innocent girl with headstrong ambitions to find her missing brother. Confident that no harm would ever come to her. When she had felt safe.

Kit opened her eyes, which were stinging with tears from her thoughts and the dry wind. Just ahead, between two spires, the sun haloed a tall, lean silhouette.

With slow, deliberate steps, Garret sauntered down the

embankment to her. Pushing back his Stetson, he exposed a patch of wheat-colored hair. "Different kind of place, isn't it?"

Kit brushed the palms of her hands against her dungarees and tried to calm the pounding in her heart. "I've never seen anything like this before."

"Neither have I." The gentle softness of his voice caused her to meet his stare. His gaze swept over her and a flush of heat burned her neck and cheeks.

Rummaging in her soul for the old panic, Kit wanted the distance it would put between her and Garret. She couldn't find it. Instead, desire churned in her. She longed to savor the taste of him. Ached to feel his arms around her. Afraid he would see her wantonness, she turned away. "I guess it's time to get back to the wagon."

"Not yet." Garret checked her retreat by placing his fingertips on her elbow.

She could have brushed off his hold with a jerk of her arm, but she found herself unable to move from the warmth of his touch.

"Kit, I need to talk."

His words closed the door on any chance of escape. Kit faced him. The thin lines near his eyes deepened with sadness as his scar lightened. Anger and sorrow. They seemed to be the only emotions Garret showed the world. He crossed his arms, and uncrossed them, finally settling on hooking his thumbs in his pockets. "I don't know how to do this."

"What?"

"Trust you." He shook his head, his jaw becoming a crowbar of determination. "I'm just going to ask you plain out. If the answer's yes, then you and Hawk ride out, and I..." He clenched his teeth and took a breath.

"I'll give you twenty-four hours before I get the law. And if the answer's no, then that'll be the end of it."

"What do you want to ask?" Kit knew the question he wanted answered.

"Are you rustling cattle?"

Tell him the truth. Tell him about Jando.

"No." A part of her heart broke as she lied by withholding the truth. But Garret couldn't keep the law out. He would tell the sheriff and Jando would escape. She couldn't risk it.

"And Hawk?"

"We don't steal cattle." A sharp pain radiated from her chest. She realized the rest of her heart had shattered.

Garret's whole body stiffened as if her words hit him a physical blow. He swallowed. His shoulders relaxed. "All right then. I believe you."

No you don't. Kit could almost hear the war going on in his head. It had been so long since he'd trusted someone, he didn't even know how to start. And the first person he chose was doomed to disappoint him.

"Kit?" Garret reached out and wove his fingers through the loose hair around her shoulders. "I wish things could be different. But I promised Ma."

"I understand promises, Garret." Kit hoped the wind would sweep away her tears. "I keep mine, also."

She turned and headed back to the wagon, the ghosts of the past separating her from Garret, keeping her silent, and alone.

Chapter Ten

The streets buzzed with activity as Garret and Cade rode into the mining town. Overhead, a banner flapped in the light breeze. Elaborate scroll letters filled the canvas, advertising the annual pre-drive barn dance.

On the upper balcony of the Calico Cat Dance Hall, two girls, dressed in feathers and lace, smoked thin cigars. One of the women leaned over the balcony, displaying a generous amount of her cleavage, and threw a kiss. "When ya comin' to visit?"

"Bessie, I'll be seeing you later." Cade pretended to catch the kiss in his hand. A rascal grin played across his face. "How about I meet up with you down at the Calico?"

"And what about Davidson?" Garret reminded, grateful for some excuse to keep Cade from the saloon girls and gambling tables. "Those two'll have him suffering Cupid's cramps in a minute."

"Wish I hadn't talked you into bringing the boy. Bessie and her friend are going to be disappointed," Cade complained.

"They don't appear to be the type to be lonely for long. There's no time today for poker, rotgut or women."

"There's never any time as far as you're concerned," Cade muttered. He dismounted and tethered his mount to the crowded hitching post. Lifting his mare's back hoof, he swore, "Damn, Pretty Gal's got a loose shoe."

Garret tied his reins alongside his brother's. Stepping around the piles of horse manure, he watched the parade of men on the street. Saloon doors swished open and closed to accept them. Places like the Calico Cat attracted good cowhands as well as bad. And offered Garret the best place to look for new hires. But he'd have to lose Cade first. "I've got some things to take care of. I'll meet you back at the store."

"Are any of those things Abigail Benton?" Cade snorted.

"She's none of your concern."

"If you're thinking of making her my sister-in-law, she sure is." Cade adjusted his sweat-darkened hat a little lower over his eyes. "Kit'd be a better choice."

"Leave her out of this." Garret's temper flared like a prairie fire.

Cade whipped back his head. "What's got you so riled? Just what did you and Kit talk about back at the red rock?"

"I did like you wanted. I asked if she or Hawk were stealing cattle."

Cade's mouth dropped open, a canyon of disbelief. Recovering, he asked, "That so? What'd she say?"

Garret dug his boot heel into the worn boardwalk. It creaked in protest. "She said both of them were innocent."

"Do you believe her?" Seriousness underlined each word Cade spoke.

"Hellfire, Cade, I'm trying to. 'Cause you asked me to and 'cause I haven't forgotten the saloon brat in me. I asked, she answered, I said I'd go by her word. But so help me, if she's lying, there won't be a rock small enough for her to hide under."

Across the street, the wagon pulled up to the mercantile. Davidson hopped down and so did Kit. Garret found himself releasing a slow breath of relief. Beside Davidson, whose jaw was just as whisker-free as her own, Kit looked like just another young boy. Inviting the boy to come along had been a good idea. And it had come from Cade.

Garret nodded toward the wagon. "You were right. Having Davidson along makes Kit seem more like a boy."

Cade stalled, one foot on the dirt road, the other still on the high boardwalk. "Thanks, Garret. That means a lot coming from you."

The chasm that had stretched between Garret and his brother that morning suddenly seemed not so deep. Garret had an urge to grab his brother's hand and pull him into a bear hug. Instead, uncomfortable with his wash of emotion, he warned, "Remember, stick close."

"Like a fly in molasses." Cade took a toothpick from his hatband and twirled it in his mouth as he moseyed toward the mercantile and wagon.

Garret headed toward the saloons and faro halls. Four years of fighting and surviving in the war had taught him one thing—to trust his gut feelings. And his gut was churning when it came to Kit and Hawk. But his gut wasn't the part of his body that was most disturbed by Kit O'Shane.

Ducking into a saloon, he paused at the doorway to let his eyes grow accustomed to the smoky light. His spur clanged on a spittoon, its brass shine hidden beneath tobacco stains.

Men stood shoulder to shoulder at the rough pine bar,

drinking and talking. He recognized a few owners of small spreads like his. A couple of wranglers from nearby ranches. Some men that had worked roundups in the past.

He waved an approaching saloon girl away. "Not here to drink. I'm just here to hire cowhands."

A cowboy at the bar laughed. "Yore gonna have to look mighty hard." Garret recognized him as one of Fredrick's ranch hands. "Ain't none of us gettin' mixed up with those thieves you hired on."

McVery, one of the ranch owners, turned to face Garret. "I reckon you've done shown those breeds the trail. I mean, old man Benton ordered 'em off your spread, didn't he?"

"Kit and Hawk are still at the Rockin' G." Garret gave each man at the bar a direct stare.

Rubbing his chin, McVery shrugged. "There's a first. Blaine going against Benton. I wonder how long it'll last."

"As long as I own the Rockin' G," Garret shot back. He looked at the skeptical faces of the men. They could afford to buck Benton. Their spreads were well established, their reputations clear and untarnished. Garret's family had a history as spotted as the old spittoon.

"Then yore gonna be mighty short of workers come this drive." Fredrick's man looked smug. "You chose a bad time to square off against Benton."

"Well now, don't be speakin' for us all," a lilting voice called from the other side of the bar. Stepping away, a man tipped his derby. The small hat looked ridiculous on such a big man. He took up a spot at the bar wide enough for two men.

Downing his shot of amber whiskey, he strode over to Garret. Clunky boots thudded through the sawdust carpet.

"Be Liam Clearny." He extended a hand crisscrossed with calluses and scrapes. Dirt stained his fingernails.

The condition of his hands told Garret all he needed to know. "I'm looking for experienced cowhands. Not miners."

One of the men at the other table hooted. "Then you can be hirin' Clearny, for he ain't no miner. Not anymore."

"You'll be shuttin' your mouth, Sean, or I'll be doin' it for ya." The Irishman curled his hands into fists and took a fighter's stance. From the silence of the other miners, Garret could tell Liam had built his strength by swinging a pickax and his fists.

Liam lowered his arms. "May God never curse ya to lay three days in a cave-in knowin' your brother's a-dyin' and it be so black ya can't even see his face. And if He should, then let's see how anxious ya are to go back into those bowels of hell."

"Leave 'em be," a miner cautioned his friend. "Liam may've left his gumption down in the mine, but he's still got his fists."

"Aye, that I have." Liam turned back to Garret. "Now, about that job."

This fast-talking Irishman didn't have a prayer. If what Fredrick's men said was true, Garret would have to offer better wages to get trail-toughened men. He couldn't afford any charity cases. "Sorry, Irishman."

Garret stood, gave McVery a hard stare, then walked out of the saloon. He had a street full of dance halls to check out. Trusting Kit was proving to be more expensive than he thought. He hoped he could afford the price.

The smell of rotgut whiskey, horse manure and sweat clung to the air. Kit couldn't get out of town soon enough, but first, she had to send her telegram. Her nephew's school could be waiting to wire her with the news she and Hawk had been praying for—Raven had spoken.

Wiping the sweat from her forehead, she dropped a sack of sugar into the wagon. Cade and Hawk made trip after trip up the storeroom stairs, lugging down heavy sacks of food. A pyramid of flour, sugar, salt and coffee waited to be loaded. She could hear Cracker's deep, gravelly voice ordering boxes of canned goods, nails and some new tools to complete the order.

She turned, expecting to see Davidson right behind her with an armful of supplies. The boy stood near the store door, empty-handed, examining a display barrel of shovels. He darted a glance back inside the store. Suddenly, Kit knew what held his attention.

A young girl sat near the store register tallying up numbers in a ledger. Her blond hair cascaded down her slender shoulders and pooled across the thick book. She sneaked a peak at her father, then at Davidson, and a smile graced her pretty face. Davidson nearly swooned.

"What's her name?" Kit asked.

Startled, Davidson stumbled. Still gripping the shovel handles, he sent the barrel on a wobbly spin. The loud clang of the metal spades echoed in the room.

Cracker stopped his litany of supplies and turned toward the door. Cade and Hawk, each loaded with a heavy sack of flour, dropped the bags and stared at Davidson. The girl hid her mouth behind the edge of the ledger but her light twitter of laughter skipped in the air.

Biting her lower lip to keep from laughing, Kit placed a firm hand on the barrel rim. The tools swirled in the giant vacant space within before settling to a slow stop. Davidson's face burned crimson.

"Sorry, I didn't mean to scare you." Kit tried to apologize but her grin kept getting in the way.

"Miranda!" the shopkeeper called, suddenly aware of the reason Davidson had nearly destroyed the shovel supply. "Go in the back and finish adding those numbers."

"Yes, Papa." Obediently, she collected her things. Just before she reached a floor-length curtain, she glanced out the window, smiled and gave a small wave with her fingertips, then ducked behind the gingham cloth.

Pointing to the sacks and boxes of food, Cade said, "That's the last of it. Load it up and we're out of here."

The old cook nodded, counting under his breath the cans of peaches. "Yep, all here." He scratched the back of his head, making the few hairs he had left on his head stand out. "'Pears Garret ain't made it back yet."

"Then perhaps Hawk and I could send a telegram?" Kit licked her lower lip. The floor vibrated beneath her feet as her brother strode across the wide store. She could sense the tension in his body and the contained anger.

Cade rubbed his hand over his mouth. "My mare did throw a shoe coming in and the telegraph office's just across the street from the farrier. But Garret told me to stick close, and looking over the town, I'm thinking he's right. A lot of drifters and no-accounts about. What really worries me is Davidson."

Davidson leaned one shoulder against the porch frame, his thumbs tucked in his gun belt. His gaze kept drifting down the street to the swinging doors of the saloons. He was a case of big behavior in a young body.

"You and Hawk go to the telegraph office on your way to the smith's," Cracker said to Cade, then sat down in a ladder-back rocker on the walk. "I'll stay here with the boy and Kit."

"And you can put Davidson in charge of me," Kit

suggested. ''Sort of the watchdog guarding the watchdog, so to speak. If I stay here near the wagon, Davidson won't wander away.''

''That might work,'' Cade admitted. ''But I'm warning the boy good and loud he's not to disrespect you.''

Cade ambled over to the young teen and spoke in a low tone. The boy's face flushed. He stopped leaning on the porch frame and stiffened his back. Every time Davidson opened his mouth, Cade jabbed him in the chest with his index finger. In a loud voice, Cade asked, ''You understand where I'm coming from, boy?''

''Yeah.''

''What was that?'' Cade barked like a cavalry officer.

''I mean, Yes, sir. I understand.''

''Good. Watch for Garret and stay outta trouble.'' Cade turned to Kit and her brother, a twinkle of amusement in his eyes. ''If there's one thing I've learned from Garret, it's how to mother. I hope the boy listens better than I do.''

Quickly, before Cade could change his mind, Kit tore a label off a can of peaches and wrote out her message in the briefest form possible.

FR. S. Lopez
San Antonio, TX
  At Rockin' G Ranch, Colorado Springs. Expect money at end of month. If asked about, inform immediately.

                                                    Kit O'Shane

She stuffed the note into her brother's hand. Hawk stared at the paper then at her. ''Raven will never ask for me.'' The love for his son shone in his blue eyes.

Kit squeezed Hawk's hand. "Time mellows the pain."

"Has it for you?" He fisted his hand, crumpling the scribbled note.

Untethering his horse, Cade waved his hand for Hawk to follow. "You know, life'd be a hell of a lot easier if you cut those braids. You wouldn't look so damn heathen."

A cold mask fell over her brother's face. "I am Cheyenne." His shoulders straightened, and the high angles of his cheekbones seemed to become more pronounced. Kit's heart ached for her brother, for the warrior he had once been.

"That so? Thinking of doing any scalping today?"

"No." Her brother remained passive to Cade's questioning.

"Damn." Cade removed his hat and ran his fingers through his long bangs. "I sure as hell need a haircut."

A cross between a snort and a laugh burst from her brother. Kit and Cracker grinned at each other. The only thing faster than Cade's gun was his charm. The patient mare plodded along behind the two men as they headed toward the blacksmith's.

The thick armor Hawk wore thinned a little with Cade. A few more weeks and perhaps her brother would rediscover the man he once was. The warrior, the gentle brother, the man who loved laughter and life. A few more weeks and they would be gone. And Garret would know her lie.

Kit balanced a small sack of beans on her shoulder. She took heavy steps back to the wagon, the small weight on her shoulders barely noticeable against the weight on her conscience.

Chapter Eleven

A group of men passed by the wagon, the scent of whiskey accompanying them. Kit's heart hammered as they eyed her. Her palms sweated, and insecurity made her long for a protector. For Garret. The men stalled outside a saloon a few yards away. Her fear mellowed but not her caution.

A cowboy reined his stallion in the street in front of her. His stare, hot with hate, drilled into her. Startled, Kit drew back.

Cracker looked up from his whittling and cursed as he recognized the cowboy. "Traynor's meaner than a rattlesnake on a hot skillet. I wish the hell Garret was here. Or Cade and Hawk. Hell, anybody."

Kit shared the old man's wish as she watched the cowboy fall in with the group of rough men who had passed earlier. Traynor had an ax to grind with Garret and her. Fear twisted a knot in the pit of her stomach.

Traynor, with his followers gathered around the wagon, sneered at Davidson. "Ya stink, boy. Comes from workin' with Injuns."

"Shut up, Traynor." Davidson, full of youthful bluster, pushed past Kit and the old cook. "Yore just sore 'cause

Kit outrode ya. How's it feel to get outrode by a woman?''

The bottom dropped out of Kit's stomach. Like Cassandra predicting the fall of Troy, she perceived the coming disaster. In one sentence, Davidson condemned her.

Traynor's wide mouth dropped open, then a sly smile twisted his lips. The gang of dirty men made a loose arc around the wagon, fencing off any escape.

The crowd tightened the arc and Kit's panic choked her. Traynor had the smell of evil about him. The glint in his eye reminded her of Jando. She folded her hands together to keep her shaking fingers still. After he finished with Davidson, he'd come for her.

Forcing his way through the men, Cracker put his hands on the tall cowboy's shoulders and tried to push him back. "Yore drunk as a polecat. Why don'tcha go soak the meanness outta ya and sober up."

"Yore the one that needs some soakin'." Traynor propelled the old cook toward the horse trough. A hard push and Cracker fell into the greenish water. His legs draped over the side, and his stained hat floated to the opposite end until a ripple carried it over the edge.

The hint of a fight drew wranglers and miners toward the wagon like a lodestone. Enticed by the audience, Traynor took in a deep breath and let his belly swell with bravado. "Ya gonna fight or turn tail, boy?"

Davidson hesitated, and Kit prayed he finally sensed the danger. *Wait for Garret. Wait for Cade and Hawk.*

The boy lunged at his tormentor. Kit heard a crack. Davidson's jaw made a bull's-eye with the belligerent cowboy's fist. A second crack echoed. The boy's head crashed against the wagon.

Winded, Davidson dragged himself up, using the wagon wheel for support. Clenching his hands into fists half the size of his opponent's, he staggered forward, swinging like a windmill.

The crowd hooted with approval. Kit cringed on the porch. The cowboy would kill Davidson then come after her. And she knew she would never be able to survive it. Not again.

Traynor danced out of range, swatting away Davidson's punches. The crowd's enthusiasm turned to blood lust when the tip of Traynor's hard boot dug into Davidson's soft belly. He staggered back, falling to his knees. Traynor sent blow after blow to Davidson's rib cage. Slumped forward, he groaned at each contact.

Cracker managed to pull himself from the horse trough. Wringing wet, he frantically searched the wagon for his rifle, buried beneath the supplies. A sack of flour broke open and sprayed fine white dust into the air.

"That's what comes of pokin' a redskin." Traynor held on to the boy and kicked him again. "Makes ya weak." Laughing, he released his battered opponent.

Davidson rolled over, blood dripping from his mouth and a cut on his forehead. He tried to crawl under the wagon for safety, but Traynor grabbed the boy's leg and yanked him back. A sadistic gleam shone in the cowboy's eyes as his boot made contact with Davidson's bruised body. The kick broke the youth to tears.

Traynor meant to kill Davidson, and no one seemed willing to stop the fight. The hard feel of her knife on her hip fortified Kit's resolve. She pulled the weapon free from the sheath. Using the hitching post as a vault, she leaped forward into the wagon bed, then jumped to the ground.

Crouched between the man and Davidson's still body, she pointed her knife at the cowboy's Adam's apple. "Back off or eat steel." Her words sounded harsh and strong, and her emotions raged between panic and aggravation at her own stupidity. Traynor pulled back, surprised at her action.

Kit weighed her options. Deep purple bruises covered Davidson's face. One eye had already swollen shut and the other was just a narrow slit. He was too heavy for her to carry and he couldn't walk on his own. The wagon hemmed her to the back. The arc of men prevented an escape forward.

Traynor recovered from his surprise and yanked Kit's hat off. Tendrils of hair fell free and cascaded down her shoulders.

Kit silently screamed, "Garret, I need you."

Chapter Twelve

Three saloons and no luck. Not a cowboy worth his salt was willing to sign with Garret. Benton and Fredrick had been mighty busy spreading the word about Kit and Hawk. The ranch owners fully expected Garret to cave in to Benton's demands. As if the old man owned his—what had Kit said?—his integrity.

He turned the corner, took a gander at the men near his wagon and knew trouble had shot another bullet in his direction. Cracker waved his double-barreled shotgun at the crowd while Kit waved her knife at another cowboy— Traynor. Dirt was cleaner than the way he fought.

Outgunned and outmanned. One wrong move, and there would be a bloodbath. Garret ducked into an alley, hoping he could save Kit and Cracker from a gunfight. Sensing movement behind him, Garret whipped out his Colt.

The irritating Irishman from the saloon stopped in his tracks. Lifting his fists, he said, "With these I've got experience. Are ya in the mood to acceptin' me employment now?"

Garret didn't have a choice. "You're hired." They hurried down the alley to the back door of the mercantile.

Together they strode past the surprised shopkeeper to

the front door. Stepping onto the boardwalk, Garret looked down on the group of miners and cowboys. Cracker and Kit stood with their backs against the wagon, surrounded by a crowd eager to see the Indian woman in their midst. Davidson lay half under the wagon, moaning.

Traynor roared to the crowd, "After I'm finished with her, she's fair game for any of ya."

"You're finished now." Careful to keep his hands clear of his gun, Garret edged around the buckboard and faced the men. Liam followed close behind.

"Good ta see ya, Cap'n." Cracker motioned toward the crowd. "These fellas are gettin' a mite tiresome."

Beside Garret, Kit waited, poised for attack. Like cursed gemstones, her eyes glittered with a lethal gleam. The silver glint on her knife contrasted with the bronze color of her skin. She reminded him of a mountain lion, waiting to pounce. At this moment, he knew she could kill.

The thought made him proud and uncomfortable at the same time. Kit was a survivor, just like he was. That trait had enabled him to walk out of Andersonville. But taking a man's life heaped a lot more guilt on a soul than stealing cattle. If Kit was capable of killing, she was damn sure capable of rustling.

The Irishman shoved his way to her side, a more-than-admiring smile on his face. "They'll not hurt a hair on your lovely head." She gave the Irishman a regal nod, accepting his respect as her due.

"Hey, Liam," the miners in the crowd called to the Irishman. "Ya got no business in this."

"Aye, that I do, seein' as how I'm a-workin' for the boss man."

Irish brogues and Scottish burrs mumbled warnings to each other. Garret had known the Irishman could fight but he must be damn good to scare a half-dozen miners into some common sense.

"I got a forty-five that can outfight any miner." Traynor stepped forward, his gaze settling on Garret. Several drunk cowhands stood ready to back Traynor up.

Cracker's rifle and Garret's forty-five summed up the Rockin' G firepower. In a gunfight, Kit's blade and Liam's fists would be useless. This standoff couldn't last much longer. The tension was as thick as a Denver steak.

"Got any ideas?" Garret asked from the side of his mouth. He didn't expect an answer.

"One." Kit lifted her chin, opened her arms to the heavens and howled an eerie war cry. The crowd silenced, people stopped in the streets. Horses neighed as though called by the haunting melody. A hawk flew overhead, its cry blending with her song.

The wildness in her soul burst forth and she transformed into a warrior maiden. Her knife was clenched in her fist, her ebony hair loose and flowing and the serenity on her face stormed his senses. He half expected to see war paint on her cameolike cheekbones. There was no fear in her song, no retreat. Kit stood ready for battle, fierce, confident and beautiful.

"Singin' your death cry, Injun." Traynor attempted to reclaim his control of the crowd.

"No." Kit lowered her chin and swept the men behind Traynor with a direct stare. "I'm singing yours."

Her words poked a hole in the mob's confidence. The circle widened, and the miners started to slip away.

"Ya ain't a-scarin' us." Traynor waved his supporters closer. "All ya are is talk."

"All I am...is the sister of a Cheyenne warrior." Kit's blue eyes froze to the color of frost. Her voice rang with respect and awe. "A man who will hunt you down to the ends of the earth and see you die slowly."

The cowboy wasn't daunted by her threat. "Well, he ain't here now, is he?" The observation made his friends a little braver. Grins replaced the concerned expressions.

Kit gave a hollow laugh. "You won't see him. At least not until he kills you." She leaned forward. Garret fought the impulse to pull her back to his side. "Or when you beg him to let you die."

The miners spread apart. Except for the two drunken cowboys, Traynor stood alone.

Kit played the men like a seasoned actress. "Whiteman skin makes strong medicine."

A smile kept tugging at the corners of Garret's mouth. He cleared his throat and rubbed his mouth to wipe it away. Like a she-wolf, Kit attacked the weakest members. Separate the miners from the cowboys and both groups would fold. The miners didn't know she was coloring up her story but the cowboys would. Fortunately, the only one sober enough to realize it was Traynor.

"She's a-lyin'." Desperation colored Traynor's voice. Sweat beaded across his forehead.

A high-pitched whistle rang out, and a tanned leather bag flew threw the air. It landed at Traynor's feet. Elaborate beadwork in bright blues and greens covered a central area. A blue feather, woven into the top, held it closed. High-noon sunlight shone on the pale white leather.

"Gol-durn. That hide's white." Anxious stares darted back and forth in the mob.

"That ain't no *cow*hide." Cracker beamed with a face-splitting grin.

Fear provided a bucket of common sense to douse the miners' anger. They drifted apart and lost the intensity of a mob.

Now that he was alone, Traynor's upper lip trembled and a sheen of perspiration formed around his mouth. The threat dissipated in Cracker's loud chortles as Traynor retreated.

"Where are ya, ya big, man-skinnin' savage?" Cracker put down his rifle and climbed down from the wagon.

Hawk and Cade materialized on the balcony just above. A woman, dressed in a white cotton chemise and black stockings, waved to Cade as he finished climbing out the window. His lips curved into an impish smile. "Bessie's sister," he explained. "She was kind enough to share her room with us."

"Get down here. Both of you." Garret didn't know whether to hug him or yell at him for being with a saloon gal.

The Indian wrapped his big hands around the balcony railing and vaulted over. Swinging back and forth, he caught the porch support and shimmied down the pole. Hawk hit the ground and looked up, waiting to see if Cade accepted his challenge.

Cade moved away from the window, leaned over the rail, and raised one eyebrow. As he turned back toward the window, the lovely saloon girl winked, the invitation clear.

"Sorry, gal. I got me a bet to win." Cade sat on the rail, spun around on his backside and made a flying leap for the porch support. His fingers latched on to the pole but his legs came around too far, slammed into the hard wood and jarred his grip. Scrambling to regain his hold, Cade landed on his backside, his legs wrapped around the pole. He stood, rubbed his backside, fished out a shiny coin and flipped it into Hawk's hand.

"I should not have left you," Hawk said as he hugged his sister. The tender smile on Kit's face brought a rush of longing in the depths of Garret's soul. How would it feel to have her smile at him with such tenderness?

"I knew you'd come when you heard my call." Kit's voice and hands trembled.

"Where the hell were you?" Garret attacked Cade, his longing channeled into his voice, making it sound bitter.

"Farrier's and—"

"You couldn't wait for me to get back?" Garret launched a cannon fire of discontent at his brother.

"Pretty Gal threw a shoe, and you weren't beating a path back," Cade snapped. "Besides—"

"Davidson needs our help now," Kit interjected as she bent down to the hurt boy under the wagon. Cade and Hawk half dragged, half carried Davidson into the wagon bed. Blood crusted the boy's upper lip. He wouldn't see out of one eye for at least a week. Tears streaked his dirty face and left watery stripes down his cheeks.

With gentle, motherly dabs, Kit wiped his face with her bandanna. She softly poked the boy's ribs. When he gasped in pain, she crinkled her eyes in sympathy. "He's bruised but nothing's broken." *Except his spirit.*

Cracker picked up the leather bag lying in the street, dusted it off, then handed it to her brother. "Ya know, that don't feel like cowhide."

"It's not." A glimmer of mischief glinted in Hawk's eyes. Giving her a wink, he tossed the bag toward Cracker. In a reflex action, he batted it to the Irishman, who flipped it back to Cracker. Cade chuckled, and even Davidson managed a smile.

"Quit teasing, Hawk." The joke slowed the pounding in her heart. Her fingers stopped shaking, and her insides stopped flip-flopping. Kit picked up the bag and threw it at her big brother's grinning face. "It's puma, Cracker. Just a mountain lion."

"One hell of a mountain lion," Hawk snorted, and patted the necklace of claws around his neck. "I was—"

"Yeah, yeah. You were only fourteen summers when you killed the mighty beast." She let her smile and easy banter show Hawk his little trick had worked. The fear had passed. Kit spread her hands to shoulder width. "It had teeth this long and breath so bad it singed your hair."

Cade and Cracker chuckled, a release from the tension of before. The Irishman blushed, but grinned. A reluctant smile tugged at Garret's stern face. For a moment, he relaxed.

Kit drank in the sight of him. He thumbed back his dark Stetson and leaned against the wagon. The tight jean material molded to his strong thighs. With his thumbs tucked into his pockets and the almost smile on his lips, he looked younger. Her heart fluttered, not from fear this time, but because of the heat building in the pit of her stomach as she met his stare.

"Get this on," Garret snapped as he tossed the slouch hat at her. "I'll do the talking."

The warmth fizzled, then dampened to apprehension as Kit spotted the sheriff striding toward them. Two men and a woman followed close behind. Cade, Cracker and Hawk formed a barricade while she hastily stuffed her hair into her hat. The charming Irishman helped Davidson find a comfortable spot in the crowded wagon.

"What the hell's going on here?" The sheriff looked over the Rockin' G riders with a baleful stare.

"Nothing. Now." Garret's tone accused the lawman of negligence. "Davidson's beat up pretty bad, but he'll live."

Peeking between Hawk's bent elbow, Kit saw Fredrick push the sheriff aside. His chest puffed out like a bullfrog. "I told you there would be trouble with those breeds."

Breeds. Revulsion lurched in Kit. She could scream slurs of her own. Murderers. Rapists.

The sheriff centered his gaze on her brother. "Mr. Benton wants an eye kept on the breeds. Where's the other one?"

Eli Benton! Land's sakes! And yes, now that she could sneak a peek at the woman, it was Abigail. Thank goodness they had never met face-to-face. Ducking her head, she wished the ground would swallow her. Instead, Garret looped his arm through hers. Dragging her from behind Cade, he presented her to the sheriff. "Here she is."

"She? She!" Abigail bolted forward. Her hat slid loose, the pink ostrich feather dipping across her face. "Daddy, is this creature a woman?" Her screeching voice drew the attention of a group of men. They sauntered over, listening in on the conversation.

"Abigail, come away. Who knows what their kind is capable of?" Eli tugged his outraged daughter to his side.

If Kit wasn't so darn mad she'd laugh.

"Garret? Garret!" Abigail kept repeating herself like a trained parrot. She clutched the cameo at the throat of her lace collar, and her voice became shrill. "Explain yourself."

Fredrick smirked. "It's clear as day what a man like Blaine wants with a squaw. She's a girl just like his ma."

Abigail's face drained of color. And, God forgive her, satisfaction fairly glowed in Kit. About time Abigail had a comeuppance. The feeling dimmed as Kit looked at the whitening scar on Garret's temple and the hard line of his jaw. Hurt glittered in his eyes.

"How dare you subject me to such embarrassment," Abigail whined. "A whore! Really, Garret."

Garret's voice remained steady, but Kit sensed the fury and pain underneath. "She's no whore."

"I want those two arrested." Eli looked like a grouse during mating season, his double chin swaying and his chest puffed out. "I want it now."

Fredrick reached for Kit's wrist. She swatted away his fat, pudgy hand. "You'll pay for that, you lousy squaw," he vowed.

Garret's fist lashed out, and he wadded up Fredrick's fancy ruffled shirt in his hand. "Don't you dare threaten her...or any of my riders." The shorter man flapped his jaw, not speaking, his face turning bright red.

"Let him go, Blaine, or I'll run ya in." The sheriff came to life at Eli's angry sputter.

Deaf to the warning, Garret refused to unlock his fingers. The sheriff clumsily went for his gun. Kit feared they were all in for another standoff.

"I wouldn't do that, Sheriff." A man from the crowd stepped forward. He moved slow and easy, but confident.

"This ain't your fight, McVery," the sheriff shot back as he retreated a step.

"I think it is." The man turned to Garret. "I drew Blaine for roundup. The Bar M and the Rockin' G'll be workin' together this drive. What's Rockin' G business is Bar M business. Seems to me, Blaine here is right. Injun or not, you can't go throwing innocent people in jail just 'cause a Benton tells ya to."

Garret turned and gave McVery a long, questioning look. "I'm shorthanded." Kit could have knocked Garret in the head with a can of peaches. *Just accept the man's help. Stop being so full of pride.*

McVery nodded, and the weathered lines on his face creased deeply as he replied, "No problem. I hired on three more than I need. You can pay me for their salaries."

"Let Fredrick go," Abigail commanded.

Now Abigail on the other hand… Kit would have no problem clonking her on the head.

Garret contemplated McVery. Finally, he nodded. "See you come sunup on the east range."

"Sunup it is." Pausing, the rancher asked, "You thinkin' of lettin' that jackass go anytime soon?"

With more than a touch of insolence, Garret slowly released Fredrick's linen shirt. The man took deep gulps of air while Abigail fawned over him with false concern. McVery shook Garret's hand. "I didn't think ya had it in ya. Glad to see I was wrong."

McVery returned to his men, gathered his crew, then headed toward the livery.

"I'm not a man to forget," Fredrick warned.

Garret gave him a nasty smile. "Good, then I won't have to warn you again about bothering Rockin' G riders."

Kit wanted to stand up and cheer. Garret had stood up to the Bentons. For her. Her elation popped like a child's balloon. She didn't deserve it. His trust. His support. In just three more weeks, Garret would know she had lied about the rustlers.

The sheriff pointed his finger at Kit. "Ya got thirty minutes to get outta town."

Eli and Fredrick helped the distraught Abigail back across the street. The sheriff trotted along behind like a dog on a leash.

Garret watched Abigail leave on Fredrick's arm and swore. All those months of sitting in the stuffy parlor, trying to balance the small teacup on his knee and make polite talk wasted. Sticking up for Kit had cut the last thread binding him to the Bentons.

Kit walked over to Davidson and fussed over the bandage around his head. Davidson just sat with his head down, all the bravado kicked clean out of him. He'd be sore for a long time, but it would take longer still for him to recover his self-esteem.

"How in the hell did this mess start?" Garret stared at Kit, his voice demanding her to answer.

Kit suddenly rushed with an explanation. "Traynor pulled my hat free. He found out I was a woman and tried to grab me. The boy jumped in to help me."

Cracker clamped his jaw together so hard Garret heard the clank of his teeth. The old man looked at Garret, at Kit, at Davidson, then down at his boots. He was uncharacteristically quiet.

Gratitude, kindness and caring mellowed Kit's tone. The smile she granted the boy could charm cards from a gambler's sleeve. "I want to thank you for defending me. Hawk," she called to her brother. "I think you ought to show your gratitude." She pointed to the claw necklace at his throat.

"My puma claws! I don't believe a word—"

Kit lowered her eyes, gave her brother a warm smile and batted her lashes just as skillfully as Abigail Benton might. "He needs something to remember the deed by."

Hawk paused, tried to give Kit an imperial stare and failed. The necklace clattered as he removed it and with solemn dignity placed it over Davidson's neck.

The aches and pains disappeared from the teen's face. He struggled to bring his sore arm to his chest and stroke the sharp talons. It had taken Kit only ten minutes to turn the humiliated boy into one part shining knight, one part mountain lion.

Garret threw up his hands in disgust. "Move out, Cracker. We're wasting daylight." Hawk jumped in the wagon and sat next to Davidson.

Removing his bowler, the Irishman offered Kit his arm

for support. "Liam Clearny at your service. Could ya be usin' a hand up?" Garret's irritation with the Irishman jumped a notch.

After a second's hesitation, Kit answered, "Thank you, Mr. Clearny." She took his arm and stepped up into the bed of the wagon like the queen of England entering a coach. Her throne became two flour sacks stacked near the springboard. Liam scrambled up behind her and nestled in between the sugar and potatoes at her feet.

A surge of emotions gnawed at Garret as he fetched his mount. If Kit could break horses, chop wood, tote flour bags and hold off a crowd of angry men without breaking a sweat, then she ought to be able to get into a damn supply wagon by herself. Garret's mild irritation at the Irishman was fast becoming a powerful dislike.

Mounting his horse, Garret waited on his brother. Cade rode up and asked, "You think there's any magic in those claws?"

Following behind the wagon, Garret watched the way Davidson kept one hand clenched around the necklace. "If there wasn't, there sure as hell is now."

Chapter Thirteen

Garret sat in the fading daylight with a ledger in his lap and a barrelful of pride in his heart. With the help of McVery's cowhands and two weeks of hard work, the Rockin' G cattle were rounded up. The herd numbered close to a thousand head—enough cattle to show a tidy profit. Enough that his break with the Bentons wouldn't push the ranch into the red.

Watching Hawk ride off, Garret mulled over some other good news. No more ranches had been hit by the rustlers. Did that mean the outlaws had pulled up stakes or were just biding their time?

Cowboys filed past Garret on their way to the chuck-wagon. Kit and Liam brought up the end. It had taken only a few days for Kit to prove herself to the plain-talking men. She had put her Appaloosa mare through the paces, culling calves while avoiding a run-in with a mean-spirited bull. The cowboys had walked away just as impressed as Garret with Kit's abilities.

Some were a little too impressed, he thought as Liam handed Kit a full plate and squeezed a seat next to her on a log. Garret slammed the ledger closed as the hair along his neck bristled. Damn that Irishman, he cursed silently as he helped himself to a plate of Cracker's spicy beans and beef.

When the sound of forks scraping metal plates ceased, Cade leaned back and patted his distended stomach with satisfaction. "Boys, we got us a real treat waiting."

A Bar M wrangler groaned, "Cade, a treat for you means I'm gonna lose money."

McVery's men snorted and hooted. No hidden animosity surfaced. Garret took a breath and sipped his coffee. Over the rim, he caught Kit's gaze. She gave him a half smile that dimpled her left cheek and started his heart thumping. Despite the campfire between them, he felt close to her, as though he could make love to her with his gaze. As though she could read his mind, she blushed.

His bushy eyebrows spiked with flour, Cracker brought a tray from the wagon to the fire. From it came the wonderful aroma of sugar and fruit. Fried peach pies.

Hungry cowhands delved into their confectionery, savoring each bite. Garret would have laughed at the sheer ecstasy on their faces, except he suspected he had the same expression. His laughter crumbled to a choked groan when he spotted Kit.

Hot steam escaped from his pastry, burning his tongue, but it was not nearly equal to the inner heat centered near his heart. He couldn't tear his gaze away from Kit. She nibbled her pie then slowly outlined her lips with her tongue, licking away the pale orange filling from her mouth. Garret wanted to feed her tidbits of pie, then kiss away the crumbs while relishing the sweetness of her mouth.

McVery sucked a peach from his pie. "I lost to Cade at Liam's fightin', Cade's shootin', Hawk's ropin' and Kit's ridin'. About the only sure bet I got is Cracker's cookin'."

Pointing toward the empty tray, Cracker teased, "Weren't me that fried them pies. It were Kit."

The syrupy filling in Garret's mouth tasted sweeter knowing Kit had fashioned it. He mumbled his thanks, along with the other men, wishing he could taste those pies every night. Wishing he could ask her to stay.

Kit took the men's adulation with a quiet smile.

"You're a remarkable woman." Liam's compliment re-kindled Garret's ire. But the Irishman had her pegged. Kit was remarkable and the knowledge turned the peach sweetness in Garret's mouth bitter.

Cutting his ties to the Bentons didn't come without a cost. Without McVery's help, Garret could never have finished the roundup. But the rancher had only offered his men as a means of putting a bur in Eli Benton's backside. Come next year, McVery might feel different. Especially if the rustling picked up again and the rest of the ranchers felt Garret's hires were the cause. He had seen the town turn their backs on his ma. Why would they treat him any different? Kit and Hawk leaving would be the safest solution. For them, for the ranch, for Cade. But what about for Garret?

He tossed his plate into the washbasin and let the question remain unanswered. The ranch and his brother couldn't afford for him to think with his heart.

Garret's gaze settled on Kit, who was smiling and laughing with the other ranch hands. He drank in the glow of the campfire on her face, the way the setting sun high-lighted her dark tresses and the soft light in her eyes as she laughed at Cracker's jokes. Passion burned deep inside Garret, and he feared the embers of that fire would never be extinguished.

Cade studied his brother studying Kit. Sparks were fly-ing between the two, and not from anger. He could see it in the way they looked at each other and in the way they brushed against each other. It made his decision over the telegram twice as hard.

That damn telegram could mean nothing—then again, it could mean a heap. "If asked about, inform immediately." Could they be on the run? Hellfire! He sounded just like Garret.

Telling Garret about the telegram would add to the doubt about Kit, just when Garret was beginning to act like—well, like Garret. After all, where did everyone think Cade had learned his charms? It sure as hell wasn't from the saloon drunks. Garret had taught Cade to try smooth talking first and a fast gun last. His big brother had taken care of the family until he couldn't take the heartache any longer. Shame and Andersonville prison had callused Garret's soul until he couldn't feel anymore.

From beneath his hat brim, Cade eyed his brother. The thick rawhide Garret had over his emotions softened each day he spent with Kit. Telling him about the telegram would only distance him from her. Like a reluctant calf, Garret needed some prodding.

Cade saddled up next to his brother and slipped his first prod into the conversation. "Dance is tomorrow night." He kept his tone low and casual. "I reckon you aim to stay with the herd since Abigail ain't gonna be there, and Kit's got a young man taking her—"

"Kit's going?" Garret ripped his gaze from the darkness that had enveloped Kit's form back to his brother.

"She's done been asked and accepted."

That Irishman! Garret growled under his breath. He should have known Liam would ask Kit to the dance. "I can't afford to let all the men off for some dance."

"Yeah, you can." Cade gave Garret a toothy smile.

"Them bets I won weren't for money. The Bar M's got to put up three men tomorrow night. All the Rockin' G men can go—except for one."

"There's no way I'm letting that bunch back into town after the fight. At least not alone. I'm going with you."

"Then who you leaving behind?"

He could leave Kit, but then what if Liam refused to go into town? Garret would be stuck at the dance while the Irishman fawned over Kit in camp. "Shortest-time man, that would be Liam."

"Ah, makes sense," Cade agreed, a smile on his face. "Too bad, Kit's gonna miss him."

Not if I can help it, Garret promised to himself.

Chapter Fourteen

The threads at the seams of her bodice showed, and the design hadn't been popular in five years, but Kit felt as giddy as a schoolgirl in her old traveling dress. It had been ages since she had worn anything except pants and one of Hawk's hand-me-down shirts.

Twirling, she examined the full skirt for broken seams or tears she might have missed. The soft calico material floated in the air, her minor repairs barely noticeable in the faded blue ripples.

Sitting on her narrow cot, Kit removed her moccasins from the protective oilcloth. Slipping on the soft leather shoes, she wiggled her toes in the rabbit fur. Tiny beads formed a wavy line along the sides. Her sister-in-law had chosen the pattern to represent Kit's long and hazardous journey to find her brother. A journey that still continued in her search for Jando.

Kit tied back the sides of her hair with a sky-blue ribbon. A few strands, not quite long enough to reach the bow, escaped to wisp around her temple and cheeks. It would have to do. Her hair was done, she had her gown and her slippers, now where was her escort?

* * *

Cade let his head fall forward onto the table. "By the time you get yourself all gussied up, the dance'll be over."

"I'm ready." Garret fussed with the top button of his white cotton shirt. Pressed and starched, the garment hindered his movements. He had half a mind to shuck it off and wear an old comfortable flannel. But tonight, everyone would be dressed in their best to mark the start of the trail drive. Cowboys in fresh washed shirts, smelling of lye soap instead of cows, would use tonight to gather memories of pretty gals. Memories that would hold them over the long hard trail east.

What would Garret use to warm the cold nights along the trail? Snatches of conversation with Kit when they weren't fighting? The one kiss in the barn? The merriment in her eyes? It wasn't enough. Not nearly enough for the lonely stretch ahead, but Garret would make those few remembrances last the months on the trail.

"Liam rode out for night duty." Cade lifted his head. "I'm surprised you waited until now to tell him."

"I had things to do." Garret knotted a red bandanna around his throat and realized if lying was a hanging offense, his bandanna would be a noose. He didn't want Kit backing down and staying at the ranch. "Kit know yet?"

"No. Guess I'll mosey out and tell her the bad news." Cade scratched the pine floor as he shoved his chair back. A wicked grin flittered across his face. It ruffled Garret's nerves. He had the feeling Cade was up to something, but what?

"I'll tell her." Garret heard the eagerness in his voice and cleared his throat. "You make sure Cracker's got the wagon hitched and everyone's loaded up."

Garret strode across the yard toward the barn, rehearsing a dozen lines and inflections, from casual to domineering, to inform Kit of her change of companion for the day.

Standing near the hitching post with his palomino, Vega reflected sunlight from the numerous conchos shells and silver buckles on his black suit. Hawk, dressed in a deerskin fringed shirt and leggings, held the reins of his horse and Cade's mare, saddled and bridled. Candus and Cracker waited in the buckboard, already jawing about the "secret" punch they were going to concoct at the dance. Cade joined Hawk and the men mounted. Except for Davidson and Kit, everyone was ready to pull out.

Pressing his lips together, Garret shoved back the barn door and marched in. With his fists on his hips, he scanned the barn, seeking Kit.

Her voice came from the far end of the barn. "You know it's not mannerly to keep a young lady waiting." A touch of reprimand and affection softened her words.

Words kept falling from Garret's mouth like an avalanche. He couldn't stop them. "Wagon's hitched. Boys are ready. Let's get a move on."

"Garret? I can't leave yet. I'm waiting on my escort." Kit stepped forward into the sunlight and Garret forgot what he had said, where he was going and damn near his own name.

A dress! He didn't know she'd even owned one, much less that she would look so beautiful in it. The modest scoop neckline, edged in white crocheted lace, highlighted the healthy glow of her smooth tan skin. Her gown, blue like a field of wildflowers, gently swayed as she approached, drawing his eyes to the fullness of her hips. From below the hem, he noticed her shoes, beaded moccasins.

His gaze lingered over the gentle hollow of her throat

and his voice grew husky. "Liam's guarding the cattle. Now shake a leg, and get out to the wagon."

"I told you I was waiting on my escort."

"And I told you Liam was with the herd." He knew immediately he had said too much.

Her eyes narrowed as she took in a sharp breath. She matched his stance, fists firmly on her hips. One foot tapped the barn floor, creating small whirlwinds of fine dust. Fury had her wound up tighter than a clock spring.

"Why, you conniving, self-righteous popinjay." Fire heated her gaze as she raked him with her sapphire stare. "If you think keeping Liam away is going to force me to stay here, hidden from the townsfolk, you can just think again. I'm going." She snapped her fingers. "I give about that much for what the town may or may not think of me."

She had it all wrong!

"Hold on just a minute. I never intended—"

"Miss Kit, ya ready?" Davidson entered the barn, his face ruddy from overwashing. His gaze flickered from Garret to Kit's face.

"We're talking," Garret said.

"We're finished." Kit gave him a tight, artificial smile, then turned to the boy. "Don't you look dapper." Her smile warmed as she took in Davidson's clean clothes and spit-shined boots.

Davidson's cheeks became splotched with red at her praise. "You look purty as a newborn foal, Miss Kit. I'm gonna be the envy of every cowboy at the dance."

"You're going with Davidson?" Garret had to mentally order himself to unclench his jaw. That woman made him crazier than locoweed.

Kit lifted her chin and shook her head haughtily. "Not

that it's your business, but yes.'' She glided forward on the boy's arm, her carriage regal.

Pivoting on his heel, Garret followed the couple to the wagon. One look at Cade's jolly face, and Garret knew he'd been had.

Cracker offered Kit a hand up to the wagon seat. "Let me help ya up.''

"I'll do that.'' Davidson stepped between Kit and the old cook. Cracker raised his bushy brows, perfect upside-down *U*'s of amused indignation. The boy held Kit's arm as she lifted her hem to step up. Garret climbed onto the springboard seat and took the reins, hoping no one noticed his obvious reaction to Kit's beauty.

"Uh, Cap'n.'' Davidson stood at his side of the wagon. "Seein' as how Miss Kit's my girl, for today anyway, I was thinkin' I oughta be the one drivin' the wagon.''

"I think that would be best, also.'' Kit turned to glower at Garret.

"Hellfire!'' Garret wrapped the reins around the brake and jumped down. "I'll tack up my horse—''

"And follow presently. There's no need for us to wait on you.'' Sugar coated Kit's tone, but Garret detected her meaning. She didn't want his company.

Davidson climbed up and took the reins. "Everyone ready?'' He glanced back at Cracker, and Candus in the back, then at Vega, Hawk and Cade on their mounts. "Let's go do some dancin'.'' He smacked the mules' backsides with the reins. The wagon lurched forward and then rumbled off, leaving Garret behind, his clean shirt coated with dust and feeling as if the wagon had just rolled over him.

Chapter Fifteen

"Now take your lady all the way home."

The fiddle music whined to an end as Davidson slung Kit around the wide pine dance floor. The fiddler put down his instrument and announced a brief interlude. Thank goodness! Her shins ached and toes throbbed. At the far end of the town hall, an opened door beckoned Kit with a shaft of afternoon sunlight.

A parade of men interrupted her glimpse of freedom. At the end of the line came a familiar caboose. Cracker smacked his lips and rubbed his hands together as he brought up the rear. The old cook and Candus must be turning a profit on their concoction. The "special brew" set up in the back had been attracting male customers all day. Everyone knew the "special" came from Candus's homemade moonshine, but Kit had learned the punch was a tradition at the trail-drive dance. Candus had told her both he and Cracker believed in preserving tradition, and their moonshine mixture would preserve just about anything.

The old-timers' business probably explained Garret's absence. He must be keeping an eye on the cook and Candus. Kit hadn't spied Garret in the crowded hall, even though he'd had plenty of time to reach town by now. Not that she had been searching for him. Her mind inserted the disclaimer while a sharp ache stung her heart.

The sight of him this morning had sent her pulse racing and wild ideas rushing through her head. The white cotton shirt had gleamed against his tanned skin. Fine lines of character near his dark green eyes contrasted with the nicks on his clean-shaven face, creating a mixture of man and boy. But her desire to spread a line of kisses along his solid jaw had told her she perceived him as all man.

"Paaartnner up." The caller stood on a soapbox, ready to begin the next dance. Couples, dressed in their Sunday best, squared off.

She searched the crowd for deliverance from Davidson's toe-crunching steps. A set of dark brown eyes were Kit's salvation. The shopkeeper's daughter, Miranda, stood near the door.

The boy had lost his heart to the girl, but after his beating had been too ashamed to ask her to the dance. He begged Kit to go with him instead, to back him up and offer encouragement. Kit had complied, reluctantly. "Go talk to her," she urged Davidson. "Or I'm going over there for you."

A sudden panic crossed Davidson's face. Then he trudged off, looking as if he were approaching the gallows instead of a pretty girl. He stopped in front of Miranda, his head down, the heel of his boot twisting on the wide plank floor. Miranda placed her hand on his arm and gave Davidson a shy nod of her head.

His dejection shifted from disbelief to joy, then settled into young male pride. He straightened, a wide grin on his face, and a swagger rolled into his steps as he led the girl to the dance floor.

At last. Kit watched the young couple and the dancers

do an allemande left, weaving in and out, forming an intertwining circle. One dancer made her grin in surprise. Cade skipped along the circle, giving each woman, in her prime or past it, a flirtatious grin.

Hawk, his attention centered on his friend, shook his head in amused toleration. His heavy braids, decorated with a blue feather and leather casings, swayed slightly. Her brother's foot tapped to the lively tune of the fiddler.

Both she and her brother had found something at the Rockin' G that Jando had stolen from them. They had found a home. But Jando still robbed them. To trail the outlaw and kill him, they would have to forfeit their ties to the Rockin' G.

Sorrow twisted the music, making it painful. Kit couldn't seem to get her breath. She wanted out of the room filled with happy families and friends. Away from the reminders of what she and Hawk could never have. With Cade and Hawk not paying attention and Davidson entertaining Miranda, Kit slipped out the door.

Strolling away from the boisterous sounds of the dance, she sought a quiet refuge. Across the street, the whitewashed steeple of the church pointed her toward a likely retreat. She skittered across the dirt road and found a refuge at the base of a giant fir tree near the church steps. Behind the thick trunk, she spread her shawl on the carpet of fallen leaves and brown needles. Sitting, she leaned against the rough bark, closed her eyes and let her thoughts drift. Garret filled her mind.

She had two nights left to build enough memories of Garret and his ranch to last her a lifetime. And she wanted more than just a stolen kiss to think of in the lonely nights to come. Much more.

Hugging her knees to her chest, she rested her chin on her tented legs. Sunlight, softened by the fir branches, freckled her face with warmth. Without opening her eyes, she could detect the passing of cloud over the sun by the sudden coolness on her face.

"So you finally got Davidson hitched up with that merchant's girl."

Her eyes fluttered open to see Garret standing over her. "I didn't know you were watching." Her heart skipped as she spoke.

"I'm always watching." His eyes flashed a gentle, but firm, warning. He squatted, letting his weight rest on his heels. A teasing smile curved his lips. "I saw you light out after Davidson matched up with that girl. Did you get your heart broke?"

The tips of her moccasins peeked from beneath her hem. Across the top of the beads, dark treads showed on the brightly colored surface. She laughed as she answered, "It's not my heart that's broken. It's my toes."

"Someone oughta teach that boy the difference between a dance floor and his partner's feet." His teasing voice sent her pulse racing. Amusement twinkled in his eyes, and a deeper heat resided in their depths. His gaze seemed to drink in her features.

"Are you up for the task?" Kit regretted the banter. Would he mistake it for a request for a dance?

Garret pulled a long blade of grass and stuck it between his even white teeth. "Well now, I just might. I can do-si-do with the best of them."

Laughter spilled from her lips. "Somehow I just can't picture you that way."

"Really? Just how do you picture me?" His voice deepened as his shoulder brushed hers.

Resting her elbow on her bent knees, Kit braced her head and studied him. No softness gentled the wind- and sun-worked lines of his face. His square jaw and angular cheekbones had developed a shadow, hiding the nicks of this morning. Muscles in his shoulders and arms pulled taut the material of his white cotton shirt. He allowed her to get her fill of him, undisturbed by her scrutiny. Her first assessment of him stood.

"I once told my brother you reminded me of the desert. That's how I see you still."

"That's a pretty bleak place." He shifted away, his shoulder no longer touching her. Shadows streaked his face.

"Yes. It's hard and unforgiving. A man—or a woman—can't afford to make mistakes and survive."

Bitterness hardened his tone. "I guess you've got me pegged good. I don't give a man—or a woman—a second chance."

"No, you don't. Not even yourself. But remember, Garret, the desert is also a place of great beauty."

His head whipped back toward her. He swallowed, and his eyes darkened, matching the needles of the fir. "When?"

She felt compelled to answer him. Thoughts and feelings she had kept locked inside her slipped from her lips. "Have you ever seen the desert after a spring rain? When the ocotillo have fiery blooms and the prickly pear are covered with butter-yellow and crimson flowers? The cliffs soak up the moisture and turn from drab tones to vibrant shades of rust and yellow. And all that beauty is more spectacular because it's so brief."

Garret had seen it. The few weeks of spring when the desert burst into color. Just as he had seen it these last few weeks. Kit was his spring rain. She made all his hidden wants bloom. "But is that enough? Could you survive there with so little?"

Her brow furrowed. "Are we talking about the desert or you?"

He didn't answer. Couldn't answer. He stared instead at the mountains, rich with evergreens instead of desolate, like his soul.

She spoke with tenderness. "You know Indians have lived in the desert for centuries. I've learned well how to appreciate the danger and beauty of such a place."

"The danger?"

"You can lose yourself, get hopelessly lost, forget your way." A shroud of sadness clouded her features.

"But not you. You know how to find your way."

"Yes." Standing, she looked back toward the town-hall steps. People mingled in tiny groups, saying goodbyes and gathering up youngsters. "We need to be heading back soon."

He could hear the protests of the children. They were no more ready to leave the magic of the party than he was.

"Not yet," he said. He needed this time. The memory of her. The smell of her. Rising, he leaned one hand against the tree, cutting off her view of the steps. She stared at his arm, then licked her lips and faced him.

Just the tip of a scar showed at her neckline. Garret recalled glimpsing the thin line when she came to him about the mare. He wondered how far it dipped beneath the white-lace edge of her dress. What accident had caused it? He rested the finger of his free hand at the point where the whiter skin met the crocheted trim. Her skin warmed his hand; he could feel her heartbeat quicken.

"Garret?" She whispered his name, her tone a combination of hesitant reservation and husky desire.

"That kiss in the barn." His mouth grew dry as he stared at the full line of her lips. As if they were forbidden fruit, he felt the temptation of their allure. And like Adam, he was determined to savor their delights. "A gentleman never kisses a lady without asking. I'm asking now, Kit."

His mouth hovered over hers. His breath caressed her lips, sending shivers of anticipation along her neck. Kit's voice disappeared, she couldn't speak, couldn't shout, "Yes, kiss me, hold me." Instead, she managed to nod and Garret claimed her.

His kiss brushed against her mouth, gentle and searching. Kit waited for the panic, hoped it would appear and save her from her exploding emotions. Her old weakness failed to show, and she found her fear replaced by desire and her panic by a longing to feel Garret's strong arms around her. She discovered the absence of her terror at the same time that Garret seemed to sense her surrender.

His hand cradled her head, his fingers massaging the sensitive skin at the nape of her neck. His lips left hers and trailed a line of kisses to her ear. His breath skipped across the swirls of her ear and her knees trembled. When he nibbled at her earlobe, then gently sucked, her knees gave way. She clung to him. Her arms wrapped around his neck to both support herself and give in to her need to have him close. Cautiously, she kissed his neck. The salty taste of his skin made her ache for more. She nipped at the skin below his ears and Garret's arm crushed her to him.

He ran his jaw along her cheek and the stubble on his chin sent gooseflesh down her neck and across her chest. As though tracking the path of her sensations, Garret's kisses followed. Heat flared from between her legs and she could feel his hardness nestled at her core.

Lean muscles pushed against her soft skin. A rough, callused hand tenderly cupped her breast, massaging the bud until it was hard and firm. Powerless to stop her wanton urges, she leaned into his touch and heard him groan as her leg brushed between his. She realized that in her abandon she had gained a hold over Garret.

He couldn't get enough of her. Garret kissed the hollow of her throat, licking the spot where her pulse beat. The treasure of her breast lay in his quivering hand, and he longed to kiss his way to its hardened tip. Instead, he splayed his fingers along the gentle curve, regretting the thin calico cloth and chemise preventing him from tasting her sweet nectar. The scent of wildflowers surrounded him as he skimmed her neck and shoulder with kisses.

"Stay, Kit. Stay here with me." The words were out before he could think. "To hell with the town and Benton and anyone else. Stay with me, Kit. Be my spring shower."

She stilled in his arms. Her hands slid from his neck and rested on his chest. Lowering her head, she hid her face. "I can't, Garret."

"I don't know what your secrets are, but they don't matter to me. You didn't learn to speak the way you do on a reservation." Garret trailed a finger down the crest of her nose and rested it on her lips. "You and your brother wouldn't be the first to ride into a town with a new name. Whatever happened in the past is the past. Leave it behind and start fresh at the Rockin' G, with me."

"I can't, Garret." Tears she couldn't hold back meandered down her cheeks. Wiping them away with the backs of her hands, she broke her contact with Garret's body but not with emotions his kisses had unleashed. She wanted to fall into his arms and bare her soul. Only her fierce loyalty to her brother stopped her. "Hawk and I must ride on when the drive begins."

"Why?"

Because we have to kill a man. Kit stepped away from his embrace and from any future with him. "My path was set long ago. Remember what I said about losing your way in the desert. If I stayed, I would lose my way. I couldn't...." She paused and bit her lower lip, the words sticking in her throat. "There are things about me, about my past."

"That I don't care about." Garret fought for her to understand his feelings. He leaned forward, ready to claim her with his lips as well as his heart.

"No." Kit held up her hand, halting the kiss she so desperately wanted but didn't deserve. "I have to leave." Any chance at happiness with Garret was destined for failure. His kisses and touch could wipe away her fears from the past but not the ghosts that haunted her dreams. Her slain friends cried for justice.

His jaw clamped shut, and the scar on his temple turned a stark white against his tanned skin. He nodded his head and gave her a narrow stare full of hurt. "Have it your way then." He dropped his arm, and in a softer tone added, "If you change your mind, you know where to find me."

In my heart. Retrieving her shawl, Kit shook it clear of pine needles and leaves, but the deep ache in her soul would not be cleared so easily.

Chapter Sixteen

A mix of longhorns and shorthorns plodded into base camp. Kit watched her brother lope in behind the tired cows. The moment she saw Hawk's eyes, she knew he had found something. Like shards of broken glass, her brother's gaze cut into hers. As a Bar M cowhand swung the gate shut on the penned animals, Hawk dismounted and strode toward her.

"I found him." Hawk hissed the news as he took her elbow and led her away from the cowhands branding cattle. "About forty miles north of here. Jando's in a canyon, ready to make a move on Blaine's herd."

A wash of panic swept through her. The urge to flee captained her emotions. Kit gripped the handle of her knife. No matter how the sight of the fat man made her cringe, she could not let Hawk go alone. This was as much her fight as his. "When do we attack?"

"Tomorrow." The ruthless glint left Hawk's eyes. Empathy deepened his voice. "My sister, you stay here. I will return for you."

"No." She clenched his wrist. "If you leave me, I'll just follow." Closing her eyes, she summoned every bit of courage and determination in her soul to war against her fears. It unsettled her to realize just how close the battle was. Only her loathing of Jando equaled her dread of the man.

"There is too much danger." Hawk paused, then added, "Perhaps you should return to your father."

"No." Kit shook her head and implored her brother to understand. "I would live the rest of my life in a world controlled by Father. Protected. Isolated. Alone. Mama thought she could live that way, but in the end, she regretted it. That's why her last words were about you. I have to see Jando dead. It's the only way I can rest or my nightmares will be with me forever."

"I can argue with my sister, but not with the will of the spirit world." Hawk's mouth became a thin, straight line. "The voices of our mother and those of the village cannot be ignored."

"Tomorrow we find Jando." Kit stared at the high-noon sun. In less than twenty-four hours Jando would either lie dead, or she would. The threat of finality swept over her. Regret lodged in her throat. Suddenly, she had a lifetime to live before the sun rose again.

She scanned the rolling hills and spotted the solitary rider on the knoll. After her refusal yesterday, Garret had ridden straight to the herd. He hadn't spoken to her since he had asked her to stay.

Holding her hands in his, Hawk turned her to face him. "You look at Garret Blaine as a woman does her husband."

The strain of last night and the threat of tomorrow made her weak. She couldn't contain her turmoil. In a soft voice, she admitted, "Garret asked me to stay on after the trail drive." Looking into her brother's eyes, she stressed, "He wanted me to stay with him."

"My wife is dead, my son is lost to me. You are all

the family I have.'' Hawk sheltered her stiff body in his arms. ''I will speak true, but my words may cut your heart. Garret Blaine wants a woman to share his bed, but a Benton to share his name.''

''I know,'' Kit admitted. ''I won't make the same mistake my mother did and trust the wrong man.'' Hawk was right. Garret lusted after her, desired her. She knew that from their kiss.

But does he love me? Kit pushed the thought away. She didn't want to know the answer or to cling to a hope that he might. Only one thought needed to fill her mind, killing Jando. She spoke with conviction. ''I've already told Garret I couldn't stay.''

''You will forget this sadness.'' A ferocity accompanied Hawk's order.

''Yes, Hawk. I will forget,'' Kit promised, but feared she had uttered a lie. Side by side, she and Hawk returned to the branding fire and working cowhands.

Cade, astride Pretty Gal, wheeled through the herd, his cow pony dancing between the sharp horns and bulky bodies. The herd parted and a gray-white bull with a six foot spread of horns slashed the air in anger. The bull's natural cussedness combined with the orneriness of age made the animal a creature to be respected and left alone. Without missing a beat, Cade guided his mount in a wide berth between himself and the old mossy point longhorn.

Crossing the corral to a group of complacent cows, Cade let out a loud cowboy yodel, culled a calf and herded it over to the fire. Liam tackled the animal and toppled the calf in record time.

''Cade, he will never make a good Indian.'' Hawk pouted his lips. ''Too loud.''

''Maybe, but he makes a good friend,'' Kit added absently.

Hawk's sharp intake of breath made her look up. The square line of his jaw became rigid. "I cannot say the same." He stabbed the embers with the branding iron. Ashes and red-hot dust flew into the air.

"We could tell Cade and Garret the truth." The part of Kit that feared the outlaw hoped Hawk would seek aid. She was a lousy shot with a Colt and not much better with a rifle. Adding the firepower of the Blaines would bolster Hawk's chances. The stronger part of her, the part forever marred by Jando's evil, craved satisfaction and wanted the rustler to suffer. That, Garret would never allow her or Hawk to do.

"Jando desecrated the Cheyenne, he will die like the dog he is." Hawk uttered the sentence like a judge at a hanging, no reprieve or pardon possible. His eyes glazed to dark blue, a hate-filled fire in their depths.

Cade dismounted near them and called, "My stomach's bellerin' louder than them calves." Dust puffed from his shirt as he walked toward them, patting his breastbone. "Let's mosey down and get some vittles."

Kit gazed at the buckboard nestled in the shade of the cottonwood trees. A wispy plume of smoke twisted upward, carrying the tantalizing scent of stew. She nodded to her brother, knowing he would understand the slight motion meant more than just an agreement to eat. Come sunup, she and Hawk would hunt down Jando, alone.

"Ah, you're the picture of loveliness, Miss Kit," Liam whispered as he joined Kit, Hawk and Cade.

Instead of building her confidence, Kit found herself floundering and wished the words were spoken not with the lilting accent of the Irishman, but with the slow, seductive drawl of Garret Blaine.

Garret reined his gelding to a stop and jumped from the saddle. His gaze fixated on Kit. He had meant to remain on the hill, studying her with his telescope, but the instant Liam had joined her, Garret had spurred his horse to camp.

That Irishman had more charm than he needed. Wistfulness bent the ugly possessiveness in Garret's heart. Why couldn't he find the words to make Kit stay?

He finished with his horse and neared the fire. A few of McVery's hands were mopping their plates with Cracker's biscuits. None of them spoke, they just nodded in acknowledgment and finished eating.

Davidson, dressed in a burlap apron, dropped the potato he had been peeling. He walked past Garret as if he weren't even there. "Howdy, Miss Kit." Davidson scooped up a blue enamel plate, filled it with food and shoved the overflowing plate into Kit's hand. The three fistsize biscuits rimming the edge formed a dam for the stew.

"Thank you." Kit gave the eager youth a genuine smile. Her smile suited her, no artful coyness, just an open friendliness. It brought a light to her sapphire eyes that Garret longed to see.

Kit glided to a seat near the fire and nibbled at her food. Cade looked at Davidson expectantly, his hand outstretched for a plate. The boy didn't give him a second glance. Instead, he fixed himself a plate then plopped down next to Kit.

Leaning his hip on the wagon wheel, Garret allowed his gaze to caress Kit. Sunshine kissed her skin, making her eyes more vivid. He detected a hint of indulgence as she spoke with Davidson and, as always, a core of mystery.

"'Pears you and the boys are on your own for grub,"

Cracker commented dryly. "My helper here's takin' a break."

"I earned it," Davidson said.

Cade and Hawk took a plate from Cracker then lit on their heels around the fire. The cook passed Garret a dinner plate.

"Thanks." Garret took the plate but it wasn't physical hunger that gripped him. A craving for Kit's touch and the sweetness of her mouth gnawed at him.

"Kit," Cade called out. "Move over and give Garret a seat."

She bit her lower lip and gulped a mouthful of food. "Sure." Her voice sounded hoarse and dry. Sliding over to the far edge, Kit scrunched her shoulders and cleared as much space as possible. Her gaze locked on her brother's.

A mountain lion's sneer looked less deadly than the one Hawk shot in Garret's direction. So she had told Hawk about yesterday, but how much?

Had she mentioned the kiss? Had she admitted she had melted in his arms and returned his passion? Had she told Hawk about Garret's plea for her to stay? She must have told her brother she had politely declined the offer or the Indian would be at Garret's throat.

He sat down and stuffed a forkful of stew into his mouth. The tender bites of beef and vegetables became dry and tasteless. The only sensations Garret could concentrate on were the luscious heat of Kit's hip against his own, of the unique aroma of honeysuckle and dust coming from her skin, and the allure of her dark red lips as she licked biscuit crumbs from her fingertips. He groaned and rubbed his jaw, the overnight stubble scratching his palm.

Kit stirred her fork in her plate, not eating. Garret almost put down his plate to gather her in his arms, but then he remembered she wasn't his, didn't want to be his. He took a sip of water and wished it was whiskey. Anything that would make him forget the ache in his body and the emptiness in his soul.

"Cap'n, when ya gonna let me do some cowboyin'?" Davidson repeated his daily plea.

"When you get some common sense, boy." Talk didn't come high on Garret's list right now. He wanted to enjoy the torture of being close to Kit. "I'll give you a go at the fall roundup."

"Fall!" From the boy's expression, September was years away instead of only months.

"You keep pestering me and it may not be at all." Garret tossed his nearly full plate onto the wagon tailgate. "Boy, did you remember to check on the remuda horses?"

A long pause answered him. Davidson replied nervously, "Yes, sir."

His gaze refused to meet Garret's direct stare. The boy couldn't even lie. Venom made Garret think, *Now there's something Kit can teach him, how to lie.*

"After I talk with Vega, I'm going to look over that rope corral and the hobbles." Garret put the boy on notice then left, anxious to put some space between himself and Kit.

Kit watched Garret's broad shoulders as he walked away. There was a strength about him, both of body and character, that tugged at her soul. Sometimes, she could almost see the weight of responsibility he carried without complaint. At other times, she had to fight the urge to run her fingers over the severe planes of his face and massage away the worry lines.

"Can't ya talk with him, Miss Kit?" Davidson cajoled as he stood.

"I doubt there's anything I could say that would change his mind."

The boy's sorrow tore at her heart. Stuck at the chuck-wagon, he was missing all the excitement of roundup. Garret was carrying his lesson too far. There wasn't an ounce of forgiveness in his powerful body.

"If I just showed the Cap'n how good I am," Davidson complained like one of the branded calves. "I just made a mistake in town. I won't do it again."

"Hell, no." Cracker removed a Dutch oven from the embers. As he lifted the lid, the sweet aroma of berry cobbler blended with the smoke of the campfire. "Ya ever that dumb again, and I'll shoot ya myself."

Turning to Davidson, she tried to lessen the brunt of the punishment. "I'm sure in time you'll be able to make Garret see your worth."

She didn't know if she spoke about the boy or herself. Had Hawk been right about Garret? Had he offered her a lifetime at his side or a short-term agreement? But what did it matter? She couldn't stay either way, but her heart lurched at the thought he might really care for her and broke with the possibility he wanted nothing more than a blanket woman.

"It just ain't fair." Davidson ripped off his apron, his face flushed with anger and despair. Running toward the creek, he fled his persecutors.

"Everyone deserves a second chance." Her words advocated Davidson, but really, she spoke for herself. What would she give for another chance to tell Garret she would stay?

No, she would leave the Rockin' G with the memory of a gentleman asking a lady for a kiss under a fir tree. Kit would miss Garret's tenderness, his strength, his passion.

"Cade, ya best get over to the corral." McVery rushed over to the cook wagon, his face red, his chest heaving with exertion. "It's the boy. He's tryin' to cut calves."

A cold churning started in Kit's gut. "Cade, do you think Davidson is foolish enough to tackle the mossy point."

The deadly white pallor on Cade's face gave her all the answer she needed.

Chapter Seventeen

Chili's persistent yapping sent a tingle of premonition down Garret's spine. He raced toward the penned cattle, his long legs outdistancing Vega, his foreman's. Pushing his way to the rail, he searched for the cause of the commotion and prayed Kit was far from it.

The sight of her, standing near the corral, stifled the anguish clawing at his throat but stirred the deep emotions he held in check. She turned to him and tugged at his sleeve. It might as well have been his heart. "Davidson's trying to prove himself to you by showing off."

Davidson, astride a sweat-streaked pony, tore through the herd. "Watch this, Cap'n." He swung his hand in the air as if to grab Garret's attention and physically hold it, then barreled through the cattle. Making the most common mistake of a greenhorn wrangler, the boy followed first one animal, tired of the chase, then another, instead of singling out one calf. The only thing he achieved was to rile the cattle and Garret's temper.

"Hightail it out of that corral." Garret swung his leg over the rail, ready to haul the boy out of the saddle. One spook and those docile cows would turn into a mass of stampeding hooves.

Instead of taking the warning, the boy, lasso in hand, stared down the biggest bull Garret had ever laid eyes on. A combination of moss and blood stained the tips of the bull's yellowing horns. Scars raked the animal's back and sides, testimony to battles fought and won. The old bull had overcome obstacles to survival in the wild—wolves, mountain lions and the harsh elements. Dropping his head, he swung his deadly weapons toward the latest obstacle in his path, Davidson.

The boy spurred his horse forward, barely skirting the curving horns. Clods of mud and cattle chips pelted the air. A hard patty collided with the bull's eye, and the animal pawed the earth with a massive hoof.

Cows hugged the rim of the corral so thick, Garret could have walked across their backs. Calves yelped and bawled when their mothers stepped on them. The cattle's mooing changed to short puffs of air, a sign of agitation.

"That boy's gonna stampede the herd," Cracker croaked as the bull let the tip of his horns score the ground.

Davidson reined his pony into a tight curve. The small-boned horse obeyed and pivoted on her back legs, nearly bending in two to comply with her rider's commands. The boy leaned to the inside as the pony twisted, and his weight threw off the horse's balance. True to her training, the cow pony paused and allowed her rider to regain control.

That second of hesitation was all the mossy point needed. Like a freight train of death, the bull charged. One horn sank deep into the pony's gut. The agonizing scream of the horse silenced the cowhands and the teen.

Death hung heavy in the air. Garret smelled it, Davidson gagged on it, and the mossy point inhaled the aroma like sweet perfume.

The bull shook his head, pitching the boy forward in the saddle, slitting a deep gash into the pony's underside. Garret's heart pounded as he watched the bull toss his victims in the air.

The horse landed with a thud on the ground, thrashing from the pain. Pinned beneath the weight of the pony, Davidson kicked at the writhing horse, trying to free himself. "Help me, Cap'n!" Davidson half cried, half screamed his plea.

Cade lifted his gun and aimed it at the bull. Garret shouted, "Fire that gun and the whole herd might stampede."

It'd take a mess of luck and a whole lot of prayers to get Davidson out of that corral alive. Garret had never considered himself lucky, and he hadn't prayed in years.

Davidson's shouts became louder. The cow pony neighed. The bull's temper crescendoed. He attacked again, causing both horse and rider to somersault.

"Damn!" Garret jumped over the top of the rail. To hell with caution. If he didn't get in there quick, there would be nothing left of Davidson to save.

Before Garret could make an attempt, Cade jumped the fence, cursing and shouting to draw the bull off. Like a wolf protecting his prey, the mossy point refused to budge from the near corpses. Unrelenting, Cade tossed his hat in the beast's face and advanced.

"You're too close." Hawk warned as he vaulted the fence. The bull took advantage of Cade's daring. A short charge and he cornered the cowhand against a moving wall of cows. Hawk shed his vest and waved the beaded garment, trying to turn the animal toward himself. But the bull didn't make the same mistake Davidson had, he was single-minded. His gaze stayed on Cade.

The bull intended to kill the Indian, Cade, Davidson,

anyone who came near it. To hell with the herd, to hell with the drive. Slipping into the corral, Garret lifted his gun and sighted between the bull's bloodshot eyes.

A blur of black and white knocked his arm, the impulse to pull the trigger already racing to his finger. Every bit of iron will he possessed erupted to stop the action when he spotted Kit, bareback on the Appaloosa, between his bullet and the bull. His hand twitched, his finger trembled, but he checked the action that would put a bullet in Kit's back and a wound in his heart. Cade's favorite gal, Lady Luck, for once bestowed her gifts on Garret. And he would be forever grateful.

His gratitude splintered as Kit cut between Cade and the bull. She flashed her red bandanna like a Mexican matador, daring the animal to attack. The bull changed direction, ready to answer her challenge.

Space and time slowed. He felt the spray of dust from the bull's pistonlike legs. Smelled the horrible stench of the hurt pony's spilled guts. Heard deep murmurs of pity and awe from the cowhands. But his fear centered on the slight figure on the running horse.

With just a hair's space between her rump and the deadly horns, the Appaloosa teased the bull with the coyness of a saloon girl. A touch of daring, a taste of playfulness. Just the recipe to send the bull into a frenzy.

"Help Davidson," Kit shouted. Clinging to her mare's bare back, she guided the horse with her knees and a handful of dark mane. The Appaloosa's dappled backside swung clear as the bull charged.

Garret sprinted to the downed horse. Hawk and Cade were breathing down his neck in seconds. The Indian withdrew his blade and sliced the animal's throat, putting an end to its suffering at last. Cade and Hawk strained to lift the dead animal while Garret pulled Davidson free.

From the corner of her eye, Kit caught a glimpse of Cade and her brother with Davidson. Thank God, the boy was safe. But where was Garret? Her only thought when she cleared the fence was to prevent him from risking everything he had worked so hard for.

Her mare pivoted, backed up, then broke into a gallop of her own accord. Her horse's attention still rested with the bull's movements. Kit tore her worries from the tall rancher and focused on the angry mossy point.

Hemmed in by the jostling cows, she couldn't get enough room to jump the fence. She sensed the bull and kicked with her left leg. The mare responded immediately and banked to the right. Hooves thundered past, the bull plowed into the fence post, but after a few shakes of his ugly head, he was ready for another attack, leaving her no time to plan any escape beyond the moment.

"Kit, this way." Garret waved to her from inside the gate. At his side, the long barrel of a Winchester gleamed in the late afternoon sun. "Now." His voice rang with an ominous authority, offering her no choice but to obey. Her heels dug into the mare's belly, transmitting the need for one last burst of speed.

The Appaloosa answered quickly. Petite and fine-boned, the mare had a heart and will to please. She gave Kit every last bit of stamina left in her long, graceful legs. Wind ripped Kit's breath away. Strands of the flying mane stung her cheeks. The thundering of hooves gave her hope and fear. Hope that the mare would not give out, fear that the charging bull behind her would overtake them.

The gate swung open, and cows and calves spilled from the corral. Weeks of work gone. Garret's hope of a successful drive disappeared in the dust of the escaping cattle.

The late afternoon sun gleamed on his rifle. Cattle raced past him, eager to leave the tension of the corral and un-

mindful of the lone man in their way. Garret didn't flinch.
He moved with deliberate steps toward her, his rifle level
and sighted.

Kit could hear the nerve-racking snorting of the bull
behind her, his breath closer, the sound of his hooves
nearer and nearer. The mare stumbled and Kit's heart
dropped. She arched her back, expecting to feel the hot
pain of the mossy point's horns as they impaled her.

A bullet cracked in the air. Kit registered a second of
silence. The cows stopped shuffling in the corral, the
bull's heavy breath no longer followed her and she could
hear her own heart beat. Garret stood almost abreast of
her horse. Smoke circled his rifle barrel.

Then chaos.

Like a brown tide of hide and hair, the cattle stampeded. In one mindless mob, they headed for the open
gate—straight over the carcass of the dead bull and toward Kit.

Garret reached up, grabbed a handful of the running
mare's mane and pulled himself up behind Kit. Clicking
her tongue, she urged her mount on to the gate.

Candus and Cracker stood by the rail, ready to close
the gate as soon as she cleared it. The few feet stretched
out in front of her like miles. Garret encircled her waist
with one arm, reached across and held on to her horse's
mane with the other. "Come on, Kit, don't give up now."

Cocooned in the warmth and smell of his body, she
leaned low against the horse's neck. The mare was tired
and carrying double. But Kit asked for more, begged for
more with her motions and the urgency in her voice.

And the Appaloosa gave it. Nearly spent, she picked
up speed, squirmed her way through the mass of cattle,
cleared the gate and rounded the fence line, out of the
way of the crushing hooves of the cows.

Candus and Cracker worked to push the gate closed and stem the loss of livestock. A numbness spread over Kit's body as she stared at the dead bull. The head lay cocked at an odd angle, his massive neck broken by the running cows. A single bullet hole between his eyes oozed blood.

Sweeping her gaze from the gruesome corpse, she followed the line of beeves. Liam, Cade and Hawk, on horseback, raced up and down the flanks, driving the cattle into the foothills.

Garret slid from her mare's back. His hand wrapped around her wrist, and he yanked her from the saddle. His fingers bit into her shoulders, forcing her to look him in the face. The pale scar on his temple blazed, matching the temper in his eyes. "Don't you ever get between me and what I'm shooting again."

"Garret, I only wanted—"

"I don't give a damn why you did it." His firm grip on her shoulders eased. His hands slid down her arms and lingered at her waist, sending a twining branch of warmth and desire through her. "Don't ever do it again." He gave the order with a twinge of wistfulness and weariness. The sandy fringe of hair fell down over his eyes, giving him a vulnerability that caused Kit's heart to ache.

"I did it for you." The admission flowed from her lips, and she gasped at her words. There was too much truth in them, too many feelings to ignore. She would have risked her life willingly for Davidson or Cade or her brother, but she had jumped that fence for Garret and for his dreams.

Like an emerald's fire, a heat flared in the depths of his eyes, but not from anger. This fire burned with the heat of passion, with desire. "Kit." He whispered her name like a caress.

"Cap'n?" Candus trotted over to them, breaking the

spell. Garret pulled his fingers from her waist and brushed the hair from his eyes. "Davidson's up at the wagon, just skinned up a bit. I swear that boy's got more lives than a cat."

"If he's got nine lives, by the time I finish with him, he'll only have one left." Garret's voice sounded like rough sandpaper.

All the sentiment and tenderness in her heart dried to a hard kernel. Garret's malachite eyes harbored no shred of forgiveness or understanding. Determination cracked through her body like a mule whip, stirring up her stubbornness. "If you hadn't been so hard on the boy—"

Garret rested his fists on his hips and gave her a no-nonsense stare. "And if you hadn't covered up for him in town he might have gotten more out of the experience than just a beating."

"You refuse to listen to reason."

"No." Garret turned to walk away from her. "I'm just not going to listen to you."

Chapter Eighteen

Fury chiseled Garret's jawline as he bellowed at Davidson sitting on the wagon bed. "Boy, you killed a good horse today and came darn close to killing me and others. God knows how many cattle we lost in the stampede."

Candus pointed toward the foothills. "I figure Cade and the men aim to run 'em into a box canyon, settle 'em down for the night, then herd 'em back come morning."

Morning! Kit heard the ominous ring in the word. Hawk would be waiting for her at daybreak, not with cattle, but with revenge in mind.

"He hurt?" Not an ounce of concern mellowed Garret's tone.

Cracker shook his head, his gray eyes wide. "Ain't much more than scratched. That boy's so flexible he could scratch his ear with his big toe."

"Can he ride?" Garret bit out the question.

Davidson's quick breath and the slight shiver that ran across his shoulders mustered forth every ounce of protectiveness in Kit's body. Even though Garret didn't know it, the stampede could actually save his herd. With the cows spread out and no longer an easy steal, Jando might leave Garret alone.

Garret barked an order to Candus. "Get him a broom tail from the remuda. Davidson's riding out." The Buffalo soldier hustled to obey.

She locked her gaze with Garret's, determined to make him back down. "It's almost sunset. Do you want the boy out on the prairie alone and unable to protect himself? And where is he to go?" She couldn't let Garret just cut the boy loose.

A low growl of anger and disgust rumbled in Garret's chest. "Back to the ranch. Come sunup, he's out of here." Garret pivoted and snatched a serape from the wagon bed. Draping the thick wool cloth over his head, he kicked at a stone, following its bumpy course toward the river.

"Thank ya, Miss Kit." Davidson pumped her hand.

"Me and Kit'll take that broom tail back," Cracker muttered as Candus trotted up with a flea-bitten nag. The old cook dug out a wool blanket from the wagon then arranged it like a shawl on Kit's shoulders. With the broom tail's lead in one hand and Kit's hand in the other, Cracker led his captives away from the camp and toward the wide expanse of the prairie.

The white-haired cook freed the old mustang. His steel-gray eyebrows wrinkled into deep canyons. "Ya never shoulda butted in between the boy and the Cap'n. One night a-worryin' about where he was gonna call home coulda taught that boy to think afore he acts."

Indecision muddled Kit's thinking. Was Garret acting in the boy's best interests? The coldness of the rancher's eyes haunted her. She had detected no mercy in their jade depths.

Cracker's large, callused hand swept the vista—the creeping shadows of the mountains over the horizon, the arc of the golden sun slipping behind the jagged peaks. "Give the Cap'n a chance, and he'll teach Davidson how to steer clear of a fight, and when there ain't no other way, how to take care of himself against a man like Traynor. Ya don't—'' Cracker's voice lowered and turned morose ''—and one day it won't be the boy's butt I'm a-carryin' out of trouble, it'll be his coffin.''

Her mind reeled with confusion. Was she doing more harm than good? ''All I did was support Davidson.''

''And not the Cap'n. The boy thinks he can go 'round the Cap'n through you.''

''But I have no influence with Garret.'' *Especially now.* A wall had always existed between her and Garret, and her refusal had only fortified it.

''Pshaw!'' Cracker shook his stubbled chin and threw up his hands. ''He cut loose that Benton gal for tryin' to ramrod this spread, but yore still here. There's got to be a reason.''

''There's nothing, Cracker. Nothing at all between Garret and myself.''

''Gal, if'n you believe that, then yore skull's thicker than Davidson's.'' The cook gave her a fatherly pat on the shoulder then left Kit with her bruised thoughts.

The air chilled as the mountain's shadow finally stretched into camp, overlapping the early fall warmth in its darkness. The campfire burned brightly in the twilight. Silhouetted in its light, Garret's tall form paced the creek bed.

He looked so alone with his worries. And she hadn't helped to ease his burdens. She had made a mistake, but one she could fix. Exhaling, Kit set her jaw in a stubborn line and headed for camp.

Her mission gave purpose to her stride. She glanced around the campfire looking for Davidson. He sat on the tailgate, shoveling food with gusto into his mouth, not a care in the world. He acted as though the whole episode had taken place years ago instead of only hours. Cracker was right. Davidson would never learn anything with her coddling him.

Kit marched over and planted herself in front of him. Widening her stance, she flipped back the blanket like a cape and rested one hand on the hilt of her knife. With the other, she pulled Hawk's necklace toward her from around Davidson's neck. One slash of the blade, and the claws slithered into her palm.

"Hey, now, I thought ya give me those." Davidson reached out to grab the necklace back.

"I was wrong." Kit's gaze drifted to the old cook's, approval lighting his eyes. "And come morning, you best be heading back to the ranch with no back talk. Understand." Kit didn't leave her last statement as a question. It was an order.

Davidson gave her a hurt-puppy look. "Yes, Miss Kit. I didn't know I had riled ya so."

"Not just me. What about McVery? Some of his cattle were in with the herd. He'll be looking for a piece of your hide, too. If you're not out of camp when they come back, Garret'll have to face off with the only man that stood with him just to save you."

The boy dropped his head. "I never thought about the Cap'n trying to help me by sending me away."

"That's your problem in a nutshell. You don't think." Kit nailed another point of guilt in the boy's self-centeredness.

"I best go apologize."

Kit pocketed the necklace in her flannel shirt and held out a hand to stop the boy. "That I can do for you. Come daybreak, you've got a long ride ahead of you."

Heading down to the creek bed to confront Garret, she rubbed the puma claws in her pocket, wishing the Indian superstition was true, that the claws could bring her wisdom. She was in sore need of some guidance on how to handle the angry rancher and her pounding heart. Sticking close to the trees, Kit stumbled through the brush.

"Davidson? If that's you, you're pushing your luck," Garret grumbled. Turning toward the stand of cottonwoods, he peered into the intertwined brush, trying to find the boy's shape.

Davidson had caused him nothing but trouble. Hell, he was more the boy's parent than boss. *I ought to wash my hands of the whole mess.* But he couldn't bring himself to do it. Garret knew what it was like to be alone.

"It's me. Kit." She slipped from the inky blackness between the trees draped in a brightly colored Navajo blanket. Just like the one on his bed. The thought came unbidden to his mind.

He didn't need a name to match the voice. The slicing pain it cut in his heart identified her. Couldn't she have supported him this one time, stood beside him instead of facing off against him? Maybe it just wasn't in her to see things eye to eye with him. Maybe they never would.

A weariness settled on Garret's shoulders. "I came out here for some peace of mind," he snapped.

"Garret, wait." Kit's gentle insistence cut into his self-righteous anger. He didn't want to hear her requests for mercy. What he wanted to do was wring Davidson's neck for placing her in danger. And he wanted to wring his own for caring so much. His heart was still slamming against his chest, his fear for Kit slowly draining away.

"I don't want to hear it." Garret summoned all his anger into a harsh blast. "Just get back to camp and leave me alone to cool down." He stomped away from the light of the campfire and the honeysuckle smell of her hair.

Leaning his back on the strong cottonwood trunk, he contemplated the moonlight skipping across the water.

Kit trailed him like a hound after a raccoon, loud and insistent. She pushed her way through the brush and nagged, "But, Garret—"

"The boy deserves exactly what he got. Don't waste your breath trying to plead his case." Garret faced the cottonwood tree, afraid of what he might do if he stared into her eyes. Afraid that he would forget reason and crush her to his chest, and if he did, she would hear the pounding of his heart. "I ought to fire him instead of just sending him back to the ranch."

"I know, Garret. That's why I'm—"

"Hellfire, he stampeded the whole herd. Ruined weeks of work." Garret slammed the tree trunk and concentrated on the feel of the rough bark on his fist. The cattle could be herded up again, but what if Kit had been injured? Nothing could have torn Garret off Davidson if she had been hurt saving the boy from his own foolishness.

"I know, Garret. I know." Her voice dropped to a gentle whisper.

"He could've killed himself, me, Cade and—" Garret faced her, suddenly tongue-tied "—and you."

"I know." A subtle smile tugged at one side of her mouth. A glint of amusement softened her eyes.

It took Garret a moment to recognize the new sensation. "You're not arguing with me."

"I know." Her smile deepened and a shadow of a dimple creased her left cheek. A smudge of dirt streaked one cheek, marking the course of a tear.

"I don't know if I have the strength for this. Agreeing, I mean."

The colorful blanket fell from her shoulders and draped across her back like an expensive shawl. Her ebony tresses cascaded down her back and shoulders, forming meanders of black against the bright background. A gentleness softened her eyes as she spoke. "I'll try not to do it very often. Agreeing with you, that is."

"Thanks." Garret pretended to study the ripples in the water and the night insects skating across the surface. Taking a deep breath, he tasted the honey scent of her skin. How could the woman ride all day, brand cattle and smell so warm and sweet.

"It's my soap." Her eyes widened in surprise.

"What?"

"You said 'honey.' I thought you were talking about my soap. I scent it with honey."

"I never said no such thing." He had to watch himself around her. She made him spill too much truth, too much of himself. Frogs in the creek croaked a lullaby. The whippoorwill added a soprano to the bass chorus. Lord, it felt good being here, with her, silent and alone.

"Why didn't you fire Davidson?"

So much for silence. "Why does it matter so much?"

She tilted her head, doing it again, agreeing with him. Making him feel connected to her. "He's just so young to be on his own, to have so much anger. What do you know about him?"

"Not much. Him and that dog wandered onto the ranch about a year ago. Both were skinny as a rail and meaner than sin. After he got his belly full, Chili gentled up some. Davidson, he's got something eating at him that won't let up no matter how much his belly's full. I just don't understand him."

Moving closer, Kit leaned against the same tree, her shoulder touching his arm, sending hot pulses of want through his body despite the thickness of his serape and her blanket. The desire to move closer and cover her body with his warred in his mind with a warning to run away as fast as he could. The battle stalled Garret's lightning-quick reflexes. He didn't move and felt like a man caught between heaven and hell.

"I think maybe you know exactly how he feels. That's why you keep him on." Kit's voice lapped against his senses like the water in the river. Calming. Soothing.

"I see we're back to disagreeing." A smile slipped onto Garret's lips.

"Davidson is out to prove he's good enough. Just like you. Determined that no matter his background, he's a man to be dealt with, respected."

"You think you got me pegged. You don't know the half of it."

"Then tell me." Her quiet authority threatened to release his guilt. "If you aren't out to show you're a better person than your mother, then what is it? What makes you so driven?"

"You're not about to let this lie, are you?"

"Now you're reading me."

There it was again, that merging of spirits that tore at Garret. A feeling he wanted to bottle up and savor the way Cracker did with that bottle of whiskey down in the wagon. The one he called "medicine." Kit standing next to him, her voice soft, her eyes willing him to open up, was a medicine. One that healed the wound in his heart and soul.

"I could never be a better person than my mother." Facing Kit, he released a trace of his past. "I hated her for becoming a soiled prairie dove, so I ran away when I was about Davidson's age, deserted her and Cade. But the worst thing I did was teach Cade to be just like his big brother, full of sass and not caring about anyone or any place."

"Garret, you were only a boy."

"That's what you keep telling me about Davidson."
Like untying a knot, Garret pushed and prodded himself
to come clean, to let the truth out of his heart. "After the
war, a lawyer down in New Orleans sent me a wire. Ma
was close to dying and he had her will. I was going to
walk away."

"What happened?" Concern thickened Kit's voice and
made Garret's shame heavier.

"Lawyer mentioned Cade was in a mess of trouble with
a gambler. I paid off his debts and then we both went and
saw that lawyer and Ma." Nodding toward the open
range, Garret continued, "Ma died handing me the deed
to our ranch. Every penny she could scrape together she
put away for this place. The only thing she asked in return
was for me to bring pride and respect back to our name.
Like when Pa was alive."

"And you have." Kit's support lifted some of the burden from his shoulders.

"How? I'm barely scratching out a living and probably
lost half the herd today."

"By standing up to Benton. Showing Davidson how to
be a man. Hiring men—and a woman—because of their
worth and not their skin color." She straightened and
pulled the claw necklace from her pocket. Lifting her
hands, she tied the claws around his neck. "Garret, you're
a good man."

Kit's hands rested on his shoulders, strands of her hair
tickled his cheek. A half smile curved her lips and fired
a deep longing in his heart. His voice sounded husky and
thick with desire. "But it's not enough to clear Ma's
shame and Pa's name. I gotta be more than good. I've got
to be the best. Like Benton."

Licking her lips, Kit nodded. "Guilt drives your life. I

can understand that all too well. I know you can't give it up. Not for anyone or anything.''

The eerie quality to her voice sent a shiver down his spine. It was as though she were speaking through a mist, reliving a time long ago. Her eyes focused on the nearly full moon, the pale light illuminating her face. She spoke in a whisper, ''I have my own crosses to bear, just as heavy as yours.''

Of course she did. Mixed-blood children suffered childhoods as bleak as his own had been. Adulthood wasn't much better. ''It doesn't matter to me you're a half-breed.''

Her finger rested on his lips. ''But it does to others. Like Benton. Men with power that you think can rub away the guilt and the shame. And despite all that, you asked me to stay.'' One finger toyed with the edge of his collar. ''You lost another button.''

His hand strayed to hers, the heat of her body sparking the space between them. ''I almost lost more than a button today.'' The ache in his body was more than lust, more than just base desire. He needed to feel her next to him, run his hands down her arms, across her body, and know she was safe.

Drained, he surrendered to his desire, clasped her hands and drew her to his chest. He wrapped her arms around his waist and rested his forehead against her own.

''Garret?''

''Sh.'' Garret released her hand to place a finger over her lips. Her arms wound more tightly around his waist. ''For just a minute, I want to imagine it's not the best cowhand on my ranch in my arms but—''

''A woman?'' The light touch of her breath warmed his chest. Staying cradled in his arms, she let her gaze search his face. "I am a woman, Garret. For tonight, I could be your woman."

Her offer stunned him, left him speechless but not motionless. He lowered his mouth and claimed hers. He tasted the sweetness of her breath and could feel the butterfly flutter of her eyelashes against his cheek. He didn't think he had the strength to release her if she asked.

Kit pressed her lips against his, offering him what she could. One night. For two years she had feared a man's touch, yet now she craved Garret's. The ugly images of Jando's hands on her body were pushed to the dark recesses of her mind and replaced by visions of Garret's arms around her, his lips exploring her body. Tomorrow, her own trail of vengeance and guilt would end. She couldn't give up her thirst for Jando's blood any more than Garret could ignore his mother's request.

The blanket fell from her shoulders as his lips ravaged hers with a raw hunger. His tongue sent shivers racing through her, creating her own hunger. She clung to him, eager to learn how to please him, eager to learn how to be pleased.

She put up no resistance as he lowered her to the blanket while his lips explored her face. He pulled the serape over his head and his last two remaining buttons popped. His shirt draped open, exposing the smooth hardness of his chest and the narrow line of hair disappearing beneath his waistband.

"Oh, Kit," he groaned as she reached for him. Explored the muscles of his chest. Brushed her fingers over his nipples. Burying his head in her hair, he slid his hand beneath her neckline and nestled under her breast. He held her fullness and ran his thumb over her breast, and a tremble racked her body. Her nipple hardened and rose to meet his gentle massage. Heat flushed her body and a demand. More.

He trailed a series of light kisses along the sensitive skin behind her ear, down her neck, and nuzzled the hollow of her throat while keeping up the mind-numbing movement of his fingers. Her flannel shirt chafed her tender breasts. She longed to feel nothing except the cool night air and the heat of Garret's touch. Then his hands were slipping her shirt from her shoulders, exposing her to the night and his touch.

The moonlight kissed her like a jealous lover. Garret wanted to impress each detail into his mind. The trail of silvery light along her hips, the erect peaks of her breasts, the contrast of her midnight hair against her skin. She nuzzled the palm of his hand. With his thumb, he traced her jaw and the outline of her full lips, swollen from his kisses. He groaned when she nipped at his fingertips then sucked on his finger gently.

Passion was replaced with reverence as he stared at the dark circles surrounding her nipples. Lowering his head, he kissed each peak, swept his tongue across the sensitive mounds and shuddered as he heard her soft whimper of passion. He ran his tongue along the thin scar that started in the valley between her breasts and curved along one perfect globe.

"Garret," she moaned as she arched to meet him. Her fingers raked his back, sending spine-tingling shocks through his body.

Fighting his building need, Garret slipped his hand beneath her loose waistband. His fingers splayed across her abdomen, then sank lower, searching for the core of her desire, and finally found her heat.

The instant his finger touched the silky vortex, Kit groaned. Thousands of new sensations, each more delicious than the one before, shocked her body. Made her ravenous for more. His finger teased her passion and she felt hot bursts of wanton desire rush forth to greet his entry and yet decry there was not more.

"Kit?"

In the midst of her desire-drugged mind, Kit heard Garret's voice. Heard the question in his tone. Opening her eyes, she saw his face looming over hers. He kissed her lips, stroked her hair back from her face. "Kit, you've got to tell me now if you want me to stop. If you want to walk away. I can't go any further without having you."

The fringe of sandy hair draped down over his eyes. Their flintlike hardness had shattered, replaced with a gentle concern. She could see the control he was exerting, the way the muscles in his back flexed, the slight tremble in his shoulders. Want and desire blazed in his eyes.

"Garret, love me. Love me like there is no tomorrow, no duties to fill, only you and I, here and now."

He lowered his head and kissed the corner of her mouth. "I don't deserve this," he whispered. "Don't deserve you." His hands tugged at her jeans while she fumbled with the buttons on his. In seconds she felt cold mountain air dance on her bare legs, then the intoxicating warmth of Garret's naked body along hers.

His hardness lodged between her legs, brushing her thighs and titillating her skin with the brief touch. Her fingers massaged his broad shoulders, skipping down his ribs then feeling the curve of his backside.

"Kit." He whispered her name as she felt his hot shaft enter her. An instant of panic seized her. Visions of men and hands and pain appeared through a mist. Then Garret's gentle movements and his mouth nibbling the delicate skin under her breast dulled the ache. Sweet waves of ecstasy assaulted her, washing away all inhibitions in their wake.

Lost in the delicious warmth of Kit's body, Garret wanted to forget the ease with which he had entered. He hadn't been the first to introduce Kit to the ways of love-making. She appeared so innocent to his kisses and touch. Yet hadn't he known she was a consummate actress?

Exquisite torture surrounded him, and he found his thoughts overflowing with the sensations around him. The smell of her honey-scented skin had him starved to taste her. Her body trembled as he moved within her, height-ening his arousal. A pillowy tightness cocooned his shaft and drove him nearly mad with passion. He marshaled every shred of self-control, determined to see her peak under his touch.

He couldn't keep his gaze from her face. Her eyes wid-ened just a bit as each new wave of passion traveled through her. Her half smile hinted of a dimple. The dark depths of her eyes swallowed him like an ocean of desire he would gladly drown in.

Her eyes suddenly flew open, and Garret felt a wave of heat envelope him. Knew she was close to the threshold as he was near the limits of his self-control. The cadence of his movements increased. Kit's breath came in deep pants, her chest rising and falling in rhythm with his dance.

Vibrations overtook Kit, drowning her in a sea of hun-ger and want. She abandoned herself to the whirlpool of sensation, followed it down, down, down to the core of her existence. Her whole body filled with need, with want. She felt Garret's firm thrust, rose to meet it and exploded.

Her body trembled from the fire. She lay consumed in the sultry heat. Garret collapsed at her side and gathered her pliant body next to his. Slowly, the intensity drained away from her, leaving behind a delicious contentment and fulfillment.

"Are you cold?" Garret asked as he tucked the serape around their naked bodies.

She snuggled against his chest, pillowing her head on his biceps. "No. I'm...wonderful." The stubbles on his chin tickled her cheek. She took a deep breath and inhaled the scent of passion on their skin and the blanket.

Garret wrapped his leg around hers, drawing her close so that he could feel her softness against him. Like a drowsy kitten, the woman beside him purred. A surge of pride and protectiveness made him squeeze Kit to his chest.

He had been with women. He had grown up in a brothel, but this was the first time he had ever lost himself in the act of lovemaking. His soul had merged to become one with his partner, become one with Kit.

Kit's gentle, regular breathing fell into the pattern of sleep. He kissed the tip of her nose and smiled. So much passion in such a delightful package. He didn't want to think of the man that had first opened her to that passion.

Cradling her body next to his, he felt life begin to tremble in his manhood, and the need grew again to lose himself in her willing embrace. He fought down the desire, sustained himself on the smell of her skin, the soft embrace of her tresses and the sweet allure of remembered passion. He couldn't take her again. Ever. She had never said she would stay. It was best. For her. For Cade. But not for him. When she left, she would take away a part of him and without her he would never be whole.

Garret lay still, watching the ever darkening sky and the brilliant lights of the stars. The sweet weariness of passion, the gentle lull of Kit's breath and the feel of her nakedness next to him made contrary thoughts impossible.

With reluctance, sleep overcame him and his dreams became filled with Kit and a future that could never be.

With reluctance, Kit pulled herself from Garret's embrace. In sleep, the scowl was gone and she gave in to her instinct to brush away the hair from his eyes. His tousled hair curled into sandy waves at the nape of his neck and around his ears. Last night, he had tutored her in passion and desire with a gentle hand and loving touch. She would be forever grateful, and sorry. Sorry that there couldn't be more between them.

Gathering her clothes, she dressed with haste and noticed Garret's spyglass lying on the ground. She had never stolen anything in her life, but this once, she would. Just to have something that had been close to Garret gave her comfort. As she made her way up the creek bed with the brass cylinder in her hand, she looked back at him. The thought to tell him about Jando and the massacre threatened to overtake her. Steeling her emotions, she concentrated on her brother. Hawk was depending on her. Blood was thicker than water. Thicker than… Just what did she feel for Garret? Whatever it was, it had to come second to her loyalty to Hawk.

A fine gray mist rose from the river water, covering her exit. Just a sliver of the rising sun cracked the night sky. Skirting past Candus and the night crew, Kit bridled her mare. When she was certain she was clear of the camp, she mounted and rode off to meet her brother, cantering toward vengeance and away from the tender memories of last night.

Chapter Nineteen

Davidson rubbed his eyes and stared at the graying sky. He hadn't slept a wink all night. The Rockin' G was the first place folks had cared about him. And he had almost blown the whole thing away with his showing off.

A rustling in the brambles caught his attention. Kit tiptoed up the creek bed, rounded the camp and headed for the remuda. He watched her lead her mare onto the prairie. Must be ridin' out to help herd the cattle back to camp. She mounted, took one look back toward the river, then headed for the north high country.

Why wasn't Kit ridin' out to help Cade with the herd? An awful thought came to Davidson. What if she was sneaking out because the Cap'n fired her for sticking up for him? A groan of pain and anguish rumbled in his chest. He had to set this mess to rights.

As he scooted off the tailgate, every muscle in his body protested. His legs felt like iron weights, his arms like fence posts, not willing to bend, creaking from the strain. But he wouldn't be put off. He shoved his feet into his boots and limped down to the water's edge. The morning air caused him to shiver and the dew clung to his wool long johns. He spotted the Cap'n sleeping at the base of

a cottonwood tree, wrapped in a Navajo blanket and serape.

"Cap'n? Cap'n Blaine?" Davidson gave a low whistle.

Garret fought as hard as he could to ignore the intrusion. His whole body lay sated, still drugged by last
night's passion. The taste of Kit's mouth lingered on his
lips. The scent of their passion permeated the blanket,
reminding him of their intimacy.

"Cap'n, ya need to wake up."

Blinking his eyes, Garret stared at the gray-and-pink
sky and felt the emptiness next to him. With a jolt, he
threw off the blanket. Kit was gone.

"Land-a-Goshon! Ya ain't got no britches on!" Davidson's young face blushed brilliant red, his jaw slack.

"What the hell are you still doing here?" Garret hunted
for his clothes in the rumpled blanket. And where was
Kit? Snagging his flannel shirt and jeans, he shoved on
his clothes and searched for his boots, his gaze sweeping
the area for Kit.

"I'm a-ridin' out. But first, I gotta settle Kit's account.
Ain't no need to fire her for somethin' I done."

"What?" As he made to get up, Garret slid in the wet
grass and fell back onto the blanket. His backside found
his belt buckle. "What are you talking about?"

"Kit." Davidson found Garret's boot near the tree
trunk and tossed it to him. "I seen her ridin' out this
mornin' and—"

Garret's foot dropped into his boot at the same time his
doubts returned. God, what a fool he was. She'd pretended
to be a boy, to be afraid of his kiss when she already had
the knowledge of womanhood, and the most believable
act of all—pretending to care about him.

His doubts multiplied as he dressed. What about her
promise that she and Hawk weren't involved with the rus-

tlers? Had last night been a way to lower his defenses?
The men were spread out looking for strays, Cade and
Liam were short-handed with what was left of the herd.
They'd be easy pickings for Hawk's gun. "What direction
was she ridin'?"

"North high country."

"Hellfire!" He pulled on his other boot and strode up
the embankment. From a high point, one or two men
could pick off his cowhands and steal the herd. Cade
would never suspect an ambush. That's exactly how Garret felt, ambushed and left for dead, only it hadn't been a
bullet Kit had wounded him with, it was her duplicity.

Turning, he shot Davidson a stern look. "Get on that
old nag and ride for the Rockin' G."

"But, Cap'n, about Kit—"

"I'll see to her." Garret wasn't in the mood for arguments, and he didn't give the boy the chance to start one.
He headed for camp, his mind reeling and his gut churning. Kit had played him for a fool, lulled him into a senseless fog to give her brother time to steal the cattle. How
could he have been so stupid? How could she have been
so heartless?

Hot embers burned in the campfire, Candus and
Cracker took turns snoring from under the cookwagon.
Garret grabbed a rifle and extra shells from the supplies
with one hand and picked up his tack with the other. Kit's
betrayal left a bitter taste in his mouth, wiping away the
nectar of her kisses. The stampede might have cost him
every penny of profit for the year, but this defection cost
him far more.

Saddling his roan, Garret shoved the rifle into the
leather sheath and the spare ammunition into his saddle-
bag. Mounting, he dug his spurs into the horse's flanks

and galloped off toward Kit and the truth of her guilt or innocence.

Davidson saddled up the broom-tail mare and hefted himself into the saddle. Tugging his hand-me-down Stetson over his eyes, he glanced all around and pondered his next move.

Cap'n said the ranch, but Davidson sensed Kit was lookin' to fade into the landscape, like she was runnin' from the law and the Cap'n. Letting out a slow, disgusted breath, Davidson reined his pony toward the north. He owed Kit, and damn if he wouldn't help her, Cap'n or no.

Garret reined to a halt and carefully scanned the ground. The Appaloosa's delicate hooves were easy to follow across the grass-carpeted prairie. And now, a larger, wider print joined the trail. Hawk's buckskin. So, brother and sister had met here and ridden west. Hidden passes and canyons littered the area, ideal places for a gang of thieves to hide stolen cattle.

The trail disappeared near a wall of igneous rock. Looking upward, Garret squinted as the morning sunlight danced off the specks of mica and quartz, turning the sheer rock face into a glittering tower. Besides a hawk in a twisted piñon tree, he saw no signs of life. The tracks didn't go around the cliff, so Kit and Hawk must have ridden up the mountain.

Garret allowed his horse to pick a path through the talus slope. The loose rock made footing for him and his mount treacherous. Pushing, prodding and cursing his horse, he led his gelding to a stand of scrub brush and juniper trees. The horse would stay put, at least until the water and grass ran out.

A ledge, barely wide enough to place one foot, skated the rim of the cliff and disappeared through an arch of tumbled rocks and boulders. Garret followed it around the bend and along the edge of the precipice. On the windward side of the canyon wall, the path branched.

One arm rimmed the canyon, widening and twisting between slumped rocks and trees. The other dipped into a broad pass that descended gradually into a boxed valley. Lush grass coated the canyon floor while a snow-fed stream meandered through the rich soil. Douglas firs and ponderosa pines edged the transition of mountain to meadow. A sizable herd of cattle grazed at the far end of the grass. Smoke from a campfire circled upward and dissipated in the thick branches of the trees.

Like the eye of a needle, a pass opened to the prairie, the brown grass visible through the wind-carved entrance. The canyon was a perfect hole-in-the-wall. Nearly undetectable from the prairie side, but wide enough to herd small bunches of cattle through, and filled with grass to feed the stolen livestock.

And Kit and Hawk had known right where it was.

A finality sunk into Garret's thoughts. Kit had to be in cahoots with the gang. How else could she ride straight to the encampment? Her betrayal split him like an ax— one half demanding retribution, the other seeking some way to save her from herself. Either way, Kit O'Shane left Garret hurt and bleeding from a wound he didn't think would ever heal.

Once he knew how many rustlers were camped below, he'd gather a posse and clear them out. But Kit was his to deal out justice to. And he would show no mercy.

Heading for the ring of makeshift tents and the blaze of the fire, he crawled, wormed and stole his way to the outskirts of the camp. His gaze swept over the mixture of roughly dressed men, searching for one figure, for one woman with coal-black hair and a heart to match.

A dozen men sprawled around the fire, drunk or suffering from hangovers. They all must have wintered hard by the look of their outfits. The only places filthier than their wind-hardened faces were their clothes. Fleas would think twice before nesting with that lot.

An enormous man sat near the fire. Saclike jowls sagged on either side of a tiny mouth. Rings of dirt marked each roll on his neck, nearly hidden by double chins. Depravity covered the man like a funeral shroud.

As he sneaked back toward the trail, Garret spotted a string of horses tethered to a line just to his left. Already saddled, the animals waited, ready for a quick getaway.

If he could drive out the horses, then the rustlers would be stuck in the canyon.

"Drop those guns and raise them hands."

Garret turned and stared down the barrel of a rifle. Slowly, he dropped his weapon and lifted his hands. Two cowboys, one built like a beanpole, the other like a bulldog, leveled their guns at him. Neither had seen the wet side of a river in months. The stench of whiskey and unwashed bodies polluted the air.

"Levi, get his gun." The string-bean cowboy leveled his rifle at Garret's gut.

The bulldog-faced man slipped the forty-five from Garret's belt and grabbed the dropped rifle. "Whoo-ee. Jando is gonna have some fun with him." Levi smacked his lips and gave the other man a wink. "We gots us some entertainment."

The brilliant light of midmorning flashed off the hard granite slab Kit hid behind. Heat radiated from the rock and warmed her face but could not touch the frozen core of her soul. Fear kept her huddled behind her hideout. She longed to cuddle up next to Garret and feel his arms supporting her, hiding her from what waited in the canyon.

She had to forget Garret. The future didn't lie in his strong arms and tender kisses. Her quest rested in the midst of the outlaws. Lifting her head, she concentrated on her brother, coming toward her in a half crouch.

Hawk sat on his heels, balanced his rifle across his knees and asked, "Is it him? Is he the one?"

Kit braced her hands on the serrated edge of rock and willed herself to spy on the encampment below. Pulling Garret's spyglass from her pocket, she used it to view the encampment. Even from this height, she could recognize the man below.

Bile rose in her throat as she stared at the fat man near the flame. His belly lay in folds down his massive chest. He yanked a whiskey bottle from one of his men and guzzled the contents. Amber liquid dripped down his mouth and rippled over his double chins.

Jando! An acid taste coated her throat. She choked out the words. "It's him. He's the one that murdered Warms-the-Heart."

Her words evoked a pained snarl from Hawk. His eyes centered on Jando, his hands opening and closing into fists as though they were choking the life from the man. A murderous light clouded his eyes. "My wife will be avenged. My son will know his father died a warrior."

"Hawk…" Kit scrambled to her brother's side. His words conjured up nightmarish images. Hawk accepted his death too readily, as though as a reward to be sought out instead of avoided. "I don't want you—"

He placed the palm of his hand over her lips. "I will do what I must, my sister, to avenge you, my family and tribe. Do not ask less of me."

She wanted to ask him to live. To ride away and find

Garret, ask for help. But they were too close to their quarry. Vengeance fueled the cankerous wound in her brother's spirit.

"I understand." She gave in with reluctance and knew that tonight marked the end of their long ride. Death would be served with a soul, Jando's or theirs. Dying wasn't what turned her legs to trembling sticks and made her break into a cold sweat. She needed to know that she would never suffer the fate of her sister-in-law. The tortured body haunted her dreams. "I need you to promise me something. If Jando captures me—" she dug her fingers into Hawk's wrist "—promise me you'll kill me."

Hawk jerked his shoulders back and sucked in a deep breath. He stared straight ahead, every line of his profile taut and stern. Placing one hand over hers, he lowered his chin and closed his eyes. "This I will do, my sister. My bullet will find your heart."

"Like hell it will."

Davidson limped forward from the bend in the trail. A rainbow of yellow, black and blue mottled his face. He braced one hand against the mountain for support. Pointing toward Hawk, he ordered, "Ya just best get away from Miss Kit. I ain't a-gonna let ya put no bullet in her back."

Like a mountain lion, Hawk pounced to his feet. One hand yanked on the boy's collar, the other clamped across Davidson's mouth, pulling his chin tight against his neck. Kit could hear his struggled breaths. His dark eyes widened, and his fingers fumbled for his gun.

She pulled the rusty forty-five from his holster and spoke in a low voice. "Hawk is going to remove his hand. You are not to raise your voice."

The boy fluttered his eyelashes, unable to nod because

of Hawk's firm hold. Kit sat back on her heels and asked, "How did you find us?"

Hawk released his hold. "Trailed," Davidson rasped while rubbing his neck.

"You followed us," Hawk accused.

"Nope, not you 'xactly." The boy rotated his shoulder and scooted away from Hawk's reach. "I trailed the Cap'n, and he was a-trailin' you." He looked straight at Kit.

"Blaine is here?" Hawk lifted his head and searched the trail for a sign of the ranch owner. Nothing moved on the narrow path. He waved the end of his rifle at the trail. Kit understood and nodded. Hawk scurried along the path, pausing to check the camp below and trail ahead.

A feeling of remorse slammed into Kit's core. She wanted Garret here, wanted to pour out her story, yet she knew she'd find no mercy or compassion. Garret had trailed her here, to the midst of the rustlers. He must know she had kept the information to herself. Know that she betrayed him.

Davidson worked his jaw, testing it to see if Hawk's stronghold had damaged it any. "That old nag took twice as long to get here. Ain't seen hide or hair of him, though."

Her heartbeat quickened. Garret was somewhere along the trail, maybe spying on her now. The summit of the canyon was littered with boulders. Several Douglas firs balanced on the edge, held in their precarious position by roots and tenacity.

Davidson wrinkled his brows. "How'd ya know where these outlaws was holed up, anyway?"

Her brother's return saved Kit from explaining. He rushed forward, a scowl on his face. "We got trouble."

"Did you find Garret?" A sliver of hope shot through her heart.

"Yeah, I found him." Hawk paused. "And so did Jando."

He twisted and pointed down in the camp.

Kit could make out a group of men emerging from the dense forest. Garret marched in front of two men, their guns aimed at the small of his back. They presented him to Jando. An evil ripple of laughter began in the fat man and spread to the drunk rustlers.

"Oh my God." Kit could feel the fibers of her body burn. Panic seized her mind and sent frantic orders. Flee. Hide. Cry. Fight. Garret had a few more hours to live, if he could stand the torture.

Davidson made a grab for Hawk's rifle. "We gotta save the Cap'n."

"Shut up, boy, or you'll have them after us." Hawk slapped Davidson away.

"Hawk, we can't leave Garret down there. You know what they'll do to him."

Beneath his vest, the muscles in Hawk's shoulders tightened, as though he were hardening his body to the screams that were sure to come. "I could lose Jando by saving Blaine."

"Don't let your thirst for revenge turn you into a man like Jando." With one hand on his shoulder, she turned Hawk to face her.

"Are ya gonna help the Cap'n or not?" Davidson queried. "If'n yer not, then I reckon it's up to me."

A tedious smile quirked Hawk's lips. "Then Blaine is doomed for sure."

"We'll help," Kit answered for her brother. "Davidson, you must ride to camp and get some backup."

"But them varmints might shoot the Cap'n afore I gets back."

"They won't." Hawk's eyes became flat and expressionless. He nodded toward the camp. Men crowded around the campfire, stoking the lazy embers with wood and logs. The flames leaped into the air. Garret stood near the bonfire, his shirt in tatters at his waist. "Remember Kit's story about skinning a man alive?"

Davidson nodded and gulped.

Kit looked at her brother and whispered, "It wasn't all make-believe."

Chapter Twenty

Ahead of Kit, Hawk forced Davidson to duckwalk away from the boulder, keeping low and out of sight of the searching outlaws. When the trail switchbacked and the mountain wall shielded them from the rustlers below, her brother stood, pulled Davidson to his feet, then set off at an easy jog into the firs.

At a break in the thick-needled branches, Kit snagged Davidson's elbow. She laid her arm over his shoulder, allowing him to use her finger like a rifle sight. "That's the pass into the canyon. It's well guarded. We'll try to clear it. If we do, we'll leave a sign."

"Gotcha," Davidson replied. "But won't the Cap'n be a sittin' duck down there when the shootin' starts?"

Garret'll probably be dead by then, or wish he was.

Kit licked her dry lips. "Cade will think of something. Now, let's get you out of here."

At a thorny wall of cypress trees, the Appaloosa and buckskin grazed on the sparse grass. Neither snickered a greeting. Both were accustomed to their owners' need for silence.

Her brother moved with calm urgency, each movement sure and methodical. He tightened the mare's girth, adjusted the bridle, pulled his own revolver and checked the chambers. Handing the loaded weapon to Davidson, he warned, "If they see you, aim to kill."

"Yessir." Beads of sweat formed across the boy's upper lip as he gingerly holstered the gun. Davidson pulled himself into the saddle. His Stetson fell back, held at his throat by a coiled string. Sunlight splattered his face through the shade of the trees, displaying the dark bruises on his pale face. He looked so young. Too young to be Garret's only hope.

There was only one way to save Garret—Kit needed to stall the outlaws long enough for the entire Rockin' G crew to ride to the rescue. And to do that, she must offer Jando something more entertaining than skinning Garret. Something that he couldn't pass up.

The sun hung in the east, still hours away from high noon. Time was the enemy. Garret could be dead before the sun passed overhead. She ran her fingers over her lips, remembering the touch of his kiss.

"Hawk, take the glass." She passed it to her brother. "I want to make sure Davidson gets down the mountain. I'll meet you back at the overlook."

Indecision clouded his face. "I will wait."

"One of us needs to keep an eye on the outlaws."

Hawk glanced over his shoulder at the mountain. "I can move faster. Stay off the trail until you hear from me."

Without Kit or Davidson to encumber him, Hawk leaped from ledge to ledge, taking the faster, but more dangerous, route back to the mountain peak. His dark hair streamed over his shoulders, the blue feather fluttering in the breeze, and then he disappeared from her view.

Her brother would tie her to a tree if he caught on to her plan. He must be far down the trail before she made her move. A prayer formed under her breath for Hawk, for Garret, for Davidson and for herself. The next few hours were the difference between life and death, between peace for her brother's persecuted soul and a life consumed with hate.

"On the prairie," she advised Davidson, "give the mare her head. It's a hard two-hour ride back to camp."

"I'll do it in half the time, Miss Kit." Not an ounce of doubt softened the boy's statement. His youth forged an immortality within him.

"I know you will." Kit whistled softly. The horse responded to the signal and trotted off. Davidson bounced in the saddle until he could regain his balance.

She watched the boy ride off. For a moment her courage flagged, and she thought of hiding out in the wind-carved alcove. Safety and self-preservation tempted her.

Her fortitude surfaced. Jando would claim no more victims. The vow made long ago at her sister-in-law's grave echoed in her head.

Like a windup toy, her legs moved automatically with stiff-kneed steps back up the trail. At the trail's fork, she unknotted the dirty bandanna from her neck and wrapped her knife in the thin cotton. Stripping the leather thong from her hair, she fixed the blade just under her breasts.

Marching down the trail toward the encampment, she spoke to the clear blue sky and the dark shade of the evergreens, just to hear herself speak. "No matter what it takes, today the devil will claim Jando's soul or mine."

The rough hemp rope that bound Garret's hands abraded his wrists. He wiggled his numb fingers to pump blood and felt the painful tingle of feeling return. Heat singed the hair on his chest and sweat drenched his body.

The fire crackled. Cinders fell like black snow, stinging his shoulders and face.

"Find anyone else?" The beefy man's voice possessed the quality of a locomotive, loud, grating and powerful. He sat near the fire, his eyes staring into the dancing flames.

"Nope." The tall outlaw shook his head. "But we found two saddled horses stashed down the trail. One's so flea-bitten ya could barely call it a horse."

Davidson. Garret didn't know if he should feel elated or depressed. *Ride for camp,* he prayed quietly. *For once, use some common sense.*

Somewhere between the pines and the treeline, Davidson must be watching. Was he alone, or were Kit and her brother with him? And if they were, as friends or enemies? They hadn't appeared in the camp and he hadn't heard any of the outlaws refer to Kit or Hawk. What was their connection to the gang of cutthroats?

Jando stared back into the flames, the orange light reflected in the dark pupils of his piglike eyes. He boomed, "I think we need some answers, boys. And I reckon I know how's to find them."

Like vultures after a kill, the renegades converged near the fire. A few wet their lips, anticipating the entertainment. These men were outlaws to humanity as well as the law.

Still seated on the deadwood, Jando picked up a blade. "I ain't worried about whose out there." He waved the heated knife toward the trees. "We'll find 'em. What I want ta know is how ya got in here and why."

"I stumbled onto your camp by accident," Garret answered in a half truth.

Jando raised one thick eyebrow and chuckled. The rows of chins vibrated with his amusement. "And weren't ya just lucky to find us so hospitable.'' His humor faded. ''Who do ya work for?''

''I draw my pay from the Rockin' G.'' Garret continually scanned the canyon for some sign of rescue. None appeared. He was on his own. ''I was lookin' for strays. Saw some tracks and followed them here.''

''Yore a-lyin'.'' The fat man's small eyes gleamed with evil. ''You didn't come in the prairie notch. My men woulda seen ya afore ya walked ten paces. And ain't no beef gonna climb the mountain.'' He laid the blade back into the fire, his love for the steel evident in the way he caressed the knife. The blaze reflected in his eyes turned them into gates of hell. From their depths, Death grinned at Garret.

He would never leave this canyon alive.

The best he could hope was to give Davidson enough time to hike back to camp and warn Cade about the outlaws. At least the herd would be protected.

''All right then, have it your way.'' Garret spit out the words. ''Me and some cowhands stumbled onto your camp. While they rode into town to gather up a posse, I stayed to make sure you didn't pull out before the sheriff returned.''

''Ain't no sheriff comin'.'' Jando lifted the knife blade from the fire. Grunting from the strain, he maneuvered his enormous bulk over to Garret. Sage and another rustler clamped onto Garret's arms. Jando held the blade just above his back.

''How can you be so sure?'' Garret taunted.

''I seen cattle dust a-risin' a mile high yesterday. The Rockin' G's herd stampeded. Blaine's got to have every cowhand drivin' them cows back to camp. Except for you. I want to know why. You best commence to talkin' and I'd best like what I hear.''

"When hell freezes over."

"Ain't that funny? It just did." Jando pressed the hot steel over Garret's exposed skin. An eruption of pain lanced across his back. Fingers of hot lava branched across his shoulder blades. The smell of burnt flesh lingered in the air. Summoning his self-control, he forced his legs to remain strong, his knees not to buckle. He focused his wrath on the fat man and Kit. Somewhere she was watching, and she would pay for every pain twice over.

"If'n ya rode in with somebody, they ain't a-movin' in or out of this canyon. There ain't gonna be no sheriff, ain't gonna be no cavalry. I aim to take that herd and I want to know what's going on in that camp." Jando's lower lip folded over, and his whiskey-coated breath stung Garret's seared skin. He placed the knife back into the flames and watched the blaze caress the blade.

An iron bar seemed to encircle Garret's chest. He fought to breathe. Clenching his teeth, he rumbled, "Cade's not about to let you take the herd."

Jando crowed, "Those boys is gonna be dead tired. And I do mean dead…tired." Hoots of morbid laughter greeted his play on words. The fat man basked in his men's applause.

"This is gonna be the easiest steal ever," Sage taunted.

"But not the best," Levi countered. "Nuthin' beats that Indian village."

Cackles of laughter cracked the air. Jando yanked Garret's hair back. The smell of whiskey and rotting tobacco overpowered the smoky scent of evergreen firewood.

These weren't men. Garret couldn't even consider them animals. Savagery and depravity cloaked their souls in a duster too heavy to throw off, too stiff to break free of.

Whatever had been human in these outlaws had been buried on Boot Hill, without a look back.

As though looking in a crystal ball, Garret pictured the next few hours. The exhausted Rockin' G cowhands would ride into camp, covered in dust and eager for a hot meal and a good eight hours of sleep. Cracker and Candus would offer to take watch, giving all the men a chance to rest. With only a skeleton crew on guard, Cade didn't stand a chance.

"I can help you take that herd," a woman's voice called out from behind the crowd. The sound made Garret cringe. He should have known.

"What the hell!"

The desperadoes parted, and Garret cursed under his breath. Kit hitched one leg on the tree trunk and draped an arm across her bent knee.

"Grab her!" Jando shouted to his stunned men.

"Sage, I suggest you just hold up a spell." Her use of their names halted the men like a forty-five slug. She spoke loudly, hoping the echo would carry to the upper rocks. "My brother's holed up on the rim with a rifle aimed right at you, Jando."

"Sure he is." Sage reached for her with his dirty hands.

A rifle shot cracked the still air. Sage's hat flew off and rolled across the ground. Jando barked an order. "Hold her and find that bushwhacker."

"You won't find Hawk." Her words stalled the outlaws. "He's been spying on you for almost a week and you never even knew he was there." Kit squeezed all the bravado she could into her voice. She pointed to Jando and said, "Me and you, we're after the same thing."

Jando studied Kit with heavy-lidded eyes. A line of drool formed along his pouting lips. "Which is?"

"The Rockin' G herd. Me and my brother have been

working for a chance to rustle some cows. But if we throw in with you, we can get a share of the whole herd.'' Kit straightened and strode over to Garret's body. She toed him in the ribs with the tip of her boot. ''And this here's the way we can get it.''

Jando's voice deepened with distrust. ''I don't need you or him to get those beeves.''

''That's where you're wrong.'' She gave Garret and the outlaw a smug grin. ''Who do you think caused that stampede? Me. Hawk and I thought to take out a few men and run off with some of the herd. Now we've got a better plan.''

''Why should I listen to you?''

'''Cause you ain't got nobody that can ride into camp and tell Cade Blaine his brother's been captured by a gang of rustlers. Who else've you got but me that can lead those cowboys right into an ambush?''

''What makes you think those cowhands are going to listen to you?''

Kit knelt on one knee next to Garret and trailed a finger down the hard muscles of his chest. '''Cause this here's Cade Blaine's brother, and every man in camp thinks I'm Garret Blaine's woman.''

Chapter Twenty-One

The stench of Jando's whiskey-washed breath and un-clean clothes almost made Kit choke. His lecherous grin started a ripple in her courage that threatened to build into a wave of panic. Sliding her thumbs into her jean pockets, she stepped closer to Garret.

He lay sprawled on the ground, bare-chested. A patch of skin, the size of his hand, puckered red from the burn. Sweat-streaked hair curtained his brows and a shadow of pain glazed his eyes.

His powerful thighs acted as pistons to pull himself to one knee, then he staggered to his feet. His stare fixed on her, and beneath the pain, a wildfire of hatred burned in his eyes—directed straight at her.

Hurt and anger ground emotion into his voice. "One of my men dies because of you, and I'll hunt you and your brother down no matter how long it takes."

So like her brother. The words virtually the same as Hawk's pledge over his wife's grave. *I'll hunt you down, no matter what it takes.* Garret would be no less deter-mined than Hawk in his vendetta. Nor could she. She had to push away her desire to comfort him and explain away her actions. Jando had to die. Today. By her hand or by Hawk's.

An iciness crept into her veins and frosted her tender impulses. Like a slow freeze, her emotions stilled. A quiet determination soothed her rippling courage. "You'll be taken care of, after we've used you to set a trap."

Wetting her lips, she sauntered over to Garret, pressed her body against his and hoped he would feel the knife tied beneath her shirt. He would be on his own when she made her move. Whether he lived or died would depend on his own ingenuity.

In a breathy voice, she teased, "You've got to make the most of your chances in life, Blaine. Remember that."

The tickle of Kit's breath on his ear and the feel of her warm body, ravaged Garret's soul. Desire was smothering the hate and vengeance in his heart.

Like a cat begging to be stroked, she rubbed against his chest. A purr vibrated deep in her throat. The perfume of her skin mixed with the sharp smell of his own blood.

Her skin felt soft, silky— The hard press of steel pricked his skin. Beneath the supple mound of her breast, a bony hilt pressed into his rib cage. A knife! Her words rang in his head. Was she offering him a chance of escape or warning him he didn't stand a chance?

She studied him from beneath her thick fringe of coal-black lashes then pulled away, leaving Garret in a fog of honey scent and confused emotions. Turning toward the outlaws, she asked, "So, Jando, you gonna let me and Hawk pull in with you?"

Sage grabbed his crotch. "I got somethin' the breed can pull on." His heavy laughter hammered against the anvil of Garret's self-control. He wanted to wipe the smirk off the tall cowboy's face. Wanted to shake the arrogance from Kit's cold features.

She flicked a long strand of hair over her shoulder and gave Sage a withering stare. ''I thought Jando led this outfit. Looks like things have changed.''

''Nope, things haven't changed.'' Jando slapped Sage on the back and grunted as he walked toward her.

But they had, Kit thought. Two years had changed them all.

Two years had tanned her a tough hide of revenge and anger. She cloaked herself in it now and clenched her fingers into fists to keep from pulling her blade and sinking the steel into Jando's heart. If possible, that pleasure belonged to her brother.

The last two years had scratched deep wrinkles into Jando's leathery skin. Gray swam through his hair with wide, deep strokes. His teeth had turned to the color of mud. He reeked of old sweat and urine. The pallor of his skin and his labored breathing signaled bad health. Jando had courted death so often, he didn't even realize how close the Grim Reaper was to his own throat.

''Yer brother can't take us all,'' Jando noted.

''Two bullets and a promise are all I need.'' Kit lifted her face to the hot sun. It glared almost directly overhead. With hard riding, Davidson might be only an hour away from base camp. She imbued her words with arrogance and self-confidence. ''Hawk promised to shoot me before he'd let you have me. The second shot's for you, Jando.''

As if on cue, a rifle shot landed at the big man's feet. A spray of dust and sod flew into the air. Guns whipped from the rustlers' holsters. Silence entombed the canyon. Birds, crickets, even the sound of the water in the river seemed to become mute.

Narrowing her eyes into slits, she met Jando's leer with a direct stare. ''You know I can deliver that herd.''

''I know ya can deliver.'' Jando spoke with a thin veil

of anticipation. His stare darted to her breasts, and she shoved her hands deeper into her pockets to keep from hugging herself. Her scar stung, as though freshly cut. "Ya got a deal, woman. Let's hear your plan."

"In a few hours, Cade will have the cattle herded toward camp. The men will be so tired they can't see straight, let alone think or shoot. I'll ride out. Tell them Garret's been hurt and lead them here. Your men can ring the canyon top. The Rockin' G cowhands will be dead before they know what's happened."

"I like it." Jando's belly jiggled with evil joy. "Sage, stake out Blaine near the fire."

Sage's palms landed in the exact same spot as Garret's burn. His lips quivered, and he twisted his jaw as though swallowing the cry of pain. His flintlike gaze drilled into Kit. "You'll pay for this. You'll pay high."

I've already paid too much. Kit followed behind Sage, her eyes fixed on Garret's scarred back, and wondered if the price of vengeance hadn't just become too expensive.

Hawk glided from shadow to shadow, moving downward into the canyon. He cursed his sister in one breath and prayed to the gods to spare her in the next. To have her so close to the man who had ravaged his village set Hawk's blood singing in his veins. Singing the white man's death song.

Jando's final breath must be slow and painful, but Hawk would not allow the white man to destroy Kit. Once Hawk had his sister stashed in a safe place, or better yet, tied to a tree, he would return and extract his retribution.

He understood her need to be a part of Jando's execution instead of a silent witness. He also understood her need for the promise. To shoot Kit would demand every ounce of caring and control Hawk possessed, but he would find the strength to pull the trigger.

His sister had withstood the terror, heard the screams and seen each bloody swipe of the knives. Guilt hung heavy on his shoulders. For him, there had only been the overpowering, oppressive silence of the village. No joyful shouts to greet the hunting party. No beautiful wife and giggling son to wrap in his arms. Only Kit's frightened, shaking figure rising from the lake. Only the sight of his wife, mutilated along with the other village women.

The sun shone directly overhead, mottling the shade, but Hawk burned with the fire of his hate. He sacrificed himself as willing tinder to the emotion.

Staying close to the moss- and lichen-covered ground, he traveled lightly, barely making an impression on the damp soil. Near the line of saddle horses, he found a pyramid of rock and debris that had slumped from the high cliffs.

Slipping between two tabular stones, Hawk melted into the dark recess. He kept his ears open and his eyes focused on his sister. His rifle aimed at her heart. If he couldn't rescue her from Jando's cruelty, then he would spare her the torture.

Cade pressed his heels into his mare's flanks. Pretty Gal turned her head, gave a disgusted snort, then lengthened her stride. Liam, riding next to Cade, stood up in the stirrups then eased back down into the saddle. The ex-miner's face twisted in discomfort. Swinging a pickax and shovel might build calluses, but not where it counted for a cowboy.

"I'm lookin' forward to a long bath, a good meal and a soft bed," the Irishman said.

Cade chuckled. "Well, when we get back to camp, you

can take a dive in the river, Cracker can whip up a pot of beans, and you can throw your tucker down on the hard ground for a few hours' sleep before it's time for watch.''

Liam sighed, patted his derby firmly onto his head and replied, ''Like I was sayin', a fine, invigoratin' bath, a fillin' supper and a place to lay me head.'' He twisted in his saddle and surveyed the slow-moving cattle. ''I will say I'll be glad to see the last of these beasts.''

Cade laughed. ''You and me both. If Garret didn't need me on the ranch, I'd be gone in a minute.''

''And what would you be doin'?''

''Running a saloon. Something grand with a fine mahogany bar, gilded mirrors, gaming tables.'' Cade shook his head. That kind of outfit needed a lot of capital. There was no way he'd ever see that kind of money working as a cowboy for twenty-five dollars a month.

''Perhaps after your brother is sellin' the cattle—''

''Not likely.'' Cade threw his thumb over his shoulder toward the cows. ''We lost a good number in that stampede.''

Liam craned his neck to catch a glimpse of the cowhands sweeping the sides of the drive. ''Perhaps next year things will be better for you and your brother.''

''It wouldn't matter. Garret's got it into his head that I'm a rancher.''

''Aye, that's big brother for ya. Always a-tellin' ya what ya oughta be doin'.'' A wistful note entered the muscular Irishman's lilt. ''It's what I'm missin' most about me brother, Frank. I fussed at his henpeckin' when he was alive. Now I'm wishin' I could hear his voice again.''

A red flush of anger brightened Liam's face. ''I didn't even get a chance to give Frank a Christian burial. Eli Benton had the shaft sealed off and left a dozen men buried in the cave-in.''

"Your brother probably didn't survive the cave-in."

"I did." Liam's shoulders stiffened. "No one will ever know what those men endured. Or for how long." He turned to face Cade, a look of wisdom in his eyes. "Someday you'll be missin' Garret's motherin'. There's a bond a'tween brothers that even death can't sever."

Cade gave Pretty Gal a soft kick and the mare reluctantly broke to a rocking lope. Hell, he didn't want Garret dead, he just wanted his big brother to let go of the apron strings and allow Cade to ride his own trail. One that didn't head toward a ranch and a prairie full of four-legged beeves.

A small speck of dust, moving toward him with breakneck speed, appeared on the horizon. Cade pointed. The Irishman nodded and quickened his horse's pace to catch up with Cade. "Are ya thinkin' it be friend or foe?"

"Only one way to find out." Cade laid a rein on Pretty Gal's neck. His mount dutifully galloped forward. The tiny speck became a horse with a rider. He recognized Kit's Appaloosa, but the rider held on like a greenhorn, stiff and... Hell, it was Davidson. Cade raced out to stop the boy before he rode straight toward the herd.

Kit's mare stumbled to a halt, her sides flecked with sweat, her nostrils flared. Prairie dirt covered Davidson and the Appaloosa. The boy tumbled from the saddle and lay on the ground.

Cade dismounted. Liam rushed forward, a canteen in his hand. Davidson grabbed the canteen and water ran over his dry lips. "You gotta...come quick. It's Garret. Captured. Rustlers in a canyon, 'bout an hour ride. Kit and Hawk are—" Davidson sucked air into his lungs. "They're on the rim. Watchin'."

"We can ride back and round up the rest of the men." Cade put his hand on the saddle horn to remount.

''Ain't no time.'' Davidson wheezed, then staggered to his feet. ''That rustler, Kit knew him, called him Jando. He's a bad one.''

Cade swore. Garret had been partially right. They may not be stealing, but if Kit knew the outlaw by name, then she and her brother must have some tie to the rustlers. Hindsight provided cool-headed logic. He had to free his brother. ''Where are they holed up at?''

''Boxed-in canyon. Only one way in and one way out. Kit said Jando kept it guarded and to look for a sign.''

''How many men?''

''Counted 'bout fourteen. Maybe a few more.''

Liam tallied the cowhands with the herd. ''We've got eight, nine counting Davidson. We're outnumbered.''

Cade rubbed his lips and spit out drive dust. Hellfire. The discontented sounds of cattle irritated his ears.

The herd plodded past him, tired and hard-pressed from yesterday's stampede and today's drive back to camp. That was when they were the most dangerous. Anything could send them off again in a mindless run, crushing everything in their path, cowhands, horses, even other cattle. Everything.

Everything! Cade jumped into the saddle. ''They may have us outgunned, but they ain't got us outnumbered.''

''Have ya gone daft, man?'' Liam answered. ''What are ya talkin' about?''

''Cattle, Liam. Cattle. Gather the men and get them ready.''

''Ready for what?''

''A stampede.''

Chapter Twenty-Two

Pain slashed through Garret's burn as Sage shoved him near the fallen tree. Lichens and shelf mushrooms scratched Garret's arm and ribs as he fell, but he spared his back.

Keeping his ears open and his instincts cued, he waited for any tidbit that might lead to an escape. Opportunities weren't hopping into his lap. His best and worst chance of rescue stood a few feet away, casting him sidelong glances from beneath her dark lashes. Kit had a weapon and the smarts to cut the bonds, but did she want to?

She moved like water in a hot skillet. Never keeping still, pacing from one side of the fire to the other. Perspiration glistened on her forehead and upper lip. The thin cotton of her shirt molded to her spine and breasts. She iced each man that came her way with a one-lip snarl, but Garret sensed her raw nerves and anxiety. Her eyes betrayed her. Dark, like a sky before a winter blizzard, full of uncertainty and ringed with fear.

She dealt her hand with the devil, now let her play it. Garret wanted to feel contempt in his heart. Wanted to, just couldn't.

Each time he caught her glancing toward him, he read

the indecision in her azure eyes and knew she was worrying away her self-confidence. Jando possessed a bloodhound's sense for sniffing out fear. One mistake, and she would be at the mercy of the outlaws. That crew didn't strike Garret as knowing the word *mercy,* much less showing it.

And where was Hawk? How many times had he asked that in the last few months? Garret answered his own question. *Too damn many.* Even if Hawk wanted in with the outlaws, he would have tied Kit to a tree before he allowed her within gunshot of this crew.

This whole scene stank of Kit O'Shane's stubbornness laced with a dash of foolishness and a handful of daring. Just like the fight in town, and the old mossy point. This time, Kit might have bit off more than she could chew. Despite himself, Garret hoped she wouldn't choke on the trouble she had heaped on all of them.

High-noon heat cooked Kit's head. The day stretched out like a Sunday sermon, hot, dry and unending. There was a limit to how much she could take, how long she could keep her panic at bay. Every survival instinct screamed at her to run and hide. Fibers shot down her spine, red-hot with the desire for justice.

Sage and two other rustlers dropped their whiskey bottles and melted into the firs. A wicked grin played across Jando's face. His big belly shook with amusement.

Jando hooked the shoulder of a young outlaw and ordered, "Go ahead, Bush, have a go at her."

The man smiled as if he had just gotten a pardon from St. Peter, then tried to grab her. A rifle shot smacked the ground. Bush halted and looked to his boss for direction.

"Go ahead." Jando waved his man forward like a mother sending a child off to school.

"I don't know what you're trying to pull," Kit warned the outlaw. "My brother is a dead-on shot."

"So far, the only thing he's done is miss." Jando's voice dropped to an ominous tone. "Strip her, Bush."

"Anything you say, boss." He took one step, his worn-down boot heel barely on the ground before the crack of the rifle sounded. A neat hole smoked at his knee. Blood pulsed from the wound. Bush fell, clutching his leg, swearing and praying all in the same breath.

There wasn't a glimmer of shock on Jando's face. In fact, a glint of satisfaction shone in the depths of his tiny dark eyes. Why? Kit backed away, uncertain of her next move. Jando had purposely sacrificed his man, had known Hawk would shoot. Even now, her brother would be scurrying to a new lookout.

A warning shot came from her left. The grin on Jando's face widened.

Sage and the other men!

"Hawk, don't shoot!" Kit cried. "He's scouting your location."

A sharp report of a forty-five blasted, answered by a deeper explosion of a rifle. Gunshots volleyed in the evergreens high on the canyon wall. Then silence.

"Hit 'im." The triumphant cry sounded from the rim. Sage lifted his hand in victory. "He's bleedin' and on the run. That Injun's a goner for sure."

Hawk! Kit staggered back, clutching her heart. A bullet of grief sliced through her. She wanted to cry but the tears wouldn't come. Shock blocked all emotions, blanketing her in a muffled world. Terrible, gut-wrenching loss permeated her.

A ham shank of an arm yanked her forward. The outlaw's chuckle crescendoed into an evil laugh. "Little lady, your hand just folded."

Her composure shattered like fine crystal. Tenacity sliced through her numbness and grief. Hawk was dead. But Jando wasn't. The outlaw was hers to deal with. Justice would be dealt.

Kit plowed her elbow into the fat man's rib cage and twisted her arm free. Ready to run, she pivoted, and stopped dead in her tracks. Nowhere to go. Rustlers circled her, their eyes gleaming with lust. A wall of grabbing hands stood between her and freedom. She backed toward the center of the circle, letting the fire guard her back.

From the corner of her eye, she saw Garret struggle to his feet. Standing, he towered over the other men, a beacon of sanity in the ring of madness around her. He took two strides before an outlaw pointed a gun barrel at his chest. Halted, he waited and watched.

She sacrificed a few moments to stare at him. His white scar snaked down his temple. His full lips twisted into a snarl. Did he think she was getting her just deserts? A pang of regret washed over her but her thirst for justice wore away any tender feelings. Her hand went to her chest, ready to pull the knife and fight to the end. She wouldn't travel alone with death, Jando would be riding by her side.

Her heart pounded, the rush of blood sounding like a crashing wave in her ear. Jando's labored breathing intensified, rumbled from his chest. Vibrations tapped at her boot heels. The ring of liquored-up men quieted. Sage turned one ear toward the canyon pass. "What's that?"

"Thunder?"

"Twister?"

Suggestions hung in the air. Everyone stared at the clear aquamarine sky.

A rustler dropped to one knee and laid his palm on the soft grass. "The ground's shakin'."

Then she heard it. High, plaintive calls. Low, disgruntled complaints. The tin pot over the cook fire rattled off the hook.

"Stampede!"

Cattle spilled into the valley along with the shouts and gunshots of the Rockin' G riders. Cade careened into camp, the sharp crack of his forty-five scattering men and cattle. Riders flanked the herd, guns blazing. Each blast set the cows plunging ahead. Mindless in their destruction.

Thank God Almighty. Garret was even glad to see the Irishman. Anything to save Kit from Jando's hands and deliver her into his own. That dark-haired hellcat's punishment was his to deal out.

The herd split at the bonfire, half stumbling over the tree trunk, the other half veering off toward the saddle horses. Garret dived to the ground and hugged the log. The white underbellies of his cattle passed overhead like furry clouds, pinning him against the bark.

Screams of trampled men and horses blended in with the low bass of the stampeding cows. Horses broke free of the rope corral and joined in the frantic migration. The rustlers scattered, seeking high ground from the gunplay and trampling hooves. Trail-drive cowboys leaped for cover and fired at the outlaws. Bullets and cows crisscrossed. Lead slugs found their marks in men and animals alike. Through the wall of furry hides, Garret kept his sight on Kit.

All around her chaos reigned. The dirty oilcloth tents collapsed under the weight of the cows. Bottles of Old Taos toppled over, their contents forming a river of whiskey. The amber liquid snaked through the long blades of grass toward the fire. Moving animals hemmed her in at the sides, the fire blocked her back. She was trapped with Jando in an oasis from the destruction.

Jando's clammy hand clenched her shirt. He slapped her and threw her to the ground. Her instincts surfaced and she jutted her knee at his groin. The big man anticipated her move, shifted, and Kit missed her mark.

"You think I don't remember you?" Jando grabbed a fistful of her hair and dragged her toward the flames. "I'm gonna finish the job I started in that Injun village." He ignored the gun at his hip and instead reached for a knife blade cooked to a rosy pink.

Panic made her strong, desperation made her daring. She sank her teeth into the arm that held her captive. The salty taste of blood flooded her mouth.

"Ahhh!" Jando turned, the blade pointed at Kit. "You got nowhere to go but to hell."

Kit backed away, drew her knife and knew she was no match for the sheer weight of her opponent. She could die by Jando's blade or the stampeding cattle.

"No!" From between the blur of cows, Garret cannonballed toward Jando. Lowering his head, he used his body as a battering ram and plowed into the outlaw's belly. The impact threw Garret to the ground and propelled Jando backward toward the fire.

Wood crackled and snapped. Ashes and cinders flew into the air and coated him. Just as Jando started to rise, the whiskey stream coursed into the flames and the gates to hell opened. Blue-white flames inhaled air, breathing in life. Then the fire exhaled with a roar.

The blast hit Jando in the face. The whiskey on his breath and the spilled liquor on his clothes ignited with a demonic swoosh of wind.

"Ahhh!" Flames washed over Jando, rippling down his arms, pooling across his chest. His screams ripped across the canyon. Tongues of fire leaped from his arms to his legs, from his back to his groin, refusing to be suffocated.

Kit crawled away from the blackened, groaning body and scrambled to her feet. Blood zipped through her veins, energy pulsed within her. She spotted her knife and retrieved it. The steel settled into her hand like the handshake of an old friend. Shots richoted off a rock near her head. Dust clogged Kit's throat but not her mind. She knew what she had to do. Take her brother's place.

Everything faded into an obscure background. Only Jando remained in her focus. His charred body became a magnet, drawing her closer. She walked among the fiery rivers, the stampeding cows and the gunshots to Jando's breathing body.

Now was the time to lay to rest the ghosts of the past. Hawk was gone, it was up to her. Her fingers curled around the cool bone hilt of her knife. Heat from the fire flushed her face and burned her skin, but it could not match the flames of vengeance in her soul. Planting her feet wide, she lifted the blade above Jando's chest with both hands and shouted, "This should be my brother's blade in your heart, but at least a Cheyenne knife will spill your blood."

"Kit."

The gravelly sound of her name penetrated the trance.

"Kit."

She blinked, and realized her fingers were cramping around the knife.

"Kit."

Awareness sifted back to her. She turned toward the insistent call.

Garret lay on the ground, just a few feet away. "Hurry, cut me loose." His malachite eyes commanded her to obey. An understated urgency vibrated in his voice.

A few minutes, a swipe of her blade, and he would be free to escape the gunfire and cattle.

The man at her feet groaned. Jando's blackened face contorted. One eye strained to open, the other melted closed. The whiz of a bullet buzzed near her ear. Rustlers seeped through the lines of cows, over rocks and trees, racing toward her. Garret would have to wait. There was a more important job to fulfill first.

From her left, she heard the unmistakable sound of metal rubbing leather. A gun pulled from a holster. Swiveling on her heels, she crouched, ready for an ambush. From the dust and smoke, Sage appeared, his gun aimed at Garret's heart.

Time slowed. Her mind and her heart warred. Vengeance and love ripped at her soul. At her feet, Jando moaned. She should have known fire could never destroy him. He was the devil's godchild. The smoky shadows of men converged toward her. She didn't know if they were rustlers or Rockin' G hands. Both were just as likely to snuff out her life. Retribution changed from a solid rock-like lump in her heart to liquid, running through her fingers as the men grew closer. Now. She must kill Jando now.

Click. She heard the gun being cocked, felt pressure on her heart, as if it were a trigger being pulled. The sound forced her to turn back toward Garret. Her hair fanned out, and between the strands, she could see Sage standing over Garret, his finger on the trigger.

Kill Jando. Save Garret. Only one. Two years of her life versus one night of passion. Vengeance screamed for Jando's blood. Her heart pleaded for Garret's life.

Kit let the knife fly. Watched her victim's eyes widen as he clutched the blade slicing through his heart. Heard the gurgle of his last breath. Sage sank to his knees, then slumped over Garret's helpless body.

Weaponless, she stared at Jando. She didn't have the

strength to choke him. He was charred, burned, singed, and yet his putrid soul refused to give up its hold on that hideous bulk of a body. What had she done? Sacrificed everything for what? For Garret.

Horses and cows began to fill in the space between her and Garret, threatening to trample him and the corpse into one bloody mass. Kit scurried over to Garret and tugged the dead body off. She pulled the blade from the crimson-stained chest and sawed at Garret's bindings.

The last twisted pieces of rope snapped. Garret's shoulders unbent. Bunched muscles cracked and snapped back into place. There was no time to enjoy the respite. Gunfire blazed. Cattle scattered at each loud bang. A horse pranced near the fire, reins tangled in the horns of a dead longhorn. Kit stepped away and turned, ready to flee.

Garret latched onto her arm and her knife fell from her hand. "Not so fast. You're not going anywhere." He dragged her toward the horse.

"I've got to find my brother."

"I'm not forgetting about him, either." Garret unsnarled the twisted reins with his free hand.

The mountain of seared flesh shuddered, then pushed itself upright. Skin blistered and peeled as he moved. Jando's one usable eye stared at Kit.

She froze. Her whole body stiffened and she stopped fighting. "My knife. I need my knife."

From the corner of his eye, Garret spotted a tall, imposing figure walking with leaden steps toward them. A bandanna wrapped around one thigh. A blue feather fluttered in his hair. Winterhawk.

Kit hadn't seen her brother or she would be tearing Garret to pieces to get to him. If Hawk made it to Kit, Garret would never see either of them again. As long as he had the woman, Hawk would find him.

"Kit, we're getting out of here. Together." Garret balanced one foot in the stirrup and mounted. With a swift motion, he swung Kit into the saddle behind him.

"Put me down." Life flooded into her, and she squirmed in the saddle.

Garret grabbed her hands and forced them around his waist. "Bullets are flying and no one's too picky about what they're hitting. You stay here and you'll wind up dead." He kicked the horse's flanks and the animal lunged forward.

The crack of gunfire came from behind him. Kit's arms constricted around his chest. Her breasts pressed tightly against his bare back, setting lances of pain in his burn. She stopped fighting. The close call must have knocked some sense into her.

"Ride." She choked out the word. Her cheek rested along the curve of his neck. Fine, silky strands of her hair formed a spider's web across his face and chest. A shudder ran down her arm.

An opening appeared in the flowing mass of cattle. Garret kicked his mount and the animal broke into a spine-jarring stride. From the canyon wall, Cade waved to him and covered Garret's escape with gunfire. The outlaws were on the run. Afraid that if he stopped, Kit would bolt, Garret made for the pass.

Out on the rolling hills, he dug his heels into the ragged mount's flanks. Kit's forehead bobbed on his shoulder. Her hands slid down to his waistband, and she wove her fingers through the loops. The soft undersides of her arms caressed his hips with the rocking movement of the horse. His body burned for her. His groin thickened. His disgust with himself and his passion for her sickened him. Only the threat that Hawk might catch up with them kept Garret from reining in the miserable mount and having it out with her.

Garret kept up the vertebrae-rattling pace, letting the miles race beneath him and his festering anger. He'd tie Kit to the cook wagon in camp, send Candus for the sheriff, then ride back to the canyon to help Cade smoke out the remaining outlaws. And find Jando. There would be an end to the man's thieving and killing—today.

"Cap'n." The call floated on the still air.

Two riders crested a hill in front of him. One waved a dark cap in the air, exposing a scalp of black woolly hair. The familiar figures of Candus and Cracker were a dose of liniment to Garret's frazzled nerves. He halted the tired horse as he crested a hill.

Riding on a swift cow pony, Candus cantered across the rolling grass. Before the horse could stop, he jumped from the saddle and clasped Garret's arm. "Davidson told us about the pickle ya was in."

Cracker, riding on a mule, reined to a stop. With one hand he yanked his cannon of a rifle from its saddle boot. "Me and Candus come out to blast them desperadoes to kingdom come." He peered around Garret's back at the figure slumped against his shoulders. "That Miss Kit?" His whiskers bobbed up and down in surprise.

At the sound of her name, Kit stirred and slipped from behind him. Garret jumped to the ground, ready to give chase. "Grab her before she makes a break." If she got on Candus's horse, she'd be galloping over the prairie faster than a jackrabbit.

Kit lay slumped on the ground. Her parched lips whispered, "Water."

"Get the little miss some water." Cracker motioned to Candus.

Hell, she was playing. Couldn't the old man see that?

Kit O'Shane was definitely not the type of woman to swoon after a close call. Garret expected her to knock the old man away and make a dash for the horses at any moment. "She can help herself. The little hellion threw in with a pack of rustlers and nearly got me killed."

Candus and Cracker cradled Kit's body. The old cook pierced Garret with a steely gaze, just as sharp as any blade Jando had tried to use. "Don't reckon she can. The little hellion here's been shot."

Chapter Twenty-Three

Garret pushed his horse for speed and glanced at the treasured cargo in his arms. Kit hadn't uttered a word. Never showed one sign she had been injured. She had grit. More than her fair share. And a good measure of mule-headed stubbornness. More than she needed.

Warmth oozed through the blanket-strip bandage, a sign the bullet wound still bled. A wash of alabaster paled her face to the color of tea with rich cream. She had lost so much blood. Fear nibbled at his heart.

The gray-white curl of the campfire appeared in the swell between the hills, offering respite from the desolation of the prairie. Garret thundered into camp.

Dismounting, he carried Kit's still body toward the wagon. Candus ran ahead, pulled a handful of blankets from the cook wagon and made a pallet on the ground. Garret laid her on the thick padding, a whimper escaped her faded red lips. Blood soaked the sleeve of his shirt.

Chili hobbled over, gave his challenging bark and waited. His nubby tail wagged. When Kit didn't respond, the old dog raised one tan eyebrow. Garret laid his hand on the canine's head. "Not this time, fella. She's got another fight to deal with first."

The old dog plopped down and rested his nose on the edge of Kit's blanket. Garret and that three-legged dog had a lot in common. All the arguing and snapping covered up a lot of caring. Neither of them had realized just how much Kit meant to them. Until now.

"Bullet's gotta come out." Cracker stated the obvious while he ransacked the wagon for supplies. He placed bottles and ointments on the tailgate, then lifted a sharp stiletto. Beads of sweat popped out like dew on the old man's shaggy brows. He laid the knife in the flames to sterilize it. A shudder ran up and down Garret's back. His burn throbbed.

Rage and anger simmered in his gut. He had done nothing to protect her. She had rescued him from sure death, and he had seen the hesitation in her eyes. The tenseness of her stance as she held that blade over the burned hulk of the rustler. Kit had wanted the obese man dead. Why? For rustling Garret's cattle? For holding him prisoner? Or for some darker reason?

As usual, every action Kit made just stirred up more questions and no answers. But getting shot. That had stirred up more than questions in Garret's heart. All his clear, logical thinking muddied at the thought he might lose her.

His arms ached to hold her again. It was the first time he had ever felt physical pain if he didn't hold a woman, didn't hear her voice, didn't touch the nape of her neck with his lips. And it had to be this woman. A pants-wearing, prickly-pear-tempered desert flower.

"Leave them. Leave them be." Kit thrashed her arms. The dark stain on her shoulder spread like a cancer and so did the ache in Garret's heart. He could lose her. Lose the only woman that made him mad as a hornet one minute, and soft as butter the next.

She shouted, "Run, my sister. Run."

Garret entwined his fingers with Kit's and brought their combined fist to his chest. He let her feel the heavy beat of his heart, let her know that she rested among the living. "Kit, it's me, Garret. Garret." He repeated his name over and over, using his voice to penetrate the fog of her delirium. Chili whined in unison.

Gradually, her thrashing ceased. "Garret?" She called his name from the darkness of her nightmare.

"I'm here." A lump choked Garret's throat as she dug her fingers into the back of his hand.

"He's killed my sister. Everyone." A tie to death echoed in her words, as though she would gratefully join those specters in her dreams.

Her eyes fluttered opened, and she clutched his arm like a lifeline. Shame cramped her face into a tearful grimace. A shiver raced up her arm, shaking her body. "Let me die. Let me join my brother."

"Kit, you're not going to die." Garret fought to keep her with him. Her eyes closed. Her fingers grew slack in his fist. "Kit. Kit, wake up."

Tears cascaded down her face, leaving tracks on her dirty cheeks. Perspiration beaded across her forehead. Bright red crept along her delicate cheekbones. He laid his palm on her head. Heat burned his hand. Her eyelids quivered. Kit had fallen deep into a fevered world. A world full of torment and despair.

A spasm shook her frail body. "Can't let them find the baby. Stay here, be quiet." Her words came out uneven and rushed. She raised her fists and pummeled Garret's chest. Butterfly wings had more intensity.

Weeping from the torment in her dream, she called out in her dry, thin voice, "Not the children!" Kit's quiet plea hushed the angry men. Her body slackened. Garret could feel her hopelessness and heard the desperation in her voice. "They're only babies." A cry so full of sorrow came from her lips that even the most hardened of men touched a finger to their eye to wipe away a tear.

Cracker stoked the cook fire with kindling. The flames cast light over her fevered blush. A frailty marked the delicate lines of her cheeks and her defiant chin. Garret brushed away strands of ebony hair stuck to her forehead. He cursed his inability to step into her delirium and fight her demons. He had to settle for stroking her face, holding her hand and offering words of encouragement.

"I'm here for you, Kit. I'll stop anyone from hurting you." He kissed her dry, hot temple and worried at the unnatural heat radiating from her skin.

She whimpered like a hurt child in his arms, her nightmares draining her remaining strength. "I should have killed him," she murmured, then lost consciousness.

"Now's the time to dig out that slug. Turn her over and hold her still." Cracker bent over her with a sharp skinning knife. A tremble shook his gnarled hands.

Garret eased Kit over onto her stomach. Her faded, thin shirt tore like paper in his hands. Candus handed him a bowl of hot water. With gentle ministrations, Garret melted the bond between the cloth and wound.

The jagged edges of the bullet hole seeped fresh blood. All he wanted was for Kit to open her eyes, give him a half smile and growl at Chili. Or jump on the black and show him just what kind of cowboy she was. Or kiss him and show him just what kind of woman she was.

He had wasted too much time on old promises and false dreams. Garret was ready to start living, start loving.

"Go ahead," he ordered the cook. Kneeling on one knee next to her, Garret braced a palm on her uninjured shoulder blade, the other at the small of her back.

The tip of Cracker's tongue showed as the old cook carved his way into Kit's wound. Her body flinched. Garret hushed her futile struggles with whispered words of encouragement. He begged her to hold on. To remember him. To remember last night.

"Almost…got…it." Cracker released a long, slow breath and held the bloody slug between his thumb and index finger.

Candus squatted next to Cracker and held out a wide, flat knife, wisps of heated air rising from the edges. The black man's gray-white brows wrinkled into deep furrows as he gazed at Kit's injury. The sizzle of hot metal and water increased the nausea rippling in Garret's stomach.

Cracker took the knife and gave Garret a somber look. "Gotta cauterize it or she'll bleed to death." He lowered the blade. Kit's body trembled. She gasped. Her fingers dug into the rough wool blankets. Garret knew all too well the pain she was enduring.

The metal seared the bullet hole closed. "It's in the good Lord's hands now, son." Cracker laid tobacco leaves over the wound, letting the medicinal properties of the plant soothe her pain, then placed a soft cloth over his surgery. "Time to see to your own pains, Cap'n."

"What?" Garret couldn't tear his gaze away from Kit's face. He feared if he glanced away, if only for a second, she would succumb to her nightmares and join the ghosts in her dreams.

Cracker took the tin of ointment and pointed to Garret's back. "Best add some oak apple juice and tobaccy to that burn." The old man applied a soothing layer of green leaves to Garret's back and a loose bandage. He barely registered the reduction of the throbbing pain, but kept his concentration centered on Kit, wishing his will alone could keep her alive.

"Rest a spell," Cracker advised.

"Later." Garret waved the old man off. What if Kit needed him, called for him, and he wasn't there? Garret pulled a thin blanket over Kit's naked back, leaving her wound exposed to the air. His mind consumed itself with each rise of her chest, each labored breath she took.

"Cap'n? How 'bout you eat a bite?"

A voice cut the fog of concern in Garret's head. He suddenly became aware of the aroma of thick stew under his nose. How had Cracker cooked up a pot of stew so fast? Looking at the sun, Garret sucked in a breath. The golden ball seemed to have skipped across the sky, the tips of the mountains just piercing the bottom.

"Later." Garret pushed the plate away with the back of his hand. The other he laid over Kit's. She had quieted. The violent shakes softened to occasional chills. Garret placed another blanket over her. What he wouldn't give to have her nestled in a warm bed instead of the cold ground.

"Cap'n." Candus placed his big knuckled hand on Garret's shoulder. "Cade's riding in."

Only his brother's name could pull Garret from Kit's side. He rose, his legs stiff from sitting in one position for so long. The skin along his burn pulled and tugged across his shoulders. Dark purple bruises along his ribs made him step gingerly toward the arriving men.

Cade thundered in with the other riders. His hat fell back, the string saving it from flying away. A warpaint of soot and dirt marked his face. And that damnable crooked smile. Cade could have come from a picnic bonfire instead of a shoot-out with a gang of rustlers.

Victory cries created a din of noise as Cade jumped from the saddle before his mare pulled to a stop. In front of Garret, Cade halted. "Damn good to see you standing, big brother." He reached out his hand.

Garret gave his brother a firm handshake and, ignoring the pain in his back, drew him into a bear hug. "Damn good to be standing, little brother."

"The cattle—"

"To hell with the cattle," Garret snorted. Cows were not the most precious items he could have lost today. He could have lost his brother, and he might still lose Kit. He had been so blind not to appreciate what he had in life instead of fretting over what he didn't have. Things were going to be different now.

"What about your men?" Garret asked.

A tinge of disbelief melted from Cade's eyes and a satisfied smile appeared on his face. "We surprised the hell out of those rustlers. Only got two men winged. I left a few boys back in the canyon to watch what's left of the herd. Figure we lost about a hundred head and ran about fifty pounds off each cow." He paused, tensing as he mentioned the injury to the cattle.

"That was fine thinking using the herd. I thought I was a goner for sure." No recrimination. No lecture this time. Cade's quick wit had rescued Garret from certain death.

"Woulda been except for Hawk." Cade relaxed and perched his battered Stetson back on his head. The rattlesnake headband was gone, and ashes flecked the dove-gray felt. He looked more like a cowboy, less like a gambler playing a cowboy.

A bad taste rose in Garret's mouth. That Indian had a lot of explaining to do. First about Jando, then about Kit.

Cade sauntered over to the cook fire. "I seen that white hide bag of his hanging on the rocks so I knew the pass was clear. Hawk's riding double with Liam." Cade tore a hunk of sourdough bread from the loaf and joined the other men eating and swapping tales.

As Garret watched, Liam loped in with a pained look on his face. Rips and tears decorated his blue chambray shirt along with dust and ash. Garret noticed cuts and scratches on the Irishman's knuckles. A good number of rustlers must have sampled a taste of those iron-hard fists. Hawk stayed on the horse's back.

"How's the lass?" Liam's first words as he dismounted were about Kit.

Jealousy washed away Garret's dam of restraint. "Kit's resting. *I'm* taking care of her." Possessiveness rang in his voice.

Hawk dismounted, holding his wounded leg as he touched the ground. Red stained the blue bandanna tied at his thigh. "Move aside, white man. I will see my sister."

"She's been shot." Garret blocked Hawk from moving forward. Light couldn't pass between their chests.

Hawk tried to pass Garret, but his wounded leg made him stumble. Instinctively, Garret supported him and steadied him to his feet. The Indian stiffened his back and brushed off Garret's helping hand. "The wound is how bad?"

"Bad enough. Cracker dug a slug out of her back." Garret's biting tone softened as the Indian closed his eyes. "She's burning up with fever, but she's been resting easy."

Hawk dropped his chin, the arrogance deserting him. "Kit is my sister. I do not care how many men stand in my way. I will see her."

Cade quirked an eyebrow at Garret and shot the waiting cowboys a sidelong glance. One word from Garret and those men would be all over the Indian like bears after honey.

"She's over by the cook wagon." Garret ended the standoff by stepping aside. Hawk limped toward the wagon, his gaze fixed on Kit's form lying on the ground.

Keeping his hurt leg straight, Hawk lowered himself to sit next to Kit's pallet. In silence, he inspected her injury, his slight nod showing his approval of Cracker's medical works.

Speaking low, Hawk brushed the hair away from his sister's face. "Kit, it is I, your brother."

Not willing to give up all rights, Garret stood over the Indian, ready to haul Hawk away if he disturbed her. At the sound of her brother's voice, her shallow breathing quickened, and she mumbled in Indian and English.

Her words made Hawk flinch. He pushed back his shoulders and narrowed his eyes. "Kit," he called to her, "I am here."

"So sorry," she whispered. Garret had to strain to hear her. "I didn't do it. Didn't kill him."

The Indian's jaw locked into a vise. He spoke through clenched teeth. "Jando lives."

"My fault. My fault you died. My fault I didn't kill him." Tears racked her body, and with a moan she tried to rise. "Hawk, take me with you. I don't want to live alone."

"Get away from her." Garret pushed the Indian aside. Hawk struggled to his feet, his hand reaching for his knife. The sheath was empty. His hand closed in a fist the size of a hammer. Liam placed one of his own shovellike hands on the Indian's shoulder.

Cade interceded. "Now's not the time for this." Glancing around at the cowboys, he added, "Nor the place."

One of the cowboys grabbed a rope off the wagon.

"That Injun knew about them rustlers. I say we string 'im up."

Garret interrupted the men's growing hunger for action. He demanded an answer from the stoic Indian. "I want to know what the hell is going on with Kit. And how you two are tied up with Jando."

Turning his back on Garret, Hawk spoke to the prairie and setting sun. "We did not steal your cattle. You cannot hold us. I will take my sister now."

"Like hell you will." Disgusted, Garret circled Hawk for a face-to-face argument. "Where are you going to take her? She's more than half-dead." Hawk's mouth twitched, the first sign of emotion since he had ridden in.

Kit pleaded to her ghosts in a mixture of Indian and English. There wasn't a man there that couldn't hear her anguish, her pain. And there wasn't a man there that wasn't moved by it. Garret could see it in their faces. In the way even the hardest, meanest cowhand placed his hand over his heart each time she cried out for her sister.

"Tell me what happened."

"I will deal with this." Hawk swept Garret with a dismissing gaze. "Kit is my sister."

"No doubt about that. You two got the same streak of mule-headedness," Garret argued. "Hers is keeping her alive. Yours is gonna kill her."

Hawk's crystal-blue eyes dulled with surrender. Each terrified sob Kit whimpered sank his shoulders like a rock weight. The cool ice of disdain melted. "If you can save her, do so."

"Tell me what I'm fighting. What happened to your sister?" Garret probed for answers, a why into the darkness of Kit's delirium.

"She does not call for our sister. She calls for her sister. My wife walks with the spirits of the dead." A bitterness and self-loathing thickened Hawk's voice. "She calls to Kit for justice for herself and our people." His fist slammed against his breastbone. "Jando should be dead."

An ugly, terrible picture began to form in Garret's mind. Sage's raucous laughter. Jando's evil grin. The boasting of rape and death in an Indian village. The scar that ran down Kit's breastbone.

The force of Kit's sacrifice hit Garret like a sledgehammer. He staggered back, away from Hawk's sorrowful gaze, away from Kit's murmuring. "My God. Your wife. Jando—"

"Raped, murdered." Hawk paused. "Mutilated."

Chapter Twenty-Four

Fire whipped through Hawk's leg as the old cook doctored his wounded thigh near the campfire. Old lessons from revered warriors schooled Hawk's features. He would never let the white men see his pain or weakness.

His pride was rooted in his heritage as a Cheyenne warrior, yet all his strength, cunning and skill had not been enough to protect his family. Shame cleared a wide, torturous path through him. And Blaine demanded Hawk bare that disgrace to the crowd of hostile men.

The rancher knelt a few yards away from the crowd, his gaze on Kit. Her soft murmurs and sobs sent a lance of guilt through Hawk. Spirits haunted her and cried for a justice he could not deliver. His frustration built as Garret laid his hand upon her cheek, then joined the council fire. Was he checking for fever or giving her a caress? Either way, Hawk didn't like the possessiveness the white man exhibited toward his sister.

Tall, immovable, patient. Hawk had once said Blaine reminded him of the mountains. Kit had argued he was like the desert. As usual, when it came to understanding people or animals, Kit had been right. The desert tore the truth from a man and made him face his demons or die. Garret did the same to Hawk.

He swallowed a deep, cleansing breath then slowly released it along with his story. "We were a small band, only ten braves and our families. Kit had just found me."

"Found you?"

A lie covered his blunder. Benton still posed a threat to him and to Kit. "She had been taken to a school in the East."

"So that's where she picked up that lingo." Cracker smacked his lips in satisfaction.

"She wished to be with the Cheyenne so sought me out. To escape the bluecoats and the reservation, our band rode high into the mountains. I begged Kit to return to her school, but she would not leave." Hawk raised his palms in supplication. "I threatened to tie her—"

"To a tree." Garret finished the sentence as he sat down on the tailgate. He knew how much good that would have done. If Kit got it in her mind to follow Hawk, there wasn't much the man could do to stop her.

Deep sorrow dimmed Hawk's eyes, even in the bright light of the fire. "She and my wife were very close. My son adored her. We lived well, we lived free." Hawk's tone conveyed pride and a love of freedom. Two emotions every cowboy worth his salt craved.

Emotions flooded the Indian's normally stoic face. Worry furrowed his brows into deep rows. Anger stiffened his jaw. He harnessed his voice into a calmer tone. "One season, we discovered a herd of mustangs mixed with stray pack animals. It was easy enough to trap them and again bring the saddle horses to the bit. But the mustangs..." A wry smile creased his lips. "Kit found she had a gift for breaking the truly wild ones."

"Or was she just too headstrong to admit she

couldn't?'' Gentle amusement softened Garret's statement to an endearing one. She wouldn't give up a challenge.

Hawk closed his eyes and nodded. He opened them and Garret was surprised to see the tears glistening in his eyes. ''That is what my wife said. She was very wise.'' The blue feather vanes in his hair created shadow scars along his cheek and decorated his face like war paint.

He spoke, dragging each word from his throat. ''We had seen signs of white men and cattle but thought best to let them be. Let the whites steal from each other. Still, we moved our camp high on the mountain.''

''Which meant you had to hunt lower.'' Garret sensed with dread what was coming.

Hawk slapped his thighs with balled fists. ''We did not know the depth of Jando's greed. Why ride so high to take a few more horses when there were plenty to steal from the lower ranches and mines? I and six braves went to hunt meat. Four stayed behind to guard the camp.''

''Kit?'' Garret wanted to hear him say she had insisted on riding with the hunters and not staying behind in the doomed encampment.

''She remained. Held by a promise to take my son berry picking.'' Each time Hawk spoke of his child, raw suffering bled into his tone.

''We returned two days later, our parfleches filled with meat. Our village empty of life.'' Hawk folded and unfolded his hands. ''The stench overtook us first. The buzz of flies shouted our welcome. Grandfathers, grandmothers, wives and children—all butchered. The women, my wife…'' Hawk's voice constricted. He spoke in a harsh tone. ''Raped, their bodies butchered. Jando not only stole our horses, he stole our lives.''

''Jehoshaphat!'' Cracker switched his wad of tobacco

Diana Hall

from one side of his jaw to the other. "You been trailing
Jando ever since?"

"Two years." A hollow, tired echo resounded in
Hawk's words. "From Cheyenne lands to Texas, and here
to Colorado. Jando likes to kill. Talk spreads. Kit and I
followed."

Garret folded his arms over his chest to keep the pounding of his heart from echoing across the camp. Tracking
meant days of hot sun and nights sleeping on the cold
ground. Of rain drenching your skin until you felt as if
you were being washed away in your saddle. And yet Kit
and her brother had persevered in their pursuit. Waiting
for the chance to kill Jando.

Back in the canyon, Kit could have put an end to it,
but she had chosen Garret's life over her own justice.
Jando had to be dead, the burns alone must have killed
him. A hollow victory, a weak taste of revenge at best.

Hawk leaned back, studied the stars, then again faced
the men at the fire. "I found Kit in the lake holding on
to a log, barely alive. For three days she lived with the
spirits of the dead, calling to them, crying with them.
Through her, the spirits demanded justice." Under hooded
lids, Hawk's gaze switched to Garret. "Kit spoke of many
things. Of the terror. The blood. Jando slashed each
woman after he raped her."

"Then Kit escaped without being..." Liam's voice
melted into embarrassment as his neck and cheeks turned
ruddy. Hawk didn't answer. Instead he kept his piercing
gaze on Garret.

Her scar. The fear when he kissed her in the barn. Her
absent maidenhead. Garret seethed with outrage, both at
himself and Jando. Kit had been violently, savagely assaulted. A weaker woman would have broken, but Kit had
the fortitude to hold on to life. That deep vein of stub-

bornness wouldn't let her cave in. Garret had cursed that trait; now he couldn't imagine her without it. Thank God she had a mother lode of it.

From across the fire, Hawk's steady gaze never wavered. Garret could read the undercurrents in his eyes and knew the Indian held his tongue to protect his sister's honor. Firelight reflected in his eyes, turning them to blue heat. "Kit does not remember much. Night is when the memories flood her."

"Why she walks in the moonlight," Garret finished. Those nighttime strolls were to find some peace of mind, not invitations. Every word Hawk uttered made Garret heavy with guilt and remorse.

A quiet respect cloaked the campfire, making it impervious to the growing night. The men shed their mistrust and anger. Their stance became less rigid and accusation left their eyes.

Liam raked his fingers through his dark hair. "At least Kit was able to save herself."

"And my son." Hawk walked and stopped a few feet from where Kit lay in a fretful sleep. His back to the fire, he separated himself from the cowboys. Afraid he would disturb her, Garret followed.

In a low, terse voice, Hawk confided in Garret. "She sacrificed herself to draw Jando away and save my son." He didn't have to mention what she gave up to protect the boy. Garret knew.

"I understand." Garret put his hand on Hawk's shoulder and gave it a slight squeeze.

The pulse along Hawk's jawline quickened. "Kit blacked out. She remembers fighting, falling into the water, but nothing else. She's never known for sure, if Jando…"

"And she won't learn from me," Garret promised. "Your son—"

"In Texas at a mission school. Raven hasn't spoken since the raid. But why should he?" Self-loathing distorted his noble features. He shook off Garret's hand. "I have yet to kill the man that murdered his mother." Kit stirred in her sleep, and Hawk limped back to the fire. He stood alone within the ring of men.

Cracker sucked his teeth then gave a low whistle. "That poor gal. She's been through hell and back."

McVery asked, "Why didn't you just go to the sheriff? Jando woulda pulled a noose for rustling."

"Because," Garret answered for Hawk, "killing a man's family isn't equal to stealing a cow."

Hawk's face fused into angular planes of anger, shame and sorrow. "Jando made my wife suffer. He will taste my blade. On this I swear."

"Jando's dead." Garret released the bittersweet news. "I saw him burned. No man could survive that."

"You are wrong, white man." Hawk's back straightened. A gleam of hatred shone in his eyes. Rage turned his arms into contorted muscles of power. "Jando lives."

Let me die. Let me die. Kit prayed from the depths of her nightmare. The massacre played over and over again in her mind, a gruesome reminder of her own weaknesses. Hawk was dead, and Jando lived. And she was to blame.

In answer, Hawk's spirit materialized in her dream. "Be at peace, little sister. Come join us."

Her brother beamed with approval, swathed in a distant light. Kit could make him happy, could atone for her sin if she crossed over. It would be so simple. Just lie back. Close her eyes. Let it happen.

"Kit!" A voice full of concern and caring startled her. "Kit, come back to me."

Peace and contentment disappeared. Confused and disoriented, she fought to regain her peace. She didn't want to come back. She didn't want to feel again.

Rough knuckles brushed the sensitive skin near her ear. A thumb traced the outline of her lips, then she tasted soft, seductive lips on her mouth.

As if by a magician's trick, Hawk vanished, the faraway blur disappeared. Sadness enveloped her. She had been so close to peace. So close to a restful sleep.

Angry, she turned, ready to blast the fool that had torn her away from her brother. Starlight swirled and coalesced into a tall, wide-shouldered figure. Features slowly became recognizable. Hair the color of the desert ground. A face marked with years of hard times and sorrow. Lips, full and wide. Malachite eyes.

From out of the glow, Garret stepped forward, his hand open, his eyes gleaming with the soft iridescence of stardust. "Kit," he whispered. She felt the rumble of his voice in her chest and heard the steady beat of his heart.

Strong fingers clasped hers and drew her into his arms. He smelled of horses, leather and camp smoke. His lips nuzzled her neck. "Kit, stay with me." His tone both ordered and pleaded.

She risked one last look behind her, straining for a sign of her brother or the beautiful light. Garret guided her chin with his thumb and forefinger. With gentle pressure he forced her to look at him. "Choose me, Kit."

"Garret?" She moved her lips and felt the cracked skin shift, but no sound came to her ears.

He raked back a strand of sandy hair. Faint lines creased the corners of his eyes. "You had me worried for a while. Thought I might have lost you."

Bewildered, Kit sought for some understanding of this latest twist to her nightmare. She studied him. Noticed his unshaven face, the missing second button, the genuine concern in his eyes. She lifted her arm. Very real pain streaked across her shoulder and dry heat burned her throat.

Tilting her head upward, she welcomed Garret's supporting palm at her neck. She swallowed hard, then questioned him, wanting him to verify her suspicion.

He leaned over, brushing her naked shoulder with his skin. "I can't hear you."

She tried again, closing her eyes as she took a deep breath and caught the essence of his male scent.

His body stilled. He lowered her head and the edge of his mouth curved upward. "Yeah, you're alive." A full, generous smile tilted his lips. "And I aim to keep you that way."

Garret's voice, his plea and presence had drawn her back from death. Why had he bothered? She was the reason he had almost been killed, the reason he stood a good chance of losing the ranch. But the question she feared the most, only she could answer. Why had she been unable to resist his call?

As fatigue conquered her weary mind and body, Kit's soul confirmed her worst fear. How could she have fallen in love with a bad-tempered, mule-headed, dry-as-the-desert man like Garret Blaine?

Chapter Twenty-Five

I almost lost her. The realization became a steady chant in Garret's head, clanging against his self-control. He ran the back of his hand along Kit's cheek as she slept, soundly and without dreams.

Conflict raged inside him. *Keep your head. You've got a herd to think about, a ranch to run. To hell with the ranch. Hold her. Tell her you need her, want her.* Cool, clear thinking took a boot stomping to the hot, driving need in his heart. Loving Kit conquered any doubts.

But Hawk stood between Garret and his beloved. Hawk believed Jando still lived. One word from her brother, and Kit would sit a horse, no matter her pain, and ride off to search for a dead man, leaving Garret with the ache of loneliness in his heart.

Vega had led a group of cowboys back to the canyon to help round up cattle. When the men returned, that would clear up any question about the rustler's fate. Someone must have seen Jando's corpse. Hawk would be proved wrong. There would be no reason for Kit to leave. Garret would have time to court her. Make her love him. Have her choose him over Hawk. *I'll find a way to make her stay.*

* * *

From the shadows, Hawk watched the rancher capture Kit's wrist. He had seen hunger in Blaine's eyes. The raw hunger of a man who desires a woman. But for what? Blaine wanted a woman who readily accepted the bridle of respectability, not one who fought the bit and retained her untamed mustang streak. Not a woman like Kit.

Hawk slowly lowered himself to the ground, keeping his injured leg straight. Let Blaine tend to Kit now, but when the time came, Hawk would ride out after Jando, with his sister at his side.

"I see no fat man." Vega twisted the tip of his thick mustache between his thumb and index finger. "No Jando."

"Jando's carcass must be rotting in some side canyon." Garret cursed under his breath as he watched the returning cattle straggle into camp, their heads hung low, the wildness run out of them. Dust from the moving animals turned the air hazy, settling a red-brown film over Garret, his men and his spirit. The smell of sweating cattle, the taste of dust and the stifling heat varnished the camp.

Hawk stood tall despite his injured leg, his arms crossed over his chest. Speaking to the broad emptiness of the prairie, Hawk let the wind carry his voice to the rolling hills and mountain peaks. "Jando, you will yet taste the steel of my blade. On this I swear."

Garret tilted his face upward and let the blistering midday sun evaporate his boiling frustration. Hawk wasn't going to listen to reason. The day he touched the rustler's cold flesh would be the day he believed the man was dead. Mule-headedness must be a family trait.

Rotating his head, he winced as the skin between his shoulders flared into pain. He was in about the same shape as his cattle, tired and hurting and in no mood to justify himself to the obstinate Indian.

"Cap'n, what we gonna do with this herd? They's so skinny they got to stand double just to cast a shadow." Cracker uttered the sentence as if it were an epitaph.

Exhausted. Men and animals.

He only had one choice he could make. "Cade, you're going to have to head up the drive."

"Me!" Cade spit a mouthful of coffee into the fire. The wood sizzled and popped, along with his eyes.

"I can't ride," Garret said. "Not yet. And Kit—"

His sister's name yanked Hawk's attention from the landscape. "Kit is—"

"Too shot up to be traipsing across the countryside." Garret wasn't about to lose this fight. "And so are you. You, me and Kit are heading back to the ranch."

Hawk lifted his chin and sniffed the air as if Garret were a piece of rancid meat. "Kit will grow strong again. As will her hatred of Jando. She will not stay long."

"You think she's going to get well fretting over that rustler?" Garret pivoted on his heel and faced Hawk. "Kit needs rest. Lots of it. I've got no say as far as you're concerned, but I'm asking you not to tell her that we didn't find Jando's body."

"Kit deserves to know the truth." Hawk struck his chest with his fist. "I will not lie to her."

Garret leaned his weight on one leg and crossed his arms. "We're both looking after Kit's welfare."

With any luck, he would convince Kit his love was stronger than any hate. That nights alone with him could replace her nightmares with dreams of a future with him. A glimmer of hope warmed his heart. He just might have a chance if Hawk gave him the time he needed.

Hawk sneered, "I will wait. For now."

Chapter Twenty-Six

"There's got to be someone else to lead the herd," Cade pleaded.

Wrapping strips of leather around the tips of two cottonwood poles, Garret patiently explained his lack of alternatives. "Not on such short notice. Liam's not experienced enough. Vega knows cattle and cowboys, but he's not a negotiator." Giving Cade a wink, he added, "Time to use your charm to get the Rockin' G a good hoof price."

"But I'll be in Dodge City. With every cent you own."

Ducking under the horse's belly, Garret checked the ties attaching the travois to the animal. He released a breath, put his faith in Cade and stood up. "With every cent *we* own."

This drive would make or break his little brother. Cade possessed the ability, he just needed to believe in himself. "I've been wrong trying to force you into a life you don't want," Garret admitted. "Sell the cattle. After paying wages, half is yours. For whatever you want."

"Gambling and women?"

Garret didn't rise to the bait. He kept calm and spoke from the heart. "If that's what you want."

"What I want is for you to be proud of me." A shade of big-brother worship softened Cade's voice. It brought back memories of happier times, when Garret had watched out for his little brother instead of ruling over him. "What if I mess up again, like in New Orleans?"

Garret rested his hands on his brother's shoulders. "You got me out of that canyon—alive. You can get these cows to Dodge—alive." He met his brother's gaze. "There are things between Kit and me that I've got to put to rights. Things that can't wait."

"I don't know if it was the knock to your head or the kick from a cow, but you're finally thinking straight about Kit."

"And about you. You're my brother, and I want the same thing for you that Ma wanted for me."

"Pride?"

"Nope, just to be happy. It took me till now to realize that's all she wanted all along. She asked me to make Blaine a name to be respected because that's what she thought I wanted. Well, I've found what I want and that's Kit, but I need time with her. I know you can handle the herd, Cade. Will you? I'm asking. It's something I intend to do more often."

"Yep." Cade's voice deepened. He slammed the heel of his boot into the dirt. "Dammit Garret, I know how much this year's sale meant to you. I'm sorry it's not gonna turn out like you figured."

Casting a glance at Hawk carrying Kit's sleeping form to the travois, Garret murmured, "It's a damn sight better than I ever hoped."

The flames of the village reached for Kit. Jando's evil laugh echoed in her ears. She fought to keep from falling into the hellish scene. Fatigue threatened to make her surrender. The laughter grew louder, the fire closer.

"They can't hurt you anymore." A gentle whisper in her ear pulled her from her terror. Like a lullaby, the voice delivered comfort. Kit clung to the promise and believed. The horrible scenes faded away, and she floated toward the realm of consciousness.

An eiderdown softness enveloped her. She snuggled deep into the plushness and detected a hint of cedar. A wet nose pressed against her cheek, and she heard a distinctive whine.

Opening her eyes to slits, Kit spotted the dog's head and realized she lay in a real bed. Sunlight glared through a glass window. A bouquet of blue columbines and red poppies sat on the sill, an old peach can as a vase. Coffee perked nearby, tempting her with its heavenly scent.

"Kit, are you awake?" Garret's voice asked. A heavy weight shifted at her side, and she heard the corn-shuck mattress rustle. A mattress? Flowers? Coffee? Where was she?

Reason and logic drained from her mind. She couldn't untangle her observations to make any judgments. Blinking her eyes, she tried to move and get a better look around.

"Ah!" Pain shot from her arm and kicked the breath from her.

Garret's footsteps hurried across a wood floor toward her. He sat next to her and the mattress dipped at his weight, shifting her closer to him. "It's good to see you back in the world of the living." He reached over and kissed her dry lips, then tucked the corner of a multicolored quilt under her chin.

"Hurt." She meant to ask more, but her voice came out like the mewing of a kitten.

"I bet you do. Cracker dug a nasty slug out of your shoulder." He caressed her cheek as he spoke in a tight voice. "You damn near died."

Garret sat back, and she got a good look at him. A thick white bandage encircled his chest. Scuffs and scrapes tattooed his arms and face. He had a goose egg on his temple varying in hue from pale green to dark blue. He looked horrible. He looked wonderful.

Her chest constricted. She found it hard to breathe and impossible to look away from the gentleness of his gaze. A lock of hair fell over his face, and she lifted her arm to brush it back. Spears of pain stabbed her arm and back. Memory of her injury lanced through her.

Then a rush of images unfolded. Jando. Garret. Sage. Hawk. Her mental anguish crushed the physical pain. The ache in her shoulder ebbed, but not the one in her heart. To have her brother dead and Jando alive stabbed her with guilt and grief. If only she had killed the outlaw, then Hawk's death would have some meaning.

"How long?" she asked.

"Six days."

"No!" Somehow she'd track down Jando on her own and kill him. She owed it to Hawk's memory. "Have to go. Find Jando. Hawk—"

"Is fine."

The information knocked the energy out of her. She fell back, surprised, delighted and ashamed. How could she ever face Hawk, knowing she had let Jando escape? "Where?"

"Out in the bunkhouse. Now, just calm down." He rubbed the nape of her neck. The fine hairs along her scalp stood on end as his touch telegraphed sensuous memories to her heart and mind.

"Hawk got shot in the leg, but he's fine. Your brother

and I brought you back to the ranch." His gaze raked over her face with a deep longing. "Back to my cabin, Kit. Back to my bed."

Garret's home! She had never been inside the cabin before. A pinned-back curtain allowed her to see the modest furnishings. Steam whistled from a kettle on a stove near the door. Cast-iron cookware hung on the wall beside it, ready for use. Embers glowed in the rock-lined fireplace across from the stove. Straddling the middle of the room, a cherrywood table filled the free space.

"I know it's not much." He gave her a wink. "But I've got plans."

Plans that she had destroyed. What about his livestock? Why wasn't his scar white and his gaze angry? He should be devastated at his loss and furious with her. "Where are the cattle?" Words still took an effort, but she had to know.

"Cade's handling the herd now."

"Cade?"

"Yeah, you know, that irresponsible brother of mine that just needs an opportunity to strut his stuff? That one." He knelt at her bedside, took her hand in his and kissed her knuckles. "I've been trying to make Cade into something he's not, and I've been trying to do the same thing to myself. Kit, I still want the Rockin' G to succeed, but I want it for us. For you and me, and the mess of children we'll have."

"Garret, no." Tears formed in her eyes. "I can't stay. You don't understand."

"Yes, I do." He crawled up in the bed next to her, sheltering her in his arms. "Hawk told me about the village and the massacre. I've lain here for six nights holding you and talking you back to me from your nightmares. Kit, Jando can never hurt you again."

"But I didn't kill him."

"Jando was engulfed by flames." Garret bit his lip, then told a half lie. "He couldn't live with such wounds. He couldn't survive." *But we never found his body.* Garret silenced the nagging reminder echoing in his head. He could understand Hawk's need to see the rustler's corpse, but that didn't mean Kit had to follow.

Her body trembled in his arms and tears coursed down her cheeks. "You don't know everything." Her uninjured hand traced the scar between her breasts. "This scar—"

Garret stopped her confession with a kiss. He wouldn't allow her to ever doubt him or his love. "Kit, when a man makes love to a woman, he knows if he's her first. I want you to know that I'm the first man that you ever gave yourself to, and if you'll have me, I'll be your last. Marry me, Kit. Stay with me. I love you."

Nightmares swirled with daydreams. Longings conquered fears. The past faded as a prospect of a future with Garret unfolded. "I've caused you so much trouble."

"Yep, you sure have." He laughed and nuzzled her ear. "I'm thankful for every minute of it. You yanked me clear out of that prison I had constructed around my heart. You made me dream again, Kit. You made me feel again."

Joy washed over her. "You did the same for me. After the massacre, I was so afraid I could never love a man, but that night with you changed all that."

He cradled her, trailing kisses down her nose, and then captured her mouth with his. His kiss tantalized her and beckoned her smoldering passion. "Tell me you love me. Tell me you'll be my wife."

"What about Benton?" She wanted him to be sure that Kit O'Shane was what he wanted.

"Who?" He smiled, a confident grin that creased the lines near his eyes. "Kit, I'm waiting."

All the love she had tried to deny flooded her with a rush of tenderness and yearning. "Garret, I love you. Nothing would make me happier than to be your wife."

Careful of her wound, Garret cradled her to him. The length of his lean body molded to hers. His lips kissed with tenderness, but she tasted a promise of his deeper hunger. Parting her lips, she darted her tongue into the warm recess of his mouth. His groan and the shudder that ran down his body thrilled her with power. Garret wanted her. Garret needed her. Garret loved her.

Their lips parted, and he caressed her with his gaze. His callused fingers combed through her hair and sifted the strands over his shaking hand. "I don't know what I would've done if you had said no. I guess I'd have to tie you to a tree to make you stay."

The familiar quip made Kit think of her brother. She and Hawk had their lives back. With Garret, she would build another to blot out the painful past, but what of her brother? "Garret, I know you and Hawk don't get along, but I love my brother, and he has a son...."

"Hawk and Raven have a home with us, here, for as long as they want it, sweetheart. This is your home, and theirs." Rising, Garret swiped a quick kiss. "Now you need to rest. I'll get you some tea, and you can tell me the address of that school in Texas so we can send for Raven."

Hawk stood outside the cabin, listening to his sister's happiness pierce his heart. Kit loved Blaine. He had feared as much. But what surprised him was the rancher's feelings. Blaine's love had been able to enter the spirit world and drive away the demons that Hawk could not. Whatever violation Kit had suffered from Jando, Blaine's simple declaration put to rest. She found completeness with Blaine at her side.

Jando had survived. Hawk sensed his evil, and there could be no rest for him. The death of his wife drove him, along with fear for his sister. If Jando did live, he would seek Kit for his own revenge.

With light steps and a heavy heart, he crossed to the barn and gathered his tucker-bag. Saddled and bridled, the buckskin waited patiently while Hawk tied the oilcloth with all his belongings to the saddle. The barn door creaked open.

"I've come to try and talk some sense into you." Garret blocked Hawk's departure with a wide stance.

"If Jando lives, he will seek Kit out and kill her." Hawk knotted the leather straps holding his tucker. "You will protect her here." Cocking his head toward the open door, he added, "And I will protect her out there."

"We can make a home for you and your son."

A home? Hawk shook his head. His home burned to the ground. There would be no other for him. But for his son? Raven loved Kit and she him. With her care and nurturing, perhaps his son would one day speak and think of his father without shame.

"Send for Raven." He exchanged a handshake and promise. "I give you my son and my sister to protect and to love. I have no more cherished gifts than these."

Giving Hawk's arm a firm clasp, Garret answered, "I'm honored."

"You should be, white man." Hawk led his buckskin outside. "You forget, and I promise to kill you."

"It's nice to know my brother-in-law is a man of his word." Garret followed him outside then glanced at the cabin. "What are you going to tell her? She loves me, Hawk, but you're her brother, and this thing with Jando goes way back. If she finds where you're really going, I'll—''

"Have to tie her to a tree?" Hawk's severe face broke into a gentle smile. He pointed toward the stand of firs surrounding the cabin. "These trees are not strong enough to hold Kit's determination. I do not like to lie, but my sister would sacrifice her own happiness to keep her word to me. Tell her I will meet up with Cade. She will believe this." He walked over to the porch, his broad palm ready to push the door open.

"And when he returns and you're not with them, what then?"

Hawk hesitated before opening the door. "Then, white man, you had best have a ring on my sister's hand, a baby in her belly and a good strong rope."

He opened the door and prepared to lie to his sister, a lie that he hoped would bring her all the contentment she deserved, and him a lone trail toward Jando.

Chapter Twenty-Seven

Gray smoke puffed from the cabin chimney, filling Garret with warmth despite the nip in the air. The homey scent of fresh baked bread and the promise of his woman's kiss lured him home.

"Supper's on." Kit waved to him from the porch. She walked to the middle of the yard, wearing his sheepskin jacket. Turning up the jacket collar, she faced the north and his heart lurched painfully. He knew who she searched for, her brother and the returning crew.

Joining her, he turned her to face him and nipped her earlobe. "I'm hungry."

The worry lines eased near her eyes and she returned his embrace. "For my stew or for me?"

"Both." His hands sought the heat of her body and drew her to him. The soft mounds of her breasts pressed against his chest and created a hard stab of want in his jeans. He explored her mouth with his, and when her lips parted, his tongue entered. Love soared through him and he clung to her as she clung to him.

"Kit, let's ride to town tomorrow and have the preacher marry us." Each day threatened his precarious happiness with Kit. When Cade and the crew showed up, she would discover the lie he and Hawk had told her. As the days grew shorter, so did his time with Kit.

Pulling from his arms, she tilted her chin and met his gaze. "I want my brother at my wedding. Hawk can give me away and Cade can stand as your best man."

Hawk can take you away. The thought brought fear to Garret. The sun hung low on the horizon, painting the sky in turquoise-and-rose light. Kit snuggled in his arms and gave a contented sigh.

"But what about a baby?" Garret tried another angle. "Since your arm healed, I've been loving you every night."

Her face flushed, and she whispered, "I promise, if I suspect I'm with child, I'll tell you and then we'll make that trip to the church. But I won't know that for a few more weeks. By then, Hawk and Cade will surely be back."

The wind whispered through the firs like spirits, warning him that his happiness had a deadline. He shivered, not from the cold, but from the ache in his heart. The feel of her soft curves, her hearty laugh and her love opened up his soul. If she left, that door would slam shut and he doubted it would ever open again. "Come on, let's get you out of the cold."

Inside, Kit hung the jacket on a hook while Garret washed up in the porcelain basin by the door. He smiled when he reached for a towel. Red gingham curtains graced the window. On his bed, covered by his mother's quilt, lay another set, not quite finished.

Kit stirred a kettle hung from the iron hook by the hearth. Her smile made him want to forget about supper, sweep her up into his arms and make love to her for hours.

"No you don't." She rose, and the fire shadowed her curves beneath her loose shirt. He could see the shape of her breasts, the hardened peaks and the flatness of her abdomen.

"Don't what?" He pretended to look perplexed.

"You know what." Her lips curved into a sultry smile. "When your eyes turn dark green, I know what you're thinking."

"Really? What am I thinking now?" Stripping her mentally, he thought of touching, kissing and loving every curve.

Kit forgot about her delicious stew and soft bread. She hungered for food that would feed the building desire in her heart. Leaning her head to the side, she gave Garret freedom to trail kisses down her neck and her unspoken consent. He lifted her in his arms and carried her to their bed. His nimble fingers unbuttoned her shirt, freeing her breasts to his touch. Cool air danced across her nipples and they puckered to hard nubs.

She arched as his mouth surrounded one sensitive peak while his hand sought the triangle between her legs. One finger entered and an explosion of heat and desire consumed her. Gently, he teased her, built her want and led her uncontrollable passion. With slow, deliberate movements, he removed her jeans.

Kit's supple body lay beneath him and Garret indulged his earlier daydreams. His hand cradled her womanhood while he discovered the taste of her skin. He outlined her scar with his kisses then ran his tongue down her rib cage and tunneled it into her belly button. She giggled. Then he traveled lower. She gasped as his mouth replaced his hand, and he tasted her sweet nectar.

"Garret, please," she begged. Her fingers tore at the back of his shirt. Buttons flew, then his shirt draped open. She caressed the taut muscles of his stomach as he used his tongue to wind a sensuous path across her stomach then along her side. Gently, she held him, her thumb caressing him. Her touch drove him to passionate madness. He craved to feel her along his naked body. Her softness against his hardness.

It felt so right to watch him. Kit lounged on her side and rested her head on one elbow as Garret removed his pants and slipped off his shirt. She loved the light sprinkle of curly hair on his chest that formed a perfect trail for her kisses. Muscles along his shoulders and upper arms spoke of power and strength, yet when he held her, she never feared he would harm her. With Garret, love overcame any panic or fear. She basked in his love.

He returned to their bed and lay next to her, his eyes forest-green in the dim light of the cabin. Taking long strands of hair, he curtained himself with her tresses.

"You're mine, Kit. Tonight, we'll make that baby." His need reached her, and she gave herself up as a willing sacrifice. His touch seemed reverent as he ran one hand along her hip and thigh. The tip of his shaft stirred and pushed against the apex of her thighs. Pleasure radiated from the juncture, and she fell back into the soft contours of the quilt.

"I'm yours, Garret. Yours." And she opened for him. Rolling on top of her, he gazed into her face, stroking her cheeks, kissing her chin. He suckled each of her marble-hard nipples, then placed his manhood at her entrance.

"Do you love me," he whispered as he glided inside.

"Yes. Yes." Kit could not hold back her declaration. Delightful aches began to pulsate within her.

"For always?" He shifted, and he sank deeper within her. Rotating his hips, he began a slow waltz of lovemaking.

Her emotions whirled and skidded, following the

rhythm of Garret's movements. "For always, Garret." Her legs embraced his waist. "For always."

Garret hoped she spoke from her heart and not from the crazed depths of passion. Looking for her pleasure and seeking her release, he began the cadence of love. With long, slow beats he built her ardor until he felt a wash of warmth surround him. Kit's breath became deep pants. Her breasts rose and fell beneath him like two jewels. She cried his name and called him her love. He wanted to hold on to this moment, but the tempest inside had reached its threshold. He quickened his pace, unable to hold back any longer. Kit arched and he kissed the valley between her breasts as he plunged inside her heated core.

Her legs tightened. Ecstasy blinded him to everything but her tiny gasps of pleasure and the sensation of warm wetness surrounding him. His love was pure, his pleasure explosive. With one final thrust, his desire exploded, pulsating inside of her.

Virgin regions of Kit's soul burned as Garret emptied his love inside her. Hot, liquid passion soared, then ebbed, in time with Garret's thrusts. Kit rocked on an ocean of passion, each crest higher, each trough deeper. She balanced on a wave of hot need. A tidal wave built inside her. Higher. Higher. Deeper. Deeper.

"Kit." Garret shouted her name, and he touched her core. She gripped Garret's arms, released her hold on her own inhibitions and drowned in his golden light. Buffeted by pleasure, she slowly spiraled upward and floated on the aftermath of Garret's lovemaking.

Garret collapsed at her side, weak from completeness, already regretting his physical separation from her. He curled her body to his. She yawned, her satisfied body demanding rest. As she drifted off, she mumbled, "Love you, Garret. Sweet dreams."

"Go to sleep, love," Garret murmured in her ear, and hoped that his life with Kit would not be a dream, but a lifetime.

Cocooned in the warmth of the quilt and Garret's body, Kit closed her eyes and wished she could stay in bed all day. But last night's dishes and supper needed to be put away, and this morning's breakfast still had to be cooked.

After finding her clothes and dressing, she indulged in one favorite pastime before heading for the cookstove. Gazing down at her partner, she softly brushed aside the curtain of sandy hair over Garret's eyes.

The weeks together had softened many of the harsh lines of his face. She hadn't seen his scar turn white— only when she insisted on using her injured shoulder. He pampered her, and she liked it.

Most of all, she loved when his eyes deepened, and the tiny lines near his eyes crinkled as he smiled, because then she knew he was thinking of making love to her. When he looked at her as he had last night, her knees melted, her spine tingled, and she was helpless to resist him. Which was good, because she didn't want to. He made her feel alive and wiped away every horror of the past.

Only one last lie stood between them—her parentage. Revealing the truth would put her and her brother's lives in her husband's hands. But they were safe hands. Gentle hands. Kit clasped Garret's large hand in her own small one. Matching finger to finger, she marveled at the length of his compared to hers, and at the magic they could do to her body.

Garret slept soundly, and well he should. They had made love most of the night. Once with a primal urgency, quick, rough and passionate. Again but with a tenderness that had brought tears to her eyes. Every kiss and caress made her feel cherished. Sunrise had crested the horizon as she found her release bathed in Garret's adoring gaze.

He deserved to sleep late today. Kit shuffled in her sock feet across the floor and closed the curtains, shutting out the rising sun. He'd wake to the smell of eggs, coffee and their love-scented sheets.

Working quietly, she covered the bread with a cloth and placed it in the warming tray at the bottom of the oven. She slid the heavy cast-iron lid back on the kettle, then found she couldn't lift the full pot back to the hook. Well, she'd leave that for Garret to do when he woke.

The stove kindling caught fire with just a touch of a hearth ember. Garret rolled over on his back and Kit found herself staring at the line of sandy hair that formed just near his belly button and disappeared beneath the sheets resting across his hips. Her fingers itched to tickle a path to that hidden region, but she denied her wanton wishes. If she wanted Garret to keep up the strenuous nighttime games, then he needed some sustenance.

She had the coffee perking and the skillet getting hot for eggs. Then, as her stomach rumbled, Kit decided to make flapjacks, as well. She stirred up the flour, sugar and soda. Added eggs, then fumed when the milk pitcher turned up empty. She'd have to go out to the stone cellar behind the cabin to get more. Hoping Garret wouldn't awaken, she slipped on his jacket and her boots, took the pitcher, carefully closed the door and headed out back.

A dark shape came loping from the barn, his tail wagging so hard it nearly made it impossible for Chili to run. "Down, boy." Kit ruffled the dog's thick coat. "And hush, I don't want Garret waking up yet."

Chili issued a part whine, part yodel then raced away toward the far gate.

Shading her eyes, Kit spotted a group of riders breaking

into a canter as they passed under the Rockin' G sign. One waved, others shouted, and Chili ran alongside, barking a greeting.

"Cade." Kit dropped the pitcher of milk and ran to meet them.

Metal clanged against wood and Garret woke with a jolt. He heard Kit shouting, Chili barking and the thunder of horses. He scrambled from bed and stubbed his toe on his boot. Damn! Where the hell were his clothes? Naked, he peered out the window and sighted a group of riders entering the yard, Kit already in their midst. They might as well have been the Horsemen of the Apocalypse. His men's arrival meant his idyllic existence with Kit had come to an end.

Where was his damn shirt? His pants? He picked up one of the half-finished checked curtains and contemplated covering his backside in the cloth just to get to her, then he spied his jeans crumpled near the trunk. Shoving on his pants and putting on his shirt at the same time, he dressed while trying a dozen different lines to explain his lie.

Garret bolted out the door, his heels not quite all the way down in his boots, the top button of his jeans undone and his shirt wide open.

Cade had Kit in a bear hug. "Good to see ya…sis?"

"Not yet." She beamed at him then flushed. "But soon."

"Yahoo!"

Garret made it down the steps, Chili nearly tripping him as the dog jumped from one man to the next.

The Irishman lifted Kit up to eye level. "Lass, it's good to be seein' ya up and about."

"Liam, I've missed you." She planted a kiss on his cheek.

Looking at Garret bearing down on them, the Irishman added, "But not much I'm thinkin'." The one time Garret wished Liam would hold on to her, he didn't. He set her back to earth.

"Home at last." Cade pumped Garret's hand, keeping him from reaching Kit. "We made a haul."

Liam slapped him on the back. "Aye, your brother used that gift of blarney to get a pretty poke. And just ta show ya there's no hard feelings about the lass..." The Irishman wrapped him in a bear hug, then added, "But if she's a mind to thinkin' again, well, I'll be here."

"Forget it." Garret broke contact with Liam and just touched Kit's elbow when she was pulled away.

Vega kissed both her cheeks. "Señorita Kit, you are the most beautiful thing I have seen in three months."

"That's because you've been looking at cows." Kit returned the greeting, then hands passed her down a line of dusty-faced men, farther away from Garret.

"Any more of those peach pies?" Several of McVery's men had pitched in for the drive. Each man grabbed Garret's hand for a hearty shake and a few words. A wagon pulled to a halt behind them.

"Not right now, but I was just getting ready to make flapjacks."

"This time a day?" Cracker jumped down from the wagon.

He gave her a cheek burn with his beard. "Now, what coulda kept the Cap'n a-layin' in bed to this hour." His eyebrows lifted.

"Leave her alone, old man." Candus rounded the wagon and scolded the cook.

A thin, lanky young man shot over the wagon gate as

if he had been primed in a cannon. He wrapped Kit in a tight hug. His tanned face creased in a wide grin.

"Thomas Davidson!" Kit rested her hands on his shoulders. "Let me look at you. I hardly recognize you."

Garret freed himself from the trail drivers and reached the wagon. Cracker clamped onto Garret's hand like a snapping turtle. "Cap'n, you're a-lookin' fine. Don't he look fine, Candus?" Garret tried to shake off the old man's two-handed shake.

"Oh, more than fine, Cracker." The old Buffalo soldier's white-toothed smile gleamed on his dark face. "Lookin' like a married man."

"I've got to get to Kit."

"And henpecked already." Both geezers hooted and purposely stood between Garret and his quarry.

"Land o' Goshen, Miss Kit." Davidson rubbed his three-hair beard and gave Garret a nod as he finally made it to Kit's side. "I'm surprised to see ya here. Seeing as how Jando ain't dead, I figured ya'd be off with Hawk a-trailin' him."

The trail had made Davidson heartier, but not any smarter. Kit stiffened at Garret's side. Her hand flew to her hip. She gasped air and whispered, "Jando lives."

Garret caught her as she collapsed.

Chapter Twenty-Eight

The nightmare returned.

In her dream state, Kit sensed the burning village around her and could smell the foul breath of men holding her down. Hawk's chubby little son raced toward the cover of the woods and safety. Raven's escape was the last memory she had of the massacre. The rest had been blissfully erased. *I'll wake up soon.*

Kit struggled to open her eyes and stop the hateful images, but her muscles wouldn't respond.

A knife slashed at her deerskin dress. Hands gripped her breasts while other unseen men forced her legs apart. Sage yelled, "Hurry up so I can get my turn."

A strange thickness pressed between her legs. Panic made her strong. She bit, scratched, anything to escape. Then pain nearly splintered her in two. Blood trickled down her leg. Jando convulsed over her.

She pieced together what her mind had fought so long to block. Invasion. Rape. The savagery took her breath away, leaving her spent.

"I'm marking this one." Jando's blade sliced her skin as her outstretched hand found her knife lying on the ground. One quick swipe at the outlaw gave her an opportunity to stagger to her feet.

Run, Kit, run. Her bruised thighs ached and each step brought excruciating pain through her womb. Men cursed behind her. Their hands pinched her naked skin as she ran.

Cresting the hill, her rapists close at her heels, she turned to fight. Her foot slipped, and she felt herself falling down the steep embankment toward the lake.

A scream tore from her throat as she fell into the water. Cold liquid filled her lungs. She struggled to kick, to rise to the surface, to breathe.

"Kit, wake up." Garret's command reached into her terror. A woman's scream nearly drowned his voice out. As she escaped her nightmare, she realized the scream was her own. She gulped for breath as though the icy water still clogged her lungs.

Arms enveloped her and Garret's anguished whisper pulled her to reality. "Sweetheart, I'm here." Tears welled in his eyes as he kissed and hugged her, then kissed her again. "I'm so sorry, Kit. I should have told you."

"You lied." She choked out the accusation.

"Kit, you were in no condition to ride with Hawk. You needed time to heal."

"Not that." She pulled away from him. "I remember, everything. Jando did rape me. You weren't the first."

Garret found his throat dry and parched as a desert. Sadness rimmed her eyes and the luster drained from the sapphire orbs. Her dark hair draped over her face, covering her shame. And that stuck in Garret's craw. Kit O'Shane had nothing—nothing—to be ashamed of.

He used one finger to tip her chin up. With his other hand, he brushed back the ebony tresses. "I told you I was the first man you ever gave yourself to. The first to make love to you. And I am. Kit, I love you. What happened before doesn't matter to me. It doesn't matter to us.''

He rocked her in his arms, comforting and soothing her. She lay limp in his embrace, crying for her loss and thankful for Garret's understanding.

Though warmed by Garret's comfort, she still felt stripped of her safety and vulnerable to attack. The shadows in the cabin became phantoms; the reflected light of the lantern in the window, peering eyes. Shivers racked her body. Somewhere in the night, Jando waited for his revenge.

''I need my knife.'' When was the last time she had held the bone hilt? She hadn't needed her weapon these last months. Garret's nurturing love had kept her secure.

''I haven't seen it since the fight in the canyon. It could be anywhere. I'll get you another one.''

''I need *that* knife, Garret.'' How could she explain the importance of one blade? That knife helped her escape Jando before. That knife could keep her safe from Jando's treachery.

The search for Jando had always been dangerous, but now that risk doubled. Jando knew their names and their faces. If he was hurt, the old rustler was canny enough to lie low in some hole-in-the-wall until he healed. Then he would come after her and her brother.

''Garret, I need to ride out to the canyon. I want to see for myself and look for my knife.

''You're staying right here.'' Garret pointed straight at his bed. ''Your arm isn't up to snuff yet, you've just had a helluva revelation about what happened in the village, and we're getting married come the end of the week.''

''But Hawk—''

"Can give his congratulations when he gets back."

"Have you heard from Hawk?"

"Nothing. But first thing in the morning, I'll send out telegrams. We'll find him."

"No!" Fear laced her tone. A flood of telegrams would only draw attention to Hawk. And danger.

Garret ran his fingers through his hair, freeing his cowlick. "Why? Kit, I can't help if I don't know what's going on."

She trusted Garret, but if Father ever found out about her rape, he would hold her brother responsible. Father had the power to have Hawk arrested, perhaps even executed. Hadn't she already made her brother suffer enough by not killing Jando? Did she have the right to reveal confidences that could put Hawk's life in jeopardy?

"There is a powerful man looking for my brother and me." This much she could tell Garret. "He would pay handsomely for information on Hawk's whereabouts."

"Who is this man?"

"I can't tell you. It's Hawk's life on the line, and it's up to him to tell you. I trust you, Garret, but—"

He shushed her protests and guided her back under the quilt. "Then that's all that counts. In the meantime, we'll bring Raven here to the ranch and raise him as our own until Hawk returns. Now, you rest."

She lay in the big bed, her head nestled on a pillow, the quilt tucked under her chin. The night sounds outside sent prickles of apprehension down her spine. Was that the wind through the firs or the spirits of the past demanding retribution? Was Jando hiding behind the cabin, waiting for a chance to kill Garret and torture her? "Garret, don't leave." She clutched his hand, every nerve alert and alarmed.

"I won't, love." He lay next to her, slipped one arm

under her neck and covered her thighs with one powerful leg. Imprisoned by Garret's protective caress, Kit lay with her eyes closed but awake to every strange sound. If only she had her knife or knew for certain that the demon from the past had really returned to hell.

The cabin door crashed open and Kit jumped. The plate of peach pies in her hand dipped. Cade made a diving catch and saved the pastries from splattering on the floor. "Whoa, sis. Getting ready for your wedding tommorow's got you jumpier than a jackrabbit in a den of wolves."

It wasn't the wedding that had Kit's nerves frayed. Every bump in the night made her heart pound and she feared Jando had found her.

She wiped her hands down her apron and wished she felt the reassuring bulge of her knife on her hip. "Garret's invited so many people."

"He's proud of you." Cade sneaked a pie from the plate. "And he just invited McVery."

"Who talked Garret into inviting half the other ranchers?"

"A shindig's a shindig." Cade munched his pilfered treat. "This wedding's giving everyone a chance to celebrate before winter sets in and we all get stuck in our cabins. Of course, some might not mind being shut up in one room for a couple of weeks." He gave her a sly wink.

Winter meant months of not knowing about Jando's survival and not having her weapon. She'd go crazy wondering, afraid that the rustler would show up at her doorstep. If she could just retrace her steps, perhaps she would remember some small detail that could put her worry to rest. "Cade, have you been back out to the canyon?"

Cade licked his fingers and screwed up his face. "You don't want to go out there."

"Hawk went."

"'Cause he's still searching." Cade tugged at her braid like a schoolboy. "But you ain't. Everything you want is standing right there by the corral. Garret ain't as good-looking as me, or half as charming, but he's a good man."

"Yes, you're right, Cade." She pointed toward the table. "Now, go on, I've got a mountain of work to finish by the time the guests arrive tomorrow."

As she shut the door, Cade murmured, "If you need us, for anything, you call. We all think a heap of you, sis."

"Thank you, Cade. I think a lot of you all, too." *Too much to bring danger to your door.* As long as there was a chance that Jando lived, there was a chance that the outlaw would find her here on the Rockin' G. His vengeance would include Garret and his brother.

Marrying Garret tomorrow would be the happiest day of her life, and it could also be the saddest. If he or Cade was hurt because of Jando, she would never forgive herself.

I can't live this way. She had to see that canyon, convince herself that Jando died, or ride off, freeing Garret from Jando's retribution.

Stubborn determination took hold. She would ride to the canyon today. Sweeping peach peelings into a tin, Kit formulated a plan. If she left now, she could make the canyon in a few hours.

She pulled herself up straight, put on Garret's old coat, hefted the tin on her hip and stepped outside. The morning sun added a bit of heat to the crisp day. By noon, the day might be warm enough to shed a coat. By noon, she should be at the canyon.

"Kit." Garret spotted her and left the men near the

corral. His green eyes lit with concern as he approached. "Is everything all right?"

She stepped off the porch and noticed a few more lines near his eyes. Worry lines for her. "Garret, I'm fine. Now get back to work."

"Here, let me take that for you." He moved to take the refuse.

She pulled away from him. "I'm just taking it out to the waste heap behind the barn. I can do it."

"Your arm—"

"Can handle this." He conceded the argument with a shrug of his shoulders. As he turned to walk back to the corral where the men were breaking horses, she called to him. "Oh, and, Garret, with all the preparations for tomorrow, I've got food everywhere in the cabin. Could you eat in the bunkhouse today?"

"Sure. I've smelled peach pie since sunrise. I'll come get you for the nooning."

"Don't bother." Kit bit her lower lip and lied. "I'll just get something in the cabin. I don't want to leave my pies." She wagged her finger at the crew. "Too many peach-pie-hungry men around." *And I don't want you finding out I'm gone too soon.*

"Especially Cade." Garret laughed, a light of humor in his eyes. Kit wanted to run to him and give him a tight hug, but held back. She couldn't afford to be weak, but conceded to just one tender moment. "Garret?"

"Yes?"

"I love you. Remember that."

"Won't have to." In two steps he strode to her side. "You're going to remind me every day, just like this." His mouth covered hers. The kiss sent the pit of her stomach in a whirl and her heart hammering. As their lips parted, she gazed into his face, memorizing the dark highlights of his eyes, the color of his sandy hair and the smell of him.

She scurried to the barn as Garret walked back to the corral. Dropping the tin, she headed for her horse then stopped. The Appaloosa had the first stall. Her absence would be easily detected. She needed a horse that had a stall toward the back and one that few people rode. But the mount had to be fast, at least as quick as her mare.

Walking down the row of saddle horses, she found her animal. The black. The stallion's powerful legs could cover the miles to the canyon faster than her Appaloosa and no one rode the animal but her.

Throwing a blanket on his back, she guided the animal to the barn door. She peeked outside. If she could just round the barn without anyone seeing her, she could walk the horse to the firs and mount there.

The crew had their gazes glued to the corral. Vega had another mustang under him, bronco riding with flourish. Sunlight reflected off the silver conchos on his wide, bat-wing chaps. Cade had a fistful of dollars high in the air, calling for bets on how many horses Vega could break by noon.

While the men haggled over the odds, Kit led the black around the barn then waited, expecting Garret to run around the corner after her and demand to know where she was going. Nothing happened. Her heart slamming against her chest, Kit led the black into the woods, mounted, then headed for the canyon. To her knife, her peace of mind and, if she was lucky, Jando's corpse.

Chapter Twenty-Nine

"Riders comin' in." Cracker chewed his tobacco as he nodded his shiny bald spot toward the Rockin' G gate.

Garret jumped down from the corral and studied the riders. "Looks like the sheriff and Eli Benton."

Cade asked, "But who's the big man?"

"Never seen him before." Garret glanced back at the cabin. He hadn't seen Kit since before the noon meal. She must be baking a wall of peach pies for their wedding tomorrow. It'd be best, while the sheriff and Eli Benton were here, that she stayed in the cabin. "Davidson, run over and tell Kit to stay inside."

"I'll tell her, sir, but that don't mean she'll listen." The young man trotted toward the cabin as the riders came to a halt.

"Which one of you is Garret Blaine?" the big-boned man demanded. He stared at the Rockin' G crew with contempt.

"I am." Garret stepped forward, aware of the Navy Colt on his hip. "What's your business?"

"You're my business." The big man draped his expensive wool coat to the side, exposing a silk brocade vest. "I'm Sam Benton, and I want to see those two Indians. Now."

Garret widened his stance and glanced at Cade to his left. His brother stood casually, his gun hand ready. Vega had made his way to cover the sheriff and Eli. Liam didn't have a gun, but he was in arm's reach of either man, and his fists would find a victim.

Thankfully, Kit remained tucked away in their cabin. He noticed Davidson on the porch, standing in front of the door. Good thinking. Hold her in if need be.

Sam Benton gave him a wicked smile. "Now, you're calling off this wedding and giving me both those breeds. I hear they've been rustling cattle."

The sheriff chuckled, his belly shaking from the exercise. "Told Blaine to hand 'em over, but he had other plans for that squaw. And so do I."

Cade made a draw for his gun. Garret moved faster. He reached up and yanked the sheriff's tin badge, hauling the overblown sack of air off his saddle. He landed in a mud hole made from melted early snow and horse urine. Garret held the man's face inches above the smelly mixture. "You ever talk about my wife like that again, and you'll be eating this."

"Blaine, that's an officer of the law," Eli Benton's high-pitched whine reminded Garret.

"He's an officer of Benton law," Liam shot back.

"And that ought to remind you of what kind of man I am." Sam Benton dismounted. Dirt wouldn't dare cling to his shiny calf-high leather boots. He stood with a wide stance, dressed in black from his felt hat to his tight riding breeches.

Garret released the sheriff so quickly, the man fell forward into the muck. "Get off my land."

Fear stabbed a hole in his bravado. Sam Benton didn't

have the man power today or tomorrow to take Kit by force, but what about next week or next month? The Bentons could hire a dozen men, two dozen men. If old Sam really wanted Kit, he would find a way to take her.

If need be, Garret would sell the ranch for whatever hard cash he could get. Then he and Kit could go farther west.

Taking his time, Sam removed a cigar from his breast pocket, used the tip of his boot to strike a match, then took deep, satisfying puffs from the stogie. His tone turned cruel. "You turn those breeds over to me now, or you'll never even smell the ink on that army contract, much less sign it."

"Hawk's not here."

"Hawk?" Sam's eyes narrowed, his upper lip curled. "Eli, I told you to be on the lookout for an Indian buck by the name of Winterhawk."

The little man squirmed in the saddle. "I didn't bother to ask his name. And you didn't mention two half-breeds, just a white woman and Indian buck."

"Get that squaw out here now. I want to see her." Sam pointed toward the cabin and crooked his finger at Cracker.

The old cook shot a line of tobacco juice that landed right on the toe of Sam Benton's shiny boots. "Don't reckon I will."

"Don't reckon you can." Davidson ran up from the open barn. "Cap'n, I can't find Kit anywhere. Her Appaloosa's here, but the black's missing."

"Hellfire!" Cade grabbed Garret's arm. "She was asking about the canyon."

Benton mounted and motioned for the dirt-covered sheriff to do the same. "Do you know where that canyon is?"

The sheriff spit out mud and an answer. "Yep, about two hours away."

"Then we're riding for that canyon."

Garret snatched the powerful man's reins, halting the bay, Eli and the sheriff. "Davidson, get me my horse." Looking Sam Benton in the eye, he added, "You're not riding without me."

The stench of death lay over the canyon valley like a coffin shroud, thick and heavy. An unnatural silence coated the steep rock walls. The black's hoofbeats sounded muffled in the light snow covering the valley floor. The pure white covering made the grotesque scene more horrible. Trepidation made Kit's heart skip a beat. Determination made her walk the black through the carnage.

Trees, scarred by fire, rimmed the charred meadow. Kit led her mount between carcasses of longhorns, their eye sockets vacant, mouths open, bodies bloated. Half-chewed heads and ripped-open bellies told Kit that the wolves, mountain lions and buzzards had already staked a claim on the dead animals.

Everything smelled of the fire. The scorched sap of the firs, the singed hides of the longhorns and the blackened earth she walked on. A putrid fog hung over the canyon. Buzzards formed a spiraling circle overhead, waiting for her to leave before landing to feast.

She tethered the black to an evergreen and headed for the center of the valley, the spot where the fire had consumed Jando. Her knife and proof of Jando's death would be near where they had fought. White bones, gnawed and scratched by meat eaters, littered the ground. Garret could be right, the predators might have made it impossible to determine what really happened to the outlaw.

Bits of wood and broken whiskey bottles outlined the area where the bonfire had been. Kit dragged her boot tip along the dirt, unearthing shards of glass, bits of bone and bullet slugs. The overpowering smell of burnt hides and flesh made her want to gag, but she kept searching for anything that would put to rest Jando's outcome. Tears threatened to erupt as hours slipped away and she found nothing.

Sitting on her heels, she dug her fingers into the black earth. She groped the tangle of dead grass roots and trash, her mind telling her to give up, her heart ordering her to continue. There had to be something that would put her unease to rest.

Her fingers grazed something smooth and hard. Desperately, she tore at the ground, darkening her nails with the ash. A glint of ivory lay exposed. Grabbing a flat rock, Kit stabbed at the hard-packed ground, sending clumps of soil flying.

"My knife." Kit clawed the last bit of the bone hilt free. The blade was broken off, but she recognized the detailed line design on the bone. An unbearable burnt stench choked her. The wind must have shifted, stirring more of the embers. "If I only knew what happened to Jando."

A wheeze sounded to her left. Startled, Kit turned and faced a rifle barrel. Lifting her gaze, she screamed, the sound echoing off the walls, carrying her terror throughout the canyon.

"He lived." Jando aimed his rifle at her. As he spoke, his burnt eye seeped liquid, his disfigured mouth drooled, and patches of his scarred skin flaked off. "And what's left of me is gonna enjoy killin' you."

Chapter Thirty

Garret beat the posse to the canyon. He reined the gelding to a walk when he entered the boxed valley. The smell of death seeped into his pores.

The rest of the men thundered into the canyon, then they, too, slowed at the sight of the dead animals. A flock of buzzards, feeding on a cow, took off and formed a circle in the air above.

"Kit," Garret called, and listened as her name repeated over and over again, drifting away, just as his chance of happiness seemed to be, also. Where was she?

"There's the black." Cade dismounted and pointed toward the grazing stallion tethered to a fir.

The sight eased one worry for Garret. Kit hadn't ridden off after Hawk. But it created another. Why hadn't she answered him?

"You find that girl and no excuses," Sam Benton ordered. "I want a good look at her and the buck." The sheriff and Eli nearly jumped out of their saddles to obey.

The breeze carried the acrid smell of burnt hide, then a voice called, "I figure I know what yore a-lookin' for."

Garret turned and his blood froze in his veins. Standing near the treeline, a gun barrel at Kit's throat, what was left of Jando sneered. His face, horribly disfigured by the fire, wore a satanic smile that showed his gums and missing teeth. "I figured you'd come ridin' for her, Blaine. Now I got both of ya."

"Hellfire!" Cade reacted by going for his gun.

"Draw it and she's a dead woman." Jando, leaning against a tree trunk, shoved the barrel harder against Kit's throat and drew her tighter in his clawlike grasp. "Throw them guns this way. Real slow."

Their guns hit the ground with quiet thuds, and so did their chances of taking Jando.

Sam Benton's face turned gray, and his blue eyes flickered with anger and hope. "Kitten?" He took a few faltering steps, then his walk became more sure. Garret saw Kit look at him for help and not at the big man striding toward her.

A few steps away from Jando, Benton demanded, "I'm Samuel Benton. Release my daughter."

Jando chuckled, his melted features more hideous in laughter. "So the great Sam Benton's got a by-blow." He pushed his girth off the tree with his backside and used Kit to steady himself.

"Katherine Angeline Benton is not a by-blow," Sam roared. "Her late mother was an O'Shane, one of the wealthiest families in Chicago."

"And the other one?" Drool drizzled down the rustler's chin. "What about the big buck?"

Remembering Kit's fear for her brother, Garret added, "Hawk's your son?"

"He's not mine," Sam shouted. "He's my wife's mistake."

"I aim to kill that Injun, too." Jando's putrid breath nearly made Kit choke. The hard edge of the Colt barrel dug into her skin. Uncertainty cut into her heart. Garret knew everything now, and the knowledge offered him a heady power. Marrying Kit O'Shane gave him nothing but a loving wife. Giving up Katherine Benton would give him the riches and influence that he had craved. Turning Hawk over to her father would buy Sam Benton's generosity.

"Looks like I got more than I bargained for." Still using her as a shield, Jando inched closer to the abandoned guns. His fire-damaged legs moved stiffly and he used Kit as a cane for his massive weight. Pain lodged in her elbow and up her shoulder.

Her free arm ached from her injured shoulder and cramped position. She swiveled her shoulders, both to ease the tightness and to avoid contact with the outlaw. Her fingers brushed her jeans and felt a bulge in her pocket. Her knife hilt.

"Let her go and I'll pay a sizable reward." Sam Benton motioned to the rustler with an impatient wave. "Name your price."

Jando nearly doubled over with laughter. "What's a man like me gonna do with money, Benton? Buy women? Don't think they'll have me at any price."

His sharp jerk stabbed his manhood against Kit's backside. While struggling to put some distance between them, she managed to retrieve what was left of her knife and palm it. All she needed was an opportunity to use it.

Jando nodded toward his hostages. "I'm savin' a shot for yer brother. And for you. It's gonna take ya hours to die. And while yore guts are fallin' out, I'm takin' yore woman—again."

"Kitten!" Her father's face turned white with anger. "Just like your mother. Trusting the wrong men. Hawk left you, didn't he, to face this criminal, and Blaine's just after money. Maybe now you'll listen to me about men and the world.''

"I aim to teach her a lesson, one she'll die learnin'." Armed with the revolver and with Kit as his protection, Jando leaned heavily on her, increasing the force on her arm. His misshapen legs shuffled backward, toward a boulder and a sturdier support. As he took a step, he faltered, and the gun barrel slipped from Kit's bruised skin.

The instant the pinching steel left her throat, she reacted. She summoned what strength she had left and plunged the broken knife into Jando's gut. The outlaw expelled a surprised breath. He teetered on his crooked legs. His hand shot out to use the boulder as a prop. The grip on her arm relaxed and Kit twisted free.

Garret wanted to curse her brashness and applaud her quick thinking. He pushed her behind him then joined his brother, diving for their weapons.

"Hold it right there." Jando lurched upward, his back using the boulder as a foundation. He aimed the Colt at Garret and Cade.

His fingers inches from his gun, Garret paused, his body tight with pent-up rage.

"It's a good thing I want to kill ya slow, now, ain't it," Jando taunted as Garret and Cade backed away. "A few minutes of livin's like an eternity when yore this close to dyin'."

Garret nestled Kit close to him and wished his mere flesh could protect her from Jando's sadistic plans.

"Garret, I wanted to tell you about—" Kit's gaze swept to where her father stood.

"Later." Garret squeezed her waist and hoped he spoke the truth, that there would be a later for all of them.

The crazed gleam in the rustler's eyes turned to blood-lust. With a smile on his face, Jando cocked the revolver. "I'm gonna kill every last Blaine and Benton."

A whoosh sounded from the timber and Jando's one good eye bulged. His mouth gaped open as an arrow pierced his throat and blood sprayed Sam's fine linen shirt. Kit screamed as Garret pushed her behind him, ready to sacrifice himself to protect her. Cade lunged for the guns, rolled to his feet and threw Garret a Colt.

From the firs, a tall, big-boned figure emerged. Through the carcasses of the dead longhorns, he walked slowly toward them, the breeze rustling a blue feather in his hair.

"You forgot about the O'Shanes, Jando." Hawk stood over the still-living rustler. Blood sprayed from the arrow wound, sprinkling dark red stains on Hawk's leather leggings. Lifting his knife overhead, he spoke in a calm, clear voice. "Now feel Cheyenne justice. I give your soul to the birds to rip to pieces."

Hawk issued a long, eerie war cry and plunged the blade deep into the evil man. Jando's body jerked, then he lay still, his evil finally conquered. Above, the circling buzzards broke their pattern, screeched and chased an unseeable prey.

"My wife has been avenged." His hands dripping with Jando's blood, Hawk turned toward Sam Benton.

"Stay away." Sam scrambled backward, colliding with Garret and Kit. "He'll kill me."

"And you damn well deserve it." Garret stepped between Hawk and Benton.

"Move aside, Blaine," Hawk commanded. "This man kept my mother from me."

"You savages kidnapped Kathleen," Sam argued.

"She joined the Cheyenne. She left only to save us from your Bluecoats." Hawk's stare drilled into Benton's.

"This I now know, because my sister had the bravery to find me and tell me. My mother's last words were of me."

"You were a mistake." Sam's voice rose and fell in accusation. "Kathleen loved me. Only me. She slept with your father out of gratitude. And you repaid that gift by allowing Kathleen's legitimate child to be mauled and raped. You planned it as a way to get even with Kathleen for abandoning you."

Pulling the bloody knife from Jando's chest, Hawk advanced toward Sam Benton.

"Hawk, don't," Kit shouted to her brother as he approached. "I know you weren't responsible for Jando."

Garret refused to budge, blocking Hawk from his blood-covered quarry. "Think of your son. If you kill Benton, you'll be on the run for the rest of your life."

"Kill that Indian." Sam Benton issued the command in a high-pitched voice similar to Eli's. Weaponless, neither the sheriff nor Eli seemed tempted to stop Hawk.

Strutting like a gobbler in a peahen house, Benton looked at Garret and the gun in his holster. "Blaine, I'm not about to let you marry my daughter. Your only hope of signing that army contract is with my consent."

Sam closed his hand into a tight fist, just as he planned to do to Garret's future. "If you protect that buck or marry my daughter, you'll never do business with the army. Kill the Indian, and I'll give you Abigail and the contract. Do it my way, and that ranch of yours will be selling all the beef and horses you can handle. Go against me, and you're finished."

There it was, laid out for Garret like a Sunday picnic. He'd have a money roll big enough to choke a cow. With old Sam's backing, and Abigail as his missus, people would be calling Garret "mister" with respect in their tone, if not in their hearts. He had a lot to gain by putting a shot in the Indian and giving Kit back to her father.

Beside him, Kit tensed in his arms, but she said nothing, and that trust made Garret smile. He had a helluva lot more to lose if he turned his back on her. She had unlocked his heart to love, and that was a key no amount of money could ever buy. "Can't do that, Sam. Hawk here has to walk my bride down the aisle tomorrow. That is, if she still wants me."

"Garret, do you want Kit O'Shane, or Katherine Angeline Benton?" Kit's gaze flickered from her father to Garret. "Father won't relent. He'll make life miserable for you."

Garret smiled and kissed her upturned face. "I want the woman I fell in love with. A pants-wearing, prickly-pear-tempered, stubborn-as-a-mule, bronco-riding woman."

"Well, that answers that question." Cade slapped Hawk and Garret on the back. "That can only describe Kit O'Shane."

Kit gazed up at Garret, then kissed him tenderly. "I love you, Garret Blaine, with all my heart."

"Kitten, you can't mean to desert your father." Sam's voice turned silky and soothing. "You're doomed to keep repeating your mother's mistakes. Blaine is just another user. Listen to me, I can make this whole episode disappear. I'll take you to Europe. No one will know what's happened. And if there are any problems to be disposed of from this affair, I'll handle that, too, just like I did for your mother."

"And lock me away like you did Mama?" Kit's voice wavered between fear and anger.

Garret now understood her wish to keep her father's name a secret. Wild-spirited Kit would wilt within the confines of any prison walls, no matter how luxurious the cell.

"Blaine, I'm offering you everything that you ever wanted." Sam Benton tempted Garret like the devil in the desert.

But Garret knew that with Kit at his side, he had found the spring rain that would shed beauty in his harsh life.

"Benton, there's nothing you have that I want." At his side, comfortable in his embrace, was the answer to every dream he ever had. Kit had rustled Garret's heart and burned a brand so deep with her love that it would never fade.

When Kit became his bride, he would finally have accomplished what his mother always wanted. For him to forget the past and build a future with a woman he loved.

"Let's go, we've got a heap of work to do before the preacher comes tomorrow." Garret hooked an arm around Kit's waist and led his men toward their horses.

Hawk turned his back on the man who had deprived him of a mother, but not her memory or her love. That lived on in his sister's voice and caring.

Joining the Rockin' G crew, Hawk looked at his sister's beaming face and knew the spirits would never haunt her again. Blaine moved his mount so that his leg brushed hers and leaned over to kiss her.

Sorrow and happiness cut through Hawk's heart. Happiness that these two had found each other after so much pain. Sorrow as he remembered his own love for his dead wife. Such love had been gifted to him once, it would never come again.

Cade offered him a hand up, and Hawk settled behind him, riding double. "Well, what do you know, me and you are gonna be family. Enjoy the ride, brother-in-law."

"*Step*-brother-in-law," Hawk corrected.

"Same thing." Cade spurred his horse and the pony lunged forward, nearly unseating Hawk. "Yipp-eee-iii-kii-yaa!"

Speaking to his sister and Blaine riding next to them, Hawk shouted, "Cade, he will never be a good Indian."

Kit laughed, her fear disappearing with the hearty sound. "You're right." Then, reaching out and touching Garret's hand, she added, "But we're gonna make a wonderful family."

* * * * *

This season, make your destination Great Britain with four exciting stories from

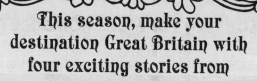

Harlequin® Historical

In October 1999, look for

LADY SARAH'S SON #483 by Gayle Wilson
(England, 1814)

and

THE HIDDEN HEART #484 by Sharon Schulze
(Wales, 1213)

In November 1999, look for

ONE CHRISTMAS NIGHT #487
by **Ruth Langan, Jacqueline Navin and Lyn Stone**
(Scottish Highlands 1540, England 1193
and Scotland 1320)

and

A GENTLEMAN OF SUBSTANCE #488 by Deborah Hale
(England, 1814)

Harlequin Historicals
Where reading is truly a vacation!

HARLEQUIN®
Makes any time special ™

"This book is DYNAMITE!"
—Kristine Rolofson

"A riveting page turner..."
—Joan Elliott Pickart

"Enough twists and turns to keep everyone
guessing... What a ride!"
—Jule McBride

See what all your favorite authors
are talking about.

Coming October 1999 to a retail store near you.

In celebration of Harlequin®'s golden anniversary

Enter to win a *dream!* You could win:

- A luxurious trip for two to *The Renaissance Cottonwoods Resort* in Scottsdale, Arizona, or
- A bouquet of flowers once a week for a year from **FTD**, or
- A $500 shopping spree, or
- A fabulous bath & body gift basket, including **K-tel's** *Candlelight and Romance* 5-CD set.

Look for **WIN A DREAM** flash on specially marked Harlequin® titles by Penny Jordan, Dallas Schulze, Anne Stuart and Kristine Rolofson in October 1999*.

This season,

COMING NEXT MONTH FROM

HARLEQUIN
HISTORICALS

"PEOPLE OF GODSWORLD!"

A voice boomed out from the huge, glittering thing overhead.

"This is your only warning. We have the means to defend ourselves. We have weapons that can shatter Godsworld like a hen's egg hit by a sledgehammer. Turn back now, return to your homes, and no ill will befall you; continue on, and you will be destroyed. This is your only warning. *All* we want to do is trade. We do not wish to harm anyone, but further advance in our direction will be met with force." The device hung silently fo̶ ̶ ̶moment longer, then swooped away w̶ ̶ ̶ ̶ ̶ faint buzz.

"It's a Devil's tr̶ ̶ ̶ ̶ ̶ ̶ ̶owed to his waiting army̶ ̶ ̶ ̶ ̶ ̶ ̶ ̶arch! In the name of the ̶ ̶ ̶ ̶

Other Avon Books by
Lawrence Watt-Evans

THE CHROMOSOMAL CODE

SHINING STEEL

LAWRENCE WATT-EVANS

AVON
PUBLISHERS OF BARD, CAMELOT, DISCUS AND FLARE BOOKS

AVON BOOKS
A division of
The Hearst Corporation
1790 Broadway
New York, New York 10019

Copyright © 1986 by Lawrence Watt Evans
Published by arrangement with the author
Library of Congress Catalog Card Number: 85-91507
ISBN: 0-380-89671-0

First Avon Printing, June 1986

AVON TRADEMARK REG. U. S. PAT. OFF. AND IN
OTHER COUNTRIES, MARCA REGISTRADA, HECHO EN
U. S. A.

Printed in the U. S. A.

K-R 10 9 8 7 6 5 4 3 2 1

Dedicated to
Benjamin C. Ray,
who probably doesn't
remember me

Religion . . . is the opium of the people.
　　　　　　　　　　　　—Karl Marx

If you ask me, to some people it's more like PCP.
　　　　　　　　　　　　—Walter Vance Awsten

Chapter One

He saith among the trumpets, Ha, ha;
and he smelleth the battle afar off, the
thunder of the captains, and the shouting.

—Job 39:25

THE brass casings gleamed golden in the firelight as he picked
up the first bullet. He handed it to a waiting warrior and sol-
emnly spoke the ancient and meaningless ritual phrase,
"Mekkit kant!"

The warrior accepted it with equal solemnity, then stepped
back to make room for the next.

The ten bullets were distributed to ten men, and each of
the chosen carefully slid the precious cartridge into his rifle.
When all had done so, they settled comfortably on the ground
to await the order to attack. Some cast occasional glances at
the eastern horizon.

Around them their less fortunate comrades, those who had
not been chosen to carry firearms in the coming battle, covered the hillside. Many of them, as they polished swords and
knives, also looked to the east.

"Won't do no darn good watching the sunrise," said the
man who passed out the ammunition. "We go on Captain
John's word, not before."

"He told us we'd attack at dawn, same as always," one of
the riflemen replied.

1

"We probably will, then," said the first. "But it's at his word."

The other shrugged and looked to the east. The sky was blue now, no longer black, and the first warm hints of pink were beginning to show. Whatever the signal, he told himself, it would not be long in coming. He cradled his rifle in his arms and looked down the slope at the waiting horses.

The tent flaps behind him parted and the commander stepped out, already dressed in his riding leathers, his sword on his hip and his helmet on his head.

"All right, boys," he called, "get your horses. We're riding out now. Got your bullets, riflemen? Habakkuk?"

"All set, John," answered the man who had distributed the cartridges. The ten chosen recipients nodded confirmation.

"Good; don't waste them. We want this village as a base; this isn't just a raid for the fun of it. Shoot to kill, and use your swords, not your lungs. We mean business, we aren't just out to scare them."

There was a muttered chorus of assent.

"Well, don't just stand there, then; get the horses!" The commander waved, and the men hurried down to their waiting mounts.

The commander's own horse was led up the slope by a young aide; it was beneath the dignity of the captain's office to fetch the beast for himself. That, at any rate, was what the Elders insisted, and that was why John forced himself to wait while the boy cajoled the reluctant animal. He would have preferred fetching his own horse, as the other warriors did, but that went against custom—and custom was very important, as no one could say for sure, in these benighted latter days when so many had fallen away from the true faith, what was mere habit and what was the one way.

Hiding his impatience, John waited.

The instant the animal was within reach he snatched the reins from the boy and swung himself into the saddle. A glance around assured him that at least half his men were astride; that was enough for the next step. The others could mount during the invocation or catch up later. This hurry would keep them on their toes; he could not allow anyone to get soft.

"Douse the fire," he ordered the boy, "and break camp. After today we'll either be in the village or we'll be dead." That said, he turned toward his waiting men and shouted, "Hear us, O Lord!"

The warriors watched expectantly.

"O Lord, it's me, John Mercy-of-Christ, who You've made the Armed Guardian of the True Word and Flesh, and I'm speaking for all these men here. We're about to go into battle, Lord, to fight against people who have left the true path, the way of the True Word and Flesh. We're fighting for You, Lord, to bring Your truth to those who have spurned it, and we ask that You bless this task, and these men who attempt it. And if any of us fall today, Lord, we know that You've got a special warm welcome waiting and an honored place in Heaven for us, because we're doing Your work. Amen."

"Amen," his men replied.

Satisfied, John took a final look at his advance unit of cavalry, more than a hundred strong, then turned and spurred his mount up the slope. "To battle," he bellowed, "in the name of the Lord!"

"In the name of the Lord!" his men shouted back. In a great rushing mob they stampeded up and over the crest of the hill.

John had not been foolish enough to make camp right atop his target, where it might be found by any idiot chasing a lost pup. Beyond the hill lay a short stretch of broken country, not fit for farming or much of anything else, consisting largely of gray stone speckled with scraggly red mosses. A mile or so to the northeast, beyond this worthless expanse of rock, a long, grassy slope led down to the marshes that edged the Little New Jordan. At the foot of that slope, nestled against the marsh, stood the village he intended to make his supply base and reserve headquarters for the coming campaign.

The village was not actually in enemy hands, so far as he

knew; its people were neutral in the current conflict. He was not overly concerned by that, save that it meant the defenses might be weak. He knew nothing about the inhabitants of the town, not even their name for the place, and cared just as little; all that mattered was that they were in a convenient location and that the survivors would presumably make decent slave labor until the Elders could convert them. After all, they were heretics. If they had not been, they would have joined with his own people, the People of the True Word and Flesh, long ago. That went without saying.

The initial enthusiasm of the first riotous charge up the slope faded quickly in the intervening rough. John had expected that, and even planned it. This would provide him with an opportunity to gather his men into some sort of order, rather than letting them gallop down in threes and fours, wasting their numbers.

"Keep together!" he bellowed. "Bring it in, keep it tight!"

Those nearest him heard and obeyed; some of those further out, seeing the inward movement, copied it.

"Keep together! Pass the order on! We strike as a single group!"

The order was passed; reluctantly, the hotheads in the lead dropped back to join the main body, while the stragglers strained to catch up. The central group was moving at a steady trot, the best pace that the dim light and broken land safely allowed.

The glow in the east had spread across half the sky, and the edge of the sun's disc was beginning to show as a bloody red line on the horizon when the leading edge of the mass of horsemen reached the grassy slope.

"Hold up!" the commander bellowed. "Hold up! No one goes until I give the word! This isn't a raid!"

A few horses were already on the slope, but their riders reined in and turned them back. It took several minutes for the whole company to gather along the brink; by the time John was satisfied that all were ready the sun was showing a half-oval.

When he was certain that all his men and horses were where he wanted them to be, and all facing in the right direction, he glanced down at the village. There was no wall or stockade; small villages off the trade routes were usually not bothered.

Despite the noise his men had made, and the delay until nearly full daylight, he saw no sign of movement below, no sign that anyone suspected he and his soldiers were nearby. No one was working in the narrow grainfields squeezed in between the hillside and the marsh. It was utterly still, and he wondered if the inhabitants might have fled.

He drew his sword, the steel shining red in the early light.

"In the name of the Lord!" he cried, and spurred his horse down the slope.

The first charge had been mere showmanship, to get the blood stirring and to fire up his men. This was the real thing, and he drummed his barbed heels on the horse's flanks, urging it to its fastest gallop. He raised his head briefly to call a final command. "Fire at will!"

Almost immediately he heard the report of a rifle, small and distant over the rush of wind around his speeding mount. Despite all warnings and imprecations, there was always at least one impatient idiot who wasted his bullet.

A moment later the foremost, John among them, were riding past the edge of the village, their steeds easily leaping the surrounding ditch and charging down the streets that ran between the neat rows of stone and nearwood houses. John glimpsed faces in windows, saw doors open and close as he galloped past; the town was not empty. He looked for a foeman to strike.

A second rifle shot sounded, then two together, and he heard a woman scream somewhere nearby. Something crashed loudly to the ground, startling him; his horse broke stride and slowed, jerking him about in the saddle.

Then a new sound, a strange, heavy, threatening sound like nothing he had ever heard before, drowned out everything but the pounding of hooves. The sound was something like hoofbeats, but far louder and more even. It reminded John slightly of an ancient steam engine he had once heard run.

He judged it to be coming from somewhere behind him and to his left. He yanked hard at the reins, struggling to turn his mount in the narrow street.

Men were screaming—men and horses, and he had seen no trace of horses in the village. Now the street around him was jammed with milling horses as his soldiers, like himself, tried to locate and identify the strange new sound.

The thunder of the charge was gone. Instead of a steady roar of hoofbeats he heard the frightened cries of wounded animals and the hoarse shouts of men, and that constant rhythmic hammering. He thought he heard his name being called, but could not be certain over the din.

He had hoped to avoid any serious losses in attacking such a small and lightly defended village; he had expected a quick surrender. It was plain that something was ruining his plans, and that if he did not regain control of events quickly the attack might turn into a disaster. Custom called for prayer at such a moment, but he did not feel that he could spare the time for that. He stood up in the stirrups, straining to see what was happening.

The lower part of the hillside was littered with downed horses and riders, some apparently dead, others still moving. Some horses, their saddles empty, were scattering and fleeing; a few of his men were fleeing after them. He could see no sign of what had wrought such carnage, unless it was the faint wisp of blue smoke that rose from a house at the edge of the village, the last house on the street where he rode, built close on the edge of the ditch.

Most of his warriors were still alive and ready to fight, but had become confused and frightened by the strange noise and the breaking of the charge. The noise continued unabated, but whatever had spread death across the slope had caught only the rearmost portion of the company. The rest were now riding up and down the village streets uncertain what to do. The enemy had not emerged to defend the town in the usual way, as John and his men had expected. Ordinarily, when the defenders remained hidden, the attackers would have dismounted and formed squads, then gone from house to house, taking prisoners, killing anyone who resisted, and raping and looting as they went. After seeing their comrades strewn dead and wounded across the hillside, however, no one was eager to dismount and reduce his chances of fleeing safely from whatever had cut those men down.

No one who had reached the village had fallen. All the dead and wounded lay on the slope, well away from the houses. The hammering noise continued, and John saw puffs of dust spewing up from the hillside, a puff with each beat, as if bullets were tearing up the turf. Startled, he realized what the noise was, and what had torn up his cavalry; old stories and childhood history lessons came back to him in a rush.

"Machine gun!" he called. "It's a machine gun! Stay clear!"

The old stories had told him about machine guns, tanks, and aircraft, about bombs and artillery and computers, and a dozen other lost secrets of warfare, all left behind on Old Earth. They had not, however, told him how to deal with such weapons.

He saw bullets ripping through downed men and horses, finishing off any that might still have been alive, and realized that the gunner was wasting an incredible amount of ammunition by keeping up the steady stream of fire. The man was a fool; if he ceased firing, he might lure more targets—John's men—back into range.

As if someone had heard his thoughts, the hammering abruptly stopped.

A good sniper should be able to pick the gunner off, John theorized, but some of his riflemen had fired their single bullets, and others were probably lying dead on the hillside. If any remained, John was not able to spot them.

Furthermore, he was not able to see the machine gunner, either.

A rifle cracked nearby; he ducked instinctively and spurred his mount forward as one of his men cried out in pain. That reminded him very effectively that the machine gunner was not the only man defending the village, nor even the only one with a gun and ammunition.

Ordinary weapons his men could handle, but someone had to stop the machine gun before the attackers could rally.

Or did he? After all, the gun was no longer firing. It might be out of ammunition. Even if it were not, it had not been turned against anyone who had reached the shelter of the village streets. Wherever the gun was concealed, its field of fire was apparently limited to the slope above the town.

As he came to that conclusion, however, he saw a window in the second story of the house at the end of the street explode outward in a shower of shattered glass, smashed from inside. One of his own warriors raised his rifle and fired, wasting his lone bullet and, so far as John could see, hitting nothing but the rafters of the house.

A dull metal snout, large and awkward and not quite like that of a rifle in shape, thrust out through the shattered window, trailing blue smoke and pointing down toward the street. That, surely, was the machine gun.

"Look out!" John cried. He was already moving, guiding his horse close to the house.

The gun fired a short burst, perhaps half a dozen rounds, and two warriors fell from their saddles while the rest scattered. The street cleared with amazing speed, leaving only John in the neighborhood of the terrifying weapon.

John, looking at the gun projecting from the window, guessed that it could not be tipped down very far. A gun like that, he was certain, would have too powerful a recoil to be handheld. It would need to be braced somehow, and in that case it could not be brought forward and held vertically out the window. That meant that if he hugged the wall of the house, right under the window, he could not be shot—at least, not with the machine gun. He was already fairly close; he urged his horse forward and even closer, huddling directly beneath the muzzle of the gun.

A man leaned out and started to look down the street for new targets; John's sword swept up and hacked a red line across his throat. The angle was wrong to get any real power behind the blow; John doubted that the wound would be fatal even if left untended. Still, the man made a wordless noise of pain and surprise and fell back out of sight. Inspired by this minor success—the first blood he had drawn so far—John gripped the hilt of his sword in both hands and brought it chopping forward against the protruding gun barrel. Metal rang loudly and the machine gun tottered back, aiming at empty sky but not visibly damaged.

Someone out of sight within tried to straighten it, and John chopped at it again, twisting it over against the window frame. He thought wryly that he would need a new sword after this; the edge would be ruined beyond recovery by such misuse.

"Ho, the True Word!" he called.

"Aye," a few voices responded; not all his men had fled beyond earshot.

"This house, last on the street," he bellowed. "Take this and you take the machine gun! I'll keep them from firing; you get inside and take the house!"

As if to disprove him, the gunner stopped trying to bring the gun to bear on anything, and instead fired a few rounds. They sprayed harmlessly across the rooftop opposite.

John laughed as he pressed his sword with both hands, forcing the gun aside. "Waste your bullets, heretic!" he called. "I don't mind!"

His horse shifted under him; he risked a glance back and saw that four of his men had heeded his call and were clustered at the door of the house, led by his lieutenant, Habakkuk Doomed-to-Die.

When he turned his eyes back toward the upper floor a man's sword arm was reaching out the broken window, preparing to slash at John's wrists. He parried, releasing the barrel of the machine gun; while the swordsman was blocking the opening the gunner would be unable to fire effectively in any case.

Fighting around the corner formed by the windowsill was awkward, but John had by far the better of it. In order to reach out far enough to strike at him or keep his blade away from the barrel of the gun the other swordsman had to put at least a hand out the window, giving John a good target, while John

could remain safely out of sight below the sill and still interfere with the use of the gun.

"Damn you, pagan!" a voice shouted from inside the
house.

Behind him, John's men kicked in the door of the house
and ran inside. A gunshot sounded, followed by a short
scream and much shouting.

The swordsman above locked blades with John, forcing
both swords back against one side of the window, and John
realized that his opponent meant to snap the blade. He pulled
his weapon clear, barely keeping his balance in the saddle.

"They're inside," someone called within the house.
"Turn the gun around!"

Desperately, John slashed at the gun barrel again, and the
blade of his sword rang loudly as it struck. That did not prevent the gunner from pulling the weapon back out of sight.

"Captain!" a voice called.

John turned and saw Habakkuk standing in the doorway.

"John, we can't get up the stairs. There are five or six of
them up there. We're going to burn them out."

John glanced back at the window. Neither the swordsman
nor the machine-gun barrel was visible. He would have preferred to have captured the gun intact, but that appeared to
be impossible.

"All right," he said, "but try to keep it from spreading. I
want this town as a base, not a ruin. If you can take anybody
alive, take them, and don't hurt them more than you have to.
I want to know where they got that thing. And once the gun's
out of the way, go house to house; take all the prisoners you
can, burn out anyone who gives you trouble, but keep enough
standing for us to use."

"Aye, Captain." Habakkuk raised his right hand in salute, then vanished back through the doorway.

John watched the window, sword ready, but saw no further activity there. A moment later the smell of smoke reached
his nostrils, and shortly after that his men came spilling out
the doorway, coughing, swords bare in their hands. One blade

was spattered with red, and only three men emerged where four had gone in.

He turned his horse, keeping one eye on the window. He heard renewed shouting inside as the defenders struggled to put out the fire. No sign of life showed at the window.

A few moments later the first two staggered out the door, choking and gasping. John's men were waiting, swords drawn; the villagers threw down their weapons and surrendered, to no one's surprise. This was not the first time John had seen smoke take the fight out of men.

A third villager emerged and was taken, but after him came a long moment of near silence. The smoke pouring from the door grew thicker, and thin streamers began to leak from the upper story.

Finally, a fourth defender dashed out, his sword ready; he was plainly not willing to give in easily. Two warriors pursued him, leaving John astride and Habakkuk afoot to watch the door and guard the three prisoners.

John shifted his grip on his sword; he was certain that the fleeing enemy was a diversion.

Sure enough, a few seconds later another man emerged. He swung immediately to the side and engaged Habakkuk, while behind him a sixth villager appeared, lugging a long, heavy metal thing. John spurred his horse and clouted this last man with his sword. The villager managed to duck at the last instant, but the blade gouged his scalp and he fell, dropping his burden—the machine gun, John was certain. One end was identical with the barrel that had protruded from the window; though the rest of the mechanism bore little resemblance to an ordinary gun or rifle, John had no doubt what it was.

Flames were licking at the doorframe; the defenders had waited until the last possible minute before making their break. John was sure that any who might remain within the house were doomed.

The three who had surrendered, upon seeing their comrades putting up a fight, attempted to join in, grabbing at Habakkuk from behind; John urged his mount forward again, trampling over the downed gun bearer to get at them, his sword flashing in the sun.

More of John's warriors, hearing the combat and seeing the smoke, were emerging from wherever they had fled, and in moments three of the six villagers were dead, another seriously wounded, and the remaining two captive. A horse's hoof had caved in the gun bearer's skull, and John saw, to his disgust, that the machine gun had been broken open somehow in the melee, scattering small bits of metal in the street.

"The machine gun is ours!" Habakkuk cried, and more of the invading cavalry reappeared. "Take the village, house by house!"

John did not bother to confirm the order; the men were obeying without his command. He stared down at the scattered fragments with regret. He had no mechanics with him. If the gun could be repaired at all, it could not be done here. Even the belt of ammunition, spilling from a box at one side, was of no immediate use; he could tell at a glance that the shells were far too large to fit the rifles his men carried. Eventually, of course, the gunpowder could be salvaged and used in ordinary cartridges—in fact, the ammunition belt probably contained a fortune in gunpowder. Perhaps a gun could be improvised that could use the shells.

A woman's scream distracted him; he looked up to see three of his men dragging her from her house, her skirts already torn away and blood running from a cut on her head.

"Keep them alive!" he shouted. "Take prisoners! I'll flog any man who kills an unarmed villager!"

One of the three men grinned at him and signalled an acknowledgment. "Yes, sir, Captain," he called. "We won't kill her, we'll just pass her on!"

"You do that," John replied. He glanced down at the pieces of the gun. "We need to know where they got this thing." He grimaced with distaste. A machine gun—obviously valuable, perhaps an irreplaceable historical relic, maybe brought on one of the founding ships all the way from Earth itself, and now broken.

He cared more for its value as an artifact than as a weapon;

this gun was a piece of Godsworld's history. As dangerous a weapon as it might be, it was not to his liking, killing indiscriminately at a distance. He preferred more personal weapons. He wiped the blood from his sword, holding it up so that the blade gleamed bright in the sun.

Give him steel, he thought, shining steel, not the dull lead and brass of bullets.

Chapter Two

Ask, and it shall be given you; seek, and ye shall find; knock, and it shall be opened unto you.

—Matthew 7:7

JOHN looked at the little group in disgust. Out of perhaps as many as two hundred villagers, only two dozen had been fit to question by the time his men had finally calmed down. He saw just five warriors; the rest were evenly divided between men too old to fight and women of various ages.

Many others were still alive, of course—virtually all the children had survived, and most of the women. John disapproved of interrogating children, and few women were fit to question after a night of beatings and gang rape. Most of the men in the village had insisted on fighting to the death.

"J'sevyu, friends," he announced. "We are good Christians, and mean you no harm; we ask your forgiveness for the violence done to you in the rage of battle, but we're fighting for the True Word and can't allow anyone to stand in our way." He looked at the faces of the captives. Their expressions covered a wide range, from fury to sullen resignation, from dull apathy to intense interest. He had seen such faces before, but they never failed to fascinate him. He tried, as he had tried before, to decide what he himself would feel in such a position; but, as always, he simply could not imagine ever being a defeated prisoner. He told himself that in a hopeless situation such as that the villagers had faced, he would have

14

surrendered quickly—after all, he who surrenders lives to fight again, and fighting on against impossible odds would be suicide, and suicide is a mortal sin. Surrender would be the only reasonable thing to do in such a position. Still, he absolutely could not conceive of what he would feel when he had actually done so. As yet, he had never faced such a situation.

"I'm sure you all know what will happen to you now; you'll be taken back to our homeland, where you'll be put to work and taught the way of the People of the True Word and Flesh. When you've accepted the True Word into your hearts, you'll join us as free and equal partners in the crusade to bring enlightenment to those who, even here on Godsworld, have strayed from the only true path to God's kingdom. I know that right now you're all hurt, you're suffering the deaths of your loved ones and the loss of your homes, you're probably full of hate for my men and for me, but I'm asking you to rise above that hurt and that hatred, to accept what's happened and to accept the True Word that we bring you. I'm no preacher, I'm not an Elder, I'm just a soldier. I can't teach you the way. But I can tell you that ours *is* the one true path, and that you can follow it with us. It'll help if you cooperate with us now, if you forgive as much as you can of what we've had to do to bring you your eventual salvation, if you can put aside your mistaken loyalties of the past and answer our questions as best you can."

Few of the expressions changed. He had expected that. He had made such speeches before, and only the youngest ever seemed moved by them. He smothered a sigh of disappointment. The aftermath of a battle was always depressing. He loved the careful planning, the preparation, and the chaos of the actual fighting, but when it came time to divvy up loot, bury the dead, and deal with the defeated enemy he invariably found himself hating every minute of it.

"All right, then, we're going to be taking you in one by one and asking a few simple questions. No harm will come to any of you, so long as somebody answers our questions. Those of you who refuse to answer—well, we'll note it down, and I can't say for sure what will happen if *nobody* answers us. Let's just see how it goes. You," he said, pointing to an old man in the front row, "you first. Hab?"

Habakkuk nodded, and led the man out of the room. They had taken over what appeared to be an inn as their base of operations; John had made his speech in the common room, and interrogations were to be carried out in the kitchen. Several carving knives had been neatly laid out on a side table; neither John nor any of his men intended to use them, but simply having them visible there would be a powerful threat.

John signalled to the men guarding the rest of the prisoners, then followed his lieutenant and his captive into the kitchen, closing the door behind him. Those few guards had been chosen as being the least exhausted, least battered of the invading company, but his last glimpse of them was not reassuring; two were leaning back against the wall, swords hanging down loosely.

In the kitchen Habakkuk had already seated the old man on the hard stone-capped stool they had selected earlier. "Well, mister," he said, "what's your name?"

"Joseph Walker-in-the-Valley," the old man replied. "And that's the last of your darned questions I'm going to answer."

"No need to be like that; we aren't planning to hurt anybody. At least, not anyone around here. We're at war with those heathen filth who call themselves the Chosen of the Holy Ghost; can you tell us anything about them? Any of them been around here lately?"

"I don't plan to answer that."

Habakkuk looked up at John, then glanced over at the display of knives. He shrugged.

"Whatever you like, Mr. Walker. So you don't know anything about the Chosen."

"Didn't say that."

"Do you know something, then?"

"Won't tell you."

The conversation went on in that vein; after a minute or so

Habakkuk switched topics, and began asking about the machine gun.

"Caught you with your pants down, didn't we?" Walker-in-the-Valley gloated.

Habakkuk shrugged again. "Didn't do you any good, though, did it?" He waved at the heavy closed door and the table of knives. "You're here just the same. Wherever you folks found that gun, you might just as well have left it there."

"Who says we found it?"

"Well, if someone sold it to you and told you it would protect you, you got swindled. You tell us where you got it, and we'll see about putting it right."

"Won't tell you."

Habakkuk sighed, and continued.

After about fifteen minutes, Joseph Walker-in-the-Valley had refused to say anything about the Chosen, the machine gun, the village leaders (if any), even the weather. With a final frustrated sigh, Habakkuk noted this down and dragged the old man back to the common room.

"This one stays," he called to the guards. Then he pointed at random at another prisoner. "You next, please; come on back."

John had watched the whole thing silently. He watched the second interview, with a warrior named Luke Bathed-in-Blood, just as silently, and the third, and the fourth. None of them yielded any useful information. The village leaders were dead, according to two of the prisoners, but John and Habakkuk had already expected that—heretic leaders usually fought to the death, since they knew they would be executed anyway for leading their people astray. Nobody admitted to knowing anything about the Chosen other than that they were there, and on the verge of war with the People of the True Word and Flesh. Both groups being heretics, as they saw it, the villagers hadn't paid much attention.

Nobody was saying anything about the machine gun. That subject alone brought either silence or refusal from every prisoner.

Every prisoner, that is, until a young woman who gave her name as Miriam Humble-Before-God.

"Where was that machine gun found?" Habakkuk asked, after a few preliminary questions.

"It wasn't *found* anywhere!" Miriam spat back.

Habakkuk stared at her coldly; John suppressed his reaction, forcing himself to remain silent.

"Then where did it come from, if it wasn't found somewhere?"

"The elders bought it, of course—and if they'd had any brains they'd have bought more weapons with it, and shot all of you, instead of just a few!"

"A *few?*" Habakkuk stared at her, quietly enraged. "Thirty-one of our men and twenty-six horses were killed by that infernal weapon, and more were wounded."

"They deserved it, attacking a neutral village!"

"There *are* no neutrals, only the People of the True Word and the heretics." He was in control of himself again. "Where did they buy it? Were there other weapons for sale?"

"They bought it in Little St. Peter, I heard."

"Where is that?"

Miriam stared at him in surprise. "Don't you know?"

"Just tell me where it is."

"*I* don't know; I'm just a village woman, I don't travel. Somewhere east of here, I guess."

Habakkuk glanced at John; he nodded slightly. "All right," Habakkuk continued, "they bought the machine gun in Little St. Peter. Where did the people in Little St. Peter get it? Did anyone say? Did they find an ancient cache, or was someone hoarding this one gun?"

"They bought it from the People of Heaven, of course; it's not ancient."

"Oh?"

"Heck, no! You think we'd trust our lives to some rusty antique? That machine gun was brand-new!"

"And your village elders bought this brand-new machine gun from the folks in Little St. Peter, and they bought it from the People of Heaven?"

"That's what I heard."

"So where did the People of Heaven come by it, then?"

"They built it, I'd reckon—and they've built plenty more, I'm sure, and when you go up against them you'll get your heads shot off, just the way you deserve!"

Habakkuk glanced at John, then at the display of knives, then back at the woman. "You think they built it?"

"Somebody must have, and from what I've heard, the People of Heaven are the ones to do it."

Habakkuk leaned back on his chair. "And just what have you heard?"

The woman was suddenly quiet. "Not much."

"How much?"

"Really, not much; just that the People of Heaven are running a protectorate, with maybe twenty or thirty villages signed up in some kind of pact without any conversions or tithes that I've heard of, and that they've got the guns and other stuff to make it work."

"Where'd you hear this?"

Defensive, Miriam said, "Well, the elders were thinking about joining, maybe; I heard my daddy talking, that's all."

"Your daddy was one of the elders?"

"Until one of your men cut his throat, he was."

"He wanted to join this protectorate?"

"I didn't say that; he voted against it. The others were all for it, said look how well Little St. Peter's doing, but Daddy thought we were just fine the way we were, and he didn't trust the People of Heaven. He thought we could get alone fine as we always had, didn't think anyone would ever bother us." Her voice broke. "I guess he was wrong." She snuffled, all her earlier defiant appearance gone.

Habakkuk looked at John again.

He, in turn, looked at the girl. She was about twenty, he judged, of medium height and pleasantly plump, with soft brown hair that was currently dirty and tangled; a large bruise covered one cheek. She had apparently not escaped the soldiers' attentions, but all in all did not seem to have suffered excessively. "Is that all you know about the People of Heaven?" John asked.

"That's all."

"How long have they been running this protectorate thing?"

"I don't know; a year or two, I guess."

"You ever hear about them, Hab?"

"Not that I recollect," Habakkuk replied.

John had in fact heard of them vaguely; one of the Elders had said something when preparing this expedition, though John did not remember exactly who it had been. The People of Heaven had recently appeared on the scene in the southeastern hills, down toward Judah; nobody seemed to know their heritage exactly, so the Elders of the True Word and Flesh assumed they were a new group, gathered by a new false prophet who had somehow won adherents to his particular brand of heresy without any claim to birthright ministry. Such false prophets had arisen from time to time in the history of Godsworld; usually their cults fell apart as soon as the leader died.

The People of the True Word and Flesh had no quarrel with the People of Heaven, so far as John knew—other than that, like all groups except his own, the People of Heaven were heretics, fallen from the true path—but for his own part he disliked protectorates. The idea of villages and towns banding together as a mere business arrangement, without sharing one faith and without proving their value in battle, seemed wrong, somehow. A nation was meant to be a single people, united in their beliefs, who had tested the strength of those beliefs against their enemies. God promised the final victory to the righteous—but how could the righteous triumph if their enemies banded together against them? And a league or protectorate could not possibly be righteous if its people were not in accord with one another.

Of course, most protectorates and alliances fell apart quickly enough; the stronger ally would absorb the weaker, or the client states would betray the protector or rebel against him. John saw the workings of God in such events. The mighty shall be cast down, he thought, so that the People of the True Word and Flesh may triumph.

He fully expected that his people would in time unite all of Godsworld in a single faith, as it had been when first men came there from Earth. The People of the True Word and Flesh were strong, because they had the true faith—and they knew theirs to be the true faith because it made them strong. Theirs would be the kingdom and the glory, John knew.

If the People of Heaven were really making machine guns, however, the day of that kingdom's coming might be long delayed, indeed.

How could they be making machine guns? Quite aside from the lost knowledge involved, and the unheard-of machining skills, where were they getting the powder? Had the legendary mother lode of sulphur finally been found?

Or was it the brimstone of Hell itself they used? Perhaps the People of Heaven were the armies of Satan, come to subvert Godsworld as they did Earth, so long ago. John had heard a heretic explain once that the reason Godsworld had no sulphur to make gunpowder was that sulphur was a product of Hell, and Godsworld was too close to Heaven for such things. Certainly Earth had been closer to Hell, and sulphur was said to be cheap and plentiful there.

But then, many things were said to be plentiful back on Earth—sulphur and iron and plastic, and varieties of plants and animals. The stories told of a black stone called coal that could be burned like nearwood, and black oil that came from the ground; Godsworld had nothing like that. Undoubtedly Godsworld had its share of things Earth had not.

None of that concerned him at present, however. The machine gun did.

"We'll want to send someone to Little St. Peter to see if she's telling the truth," he said.

Habakkuk frowned. "We don't have many men to spare for that," he replied.

"If they're really building machine guns over there, we'd better find out about it as soon as possible."

"True enough," Habakkuk admitted grudgingly.

John looked at Miriam with interest; she stared back defiantly. "Why did you tell us all this?" he asked.

"Because I want you to go and see for yourselves—and get your heads blown off by the People of Heaven."

"You're sure that's what'll happen?"

"No, I'm not sure—I'm just hoping."

"We'll send someone," John said with clear finality. "Call the next prisoner, and get someone to take this woman to my quarters; I want to keep her close at hand."

Habakkuk glanced at John, then looked Miriam over. She wasn't to his taste—he preferred his women short, blonde, and full-chested—but she wasn't bad. He doubted that the captain's interest was strictly military.

That was all right, though; a man had his own life to lead, as well as his duties. He went to call the next prisoner.

Chapter Three

JOHN sat at the desk he had appropriated, frowning. He would have preferred to wait for word from Matthew Crowned-with-Glory, the man in charge of the party he had sent to Little St. Peter, before committing himself to the campaign against the Chosen of the Holy Ghost, but that did not seem to be something he could do. The Elders back in New Nazareth would never accept it. They would not believe the testimony of Miriam Humble-Before-God, or any other heretical prisoner, without good reason. They would surely insist that the machine gun had been found somewhere, not bought—or at best, that the people of Little St. Peter had lied about where they got it. God had allowed the knowledge of such weapons to die, and would surely not now revive it only to turn it against His own people.

John was even willing to admit to himself that Miriam might have been yarning to try and distract her foes, but he could not be sure, and did not want to expend his people's resources in a long, bloody war with the Chosen if the People of Heaven were a more dangerous enemy.

True, the Chosen of the Holy Ghost were putting constant pressure on the trade routes of the People of the True Word and Flesh; they had publicly insulted and denounced the True Worders, and were vigorously proselytizing for their own false religion and its false prophet. Their conquests posed a growing threat to the security of even New Nazareth itself, and of course there was the great spiritual need to bring the light of the True Word to the darkness of the lands the Chosen held in thrall. Still, they were just another enemy, to be dealt with at any time; they were not manufacturing machine guns.

If the report of his scouting party were to prove that the so-called People of Heaven were, in fact, a greater and more immediate danger to the People of the True Word and Flesh than the evil empire of the Chosen, then he could send that report on to the Elders and postpone the inevitable conflict with the Chosen. He was not certain just what action he would take in such a situation; a consultation with the Elders would be needed. He was sure that they would defer to their commander regarding the need to rethink the situation, since it was he, not they, who was here in the field and in possession of the facts, but he was also sure that they would want to do the rethinking.

The Elders would not, however, be willing to change their plans simply on the word of a captured woman; they would need some sort of convincing evidence. John had been hoping that Matthew would return quickly with that evidence.

He had not been idle since Matthew's departure; he would not have dared to be. His old main camp had been packed up and moved into the village, which was known to its inhabitants by the oddly secular name of Marshside. Some of the villagers were on their way to New Nazareth, under guard; others had been recruited as camp servants. Scouts had been sent out, not only Matthew and his men to Little St. Peter, but others to various points along the borders and even in the Chosen empire itself. The main force of infantry had arrived two days behind schedule, and getting the cavalry back into fighting trim after their postbattle debauch had taken time as well, so the campaign had been delayed already—but not seriously. Preparations had been made, the men were ready, the village's resources were strained—the time had come when the first real assault on the enemy should be made. The plan called for a march up around the marsh and across the

Little New Jordan, taking the Chosen on their presumably undefended southeastern flank with a series of harassing raids on outlying settlements by the cavalry, while the infantry drove straight toward Spiritus Sancti.

The entire plan assumed that the Chosen had not discovered the True Worder troop movements in time to move their own main army; John had some doubts about that. He thought that he could win in any case, but knew that the victory would be very costly if the Chosen did, in fact, know that he and his men were coming. And if the People of Heaven were building machine guns, the People of the True Word and Flesh could not afford such a victory.

If the Chosen were truly as ignorant and their southeastern flank as undefended as the Elders believed them to be, then the entire war would be relatively quick and painless and would do little harm to either side—excluding, of course, those who persisted in their heresy—but John did not believe that the Chosen, who had built a respectable empire for themselves, could be that incompetent. He sighed. He did not mind fighting a protracted war; he had anticipated it all along, and accepted the Elders' plan to come around through the southern badlands because it was as good a plan as any, even if the much-vaunted element of surprise was unlikely to amount to much. The People of Heaven worried him, though—perhaps more than they reasonably should. After all, he reminded himself for the hundredth time, the People of Heaven had no known quarrel with the People of the True Word and Flesh, unless they took amiss the seizure of Marshside. Still, John wished that Matthew had returned. With no word from Little St. Peter he would have to start the march north at dawn.

He was accustomed to operating without crucial knowledge; any military commander had to be. Misinformation about the enemy's forces, inaccurate maps, lying informants, all of those he was accustomed to dealing with, but the possibility of an enemy armed with the incredible superweapons of legend attacking from behind while he fought someone else was unsettling. A machine gun in

Marshside—what if somewhere else he were to run across the superbombs that destroyed entire cities?

He pushed back his chair and arose, glancing one last time at the papers on the desk. Nothing there was really urgent, and he felt in need of distraction. He had been worrying about both the Heaveners and the Chosen for too long without a break. In the morning he would be moving again, leading his men around the marsh, and there would be plenty of minor problems to deal with, taking his mind off the major ones; why wait until then to let the burden be lightened? He was doing no good sitting at his desk and worrying. He had minor problems here in Marshside that he could attend to.

He walked out of the room without consciously choosing a destination, but knew immediately where he was going— up the stairs to the room across from his own, where Miriam Humble-Before-God was kept.

He threw back the bolt, swung open the door, and looked in, then immediately stepped back. She was not on her bed, which stood against the opposite wall. There was no other furniture in the room, nowhere else she would reasonably be—which meant that she was somewhere unreasonable.

He had not bothered to post a guard here, since there were two at the door of the house; he did not feel he could spare the manpower, and the bolt had seemed adequate. Even had she managed to open or break it, where could she have gone? She might have escaped through the window, if she could find a way safe to the ground and avoid being seen by the people in the street below, or broken through the ceiling into the attic; but again, where would she go?

It was possible that she had escaped, but he doubted it. He had had two weeks now to learn something of her personality, and guessed where she was. Almost amused, he flung out his arm and slammed the door back against the wall with his full strength.

As he had expected, instead of the bang of nearwood against plaster, he heard the thump of the door hitting flesh. He strode into the room and turned.

Miriam stood behind the door, clutching a long, jagged

splinter she had pried from the bare boards of the floor; it would have served quite as well as a dagger had he simply walked in and allowed her to reach his back with it. He had not been that careless, and robbed of her victim she looked rather dazed and foolish.

"If you *had* killed me," John pointed out, "my men would have hanged you."

"Only if they caught me," she spat back. She flung the splinter aside.

"They'd catch you," John replied as he stooped to pick up the fragment. "Where could you run?"

"Little St. Peter, maybe—they wouldn't follow me there."

"You don't know where it is." After a final glance at the crystalline edge he tossed the splinter out the window.

"It's three days afoot east of here—and your man's been gone two weeks now, hasn't he, and on horseback? Looks like something happened to him, I'd reckon."

"He's taking his time to look around, I'd say—I told him to."

"You told him to be back in ten days!"

"You heard that? Or did someone tell you? No, doesn't matter, don't say anything. Even if I said that—and I'm not saying I did—he might have had some trouble; could have been taken sick, maybe. We'll see."

"No, *we* won't; you're leaving tomorrow."

"So are you; I'm taking you north with me."

"What?" Her mouth fell open for an instant; she snapped it closed. "What are you talking about?"

"I'm taking you with me."

"Why, in God's name?"

"Thou shalt not take the name of the Lord thy God in vain," he reproved her.

"Why are you taking me with you?"

"Because I choose to do so."

"But *why?* Why don't you just rape me here and have done, get it over with?"

"I don't intend to rape you."

"You don't?" She was plainly startled. "Why not? Your men did; I thought you were just waiting for the right moment. What makes you different?"

"I prefer not to, that's all."

"Are you queer, then? I've heard that some warriors are—that must be it." Her mouth twisted unpleasantly. "Leviticus, chapter twenty, verse thirteen," she said.

"First Corinthians, chapter seven, verse thirty-seven," he replied.

"Oh, so now you're holier than the rest of us?"

"Holier than you, heretic."

She spat in his face.

He grabbed her arm with his left hand and backhanded her across the cheek with his right. "You're coming with me because I don't trust you out of my sight; is that reason enough for you? You're the only person in this stinking village with brains enough to worry me."

She glared at him silently.

He released his grip on her arm; she pulled away fiercely.

"I came up here to see if you were ready to be reasonable, and to see if you would tell me anything else about the Chosen, or Marshside, or Little St. Peter, or that machine gun—and to tell you that you're coming north with me, too," he said. "Well, I've told you, and it doesn't look like you're feeling reasonable, so I've done what I came to do." He turned and marched out the door.

She slammed it hard behind him, as he had known she would; he turned back and threw the bolt, then went on down the stairs. He hesitated at the foot, then walked on out into the street, leaving the papers and plans on his desk for later.

The guards at the door saluted, and he paused on the step between them to survey the scene.

Marshside was jammed; his men were sleeping four to a room, the villagers themselves relegated to doorsteps and kitchens for the most part. The street was full of men and boys and horses—and a few women, both villagers and camp-following harlots. It was a safe assumption that these villagers, too, could now be called harlots—the women determined to remain respectable would stay inside until the main body of troops had moved on. John recognized several of the men; his own elite cavalry—what was left of it—had been kept close to his headquarters, with the vast horde of infantry filling the rest of the town.

One face suddenly stood out, a man waving to him; John shouted, "Ho, there!"

Faces all over the street turned to look at him; he pointed at the man he wanted. "Come up here!"

The man obeyed, the crowd parting before him. He saluted as he neared his commander, and then stood at attention a yard away.

"You're Timothy Gates-of-the-City. I sent you to Little St. Peter with Matthew Crowned-with-Glory," John said.

"Yes, sir," the soldier agreed.

"When did you get back?"

"Ah . . . about an hour ago, sir; I was on my way to report." The man tried unsuccessfully to hide his embarrassment.

"An *hour* ago?"

"Yes, sir," he said unhappily. "I was tired and hungry, sir, and I got a meal and took a bath. I rode here without stopping, sir, almost killed my horse."

"Well, darn it, soldier, next time report to me *first;* another five minutes wouldn't kill you." John glared at the man.

"Yes, sir."

"You're here now, anyway. Come inside and report."

"Yes, sir." Timothy relaxed slightly; he knew he was still in trouble, but the captain was apparently not going to hang him on the spot. He followed his commander into the headquarters building and on to his office.

Timothy stood before the cluttered desk while John seated himself comfortably behind it. When he was settled, John demanded, "Report!"

"Yes, sir. We made good time at first, sir, but Little St. Peter is further east than we had been told, sir. We reached it on March twenty-fourth, and found an inn, but it was late, so we just ate supper and went to bed there."

"Did you talk to any of the locals?"

"No, sir; there weren't any there but the innkeeper. Everyone was at home—they said it was Easter there!" Timothy made a show of astonishment.

John shrugged. "Heretics," he said. "Go on."

"Well, the next day was April first, and we didn't know if they kept Fool's Day, so Matthew wanted to be extra careful; he sent Barney—Barnabas Righteous-in-Wrath—out, while the rest of us stayed in the inn and talked to people there." He hesitated. "Ah . . . we heard a lot of things, sir."

"Skip that for now." John was becoming impatient. "I'll hear the rest of the details later. For now you can answer some questions."

"Yes, sir."

"Did you see any more machine guns?"

"Yes, sir—there were machine guns mounted on the village walls, five or six of them at least. Big ones, bigger than the one they had here."

"Any others?"

"I didn't see any, sir."

"Did anyone talk about them?"

"Yes, sir—we asked. It seemed a natural thing for traders to ask about, so we did. They bought them from the People of Heaven—everyone agreed on that, sir."

John nodded. Miriam had told the truth, as he had believed all along; much as she obviously hated him and his men, he had not seriously doubted what she had said—including her motive for speaking. Five or six machine guns, bigger than the one in Marshside—an open attack on Little St. Peter would be a bloodbath. Her big mistake had been in assuming that John would be stupid enough to make such an attack.

There were other ways of dealing with enemies than frontal assault.

"Did you meet any of the People of Heaven, talk to them? Were there any of their traders or soldiers there?"

"*I* didn't talk to them, sir, but I think some of the others did. There were some of them in town, all right—very strange people they were. Tall, all of them, and there was something funny about their clothes, though I couldn't say just what it was. They talked funny, too—didn't pronounce things quite right.''

"You *think* some of the others talked to them? Where *are* the others?''

"I . . . I don't know, sir.''

"What?''

Obviously miserable, Timothy repeated, "I don't know, sir. I told you, Matt sent Barney out that first morning; well, he never came back. So the next day—Tuesday the second— Matt himself and Joey, Joseph Mother-of-Mercy, went out together. Matt didn't come back; Joey came back with a message, said that Matt was going on to the Citadel—that's the homeplace for the People of Heaven—and that we should stay at the inn and wait for him. The next day Joey and Mark Blessed-of-Heaven went out and never came back. I waited at that inn for them, sat around for days; I went out looking a few times, but never found any of them. I'll tell you, sir, I got scared after a while. Finally I decided that I'd better come back, that they were all four gone for good, and here I am.''

John sat silently for a moment, then asked, "What's Little St. Peter like?''

"Rich, sir—very rich. It's sinful, it seems to me. Every bed in the inn had a mattress as thick as my arm. Clocks everywhere, people wearing watches, the women dressed up as bright as flowers. The food's good, and the beer the best you ever tasted; a cushion on every chair! And guns, sir— there were men walking the streets with pistols on their belts. And other things that seemed like magic—you wouldn't believe me if I told you about them.''

"I'll want to see for myself.'' He leaned back. "I think the Elders better hear about all this. Our war with the Chosen of the Holy Ghost will have to wait. I think we have something more important to worry about.''

"What, sir?''

"The People of Heaven. I don't know who or what they are—not for sure, anyway—but I intend to find out.''

"Devil worshippers, maybe?''

John nodded. "That's a possibility—or maybe they're people from Earth, come to destroy us after all these years."

"Devil worshippers all the same, sir, whether from here or from Earth."

"True enough," John agreed. "True enough."

Chapter Four

I am a man under authority, having soldiers under me: and I say to this man, Go, and he goeth; and to another, Come, and he cometh; and to my servant, Do this, and he doeth it.

—Matthew 8:9

THE Elders were not pleased by the delay he requested; as John had expected, they doubted that the People of Heaven were actually a threat, or that Little St. Peter was actually guarded by machine guns on the walls. The letter answering his report suggested that Timothy might have been drinking, or that the guns on the walls were mere mock-ups intended to frighten the gullible.

John thought he recognized his maternal uncle's style in the letter's phrasing; old Lazarus Speaker-of-Gospel had a way with words. It was obvious that he and the others wanted to get on with the war against the Chosen. They did not want to hear about any threat less immediate, however dire that threat might eventually prove.

However, they had faith in their chosen representative, at least to some extent, and had not reached their current prominence by ignoring reality; they authorized him to leave his men encamped in Marshside, or wherever else he thought prudent, and get his scouting expedition over with as quickly as possible.

If John was not back by the first of June, Habakkuk would

assume command and lead the attack against the Chosen, as planned.

He had to agree that that made a certain amount of sense, but it occurred to him that if the Heaveners were even more dangerous than he thought, then he might well not return— whereupon the attack on the Chosen would be more of a mistake than ever, quite aside from the unavoidable fact that the delay would give the Chosen more time to discover the True Worder plans. Still, he might be delayed by any number of trivialities; the Elders were assuming until shown otherwise that the Heaveners were harmless and that the attack on the Chosen should proceed, with or without Captain John Mercy-of-Christ.

He doubted the wisdom of that assumption, but he knew better than to argue further. He had won his main point; the attack would be delayed while he scouted out the new enemy.

He planned quickly. Matthew's party had been dispersed, and all but Timothy had vanished; perhaps they had somehow aroused suspicion. He would need to be very careful, and to avoid any appearance that might suggest anything out of the ordinary. Matthew's party had consisted of five men; that in itself might have drawn attention. His own expedition would consist of just three, not all men. He would go himself, of course; he would take Timothy, since he already had some experience of Little St. Peter; and he would need a woman to play the role of his wife. A family group would appear innocuous enough.

He dismissed the possibility of taking any of the camp followers. There were none he could trust on such an expedition. None looked like a trader's wife, for that matter; all looked like what they were. Furthermore, they were the dregs of society, and were generally stupid and sloppy, quite likely to say the wrong thing at the wrong time. And he did not have time to send for someone respectable from True Worder lands.

That left the prisoners captured in the attack on Marshside. He would, he decided, take Miriam. He already knew her somewhat, and was convinced that she was intelligent. She had a proud bearing that would not be out of place in a trader's wife, and knew something of the area.

She hated him, but that would be no problem. Wives often appeared to hate their husbands, despite the Bible's teachings. She would nag at him, and if she got out of line he would beat her. She would not be stupid enough to expose the mission for what it was, since the Heaveners would surely kill her—if John didn't manage it before being captured or killed himself—along with Timothy and himself. That would be common sense on their part, in case her actions were part of some elaborate scheme. She might claim to be willing to die if she took her captor with her, but John did not believe it.

He would need to watch her closely, of course—but that too was in character for the role he intended to play.

Timothy could pass for a brother, a younger brother brought along to learn a trade at the family's behest.

A child or two might make the act still more convincing, but John did not think he could trust any child to stay in character.

Supplies—they would need supplies, both for the journey and as trade goods. Four horses, one for each of them and one for the packs. Good weapons—he would take one of the rifles and two, maybe three cartridges, as well as a good sword.

He sat back in his chair and planned carefully. He got only three hours' sleep that night, but the party set out at noon the following day.

Miriam had made no protest, had not commented when John explained to her why he was taking her and why she could not afford to betray him to the Heaveners. She had simply stood staring at him, accepting it. She had said nothing at all.

When the supplies were packed and loaded she was brought out by two guards; she came without protest and mounted her horse silently. Someone had found her a riding skirt—John had not wanted her to ride sidesaddle for so long a journey, particularly since she had admitted to having travelled very little. She would be sore enough, he was sure, without having to worry about sliding off, and most of the traders' wives he had seen had ridden astride. After all, it was

virgins and expectant mothers who were prohibited from riding astride, and a trader's wife would be no virgin. Nor was
Miriam, after the battle, though she had been before.

Timothy put up more resistance than Miriam, oddly; he
had obviously been badly frightened by his first trip to Little
St. Peter and the inexplicable disappearance of his comrades
there. John had considered leaving him behind, but finally
decided against it. Although Timothy protested that he had
learned nothing of any value waiting at the inn, John pointed
out that he knew more than anyone else in Marshside—for
example, just where Little St. Peter stood, and where the inn
lay within the walls.

The conclusive argument, however, was that John was quite
willing to *order* him to go, whereupon a refusal would become
desertion, to be punished by either flogging or hanging. Still
visibly unhappy, Timothy repacked his travelling clothes and
followed the others up the hillside from Marshside.

The journey was a slow one; Miriam was not an experienced rider, and although she did not complain, she kept
slowing her mount, forcing the others to slow with her, and
at times John caught glimpses of her grimacing in pain. She
invariably tried to hide such lapses, such signs of mere humanity, and John made no comment on them. Timothy did
not appear to notice anything amiss; he was only too glad to
allow his own horse to dawdle.

They camped early that evening, after covering so little
ground that John almost imagined he could still see Marshside in the distance. He knew that was nonsense; they had
gone up and down several ridges and across some badlands,
and had put enough distance behind them that even on a plain
Marshside would have been below the horizon, but still he
had the feeling that all he would need to do would be to walk
back up the slope of the last ridge and there it would be, just
as he had left it.

With that thought in mind, he considered the possibility
that Miriam might slip away while he slept, and make her
way back to Marshside. Even if his men there were to recognize her and demand an explanation—which they might

not, as one female prisoner looked much like another to veteran soldiers—she would be quite capable of devising one. An ambush on the road, John and Timothy dead—that would do well enough until he got back himself.

Or she might cut his throat while he slept and *then* return to Marshside, which would be safer for her.

Accordingly, before he settled down to sleep, he wrapped the voluminous riding skirt around her, pinning her arms to her sides, and tied it securely in place. The trailing end of the rope he then tied to the handle of the cooking pot that hung from its folding tripod over the campfire. The skirt would keep the rope from chafing her or cutting off her circulation. He thought she might well be able to work her way free in time, but her struggles, he judged, would bring down the pot and tripod with enough noise to wake Timothy and himself.

She made no comment at these preparations, and in fact had not said a word since their departure, but when he had finished she sneered at him unmistakably.

Timothy seemed puzzled by such excessive precautions, but knew better than to say anything that might be construed as criticism of his commanding officer.

John was not bothered by Miriam's derision or Timothy's confusion. He knew that he was being more cautious than might seem necessary, but he preferred excessive caution to recklessness. Fewer men died of caution.

The next morning Miriam was visibly stiff, and awkward in mounting, treating John and Timothy to a flash of leg before she got the riding skirt in place. John toyed idly with the thought of raping her after all—but morning was not the time, and Timothy was with them. Timothy would have no objections, John was sure, to anything his commanding officer might care to do, but his presence still acted as a deterrent. John mounted his horse and led the way.

They camped that night on another undistinguished hillside, and by then John had forgotten his earlier lascivious interest in Miriam. For her part, she was utterly exhausted, her entire body aching, and John saw nothing particularly attractive about his dishevelled and dirty prisoner. He wrapped her up once again, though less carefully, and took no interest in the feel of her body through the heavy fabric.

The following day was similar, save that Timothy seemed to be growing ever more nervous. John tired of coaxing his companions onward, and they made camp early.

As they were eating a sparse supper of dried mutton and beans, John asked Timothy, "How much further?"

Timothy started. "How much further to what?"

"To Little St. Peter, of course."

"Oh. Ah, not far, sir. A few hours."

"Good," John said, lifting the meat to his mouth.

"Yes, good," Timothy echoed. He stared at the road stretching out to the east.

After they had eaten and tidied up and taken turns in the bushes John attempted to chat, to get to know his companions better, and to question Timothy further about his earlier journey. Miriam would say nothing at all, however, and Timothy's answers, which had to be carefully coaxed out of him, were brief, inconsequential, and often totally inappropriate to the question. John quickly gave up. He bound Miriam in her skirt for the night and went to sleep, leaving Timothy staring at the dying campfire.

The next morning Timothy and one of the horses were gone; hoofprints were visible on the road westward, back toward Marshside. John stared after him in disgust.

"He'll hang for this," he announced.

Miriam, still tied in her skirt, finally broke her long silence with a great barrage of howling, derisive laughter.

"Oh, the great warrior, such an inspiration to his men!" she called.

John suppressed an urge to slap her; instead, he simply left her bound while he prepared and ate his breakfast. When he was done he released her and handed her the leftover scraps.

"Don't think this changes anything," he said. "We're still going to Little St. Peter, and you still can't afford to betray me."

"How can one betray an enemy?" she countered.

He made no answer, merely lifted her into the saddle.

It was midafternoon of that fourth day, the twentieth of April, when they finally reached Little St. Peter.

The town sat atop a hill, surrounded by a wall of stone braced with heavy beams of nearwood; at each corner stood a tower, and atop each tower a machine gleamed dully in the amber daylight. Looking at them, John was uncertain whether they were, in fact, machine guns; they appeared ridiculously large. There could be no doubt, however, that they were weapons. As the two travellers rode up the highway toward the western gate, the guns on either side were kept trained directly at them.

Four soldiers were lounging at the gate; one called out perfunctorily, "In the name of the Lord, Our God, state your business."

"Peaceful trade, by Christ's mercy," John replied.

"Name yourselves, and your faith."

"Joel Meek-Before-Christ and my wife Miriam, of the Church of the Only God." The Church of the Only God had been a small tribe comprising three villages along the westernmost extreme of the Upper New Jordan; John's cavalry had obliterated all three two years before. Since no one had escaped, he doubted the news had reached Little St. Peter.

"What are you selling?"

John shrugged. "A little of this, a little of that; woolens, mostly."

The soldier asked one of his comrades, "Do you want to bother searching?"

"Ah, let him go in," the other replied.

The first shrugged and pushed open the gate. "Pass, friend, into Little St. Peter, free in faith under the protection of the People of Heaven. Amen."

"Amen," John replied, startled by the open renunciation of any claim to the one true religion. He spurred his horse and rode into the town, Miriam close behind, the pack horse trailing.

Chapter Five

By the time they had made their way through the broad paved square inside the gate and found an inn, John had decided that Timothy had grossly understated the opulence of the town. He had never seen such colors and textures. Almost every woman he saw seemed to be wearing a new color—every shade of green, blue, and yellow he could imagine, and a handful of daring young things in pink. Even a few men wore colors, blues and dark greens, and those who did wear the more customary browns and grays often used shades he had not encountered anywhere else.

Strange green plants grew in tubs and window boxes on every side, including some with brown-gray stalks that looked absurdly tall and thin; he saw no red plants anywhere, nor any of the more familiar green ones. Curtains hung in every window. A few rockers stood on porches, and, as Timothy had said, every single one had a cushion—and some even had cushions on the back as well as the seat. Many were embroidered in vivid colors.

Strange plants, rich fabrics, new dyes, and incredible weaponry—John was more certain than ever that the People of Heaven were trading with other worlds. Where else could they get such things? Those tall plants were certainly nothing that had ever grown on Godsworld before.

The whole city was soft and decadent, he judged. What kind of warriors would men who sat on cushions make? Were it not for the weapons, he would have said Little St. Peter was ripe for plundering by men who still led the hard, clean life that God had intended men to live.

The guns on the towers were not the only firearms in sight; as Timothy had reported, many of the men wore pistols on their belts or had rifles slung on their shoulders. John wondered how much ammunition they actually had. He remembered the machine gun in Marshside and its feeder belt with almost three hundred rounds left, even after the wasteful spraying of the hillside during the battle; if the People of Heaven were trading with Earth or one of the other Satanic worlds, then they could probably get all the sulphur they would ever need to make more than enough gunpowder to provide every man in Little St. Peter with cartridges.

Were there any settled planets other than Godsworld that were *not* Satanic? John had never heard of any; he had been taught that all God's chosen people, the enlightened and saved, had come to Godsworld, leaving the other worlds to the multitudes of the damned. The People of Heaven could probably buy sulphur by the pound or even the hundred-weight.

He reevaluated the town in that light; the people here could *afford* to be decadent. An open attack would be suicidal.

They found an inn readily enough, just beyond the market square inside the gates; the traditional banner hung above the open arch of the doorway, proclaiming ST. PETER'S INN at the top, the customary ST. MATTHEW CHAPTER XXV VERSES 34–40 across the bottom, and *Zachariah Come-to-Grace, Prop.* in the lower right corner. A separate sign pointed the way to the stable entrance.

John lifted Miriam down from her saddle, then held all three horses while she straightened her walking skirt and removed the riding skirt. When she was fit to be seen he exchanged the reins for the riding skirt and folded it neatly, following along as she led the animals into the stableyard. A boy was waiting; John tossed him a coin, and Miriam handed him the reins. John glanced at the baggage, then at the stableboy, then shrugged. Even among heretics there was honor, he supposed; the boy wouldn't steal anything. Or if he did, if anything was missing later, John would know who to blame.

Together, John and Miriam walked through the stableyard arch into St. Peter's Inn.

The interior was in keeping with the opulence of the streets; the stone walls were covered with bright banners, lace curtains adorned the windows, and pillows and cushions were everywhere. A clock hung over the hearth, the expensive variety with a red hand to measure seconds, and although the room was relatively quiet and the red hand moving, listen as he might, John could not hear any ticking.

Honor among heretics there might be, but he wondered how such a marvel could be in so public a place without being stolen. And the cushions, as well—surely a few of those would vanish each night!

A score or so of customers were scattered at half a dozen tables, talking and drinking quietly; they paid the newcomers no heed. A nearwood bar stood in one corner, a man behind it polishing a tankard; John saw no one else, so he crossed to the bar.

"What can I do for you, sir?" the barman asked, putting down his tankard and towel as John approached.

"Are you the proprietor?" John asked.

"No, sir, Mr. Grace is away at the Citadel of Heaven today, and he left me in charge. James Redeemed-from-Sin is my name."

"Joel Meek-Before-Christ," John answered. They shook hands. "My wife and I are just in from North Dan, with a few yards of good woolens. We could use a meal and a room, but from the look of this place"—he swept his arm around to include the entire inn and perhaps the town beyond—"I'm not sure we can afford any."

"Your first time in Little St. Peter?"

"Yes."

"Quite a fine little place, isn't it? Don't worry, though; our prices are reasonable enough. We won't turn you away."

"We haven't had a successful trip; forgive my bluntness, but what's 'reasonable'?"

"What currency?"

"True Worder dollars." The money from any of the larger powers could turn up anywhere, so John saw no reason to hedge.

"Don't get those much here." He pulled out a chart from beneath the bar and consulted it, while John admired the hard, gleaming finish on the countertop—he had never seen nearwood look like that—and read the little plaque on the wall behind the barman: *Be not forgetful to entertain strangers, for thereby some have entertained angels unawares.*—HEBREWS XIII.2.

"Ah!" the barman said. "Here it is! One hundred and fifty for the room and bed, thirty for sheeting. House menu for dinner, forty-five dollars. The conversion rate for Heavener credits is fifteen dollars to one credit, if you want anything else."

John was surprised; the prices *were* reasonable—in fact were slightly less than he would have expected to pay in New Nazareth. "You use Heavener credits here? I don't know them."

"The People of Heaven—Little St. Peter's in their protectorate now, ever since St. Peter itself was sacked by the Chosen of the Holy Ghost last year. Best thing that ever happened to us, joining the protectorate—it was the People of Heaven sold us all these fabrics, that clock, everything! Here, look at this bar!" He tapped the countertop.

"I was just looking at it a moment ago," John said. "Never saw anything like it."

"It's *plastic!* Do you believe that? Pure plastic! And all they wanted for it was an even exchange in raw nearwood!"

"That's crazy," Miriam said from behind John's shoulder.

"Isn't it? But they meant it, they did it! Traded even, no strings attached!"

"They want nearwood that much?"

"I guess they do! We've been swapping nearwood for everything you could imagine! Grain, too—I understand they'll pay top price for wheat, higher than anyone else around. And those woolens of yours—they've been buying raw wool, anyway. I'm not sure about fabrics; they've got enough of their own, it seems. Beef, leather, mutton, fungusmeat, fish, and if your little lady there's got nimble fingers, they even buy embroidery! The good Lord alone can know what they want with it all—begging your pardon, folks, my tongue ran away with me. It's been mighty good for the trade here, all this stuff coming through, and what's good for business is good for me—I'm paid on a share."

"What do they *do* with it all? And how do they pay for it?"

"I haven't the faintest idea what they do with it, sir, and that's the truth, but they pay in credits, and their credits are good, solid money, good for everything they sell—plastic is just one little thing. They sell fabrics I never heard of, so fine that you can't even see the weave and with textures like nothing on Godsworld—take a look at the curtains, you never saw anything like that in North Dan. Those cushions, too. And gunpowder—they must have found sulphur's mother lode itself. You saw those guns on the walls, I reckon—the Heaveners put those up themselves when Little St. Peter signed on. I tell you, joining the protectorate was the best thing the town elders ever did here. Jesus must surely love the People of Heaven!"

"I don't know," John answered. "It might not be Jesus. Seems to me there's something sinful in all this wealth. Where'd it come from? It's a lure and a temptation, that's sure, but it's not Jesus who leads men into temptation."

The barman, who had been leaning forward over the bar, stood back, his tone suddenly unfriendly. "Now, sir, I'm not right certain that I take your meaning. Are you saying you see the hand of Satan in this?"

"No, I didn't say that—I don't know what I see. I do have

my doubts, though. There's an old saying that what's too good to be true *isn't* true, and it seems to me that all this wealth might be false, *might* have the hand of Satan behind it—but I can't say for sure. I'm just a trader in woolens, not a preacher.''

"Well," the barman said, his tone slightly more conciliatory, "I can see how one might wonder. But we do have our preachers here in Little St. Peter, and our doubters, too, and the preachers have answered the doubters. God has smiled on us, in reward for three hundred years of righteous living. If it were Satan's work, now, what Satan does is to tempt men *into sin;* and while we might've been tempted by the riches of Heaven here, there's been no sin, no one's lured us into evil. It's still honest work, cutting the nearwood or growing the wheat and trading it to the Heaveners, it just pays better than we're used to. The laborer is worthy of his hire, though— you know the Bible says that. The customs say to charge what the market will bear—and it's the Heaveners who set the prices, not us. Some of our folk have even told them, out of Christian charity, that they're paying too much, and they've changed a few of their prices, but they still pay well, because they say they want our trade and will pay high to keep it.''

"But how did *they* get so rich? What if their wealth is the wages of sin, and you're sharing in it?''

"The wages of sin is death, friend. What sort of sin could it be that would bring wealth like this instead? No, what *I* think is that they've discovered the lost knowledge of the ancients—maybe they found the Mother Ship itself, as well as the mother lode. One of our scholars says that they might have found something called a communication sat-in-light, or something akin to that—I didn't catch the words, but it's something that the ancients hung in the sky when they came that might have fallen since. It's a strange and wondrous thing, certainly, but it's a blessing, not a sin.''

"Mr. Redeemed, I hope you won't take offense at this, but *I* wonder if perhaps they haven't been trading with sinners— trading with other worlds. Maybe with Earth itself.''

The barman stared for a moment, then burst out laughing. John and Miriam simply watched until he had calmed down.

"Other worlds? Mister, have you heard the histories? Don't you know *anything?* First off, our ancestors came to Godsworld fleeing Armageddon, you know that—Earth was in its last days, and was surely destroyed long ago. And even if they escaped Armageddon as we did, the other worlds wouldn't have starships any more than we do here, now, would they? They were settled by sinners and fools—they're probably savages huddled around campfires cooking and eating each other."

"We can't be sure Earth—" John began.

"Mister, I wasn't finished," Redeemed-from-Sin interrupted. "I didn't say my piece. The *important* thing is that even if Earth is still there, even if the sinners and philistines still have starships, how far is it? It took our people *one hundred and eleven years* to cross the darkness to Godsworld! The scientists had to put them all to sleep, and the crewmen all died of old age on the way, leaving their sons to carry on until the folk were awakened. Now tell me, mister—you're a trader—what sort of trade can you carry on when every voyage takes one hundred and eleven years each way? Would you come all that distance just for nearwood and wheat?" He shook his head. "Even if Earth is still there, we won't be hearing from them again."

John stopped and considered that argument. He had not thought about it before. He knew the legends of the Crossing, of course, and how the People had been put into plastic coffins and made to sleep for over a century, but he had failed to think through what that meant to his belief that the Heaveners were from another world. The People had come to Godsworld; why couldn't others? And of course they *could*— but why should they? Not for trade, certainly, not if the journey took a double lifetime each way. Not even for conquest—unless they had been driven off Earth and had nowhere else to go.

That was foolish, though; the skies were filled with stars. Why pick Godsworld?

Perhaps Satan's empire had conquered all the rest, and was now after the only remaining bastion of righteousness; Satan was said to seek power and domination for its own sake, to hate all who opposed him. But even so, to send a conquering army out on a journey that would last centuries . . .

But would it? Maybe some way had been found of shortening the trip. John was no scholar; he knew that the original People had supposedly travelled as fast as it was ever possible to travel, but he had no idea what the limit was. Might they have been wrong about it? They had been wrong about other things—they had thought their children would live in perpetual peace and harmony, all Christians together, yet the heretics had split the congregation within three years of the Landing, and only now were the People of the True Word and Flesh beginning to see the possibility of reunification within their lifetimes.

No, that didn't seem reasonable. The bartender's explanation made more sense. John still thought, however, that there was something wrong about the entire situation, something warped and alien. Wealth appearing out of nowhere was acceptable—but for that wealth to be in gunpowder *and* plastic *and* other, less identifiable things, fabrics and strange plants and dyes, seemed threatening. A single find, however magnificent, should not produce them all.

If not Satan's people, perhaps Satan himself had decided to try new tactics on Godsworld. It was undoubtedly the Devil who had split apart the People and dragged most of the population down into heresy; perhaps he foresaw that the People of the True Word and Flesh, armed in righteousness, would soon bring the world back together if he did not find a new way to stop them. The wealth of the People of Heaven might come directly from Hell itself.

John had never believed that Satan intervened so directly in human affairs; he had always thought of the Devil, when he thought of the Devil at all, as working entirely through the hearts and minds of men. Perhaps he had been wrong.

The whole thing was a mystery, and John wanted to solve it. To do so, he knew, he would need to get to the heart of it.

Scouting out the military might of Little St. Peter was of only secondary importance. He had to find out who the People of Heaven truly were, and where they were getting their guns and wealth. To do that, he would need to see their home-place.

He had to get to the Citadel of Heaven, that was the simple truth.

"You're right," he agreed. "I hadn't thought about that, but of course you're right. Even if you made the trip asleep, the goods might not be worth anything by the time you got back."

"That's right," the barman agreed, cheerful once again.

"That must be some find they made up there."

"I guess it must be, all right."

"I'd like to see if I can get a little of it for my woolens, then—what's the road to the Citadel like?"

The barman eyed him dubiously. "It's a mighty long walk, through some bad hill country—I don't know if horses could make it."

"But you said Mr. Grace is there, and the traders come and go . . ." John was honestly startled.

"They don't *walk,* though; they take the airship over the hills."

"Airship?" John was no longer merely startled, he was astonished. After a few seconds' confusion, he asked, "Well, then, why can't we take this airship?"

"I didn't say you couldn't; you asked about the road, and where you were worried about prices before, I thought perhaps you couldn't afford the airship."

"Oh." John was struggling to think about too many things at once. In the past hour he had seen weapons such as he had never imagined on the walls of an unimportant village, and wealth beyond believing—but had had his theory of offworld intervention severely damaged, leaving him with no good explanation for any of it. And now this innkeeper's assistant was calmly talking about the fare for an airship as if it were the fare for an ordinary ferryboat. "How much is it?"

"Thirty credits."

"Thirty credits—oh." Well, John told himself, at least ancient scientific machines don't come cheap.

"That's each, if you take your wife—they don't let women ride free—and one way. Same prices coming back. No horses—you'll need to carry your packs yourself, or else pay another twenty credits to send them as freight."

"Oh," John said again. He felt control of the situation slipping away from him, and grabbed it back. He had enough money—he had expected prices to be running rampant in Little St. Peter, and had brought enough for a three-week stay. He could not risk leaving Miriam behind and the woolens would be needed to keep up his pose as a trader. That meant eighty credits each way. Eighty credits would be twelve hundred dollars; twelve hundred dollars each way would take a chunk out of his funds, but would be well worth it if it cleared up the mysteries once and for all and provided him with proof that the People of Heaven were the real threat to Godsworld. "When does it leave?" he asked.

Chapter Six

Thou art to pass over Jordan this day, to go in to possess nations greater and mightier than thyself, cities great and fenced up to heaven.

—Deuteronomy 9:1

THE airship made its pickup at midnight, the entire loading and takeoff carried out in full darkness; it did not come into the town itself, but made its stop a few miles to the southeast, in a small valley, where men with dim lanterns escorted the passengers to an unlit waiting room.

That seemed rather sinister to John. He was unable to get a good look at the airship—which, he realized, was probably the whole idea. It was simply a looming darkness surrounded by more darkness; no lights of any kind were allowed.

John wondered at that. Quite aside from its evil connotations, and even given that the Heaveners wished to keep the ship's exact nature secret, he was puzzled how anyone could steer an airship in the dark. He had only a very vague idea of what controlling an airship would be like, but he had pictured it as a high-speed craft, probably as fast as a galloping horse; he knew that he would not care to ride a galloping horse at night.

John wished that Godsworld had a "moon," as described in Genesis, to provide a little illumination. He had no clear idea what a moon was, only what the Bible said and that Earth had one and Godsworld didn't, but even a "lesser light" would have been welcome.

He and Miriam were not the only passengers; three others, all men, made the flight with them, all closed into a small, windowless chamber with golden walls that appeared to be—but of course could not be—plastic, furnished with benches upholstered in a strange, soft fabric dyed a vivid red. The other passengers ignored John, Miriam, and each other. One of them seemed to have a mild congestion of some sort, and could be heard breathing, but the others might as well have never been for all the companionship they provided.

John debated trying to strike up a conversation, but decided against it.

The two crewmen who oversaw the loading of freight and the embarkation of passengers were tall, dark men armed with pistols, men who spoke slowly and in an oddly slurred manner; John guessed, from Timothy's description, that these were People of Heaven.

As he felt the airship shifting beneath him John began to wonder if he were making a wise move. Perhaps he should have stayed longer in Little St. Peter, learned what he could there, before venturing on. The airship might be a trap of some sort—could there really be an airship on Godsworld? Such wonders were the stuff of old legends of Earth, not everyday reality.

But then, machine guns and the luxuries of Little St. Peter weren't exactly commonplace, either.

Miriam fell asleep resting her head on his arm; judging by the man's slumped posture and steady breathing, the congested fellow also dozed off. In the silent tedium, John lost all sense of time and was unsure whether he was still really awake himself.

Just when he was becoming certain that he had fallen asleep, and that recent events were all a dream and he would awake to find himself back in Marshside, the door slid open.

"Everyone off," a voice called, "we're here." John noticed that it was a Heavener's voice, with the odd slurring—the words were actually more like *"Ehwhuh awh, wuh heh."* There were some variations in speech among the various peoples of Godsworld, but John had never heard so extreme an accent.

He stood up, letting Miriam's head fall; she awoke, and muttered in mild confusion.

"Come on," John said, finding her arm and pulling her up. "We're here."

Dragging a groggy Miriam and the bundle of cloth that had occupied a third seat, John stepped out of the airship and found himself in a corridor. Startled, he looked closely, and made out a seam between the corridor and the wall of the airship. He marvelled that the pilot had been able to bring his ship in so close to the "dock," or whatever it was, that the corridor matched up to the side of the vessel with less than a two-inch gap anywhere.

He wished he were able to see something through that narrow slit, but only darkness was visible. The walls of the passageway were of the same substance as the walls aboard the airship, he noticed, the stuff that looked like plastic.

Behind him the other three passengers were waiting impatiently, eager to be off the airship and on about their business.

"Welcome to the Citadel of Heaven," said a man standing halfway down the short corridor. He spoke with the Heavener accent; John looked at him closely and noticed that the buttons on his shirt were absurdly small, less than an inch across. The texture of the shirt was odd, too, and the cut of the collar was strange. The jeans seemed all right, though they were tighter than customary. He wore a gun on a singularly narrow and unobtrusive belt, a gun not like any John had seen before—there was no cylinder, no hammer, no slide, just a smooth breech and textured grip.

"Have you been here before, sir?" the Heavener asked.

"No," John admitted.

"Straight ahead, then." He pointed down the corridor to a bright red door—hellishly red, John thought. He ambled slowly past the guard, or greeter, or whatever the Heavener was, toward the indicated door, taking in his surroundings and watching for any indication that he should take action somehow.

Behind him he heard the Heavener ask the next passenger whether he had ever been in the Citadel before.

"Yes," the man answered. "I have a trade license."

"May I see your card?"

John glanced back over both his own shoulder and Miriam's and saw the passenger handing the Heavener something small and thin, something that fit comfortably in the man's palm and gleamed silver. The Heavener accepted it and touched it to a spot on the wall that John had taken for decoration; letters appeared on the smooth surface of the wall above the spot, letters that John was too far away to read.

He almost walked into the red door at the end of the passage. He fumbled for the latch as the Heavener said, "Thank you, sir—first door on the right."

There was no latch; instead, he found a small button where the latch should be and pressed it. The door swung open and admitted him and Miriam to a good-sized room, again finished in golden plastic. John glanced around at it. How had that message appeared in the corridor? Was this stuff that the Heaveners used for their walls something other than a simple building material? Were there machines hidden on all sides? That was a frightening thought, reminiscent of nursery terror tales of the computers in the walls that watched everyone on Earth in the days before the Crossing.

The corridor had been windowless—and, John realized, he had seen no lanterns or lamps of any sort, yet it had been brightly lit. On the airship light had come from lamps set in the ceiling; he had been unsure whether they were electric or something else. Certainly they were brighter than any lamps he was familiar with; flames or filaments, however, had been hidden behind frosted glass, making their nature impossible to determine.

This room he now found himself in, however, had a window—a very large window, taking up most of one wall in a single sheet of glass. John had never seen a single pane so large before. Beyond it the sky was still black—he had lost his sense of time and wondered if dawn might have arrived, but plainly it had not.

In the center of the room a plain young woman, clad in a traditional brown dress, stood behind a sort of lectern. She smiled cheerfully.

"*Hlo,*" she said, using a word John had never heard before. She continued, speaking with the Heavener accent. "Welcome to the Citadel of Heaven. May I have your name, please?"

"*J'sevyu,*" he replied politely. "I am Joel Meek-Before-Christ, and this is my wife Miriam, from the Church of the Only God, in North Dan." Miriam, still drowsy, nodded agreement. She had not spoken since boarding the airship.

The woman drummed her fingers unevenly across the lectern, glanced down, then looked up again.

"Mr. Christ," she said, "I'm glad to meet you. None of your people have come here before; are you here as a private individual, or as a representative of your tribe?"

Disconcerted by the peculiar mistake the woman had made in her abbreviation of his false surname—which would, of course, become "Meek," not "Christ," in conversation—John hesitated before replying, "Ah . . . as a private individual—but I'm sure that my family and friends will be interested in what I tell them when I get home."

She smiled. "I'm sure they will. I take it, though, that you don't have the authority to make a treaty with our protectorate on their behalf."

"No, ma'am, I'm afraid I don't."

"Well, that's fine; we just had to ask."

"No, ma'am, I'm here to sell woolens. A fellow in Little St. Peter told me that I could probably get a good price for them here."

A flicker of doubt crossed the woman's face. "Woolens? Not raw wool?"

"No, good woolens—I've got a hundred and fifty yards of the best weave you'll find, without kinks or runs, either raw, bleached, or dyed blue."

"Well, Mr. Christ, I'm not sure that you were well advised, but since you're here, you might as well see what you can get for them. I don't know any buyer offhand; you'll have to try the old town market in the morning.''

"That sounds just fine." The woman had gotten the name wrong again; he was unsure whether or not to correct her. No one had ever before gotten his name wrong—but then, he had never used the name Meek-Before-Christ before.

"If you'll take this booklet—you can read, can't you?''

"Ma'am, of *course* I can read; it's the duty of every man to learn to read so that he can study the Word of God, and my parents saw to it that I learned my duty!" John's response was unplanned and completely sincere, a restatement of what he had been told almost every day of his life between the ages of six and ten, from his first learning the alphabet until he could recite back a chapter of the Bible after a single reading.

"Of course, I'm sorry. If you'll take this booklet, it will tell you about the protectorate that the People of Heaven operate—I'm sure that your family and friends will be interested.''

John accepted the little booklet and looked it over. It was printed on tan paper in incredibly small black type, but still clear and legible. The title was simply *The People of Heaven*.

"And if you'll go through that exit," the woman said, pointing to a brown door near one corner, "the stairs will bring you out on the main road into town. The market's just inside the gate, and there are the usual inns and hotels.''

"Thank you," John said. He started toward the indicated door, but stopped when he realized that Miriam was not following. He turned, and saw that she was still standing between the red door and the lectern, staring at the woman.

"Who *are* you people?" she demanded.

"Excuse me?" the woman said.

"Who *are* you people? What is this place? Was that really an airship? My dear Lord Jesus, what is going *on?*" She stared around. "Am I dreaming all this?"

"Ms. Christ, I—''

"What *is* that?" She pointed out the window.

John had not really paid much attention to the window; he had been aware of its presence and of darkness beyond, bro-

ken by lights, but he had not really looked at them as yet.
Now he turned and looked.

They were on the second floor of a building, apparently,
with an excellent view along a ridgetop road and of the peak
at the end of that road. A walled town surrounded and covered the peak, lit by the usual miscellany of torches, lanterns,
and an occasional incandescent lamp.

At the far side of the town, however, was a building, perhaps a fortress, that towered over the commonplace houses
and shops. Its sides sloped up for five stories, and in every
story lights were ablaze, patterning the walls with the squares
of light and dark windows; the uppermost floor John estimated at a quarter mile or so in length, the lower floors somewhat larger. In the darkness he could not tell anything about
its construction, but in the light that poured from its windows
it was clear that its sides were unornamented and plain, its
roof flat and featureless. It dwarfed the town below it, and in
fact even the mountain itself seemed to be forced down and
subdued beneath that vast blank weight.

Beside it stood something even taller, but narrow, something that gleamed silvery gold where the light from the fortress reached it; John could not decide if the thing was another
building, or a machine, or simply an object of some unknown
sort. He could make out very few details, due to the distance
and the darkness.

"What *is* that?" Miriam repeated.

"Do you mean our headquarters building?" the woman
asked politely.

Miriam turned to stare at her. "Building? That shiny
thing?"

"Oh," the woman said. "Oh, that's another airship—a
long-range one."

John was certain she was lying; the tone of her voice had
been wrong, somehow. That thing was no mere airship.

Despite the impracticality of making hundred-year journeys,
John was quite sure that the shining thing was a starship.

Two hours later John sat on the edge of his bed in a small

inn and stared at the pamphlet the woman had given him. He had read it through twice.

It said nothing about who the People of Heaven actually were, or where they came from, but only that they had "access to much of Earth's technology lost by the rest of Godsworld." They welcomed trade, and would sell weapons and ammunition to any group that joined their protectorate by signing a simple agreement. That agreement required that the member group never attack another group—not just other members, but *any* other group. The weapons were for defense only. Members were not to discriminate on the basis of religion or race—heretics, or even agnostics and atheists, were to be treated as equals. All member groups were equal in status except the People of Heaven themselves. Anyone violating this agreement would be cut off from all further trade and would have all weapons repossessed—by force if necessary.

Anyone who wanted to was welcome to trade with the members for more common goods; only weapons and ammunition were restricted.

Those more common goods included fabrics, dyes, plastics (John had never seen the word in a plural form before), medicines, and machinery such as clocks and alarms.

He glanced over at Miriam, who was curled up on a chair in the corner. She had given no further trouble after he dragged her away from her frantic questioning of the woman at the airport (strange new word, "airport"—John was not accustomed to it yet and was self-conscious in using it even when only thinking). She had come along quietly to the inn, waited silently while John roused the innkeeper, and then settled in her current position when they reached the room.

She had hoped that the People of Heaven would wipe out John's own army, but judging by the pamphlet John concluded that, despite the fearsome appearance of their weaponry, the People of Heaven were pacifists, weaklings, decadent beyond all hope of redemption, with none of the steel of faith in them.

That was the first really encouraging news he had had since the charge into Marshside.

Of course, their weapons *were* formidable, even if manned by wimps. But believers in defense only, and toleration of atheists!

There was that note that misused weapons would be repossessed by force, though—perhaps the Heaveners themselves were not weaklings, but wished their followers to be weakened, so that there would be no resistance when they exerted real authority. The "defense only" rule might just be to prevent some outlying village from involving the entire protectorate in an unwanted war against a major power, and the toleration edict might not apply in the Citadel itself.

Oh, it was tricky, trying to figure out what these people were up to, what their true nature might be, but John was certain of two things about them:

They were not from Godsworld.

They represented Satanic evil.

The former was clear from their vast alien resources—strange plants, plastics, and all the rest—even without that shining metal tower that could be nothing but a starship.

And the latter was clear from their pamphlet; they were working to undermine and destroy the Christian faith on Godsworld by allowing people of differing beliefs to interact, and forbidding their followers to war against those they knew to be in error. How could a man know the truth, if he did not see its power proven in battle? How could he believe that he had the one saving way, and allow those around him not to follow it?

He could bring this pamphlet back with him, and in itself it might well be sufficient evidence to convince the Elders that the People of Heaven were a greater threat than the Chosen of the Holy Ghost—but having come this far he was determined to venture a little further.

He had been awake most of the night, and would want to be fresh when he scouted out the enemy headquarters; he tossed the pamphlet aside, lay back, and was instantly asleep.

Chapter Seven

For the lips of a strange woman drop as an honeycomb, and her mouth is smoother than oil.

—Proverbs 5:3

HE thought it desirable to keep up the pretense of trade, so when he awoke, an hour or so before noon, rather than head directly for the looming gray fortress at the far end of town he gathered up his bundle of cloth and trudged down to the gateside market. He left Miriam locked in the room at the inn; she was still asleep, and after her behavior the night before he did not trust her in public.

An hour or two of attempting to sell his goods would be sufficient, he judged, and then he could go off to find himself lunch and work his way toward the Heavener headquarters.

He had been in the market perhaps twenty minutes and turned down one insulting offer when he spotted a familiar face in the crowd. He paused and looked toward it, but it had vanished.

He watched intently, and a moment later saw it again. This time he was able to place it. "Matthew!" he called.

Several people glanced in his direction; Matthew was a very common name, after all. The one he wanted was among them. John waved.

The man waved back, to John's relief. He had not been mistaken; this was Matthew Crowned-with-Glory, one of his missing scouts. The two of them pushed through the crowds toward each other.

They met in an embrace, slapping each other heartily on the back; John pulled Matthew out of the crowd into a quiet corner.

"What happened?" John asked when they were alone. "Where are the others?"

Matthew's expression shifted from delight to despair with astonishing speed. "Joey's dead," he replied. "I'm not certain about the others. Didn't any of them report back?"

"Timothy came back, finally—but then he deserted when I tried bringing him back here with me. He'll probably hang for it."

Matthew nodded. "Poor Tim didn't much like the Heaveners."

"What happened to Joey?"

"Oh, it was so stupid! He came out here to find me—I don't know why, not really, as I hadn't been gone that long. He didn't worry about the return fare; I had brought enough money with me, but someone stole it, picked my pocket I think, so that I was stranded here, couldn't afford the fare back to Little St. Peter, and I didn't dare tackle the roads alone, without a map or guide—and I didn't even have the money for a map anymore. I've been working odd jobs, doing what I can, to stay alive; I was hoping to save up the fare eventually if nobody came and found me."

"What about Joey?"

"Yes, I know, I was coming to that. Joey came here to see what was keeping me—disobeying my orders, I might add—and didn't think to bring the return fare, so we were both stranded. He reckoned that if we'd been robbed by someone in Citadel, then someone in Citadel owed us that money, and he wasn't picky about who it might be; so he tried to rob someone. He spotted this fellow with a bulge in his pocket that looked like a fat wallet, and a gun that looked like plastic instead of metal, without any moving parts that he could see . . . ."

"I saw a gun like that myself," John remarked.

"Well, Joey saw that one and figured it for a fake, a toy to make the owner feel like more of a man, and he tried to pick the fellow's pocket."

Already sure he knew the answer, John asked, "What happened?"

"Well, Joey was a good scout, but he wasn't any sort of pickpocket—that's not something a soldier learns. The fellow felt what was happening and pulled his gun; Joey called his bluff, but it wasn't any sort of bluff at all. That funny plastic gun blew Joey's head clean off and sprayed bits of it all over the street." Matthew shook his head. "Dang fool thing to try. I watched the whole thing, but there wasn't much I could do except claim the body and sign the petition for a Christian burial."

John nodded. "Sounds like you did what you could. And you don't know anything about Mark or Barney?"

"Well, not really. Joey told me something, but I can't swear to it."

"What?"

"Joey wasn't always the most truthful of men, sir, and he might have been funning, but he told me that he'd found Barney, and that he came looking for me to tell me that Barney had gone over to the enemy. He'd been so taken with the way they lived in Little St. Peter, with those fancy clothes and cheap guns and all, that he'd deserted and settled down there—Joey had found him by accident, and Barney had tried to talk Joey into staying with him. So Joey left Mark in charge in Little Pete and came looking for me, and you know the rest. Mark was supposed to watch the airship place, but if you didn't see him there I reckon he gave up and moved on."

"I didn't see him."

"Well, then, he's probably dead, deserted, or lost somewhere."

John nodded agreement.

Heathen pacifists they might be, but the Heaveners and their followers were proving dangerous enough—out of a five-man scouting party they had killed one, trapped one, subverted one, driven one to desertion, and the fifth had vanished—and it had all apparently been done without anyone ever suspecting the scouts' true nature.

"So how long have you been here?" John asked.

"I'm not sure," Matthew admitted. "What day is today?"

"Monday, April twenty-second," John replied.

"It's been nearly three weeks, then, sir. I arrived on the second or third, I'm not sure which."

"Have you investigated that headquarters building?"

"Ah . . . no, sir. I felt my first duty at this point was to return to Marshside with what I knew, not to risk getting myself killed."

"I can't fault you for that," John agreed. "Fools rush in where angels fear to tread—and you're no fool, Matt."

"Thank you, Captain."

"Somebody has to get in there, though. I won't ask you to go—after three weeks here you've done enough. I'll go myself."

"Do you think that's wise, sir?"

"It may not be. Look, I'll give you the fare back to Little St. Peter; if I'm not back by noon tomorrow you use it. I have a prisoner from Marshside, a woman, at the inn here—the Righteous House. She's locked in an upstairs room. Take her back with you. We left three horses in the stable at St. Peter's Inn, under the name of Joel Meek-Before-Christ. You talk to a man there named James Redeemed-from-Sin, and he should let you have them. You ride back to Marshside and report to Lieutenant Habakkuk. Understand?"

"Yes, sir."

"Good." He counted out the money, then passed over his trade goods as well. "Here, take these darn woolens and see if you can sell any, and I'll go take a look at that fortress."

"Yes, sir." Matthew looked at the bundle. "What should I do with them?"

"Sell them—here in the market. You should get at least fifteen Heavener credits for them."

"Yes, sir." He accepted the woolens unhappily.

"I should see you back at the inn around sundown, I think."

"Yes, sir."

John stepped back, then turned and strolled off in the direction of the headquarters building, leaving Matthew standing in the market looking confused and dismayed.

To his surprise, there were no guards. The strange glass doors were not only not locked, they stood open invitingly. He wondered if he had been misled by the building's massive appearance; perhaps this was not actually a fortress at all, despite the thick walls of smooth concrete. He ambled in, trying to look casual, as if he belonged where he was; nobody seemed to notice.

He found himself in a brightly lit chamber—too brightly lit, and in an oddly yellow-greenish light that seemed to come from the entire ceiling. Three passages led off in various directions, and half a dozen closed doors were located in the various walls. The floor was covered by thick golden carpeting, more luxurious than anything he had ever imagined; the walls were tawny plastic, the doors a darker shade of the same color. There was no furniture, and no people were anywhere in sight.

Puzzled, he chose a corridor at random and walked on into the depths of the building.

The corridor led past dozens upon dozens of doors, across intersecting corridors, endlessly; whenever he thought he saw the end of the passage through the harsh glare of the yellow-green lighting it turned out to be merely a corner.

His eyes adjusted to the odd illumination after a time, and he was able to notice details. None of the doors had handles, and there were no signs to indicate what might lie behind any of them; instead, a small red square of what appeared to be glass was set into the wall beside each one. The corners, he realized, were mostly to the left, so that he was actually following a large rectangle around and around; he had come in on one of the intersecting passages, but he could not identify which one. If he continued to turn only at the ends of the corridors, he would retrace his steps over and over forever.

He had just reached this conclusion after almost fifteen minutes' walk, and was about to pick a crossing passage at random, when a door a few paces ahead of him slid open and a woman stepped out.

He stopped, prepared to salute a lady, but did not nod his courtesy after all; this woman was obviously no lady. She wore a garment of rusty orange that accorded well with the yellow-brown walls, and with her sallow skin as well; it covered one shoulder, but dipped down on the other side well onto the curve of her breast. The skirt was a respectable near-ankle-length, but slit up either side, and the entire dress flowed as she moved, shifting about her so that John had occasional glimpses of far more of her anatomy than he felt he had any right to see.

"Hlo," she said. "My name's Tuesday; what's yours?"

"Joel Meek-Before-Christ," he answered shortly, cutting off his natural tendency to add, "At your service." He was not ready to serve harlots. She had used that odd greeting he had first heard at the airport; he guessed it was a Heavener peculiarity. She had also given a blatantly false name—John knew of no one in the Bible, not even in the Apocrypha, named Tuesday or anything that resembled Tuesday. He looked her in the eye, refusing either to gawk at her body or to turn his gaze away in embarrassment, and noticed that her eyes, like her greeting, had a peculiarity of their own, a very strange one indeed; each had a fold of skin at the inner corner that made them seem unnaturally far apart and somehow crooked. Her hair was very black and straight, and her skin an odd color. Distracted by her outrageous garb, he had not seen at first that she was apparently a freak.

"Joel," she said. "Nice. Come here."

"I'm busy," he said, and turned away, intending to retreat back to the last intersection he had passed.

"Sure you are," she said. "Wandering around like a lost satellite. You've gone past my door four times now." She had the Heavener accent even more strongly than most, in addition to her other quirks.

"I have?" He turned back.

"Yes, you have. Come on in, and I'll tell you about it."
She motioned at the open doorway.

John considered quickly. He had no idea who this woman
was—though her occupation was certainly obvious, probably
something she had been forced into as a result of her physical
peculiarities, which would have precluded a respectable
marriage—but he also had no idea of where he would find any
useful information. He had expected to find the building full
of people he could follow, signs he could read, and other in-
dications of where things were; these empty, featureless corridors had thrown him badly off stride. This whore might well
be able to tell him something of what was going on. He had
never had much contact with whores, but his impression was
that most were not particularly bright, and could be manip-
ulated readily.

"All right," he said. He followed her through the door; it
slid silently shut behind him.

Chapter Eight

*But her end is bitter as wormwood, sharp
as a twoedged sword.*

—Proverbs 5:4

THE room was furnished to a degree of luxury John had never
before imagined. The floor was broken into curving sections
at various levels one step up or down from one another, all
covered with thick red carpeting so soft and lush it seemed
more like a low fog wafting about their ankles. The walls and
ceiling were opalescent and softly glowing, and there were
no windows. Velvet cushions in a hundred shades of red and
gold were scattered about, ranging in size from puffs the size
of his hand to pillows big enough for two to sleep on. Some
were gathered together into couches, and John could not tell
whether they were mounted on a frame of some sort, or
merely arranged.

Pearly tables of various sizes and shapes—all curved—
floated at various altitudes; John looked for the wires that
supported them, but could not detect them. Several held bottles, glasses, or platters of multicolored crystal that contained
strange food and drink.

There was not a single hard corner or rough feature anywhere in the entire chamber, no surface that was not either
gleaming smooth or upholstered in rich fabrics. The woman,
sleek and smooth in her flowing dress, fit in well with her
surroundings; John, in his rough leather jacket and worn
jeans, did not. It was all appallingly decadent.

"Would you like something to drink?" she asked.

"A little water, maybe," he replied, to be polite.

"Oh, no, you must try this!" She handed him a stemmed glass of something a very pale blue in color.

Reluctantly, he accepted it and took a sip. He choked, gasped, and spat it out immediately.

The woman giggled.

He glared at her; when he had recovered his breath he asked, "What *is* that?"

"Just a liqueur." She saw his anger and forced herself to stop smiling.

He stared at the glass in his hand. "Liquor? You mean distilled spirits?"

"That's right."

"I can't drink that! Strong drink is sinful!" He started to fling the glass away, then caught himself and placed it gently on a nearby table.

"You drink wine, don't you?"

"That's different."

"It's still alcohol."

"Only a little. That stuff—it *burns!*"

"You're not used to it, that's all. It's only about eighty proof." She sipped deeply at her own glass, then smiled.

He shook his head. "I'm sorry, I can't drink that." He was more certain than ever that the Heaveners were not native to Godsworld; he had never heard of anyone on Godsworld, not even the most radical of heretics, who condoned strong drink. God had given mankind the gift of fermentation, so that alcohol might ease the strains of life, but it was Satan who invented distillation, to turn the blessing into a curse.

Not that distillation didn't have its uses—alcohol made a good fuel for lamps or even some machines, but not for men.

"Oh, I'm so sorry," Tuesday said. "Against your religion?" The phrase seemed almost mocking, somehow. "Try this, then." The new beverage she offered was richly red.

John sipped it warily; it had a tangy, fruity taste and no alcoholic content that he could detect. "What is it?" he asked.

"Just a fruit punch." She smiled enigmatically.

"Thank you," John said, sipping again.

His hostess raised her own glass, still half-full of the blue liqueur, then sank back onto a pile of cushions. John had not noticed them there behind her; it was as if they had slipped into place as she descended.

He found a large cushion of his own and seated himself gingerly. The thing seemed to shift about to accommodate him more comfortably, but he convinced himself that was merely overwrought imagination, brought on by the tension of being in the enemy's headquarters and being confronted by these strange events and this strange, freakish woman. "Now," he said when he was settled, "you said you'd tell me all about this place."

"Well, no," she answered. "I said I'd tell you about being lost and going in circles." She shifted, leaning to one side; her dress slipped back to reveal most of one thigh.

"Tell me, then."

"You're not from the Citadel, are you? No, I can see you aren't. You came here from one of the other villages, probably one well outside Dawes' little protectorate. You wanted to find out what was going on here—so you walked into this building, which is conveniently left open and unguarded, and then wandered about until I found you. Am I right?"

"Yes," John admitted.

"Well, it's not surprising. But there isn't anything of any importance on this level, you know. You need to know which door leads up or down, to where everything important is."

"What *is* on this floor, then?" He sipped his drink.

"Oh, a lot of storage rooms and meeting rooms and machinery, I suppose. Mostly it's just corridors for people like you to get lost in, and a lot of hidden machines watching."

"Then what are *you* doing here? And all this?" He gestured at the room around them.

"Oh, I had this whipped up for my amusement. I don't really belong here, you know—I just came to see if there was anything entertaining on this world of yours. Dawes would have preferred to keep me out, but I'm a stockholder—she can't.''

John wondered what sort of stockholder she might be; this woman did not look as if she had ever handled sheep or cattle. Another question came first, though. ''Who's Dawes? That's the second time you've mentioned that name.'' Dawes was not a real name, any more than Tuesday was, but he guessed it to be a nickname of some sort.

''Don't you even know that? Ricky Dawes—America Dawes, that is—is the executive officer of the entire operation on Godsworld.''

''What does that mean?'' He ignored the weird name for the moment; it was obviously pagan, but that was hardly surprising under the circumstances.

''She's in charge—she controls the People of Heaven.''

''She does? *She?*'' John, without really intending to, made his true question very clear with his emphasis on the feminine pronoun. He regretted it immediately; some women, he knew, were discontented with Godsworld's recognition of the natural superiority of the male.

''Yes, *she* does.'' Tuesday seemed more amused than angry, but John decided not to pursue that; arguing with women about the proper roles of the sexes was likely to get nowhere and provoke animosity that he would do better without. He drank the rest of his fruit punch as he groped for another question.

''You know,'' Tuesday said, ''I'd rather talk about you— if we have to talk at all.''

John shrugged.

''Have you had many women?''

Shocked at the bluntness of the question, even from a whore, John replied, ''I don't talk about that.''

''You don't?'' She smiled.

John was beginning to dislike her smiles. ''No,'' he said.

''Do you *do* anything about it?''

He said nothing, simply sat and frowned at his empty glass. He refused to say anything in reply to such direct obscenity.

"No?" She grinned, openly mocking now. "Are you a virgin, then? Or do you prefer men?"

This was the second woman to question his manhood within the past few days; he had dealt calmly with the first, but that was before the strains of his scouting expedition. He forced himself to put his empty glass down gently, then stood up. "I did not come here so that you might insult me."

Her grin broadened. "Oh? Where *do* you go to be insulted, then?" She stood up in turn, and reached up to the single shoulder of her gown.

"I'll go now," he said. He turned, but the door was closed.

She twisted something, and the dress fell away completely, leaving her naked. "I guess there's no harm in this," she said, still smiling, "since you don't know what to do with a woman."

He turned back to face her, rage mounting within him. He tried to remind himself that anger and lust were mortal sins, but the woman stood mocking him with her stance, hips thrust forward, her hands out in a displaying gesture. He growled wordlessly.

"Take it or leave it," she said.

He lunged at her; she fell back onto the cushions, laughing, and her hands groped for his belt, unbuttoned his pants. He no longer cared whether she was cooperating or not; he intended to prove his mastery over her. As he pushed himself between her legs she wrapped her arms around him, one hand on his back and the other on his neck; he felt a sharp sting where fingers brushed his neck, but ignored it.

Only when he was finished did the possibility of poison occur to him. He pushed himself up and rolled off her, then felt at the back of his neck.

There was a small twinge as he touched one spot; he drew back his hand and found a small smear of blood on his fingers.

"What did you do to me?" he bellowed.

"What?"

"My neck—what did you do to my neck?"

"Oh, stop shouting, it's just a little pinprick."

"It's not poisoned?" He calmed somewhat, and his voice dropped.

"No, it's not poisoned; why would I want to poison you?"

"I don't know; why did you jab me? What did you do it with?" He was genuinely puzzled.

She held up one hand languidly and showed him the tip of her index finger; a thin metal wire, the tip sharpened like a needle, projected from it at a peculiar angle. He could not see what held it in place.

"What's that?"

Her satisfied smile broadened. "It's called an empathy spike. It's wired into my nervous system—into my brain. When I used it to hook into *your* nervous system, I felt everything that you felt."

"You read my mind?"

"No, stupid—it only picks up your physical sensations. I felt what your *body* felt, not your mind."

"Oh!" Once again, John was shocked—horrified, in fact. The concept was strange, but once he grasped it he loathed it immediately. It was the most obscene thing he had ever heard of. This woman had violated his privacy in a way he had never imagined, *could* never have imagined. It was bad enough that he had copulated so thoughtlessly with a freak, but it was infinitely worse, somehow, that she had felt his own sensations as it happened. He pulled away from her, instinctively curling himself into a semifetal position. "That's disgusting!" he spat.

"Oh, it's fun!" She giggled, then rolled over onto one elbow. "It's so much more fun with the spike!"

"It's disgusting!" he repeated.

"You think so?" She grinned. "I'll have to introduce you to Isao sometime—if he lives long enough."

"Who is this Esau?" That was a name he could understand.

"Not Esau, Isao—it's Japanese, I think. He's painwired. He has his pain nerves hooked into the pleasure center of his brain; he feels every injury as pure pleasure. One of these days he'll get carried away and kill himself; he's already had to replace all his fingers and toes—and a few other things.''

"Oh, Jesus!" John was suddenly unable to accept his situation. This was not possible; God could not permit such things to exist. This impossibly luxurious room, this woman who spoke so casually of the unspeakable, this entire building and all the People of Heaven, were abominations. It all had to be a nightmare. He fought down nausea and willed himself to wake up somewhere else.

"Hey, don't take it so badly!" Tuesday said. "I just thought it would be interesting to try it with a Godsworlder, someone different—and don't feel badly that you did it, because I put aphrodisiac in your drink; you couldn't help yourself." Her almost apologetic tone suddenly gave way to another giggle. "You were pretty good, too—awfully quick, but you put your heart into it, you know what I mean? And with the spike I don't mind if it's quick."

John said nothing; he lay there, unable to awaken and convinced that it was all real after all, trying to gather up the shattered fragments of his thoughts.

"Hey, are you all right?"

He did not answer.

She said something totally alien; John was not even sure it was words. He closed his eyes, straining to think.

"The computer says that you're okay, just upset. I can't wait around all day, Joel; that wouldn't be any fun at all. I think you can find your way out if you try; I'll leave the door open." He heard her moving about, heard the rustle of clothing.

"Wait," he said.

"Why?" she asked.

"Where are you from?"

"Me? Ho Chi Minh City. Why?"

"No, I mean, where are the People of Heaven from?" He opened his eyes and saw her ankles; a skirt hung above them, cut like the one she had worn before, but this one was a different color, a deep rich brown.

"Earth, mostly; they're a wholly owned subsidiary of the

New Bechtel-Rand Corporation. It was fun, Joel." She walked away; her ankles vanished from his field of vision.

He lay there for a few seconds more, then uncurled and got slowly to his feet. As she had promised, the door to the corridor stood open. He walked unsteadily out into the passageway, chose a direction at random, and began looking for the exit.

From Earth? As far as John was concerned, such monsters of decadence could only be from Hell, and he had every intention of destroying them before they could harm Godsworld any further.

And the woman who had seduced him and used that infernal spike on him—if that whore was merely a "stockholder," which he guessed to be something like the Satanic equivalent of a deacon, then this America Dawes could be no less than the Great Whore of Babylon herself.

Could the spike have been poisoned after all? He felt weaker than mere emotional distress would seem to account for. But then, he had just . . . raped? Attacked? He had just had a woman, and he had been drugged; the unknown aphrodisiac might have side effects.

If he had been poisoned he would fight it off. He drew strength from his fury. His uncertain walk became his usual firm stride, and ten minutes later, after a few false turns, he found the lobby he had entered through. He left the building and marched toward the inn.

Chapter Nine

Who is this that darkeneth counsel by
words without knowledge?

—Job 38:2

LAZARUS Speaker-of-Gospel cocked his head sideways and stared at his nephew in annoyance.

"You're sure of all this?" he demanded.

"Yes, Elder," John replied, "I am. You've heard Matt's testimony as well; I'm sorry that the heretic Miriam Humble-Before-God won't speak, and that we couldn't find any of the other surviving scouts, but you have the sworn word of two good men, good Christians, and good soldiers. Isn't that enough?"

"I'm not sure; by your own admission you were drugged by this woman, and Matthew never heard anyone claim to be from Earth, nor saw any of the shameful perversions you insist took place."

Hiding his own annoyance, John said, "He saw the guns, though, and rode this airship of theirs, and can swear that these people are strangers to Godsworld who live in sinful luxury and decadence. Three years ago the Citadel of Heaven was just another heretic community, up in the hills—now it's the home base of this growing protectorate that uses Earthly weapons and preaches against evangelism. Even if these strangers aren't Satan's minions sent from Earth—and I believe that that's exactly what they are—they are an evil force

74

we've got to destroy." Beside him, Matthew nodded agreement.

Lazarus sighed.

At the end of the council table Jacob Blessed-Among-Men barked impatiently, "Enough of this! These people are obviously a threat, and we have to destroy them; John's right about that. So what are we going to do about it?"

"Can't it wait until after we've fought the Chosen?" Simon Called-to-the-Truth whined.

"Their power is growing steadily," John said. "Marshside was on the verge of joining their protectorate when we captured it; if we'd been a month later, we might've faced not just one machine gun but a dozen."

"And that's something that troubles me," old Isaac Fisher-of-Men said, shaking his head unsteadily. "What could you and your men—fine as they are—*do* against the weapons you say these people have? John, you lost what—thirty men against that one machine gun?"

"Thirty-one," John admitted. "And two more who died later. But, Elder, we were taken by surprise; we were charging down an open hillside, making ourselves perfect targets. We wouldn't be doing that against the People of Heaven; we know what we're facing this time."

"Do we? John, you may be a good soldier, but you don't know everything; there were weapons back on Earth that make machine guns look like children's slings. What if these people have them?"

"Why should they? They didn't come here to fight a war; they came to subvert us, lead us into the temptations of material wealth and sensual pleasure. If they have other, mightier weapons, why have they kept them secret? Why not let it be known, so that we would be more frightened than ever? Maybe Earth has lost some of its wonders, just as we have; maybe they couldn't bring that much with them. *I* don't know their reasons, but I don't believe they have any of these miracle weapons."

"Still," Lazarus pointed out, "you'd be leading men with swords up against machine guns."

"I would be leading men with swords and rifles and bombs and whatever shields we can devise up against machine guns—men armed with steel and with steel in their backbones, the steel of the one true faith, against guns manned by soft and decadent weaklings!"

"We don't need speeches," someone muttered; John did not see who had spoken.

"The men of Marshside fought well," Lazarus said. "They weren't weaklings."

"They weren't the People of Heaven, either—they hadn't even joined the protectorate yet."

"So you want to take all our guns and ammunition and men, all the explosives in New Nazareth, and attack the Citadel of Heaven with them, sneaking them in where the roads are so bad travellers ride this ungodly airship," Simon said derisively. "Fine—what are we supposed to do if the Chosen attack while you're leading your men up through those hills?"

"I hope to have the armies of the Chosen with me," John replied.

"What's he talking about?" Simon demanded, looking back and forth at his fellow Elders.

Lazarus sighed again. "I hadn't told them about that part, yet, John," he said. "I figured we'd best start with the easy part."

"Elders, I want to make a truce with the Chosen of the Holy Ghost. After all, they're as threatened by the People of Heaven as we are; I think we should put aside our differences until this greater threat has been destroyed. You've pointed out yourselves that our army, fine as it is, might not be enough against these diabolical weapons the Heaveners use—but if we had the Chosen marching beside us, our numbers doubled, nothing on Godsworld could stand against us."

"I don't like this," Simon said. "I don't like it at all. They're heretics."

"They're still Christians, though," John insisted. "The People of Heaven aren't."

Old Adam Bearing-the-Cross, who had sat quietly beside Jacob Blessed-Among-Men throughout the entire session until now, spoke up. "Our ancestors put aside their doctrinal differences in order to come to Godsworld in the first place," he said. "They hoped for a miracle that would show them how to resolve those differences permanently, and that miracle never came—but can we do any less to preserve Godsworld than they did to create it? I don't say that I believe every word John has said about these people—it's hard to imagine offworlders sleeping a hundred years to come here and make trouble—but John obviously believes it, and he's a good man, an intelligent man. If he tells us these people are a real threat, and that stopping them is more important than showing the Chosen the error of their heathenish ways, then he's probably right. I say we make the treaty."

"I agree," Jacob said. "After all, we can always take care of the Chosen later; this way we'll know more about how they fight."

"And they'll know more about the way *we* fight," Isaac pointed out.

"We know enough about how they fight now," Simon said. "Can't we deal with them first, and *then* attack the Heaveners?"

"We need their strength," John said.

"Vote!" Paul Bound-for-Glory called.

"All right," Lazarus said. "All those who favor treating with the so-called Chosen of the Holy Ghost to form an alliance to attack the so-called People of Heaven, vote aye. Paul?"

"Aye."

"Thaddeus?"

"Aye."

"Simon?"

"No."

"Isaac?"

"I'll abstain."

"Tom?"

"Aye."

"Jake?"

Simon objected, "You're not taking them in order."

"I don't have to," Lazarus replied. "Jake?"

"Aye."

"Adam?"

"Aye."

"And reluctant as I am, I vote aye, too," Lazarus said. "That makes six for, and with an abstention that's a majority. God's will be done, amen. If you others want to go on record you can, but that's all we need. Anyone?"

No one spoke up; after a brief pause, Lazarus continued. "All right, then—someone get John a white flag and a cross, and he can head out for Spiritus Sancti right now."

"Thank you, Uncle Lazarus," John replied.

The party that had ridden full speed from Marshside had been made up of John, Habakkuk, Matthew, and Miriam—John had brought Matthew and Miriam to support his testimony, and Habakkuk to report on the current state of the army at Marshside, reaffirming the soldiers' faith in their leaders and their readiness to fight any foe. The party that gathered for the journey to Spiritus Sancti, an hour after the meeting of the Elders, included John, as spokesman; Habakkuk, as second; a civilian by the name of Peter Light-of-the-World to speak for the Elders; two soldiers as honor guard; and Miriam, because nobody had any better idea of what to do with her. Matthew was to return to Marshside with Lieutenant David Saved-by-Grace, who would be taking charge of the army there until John's return—John and Habakkuk had left a mere underlieutenant running things, and the Elders deemed that unsuitable.

It was the third of May when the party reached Spiritus Sancti under heavy guard and was led into the presence of the Anointed.

When Peter had run through the required formalities and made introductions, John came directly to the point. "We have come here in hopes that we can convince your people to forget, temporarily, their differences with the People of the True Word and Flesh, and join with us against a common foe."

The Anointed sat back on his cathedra; the chair creaked

beneath his weight. "And who would this common foe be?" he asked.

"The so-called People of Heaven, and their infernal pagan protectorate."

"I don't know a thing about them; they're on the other side of the New Jordan, and I don't concern myself with anything over there."

"Well, sir, whether you know it or not, they're a growing threat to all of Godsworld, on both sides of the New Jordan, from Asher all the way to Simeon."

"Oh?" the Anointed said politely.

"Yes, they are! They're from Earth, agents of Satan come to destroy us."

"Oh?" the Anointed said again. "What makes you think so?"

"I've visited their capital, and they told me as much. They have the lost arts—they have an airship, they have machine guns, and they're fabulously wealthy. They're expanding rapidly; it won't be more than two years before they start nibbling away at your own southeastern territories. They've already taken Little St. Peter, and St. Peter itself is a part of your domain, isn't it?"

"It is—but if I were concerned with *Little* St. Peter we'd have taken that, too. Still . . . agents of Satan, you say?"

"Their women are wantons, their men cowards; their leader is a woman. The towns they 'protect' become soft and decadent. They have no faith—they insist their client towns accept any sort of heresy."

The Anointed nodded. "And your people intend to put a stop to these abominations?"

"With your help, yes."

"You propose to put an end to your plans for a war against my people?"

"We propose an alliance until the last of the People of Heaven is destroyed; I can't promise any more than that."

"And if I accept such an alliance, whose command would our armies fight under?"

John glanced at Peter and Habakkuk, then turned back to the Anointed. "That remains to be negotiated."

"I see." He nodded again. "Is that everything?"

The True Worders looked at one another. "I think so," John said.

"All right, then. You folks can wait in the yard; I need to pray and talk to my advisors. I'll let you know my decision before supper. God be with you." He pushed his swollen body up out of the chair and plodded heavily from the room.

The Chosen guards herded the True Worders unceremoniously out before they could protest, out to the yard in front of the Anointed's house where rows of benches were available for petitioners.

After a moment of rebelliousness, John shrugged and sat down. He was in the enemy camp; he had no say here. He could not even use the standard diplomatic threat of war to demand better treatment, since what he wanted most of all was to avoid a war against the Chosen.

Miriam sat beside him, pressing up close; startled, John turned and looked at her, even as Habakkuk and the others, noticing her actions, discreetly took benches well away from the pair. She smiled winningly.

"What do you think you're doing?" he asked quietly.

"Oh, I'm just enjoying myself," she replied in a near whisper.

"You are?"

"Sure—I knew you were a coward and a hypocrite all along, and it's nice to have proof."

John felt his face going red, and glanced at Habakkuk. Habakkuk politely looked the other way; he had seen the red and assumed that his captain was blushing at something the girl had suggested.

"A coward?"

"Yes, a coward. You claim that you command an army of the Lord's own men, the only followers of the true religion on all Godsworld, but before you go up against the Heaveners—men you called decadent weaklings—you want to make sure you've got the help of the biggest bunch of heretics around. The big brave warrior!''

"They have machine guns,'' he reminded her.

"A lot of good machine guns did Marshside!''

Annoyed, he pushed her away and sat brooding silently.

The sun was well down the western sky when a messenger summoned them back into the Anointed's presence.

"I've decided,'' the Anointed said without preliminaries, "that I can't afford to risk my people by getting them into a war that's none of our business. You may be right about the threat these heathens present, but we'll just have to trust in the Lord to protect us. We won't join your alliance.'' He paused, watching the True Worders' faces for reactions, then went on. "However, since these 'People of Heaven' may be a real threat someday, we *will* swear to remain neutral in any war you poor heretics may wage against them; we won't harm any of you so long as you fight the Heaveners.'' He shifted in his seat and leaned forward. "In fact, we'd be glad to arrange a truce, whether you fight the Heaveners or not, so that our two peoples won't be weakened by fighting each other. We don't want to make it easy for the Heaveners to wipe us both out later.''

John said, "I hope you'll reconsider—''

The Anointed interrupted him. "Boy, when I speak from this cathedra, it's final—I don't reconsider. You got that?''

John opened his mouth, then closed it again and nodded.

"Good. We've got a couple of rooms for you down the street; you stay there tonight, but be out of the city by noon tomorrow. Got that?''

John nodded again.

"Good. Thanks for coming; tell your Elders to send me a message if they want that truce, and I'll lay off you as long as you fight the Heaveners, truce or not. Now get out of here, and God be with you.'' He waved, then sat back and watched as the True Worders departed.

The rooms were in a boardinghouse, but the matron refused to serve heretics, so that supper consisted of cold trail provisions. After everything was eaten and the food had had time to settle, John, Habakkuk, Peter, and Miriam gathered in one room to talk—or rather, the three men were to talk; Miriam was just there.

"I don't like it," Habakkuk said.

"Which part?" Peter asked.

"Any of it."

"The truce offer isn't bad."

"It's interesting, certainly," John agreed.

"It's a trick of some kind," Habakkuk insisted.

"I don't think so," John said. "The Chosen have been careful about treaties; they don't break them without provocation. I think that the Anointed means what he says."

"Why? A few months ago the Chosen were practically *begging* for a war, blocking our trade routes, taking hostages . . . why would they want peace now?"

"There's only one reason anyone *ever* wants to avoid a war, Hab; they think they'll lose. A few months ago the Chosen didn't know anything about our army; I would guess that they've learned a little since then. They may have spies, or maybe someone from Marshside talked to them. Or maybe it's something here in Spiritus; maybe there's been trouble in *their* army. Anyway, they think they'll lose if there's a war, that's plain."

"You're right, John—that's got to be it. And that's why they want us to fight the Heaveners—so they can take on the survivor while he's still weak."

John nodded. "I'd say so."

"But in that case, we need to attack the Chosen *first;* after we're done with them we can worry about the Heaveners. The Chosen are a lot closer to home, John, and, truce or not, they've been our enemies for years, while the Heaveners don't even know yet that we exist. If we take the Chosen now, then take a year to rebuild, we should still be able to take on the Heaveners; but if we take the Heaveners now, as soon as they're defeated the Chosen will take us from behind, before we can get our men back across the New Jordan."

John shook his head. "I think you're right about most of that, Hab—but I'm not sure that we *will* be able to take on the

Heaveners after a year's rebuilding. If we don't get them now we may never have the strength.''

''You don't have the strength now!'' Miriam spat.

The three men looked at her.

''You'll never take the Heaveners on; none of you have the guts. They'd blow you all to bits, squash you like bugs.''

''Oh, shut up,'' Peter said.

''Why? Will you hit me if I don't? You're all so brave against a woman, but when it comes to facing those machine guns you'd probably all turn and run! Where's the strength of your faith now? I thought God was on your side!''

''God *is* on our side,'' Habakkuk said calmly. ''But God helps those who help themselves. We mustn't *depend* on miracles; that would be the sin of pride. We can only accept them when they come.''

''And if they don't come, you'll just let these Heaveners walk all over you? You won't defend Godsworld against the heathen unless you're sure you can win? Oh, I am just overwhelmed by your integrity!''

''Shut up, woman,'' Peter said again.

''Some defenders of the truth! You're afraid of the truth when you hear it! Godsworld is going to be taken over by the Heaveners because *you* haven't got the guts to fight them—and when they do run everything, and they don't have to play nice anymore, I'll watch them skin you alive and I'll laugh!''

''Why would they skin us if we *don't* fight them?'' Habakkuk asked placatingly.

''For your effrontery in claiming to have the true faith, when you won't fight for it!''

Peter slapped her; to his astonishment she responded by punching him in the belly with her closed fist. He doubled over as John and Habakkuk grabbed her.

When order was restored and Miriam securely bound to one of the beds, John said quietly, ''She's right, you know.''

''About what?''

''We have got to fight the Heaveners. They're the real threat to God's way, and we all know that. Even if we don't have a chance, how can we call ourselves Christians if we don't fight for what we believe? We know the Chosen aren't a real danger now, but the Heaveners are. We have to fight them. God will see to it that the Chosen don't stab us in the back—or that if they do, we'll triumph in the end all the same.''

Habakkuk shook his head. ''I don't like it, John.''

''It's what's right, whether you like it or not. And besides, if we wipe out the Heaveners we may capture some of those weapons they have—if we do that we can handle the Chosen even if we've lost half our army. I'll send messengers out, see if we can recruit some allies other than the Chosen, but even if we can't, by September I intend to be the lord and master of the Citadel.''

Chapter Ten

> *Then said he unto them, Nation shall rise against nation, and kingdom against kingdom.*
>
> —Luke 21:10

IT was amazing, John thought, how readily the small tribes signed up when they were promised booty and did not need to choose sides between empires. Faith did not come into it, really, although his messages had made an appeal to defend Christianity. Ordinarily, when one side was recruiting allies, the other side would be also, so that the small tribes would not join for fear of later reprisals against the losing side; the Heaveners, however, seemed totally ignorant of the preparations being made against them. Furthermore, they had a reputation for incredible wealth—which meant good looting—and no reputation at all for fighting. The True Worders had been a long-standing threat for most of the small tribes; the Heaveners were newcomers no one had learned to fear. With the Chosen swearing neutrality, John had had no trouble in picking up dozens of volunteer companies.

Of course, he had made a point of the decadence and evil of the Heaveners, while downplaying their armament.

His own armament had increased significantly; bombs that would probably have been of little use wasted in open battle against the Chosen would be quite effective against the hillside defenses of the Heaveners, so John had appropriated the entire True Worder stockpile.

The result of his preparations was the largest, most heavily armed army Godsworld had ever seen, all prepared in incredible haste under his command. By the third of August John was finally satisfied; on the morning of the fourth of August, after the necessary invocation and brief dedicatory service, he led his troops out of the immense camp one day's march east of Marshside, and on toward the Citadel.

In the hectic days of gathering and equipping his forces he had had no time for lesser concerns; as a result, Miriam rode beside him. He had never decided what to do with her; for some reason he could not define he was reluctant to send her to New Nazareth as an ordinary captive, to work and be taught the true faith. He told himself that she could be useful, and simply brought her along wherever he went, even though, in fact, she had as yet been of no use whatsoever.

He called a halt at noon, for lunch and a rest, and watched with pride as the vast company neatly settled to the ground. Glass-tipped spears flashed redly in the sun; harness jingled and blades rattled. A murmur of voices began.

Satisfied, he swung down from his own mount and was reaching for his provisions when he heard the sound, low and harsh, but growing quickly louder. It was a little like the whir of a spinning wheel at first, but by the time he looked up to find its source it was already rising into a screaming roar.

Motion caught his eye; he turned just in time to glimpse something huge and glittering. Before he could focus on it it howled directly overhead, the sound plummeting from an ear-piercing shriek to a dull rumble. He whirled, trying to follow it, but it was gone over the horizon before he could make out anything but a shining blur.

The murmur of voices died, then was reborn as a babble that quickly mounted into shouting chaos. The one question that he could hear clearly, over and over, was, "What was that thing?"

John felt a cold uneasiness in his belly as he remembered Isaac Fisher's words: "There were weapons back on Earth that make machine guns look like children's slings."

Then the thing reappeared on the horizon and swept toward him again; the sound followed a moment later. John began a loud prayer. "O Lord, we are gathered here to fight in Your name . . ."

He paused; something was happening. A small piece of the thing was splitting off, dropping down toward him. He forgot his prayer and started to call a warning, but his voice was drowned out by the roar of the thing passing overhead.

The smaller part did not pass overhead in a flash; instead, it slowed and dropped nearer, until it was hovering over the army's vanguard. It was almost flat, roughly triangular, and black and silver in color—silver around the edges, black at the center. John could not be certain of its dimensions against the empty sky, with nothing to give it scale, but judged it to be four or five feet across.

"People of Godsworld!" The voice boomed out suddenly, coming from the hovering device; John started, as did almost everyone else.

"People of Godsworld!" the voice repeated. "You are marching against the People of Heaven, thinking to destroy the Citadel and loot the protectorate. This is your only warning; we have the means to defend ourselves. We have weapons that could shatter Godsworld like a hen's egg hit by a sledgehammer. Turn back now, return to your homes, and no ill will befall you; continue on and you will be destroyed. This is your only warning. We do not wish to harm anyone, but any further advance in our direction will be met with force." John noted that the voice had only a slight Heavener accent. The device hung silently for a moment longer, then swooped away with only a faint buzz.

"It's a Devil's trick!" John bellowed as the thing shrank into the distance. "Forward, march! In the name of the Lord!"

With some scattered hesitation, his men got to their feet; with more hesitation they formed lines. John saw, with some distress, that a few were falling out, stepping aside, even turning to run. He drew his sword and waved it over his head. "In the name of the Lord, we march on!" he shouted as he spurred his mount forward.

The horse took a few steps, then stopped and shied as the larger flying craft came roaring up at them again from behind the eastern hills. This time it was lower in the sky than before, and seemed to John to be diving directly at him; without thinking, he slid sideways off his horse to the ground, rolling as he hit.

Something flashed, and men screamed behind him. He struggled to his feet, sword still in his hand, and looked around for an enemy he could strike—or for something he could use against his flying foe.

The enemy was gone again, but this time its passing had not been harmless; supply wagons were ablaze, and John could see men lying sprawled at the roadside, blood running freely. Screams and shouts battered at him.

Then the wedge-shaped thing was back, and the voice announced, "This land is under the protection of the People of Heaven; you have fifteen minutes before further action will be taken against intruders."

John shook his fist at it, sword flashing. "Darn you! *Damn* you!" There was no way he could strike at it. He had never thought before about the difference flying machines could make in a battle.

Habakkuk was shouting something at him; without bothering to listen, John shouted back, "We march on, those of us who dare to fight for the Lord!" He remounted his horse. "We have fifteen minutes to find cover! Those of you who are too cowardly to face the Devil's minions, turn back now; the rest of us will pray for your souls when we've triumphed!"

He spurred his mount forward again; when he had gone a few yards he glanced back and saw that his army was ripping itself in half. Some men were following him, pressing forward, while others had turned back. There was no pattern or order to it, simply two mobs sorting themselves out from one another.

He kept his horse walking forward; Habakkuk was, as usual, at his right hand, and to his surprise he saw Miriam following close on his heels.

"What are you doing?" he called.

"I want to see what they do to you," she called back. "I've been waiting for this for months!"

He had calmed considerably, as he always did when the actual instant of crisis was past, but her reply irritated him anew; he turned away and ignored her. Instead of worrying any further about Miriam, he called to Habakkuk, "Go back with them—see if you can turn them around when they're over their initial fright." He pointed at the retreating half of his army.

"Yes, Captain," Habakkuk said; he saluted, then turned his horse and spurred it to a gallop, back toward Marshside.

By the time the fifteen minutes were past the two groups had separated completely, a widening gap forming between them, and Habakkuk was in the midst of the retreating group; he was not yet trying to turn them, but merely riding along until the moment seemed right. At the head of his own half John was trying to pick up the pace, as his reduced force was still far from any decent shelter, anything that might shield them from whatever mysterious power had sliced up a dozen men and set threescore wagons ablaze.

The triangular thing had hovered overhead the entire time, occasionally changing position; now, as it hung close above the center of John's loyal troops, the voice suddenly called, "Cover your eyes! Cover your eyes!"

John glanced up and then, without thinking, covered his eyes with his arm.

Even so, he saw the flash; the light seemed to burn into his eyes, pouring around his forearm and even through it, so that for an instant he could see the shadow of his own bones.

Then the shock wave hit him, and everything vanished.

He awoke slowly and painfully, blinking unsteadily up at the uncomfortably bright, greenish yellow glow of the ceiling.

That glow answered the first question that anyone asks when waking up somewhere different from where he or she went to sleep; John knew where he was, he was inside the Heavener stronghold.

That left a myriad of other questions, however.

How had he come here? What had happened to his men? It

seemed obvious that his army had been soundly defeated; where did that leave his people? What had that flash been? Why had the flying thing shouted a warning to the attacking troops to cover their eyes? What was he doing here? And just where in the Heavener fortress was he, and how could he get out?

He turned his head; his neck was stiff, but he ignored the sharp twinge of pain.

He was lying naked in a bed, covered by a soft white sheet and surrounded by more of the familiar and hated golden plastic walls that seemed to be in everything the Heaveners built. A small table stood nearby, and the walls were dotted with various mysterious panels and protrusions. The bed was not flat; it seemed to be fitted to his body in a wholly unnatural way. It was extremely comfortable, which immediately made him suspicious. Life was not meant to be comfortable; the pleasures of the flesh were snares and delusions. They weakened a man's will.

"Please do not attempt to get out of bed," a pleasant voice said from an unidentifiable source; it had only a trace of the Heavener accent, and John was unsure if the speaker was a man or a woman. He turned his head back the other way, looking for whoever had spoken, but the tiny room was empty save for himself, the bed, and the table. There were two doors, one opposite the foot of the bed and one to his left; to his right the center of the wall contained a large panel that might have been a shuttered window.

"Who said that?" he asked; his voice was a faint croaking. He swallowed, coughed, swallowed, and asked again, "Who said that?" This second attempt was better, but still thin and hoarse.

"Who said what?" the pleasant voice asked.

"Who are you? Who am I speaking to?"

"I'm Cuddles; I run things around here."

Another of the absurd Earther names, John thought. "Where are you?" he demanded feebly.

There was a pause before the voice replied, "I'm right here."

"Let me see you! Show yourself!" John's breath gave out

after making this demand; he coughed feebly, then lay back to recover. He was still not at all sure what had happened, but he had apparently been injured somehow. This place was the Heavener infirmary, he was sure.

A panel on the wall beyond the foot of the bed glowed oddly, then seemed to vanish, leaving an opening into another room. A bland face smiled down at him. "Here I am," Cuddles said.

John still could not be certain of the speaker's sex; the face was beardless, the black hair worn at a moderate length, the features fairly delicate but not clearly feminine. The skin was oddly dark, as if heavily tanned.

"Come in here!" John demanded.

"I can't do that," Cuddles replied. "But someone will be there very soon. Here he is now."

The door to the left slid silently open, and John turned in time to glimpse the corridor beyond as a young man wearing a short white gown and white pants entered.

"Hlo," he said. "I'm Liao Hasan." The name was utterly incomprehensible to John, merely noise, even less meaningful than the other Earther names he had encountered. "I'm glad to see you awake." The man had the thickest Heavener accent John had heard yet, and also had the same odd skin hue and eye formation as the woman who called herself Tuesday. That startled him; could Tuesday have been, not a freak, but a member of an unfamiliar race? John was familiar with the half-dozen varieties of dog on Godsworld, and had heard that on Earth there had similarly been three separate races of people, white, black, and brown, descended from Noah's three sons, but he had never before encountered any kind but his own; none of the original colonists had been Hamitic or Semitic, though John had never heard any explanation of why the Japhetic race should be the only one to accept the true faith.

This attendant and Tuesday were surely not black, and even calling them brown would be a gross exaggeration, but perhaps they were another human variant that Godsworlders had forgotten.

"Who are you?" John demanded. "What am I doing here?" His voice cracked on the final word.

"I'm Liao Hasan; I'm a medical assistant here. You were brought here badly burned after your army was nuked three weeks ago; we've regrown your skin and repaired what other damage we found."

John ignored the claims of miraculous healing. "Nuked?" he asked.

"Yes, nuked; your army was destroyed with a clean fusion bomb. Intense heat in a very small area, but only a small shock wave, and virtually no fallout or secondary radiation at all—there's no fission, it's just an overload of a fusion power plant, not really a bomb at all."

John did not pretend to understand any of this explanation. "What happened to the others?" he asked.

Hesitantly, the man said something that John could not make out.

"It is not polite to speak in a language the patient does not understand, sir," the neutral voice replied.

"Ah . . . all right, Cuddles, have it your way. Answer my question. Am I authorized to tell him that?" John noticed that the "medical assistant" did not look at the window when he spoke, but simply addressed the air over John's head.

"Yes, sir," Cuddles replied calmly. "There are no additional restrictions on information for this patient."

"Well, we aren't sure how many people you had there to begin with; the central part of the advancing group was vaporized. There were even a few burns in the retreating group—that was a serious miscalculation. Out of the advancing group, we saved one hundred forty-seven men and one woman. Oh, and two horses. We aren't as good with horses—there aren't any back home."

"One hundred forty-seven men?"

"That's right."

"I had . . . well, after the split, I reckon I had six thousand men."

"I'm sorry."

John struggled to grasp the scope of the disaster. "The others are *all* dead?"

"It's possible a few fled before our rescue team arrived; I can't say for sure. The only reason you survived was that you were well ahead of the main body. The woman and about half a dozen men were up front; the rest were at the back. We were trying to avoid the retreating group."

"So I'm in your infirmary now?"

"We call it a hospital, but yes."

"And you're a doctor?"

"No, I'm a medical assistant—a nurse."

John stared for a moment, then dismissed the incongruity of a man claiming to be a nurse.

"Who's Cuddles? A doctor?"

"Oh, no, of course not! It's a *comsim.*" The final word was not any part of the Godsworlder version of English; the "medical assistant" pronounced it even more strangely than he pronounced more familiar words.

"A what? Say it slowly."

"A *comsim,*" the young man repeated carefully.

John dug back in his memory, picking through the faint memories of childhood lessons about Earth and man's history there.

"Comsymp?" he asked. "Communist sympathizer?"

"No, no, *comsim;* computer simulation. It's not real, it's just an image the machines use to talk to you."

"Oh!" John had heard stories about machines that talked, machines that thought, or flew, or swam, or whatever, but he had not always believed them completely. He looked at the window; Cuddles smiled and nodded.

"Yes, I am a computer simulation," Cuddles said. The image suddenly distorted and then reshaped itself, and John abruptly realized that what he had taken for a window was a screen of some kind on which the image of a face was projected.

"Cuddles, do you need me here?" Liao Hasan asked.

"No, I do not think I do," Cuddles replied. "If the patient has no objection, you may continue your rounds."

"Do you mind if I go? Cuddles will take better care of you than I could, anyway, Mister . . . I didn't get your name."

With his army destroyed, John saw no need to dissemble—and he did not seriously doubt that his army was defeated, though perhaps not as thoroughly obliterated as the Heaveners claimed. "John Mercy-of-Christ, Armed Guardian of the True Word and Flesh," he replied.

"Mister Mercy-of-Christ. Glad to have met you." He turned to go.

"Wait!" John croaked.

The medical assistant turned back.

"What happened to my people?"

"I told you . . ."

"No, not the army; I mean my tribe."

"The True Worders? Oh, they've joined our protectorate as a client state; the treaty was signed four days ago. Cuddles can show you the tapes, if you like."

John looked back at the screen; the computer's bland artificial face gazed mildly back as Liao Hasan departed. "Would you like to see the tape of the treaty signing?" it asked.

"Yes," John said, unsure of the proper way to address a machine.

"Do you have a preferred format?"

"Ah . . . no."

"Very well." The face vanished from the screen, and John found himself looking at a gathering of people at a peculiar angle, as if peering up through a basement window. He was shocked to recognize all the Elders, and Habakkuk, on one side; on the other were various strangers in peculiar brightly colored clothing.

The sounds of formal conversation swelled to fill the room, and John watched in horror as each of the Elders in turn first signed a paper, then pressed his hand to a metal plate. Finally, Habakkuk's turn came, and the ceremony hit a snag.

"This says 'Armed Guardian of the True Word and Flesh'; that's not right," said Habakkuk's familiar voice. "We don't know for certain John's dead, and you haven't deposed him. I'm just Acting Guardian."

"Just sign it and add 'Acting' after your name, then," Lazarus replied.

"Let's get it over with," Jacob called.

Uncertain, Habakkuk glanced about.

"Listen, even if John turns up alive, do you think we'll keep him around after what happened?" Paul Baptized-in-Fire demanded. "You're the Armed Guardian now, Habakkuk, like it or not. Sign the treaty; they want a military authority, and you're the best one we've got."

"All right," Habakkuk said as John struggled to rise to a sitting position. He accepted the pen and signed.

"Stop!" John called.

The scene vanished instantly, leaving the blank wall panel.

"You said that was four days ago?"

"Yes."

"Oh." John sank back. A thought occurred to him. "You said a hundred and forty-seven men survived; what happened to them all?"

"One hundred and six were treated and released, and I have no information on their subsequent actions. Thirty-eight, including yourself, are now conscious but still hospitalized; all are due to be released shortly. Three are still comatose; one of those three may not survive, or at any rate may have suffered irreversible brain damage. Of the total, sixty-two ignored the warning to cover their eyes and may still be suffering impaired vision."

"What about the woman?"

"Miriam Humble-Before-God has been conscious and fit for release for over a day now, but refuses to leave until you do, Mr. Mercy-of-Christ. She left a message for you, to be delivered at your request."

"What's the message?"

The reply was not Cuddles' voice, but Miriam's shriller one. "I told you I'd see you all fry, you bastard! You lived through this one, but I'll see you die yet—you aren't rid of me!"

"Oh, Jesus," John muttered, fighting back tears of rage and frustration, "how did it come to this? What have I done wrong?"

Chapter Eleven

Out of the mouths of babes and sucklings hast thou ordained strength because of thine enemies, that thou mightest still the enemy and the avenger.

—Psalms 8:2

THE clothes they had given him upon his release were strange, and so comfortable that John felt as if he weren't wearing anything, which he found disconcerting as he made his way up the street. Miriam followed close behind, but he ignored her. He was a warlord no longer, and therefore could have no prisoners, and was not ready to deal with Miriam on any other basis. She still hated him, yet she followed him without taking any openly hostile action against him. He had serious doubts about her sanity; in his opinion, a sane person would go on about her life—or rather, since her old life had been wiped out, would go about building a new life. The Citadel, with its insistence on treating strangers as equals, was probably the best place on Godsworld for doing that. Miriam's clinging to her pointless enmity, the last vestige of her old world, struck him as senseless. The People of the True Word and Flesh had been defeated, had become just another client of the People of Heaven; what more did she want?

His enemy, on the other hand, was triumphant, and John was determined to reverse that. An open attack had failed, and obviously had had no chance to begin with against the Satanic weaponry the Heaveners used—little wonder they were willing to sell machine guns when their own armament was so much more powerful! There were other methods besides open attack, though. After much careful thought and study, and some indirect questioning of the machine that called itself Cuddles, John had come to the conclusion that there were no more than five hundred of the Earth-born Heaveners on Godsworld; they controlled thousands of Godsworlders, true, but the Earthmen and Earthwomen were, relatively, only a handful. If he could bring their followers to see them in their true light, as agents of Hell come to destroy Godsworld, John was certain that he could bring even the corrupted and decadent population of the Citadel to rebel. After all, just a few years before the Citadel of Heaven had been an independent city-state; some vestige of pride and Christianity must linger.

It puzzled him that the Earthers had made so little effort to conceal their actual origins. Surely they knew that the people of Godsworld were aware of Earth's evil nature!

Against a popular uprising their weapons would not be enough; they could not bomb their own homes, after all. Even if they were able to hold out indefinitely in their fortress—their Corporate Headquarters, Cuddles had called it—they would have no further influence on Godsworld, and that would be enough to satisfy John.

All he had to do was stir up a rebellion.

He turned and entered the Righteous House inn, Miriam close behind.

The Heaveners had given him money—reparations, they called it, a word he had never heard before. He was able to book a comfortable room and order himself an ale without worrying about the cost. With the cold mug in hand—chilled by a Heavener machine called a *frizh*, instead of with honest ice stored from last winter—he settled at a large table, annoyed by the softness of his chair's upholstery and the gentle feel of his own clothes.

Miriam, after buying herself wine with her own reparations money, sat down two seats to his left.

John knew exactly what he wanted to do, but he was not

quite sure of how to go about it. He was not a preacher. He had had some experience in speaking, in telling his troops what he wanted and firing them up for battle, but that was not the same thing as trying to convince someone of something. The men had been a captive audience, already proud and eager, and had respected him and known him; now he would be speaking to strangers, individuals or small groups at most, most of whom would be reluctant to believe him, and all without the madness of crowds to help him.

He sipped his ale and tried to prepare himself, planning out what he would say.

Twenty minutes after he sat down, as he had known would happen as the inn filled up with the lunchtime crowds, a young man sat down on his right. "Excuse me, sir," the fellow said. "I hope you don't mind if I sit here."

"Go right ahead," John said. "Glad of the company. Joel Meek-Before-Christ is my name." He put out a hand.

The other reached across to shake it. "*J'sevyu*, Mr. Meek," he said. "Aaron Blessed-of-Heaven."

"Really? I knew a family by that name, back in North Dan. Kin of yours?"

"I can't say; my folks are from Naphtali, but we aren't traced. Don't know anyone in Dan, North or South, but they might be kin somehow."

"Naphtali? What brings you to the Citadel, then?"

"Oh, *I'm* not from Naphtali; when I was a baby my folks' village was burned in a border war, but they slipped out and headed this way. We've got a place in the hills a few miles east of here; I'm in town for some supplies." The man's initial formality had faded away.

"What do you think of this place?" John asked.

"The inn?"

"The whole town."

Aaron shrugged. "It's a town. It's nice enough, since the New Heaveners arrived, but too crowded for me."

"New Heaveners?"

"The tall ones who talk funny. The folks around here have always called themselves the People of Heaven, ever since I was a baby, anyway, but they were just plain folks until the new people showed up a few years back and started trading.''

''Where'd these new people come from?''

Aaron shrugged again. ''Couldn't say. I've heard rumors, but you can't trust those.''

John looked down at his mug for a moment, then back at Aaron. ''I'll tell you, Mr. Blessed, it happens I know where they're from—I was in their headquarters for something, and I found out. Wasn't any chance I misheard or misunderstood, either; they're from Earth.'' He watched closely to see how Aaron took this.

''Well,'' Aaron said, lifting his mug, ''that's the rumor I'd heard. I don't know what they're doing here, then—what we've got here that would be worth the trip.''

''I think that's plain enough, Mr. Blessed—it's us they're after. They're not Christians, you know—when our people left Earth they were the last true Christians around, though there were still some heretics claimed the name. The people of Earth all sold their souls to the Devil centuries ago, and now they've come here to collect ours, too.'' John kept his voice low, but a certain intensity crept into it.

Aaron glanced at him, surprised by that intensity, then took a healthy swig of ale before answering.

''Mr. Meek, I can't say you're wrong—but does it matter? Seems to me that we've done a pretty fair job of consigning our own souls to perdition right here on Godsworld. Jesus said to love our neighbors, but I'm here now, instead of down in Naphtali, because some of those loving neighbors didn't like the way my grandpa said his prayers and burned him out. They hanged him, as a matter of fact—him and sixteen other men—and raped my grandmother and all the other women they could catch. That's not any sort of neighborly love I know. Now, these Earthers, if that's what they really are, have come here and paid us all good prices for what we could trade, sold us what we wanted at fair prices, and they haven't burned any villages or hanged or raped anybody, so far as I've heard. That's no sort of evil I ever heard of; it's more my idea of a good neighbor. If they aren't good Christians, and that's as may be, I figure that's their own concern, so long as they don't try and stop me and mine from being what we are.''

"They killed six thousand men last month—fried them, out on the plain, and took over their homeland.''

"The True Worders?'' Aaron frowned. "I heard about that—a bad business, no doubt about that. But those men were coming here to attack us; they were offered a chance to turn back, and a lot of them took it—and those who did weren't hurt. Seems to me that when someone's attacked he has a right to defend himself. And the Heaveners didn't take away the True Worder homeland; all they did was sign a treaty to defend it against the Chosen of the Holy Ghost, or any of the other troublemakers up that way.'' He paused, drank more of his ale, then looked at John. "You said North Dan,'' he said. "Were some of your folks in that army? Most of North Dan's True Worder land now.''

"*I* was in that army,'' John admitted. "I was wounded.''

"And they brought you here to patch you up? Now, you see what I mean? That was just plain neighborly—good Samaritans, these New Heaveners. The Samaritans hated the Jews, you know, but in the parable a Samaritan helped a Jew—you can't judge everyone just by where they come from. Did you ever think that maybe the New Heaveners were outcasts from Earth, same as our ancestors were? Maybe they came to Godsworld looking for the true path, hoping we could show it to them. Fine welcome your people gave them! I don't know if that's the truth, but it could be. I'll judge them by what they do, not by what our ancestors told us about Earth.''

The possibility that the Heaveners did not represent Earth as a whole had not occurred to John, but he refused to be thrown off by it. "Look at what they're doing, though,'' he said. "They've turned this town into a fleshpot. Look at these cushions, these colors! It's disgraceful—decadent!''

Aaron waved that away. "Horsemold,'' he said. "What's so decadent about a few cushions? You know, life is hard here on Godsworld, because God didn't intend people to live here—He meant for Man to live forever in the Garden, back on Earth. The Bible says so. Man was thrown out of the Garden, and eventually he came here, and we've done the best we can with a hard lot—but the way we live now, our ancestors who first came here would call hard poverty, Mr. Meek. I've seen old pictures, from right after the Crossing—the Reverend Fuller, who became Adam Full-of-Grace, kept what they called an album, and there's a fellow out our way still has it. Back then, before there were so many people and before the ship fittings got so spread out or lost, folks lived better than the people here in the Citadel, the ones you call decadent, live now—and a hundred times better than most of the poor villagers out there.''

John was becoming confused, frustrated, and angry by this young man's easy countering of his every point. ''They were still weak then!'' he almost shouted. ''They had just come from Earth, and the stink of decadence was still on them! God made life here hard to purify men, to work that softness out of them, and that's what it's done; and you want to let these Earthers let it all back in, make us weak again!'' He was leaning toward Aaron, frowning ferociously.

''Mr. Meek,'' Aaron said, ''I don't want to argue with you; you take it how you will. I'm just saying that I don't have any quarrel with the Heaveners.''

''And I'm saying that as a good Christian, you should! We need to defend ourselves!''

''I don't feel, Mr. Meek, that I need any defending against the Heaveners. If they do me wrong, or if I see them do wrong to another, then I reckon I'll reconsider, but I don't see that they've harmed anybody that didn't attack them without reason. Nobody's forced me to trade with them. And as for comfort making them weak—how weak can they be if they wiped out an army in fifteen minutes?''

''They did that with hellfire!''

''No, sir, they did it with a weapon that was designed and built by men—just men, not demons.''

''Men too weak to fight for themselves, though—they need machines to do it.''

Aaron finished his ale. ''Mr. Meek-Before-Christ, I enjoyed meeting you," he said as he stood up, "but I think I had best move along now. Have a good day, sir, and God bless you." He nodded politely and walked away.

John watched him go, seething with suppressed anger. His first attempt at recruiting had been a dismal failure; the boy had had a smart answer for everything. Still, he was just one man; the Citadel was filled with others, and John was sure that he would find plenty who would rally to his cause. He glanced around the room.

Most of those present had heard a little of the argument, and were now steadily ignoring him, while two seats away Miriam was grinning at him in triumph. She leaned over and whispered, "All you're going to do is get them mad enough to hang you—so you just keep it up, Captain John!"

She sat back, smirking.

Chapter Twelve

Put not your trust in princes, nor in the son of man, in whom there is no help.
—Psalms 146:3

EVEN after a week and a half of intensive efforts John could see no sign at all that he had angered the Heavener authorities with his harangues. Unfortunately, there was also no sign at all that he had won a single convert, or even planted any seeds of doubt that might later bloom. The people of the Citadel, either native or visitor, simply refused to worry about any dire purpose that might lie behind the generosity and goodwill of the New Heaveners. The only actual result that John could detect was that after a week or so a few people were beginning to refer to them openly as "the Earthers."

He knew when to cut his losses; besides, just because he saw no evidence, that didn't mean the Earthers weren't mad at him. On the eleventh day, the fifteenth of September, he bought a ticket on the airship and headed for Little St. Peter.

He had not given up, however. The people of the Citadel had been too thoroughly corrupted to be saved, true, but the rest of the protectorate might not be so far gone; he admitted to himself that most of the client populations were probably as deluded as the people he had spoken to in the Citadel, but there were probably still some men who held to the true ways, and at the very least he could hope to organize some sort of resistance *somewhere*, even if only mercenaries from outlying areas. Open warfare was not possible, but quick raids and harassment could be effective. If he made life sufficiently difficult for the protectorate's client states, no more would join and some might drop out. The spread of the Heavener contamination would be stopped and the evil contained, even if not destroyed. The Heaveners could not expand peacefully if no one was willing to sign up, and if they switched tactics and tried to expand by force their evil intent would be out in the open, and John could exploit that, perhaps even foment the popular rebellion he had expected initially.

With that all thought out he boarded the airship in a mood of guarded optimism, ignoring Miriam, who was still following him.

She was not willing to be ignored, however, and shortly after the airship took off she demanded, "Fleeing for your life, Captain?" She spoke loudly enough that two of the five other passengers glanced in her direction.

"No," John replied calmly, "just looking for more promising ground to seed."

"I hope you find some, Mr. Meek/Mercy—I'm still looking forward to seeing the Heaveners finish you off."

"If you want me dead so much, Ms. Humble, why don't you kill me yourself? You tried once, but since then you've passed up a dozen opportunities. Try it again and let's get it over with—I'm tired of seeing you following me around."

"Oh, no; I want no blood on my hands. When I tried to stab you I was still mad with grief—and besides, I thought I was defending myself, I thought you planned to rape me; I didn't know you were queer. Vengeance is the Lord's, and He'll take vengeance upon you when He's ready—but I want the pleasure of seeing it happen, as a comfort for my own suffering."

"You don't seem to remember the fifth chapter of Matthew's gospel," John said. "Taking joy in another's suffering is not Christian. I have no further quarrel with you; leave me alone and I'll trouble you no more. Let what is past be past."

"And what of yourself, then, if you're so concerned with good Christian behavior? Aren't you seeking your own vengeance? Haven't you killed people, and aren't you planning to kill more?''

"I am fighting to save God's truth from its enemies, woman; the things of this world, even the lives of men, aren't as important as the life of the soul."

"You're so certain that the Heaveners are evil?"

John looked at her closely. "I thought you wanted me to fight them, so that I would be killed."

"Oh, I do, and I think that you'd fight them regardless of whether you thought they were evil or not. They're your enemies; they killed your men, destroyed your stinking little empire. You'll fight them anyway; you're not one for loving forgiveness."

"Matthew five, forty-four—I do believe that, and I would forgive them and welcome them with all my heart if I didn't know them to be agents of Satan. They did destroy the People of the True Word and Flesh, the last bastion of the one purely true way of God—what more evil do you need?"

"Your people destroyed themselves, by attacking a more powerful foe—*you* destroyed them, by attacking the Heaveners. There's no evil in defending oneself. It may not be the Christian way—one could turn the other cheek—but it's not evil."

"If it's not Christian it *is* evil."

"I don't believe that."

"I do. Christ said, 'He that is not with me is against me'— Matthew, chapter twelve, verse thirty."

"Well, we don't know for sure whether they're Christians or not—Matthew, chapter twenty-four, verse fourteen, the gospel shall be preached to *all* nations. What evil have the Heaveners done? Why attack them so foolishly in the first place?"

"You need to ask? They wallow in the sins of the flesh; their homes are full of sinful luxuries, and they take their pleasures without thought. When I visited their headquarters a woman who gave an obviously false name so that she wouldn't be held to account, forced herself upon me, seeking a moment's relief from her lust—not even an honest whore, as she took no money, but simply humiliated me for her own amusement. These are the people of Sodom and Gomorrah, come again.''

''And you're no Sodomite yourself?''

''No.''

''I almost believe you,'' she said, staring at him. ''This woman . . .'' She trailed off.

John waited for her to finish her question, but when she did not he simply let it drop and turned away. He had had enough of the conversation in any case.

At Little St. Peter John left the airship and hired a ride into town; as the wagon crawled up the slope he looked around for Miriam, but saw no sign of her in the darkness. He wondered if he had finally managed to lose her.

He quickly dismissed her from his thoughts as unimportant, however, and concentrated on his plans to organize a guerrilla resistance against the Heaveners.

He remembered James Redeemed-from-Sin at St. Peter's Inn, who had spoken so strongly on the Heaveners' behalf; that, he decided, would be a very bad place to start. Accordingly, when the wagon dropped him in the market square, he asked a few questions and found himself a room at a small boardinghouse, owned and run by the widow Worthy-of-Heaven.

In four days he found only one man who was willing to fight the Heaveners. Jonas Dust-to-Dust was perhaps not the most desirable recruit he had ever seen—fifty years old, but as bent and wrinkled as a man of eighty, not very bright, and apparently ready to hate just about anybody, particularly if there was money or food to be had by doing so.

He was, however, a start, and he did happen to make one very useful remark.

''Seems to me,'' he said when John had explained the situation, ''that if you want to put together an army you should go where there's already some soldiers. All we got here in Little Pete is those fool guards on the walls, that work those big guns, and they ain't really soldiers at all.''

John accepted the truth of this immediately. While it was true that he would have preferred to turn the people of the protectorate against their masters, it would be far faster and easier to find soldiers elsewhere. He had had no trouble recruiting allies for his disastrous first attack; surely he would be able to find ready allies for a guerrilla war. The Chosen had seen what happened to their hated enemies; they might now be frightened enough to help. With Jonas in tow, he spent most of his remaining reparations money on three horses and set out for Spiritus Sancti.

No one in the protectorate paid much attention to them, but within an hour of crossing the border into the territory of the Chosen of the Holy Ghost they were surrounded by armed men, taken prisoner, and herded onward toward Spiritus Sancti.

John did not resist this treatment; he simply announced, over and over, that he carried an important message for the Anointed.

Jonas was less cooperative; despite John's example he put up a fight, knocking two men to the ground before someone broke his jaw with a rifle butt. He was bound and flung across his horse's back. John was permitted to ride upright, though the soldiers did confiscate the long knife he had bought in Little St. Peter as a replacement for his own sword, which had somehow never been returned to him after his hospitalization.

To John's disappointment, they were not taken directly to the capital; instead, they turned off the main road and found themselves in a military outpost. Here, after delays that John struggled to take calmly, he was dragged before a harried-looking captain, leaving Jonas to wait his turn.

"Name?" the captain asked wearily, without looking up from his desk.

"John Mercy-of-Christ, former captain in the army of the People of the True Word and Flesh," John replied. "I have a message for the Anointed."

The captain looked up. He stared at John for a moment, then commented, "You're not in uniform."

"I said *former* captain, sir; I was relieved of my command."

The captain sat back, folding his hands behind his head. "Mr. Mercy, I sure hope you know what you're doing. It's traditional to use 'retired' or 'discharged' officers as spies; you could be hanged for espionage if you're not careful."

"I'm not a spy, sir; I have a message for the Anointed. I came into your territory openly, I haven't done or said anything out of line; what else am I supposed to do? I *was* relieved of my command, for leading my men into a massacre; should I lie about it, or wear a uniform I'm not entitled to? Besides, I haven't *got* a uniform; it was burned. They took my sword, too."

The captain leaned forward again. Even if he had not recognized John's name, he had certainly heard of the massacre the True Worders walked into.

"What's this message?" he asked. "Who's it from?"

"It's for the Anointed, from a group who want to keep the protectorate run by the People of Heaven from getting any bigger than it already is; I can't tell you the details, but we're hoping for some help."

"You didn't do very well with your first try—that is, if you were really in command of that attack."

"I was, sir—and that's why I won't try a frontal assault again. There are other ways, though."

The captain stared at him. "How many of you are there? The True Worders are too scared to fight; you must be an independent operation, right?"

"Well, sir, we aren't connected with the traitors in the True Worder government who sold out to the Heaveners, that's true. As for how many of us there are, even if I told you, would you believe what I said?"

"Probably not," the captain admitted. He thought for a moment, still staring at John.

"All right," he said at length. "If your buddy bears out your story, I'll send you to Spiritus Sancti with a recommendation that you be given a chance to talk to the Anointed. And if you are what you say you are, Mr. Mercy-of-Christ, I hope you get what you're after and wipe those bastards off Gods-world." He motioned, and the two guards led John away.

Jonas apparently managed not to ruin John's story; the following morning the pair was on the road again, this time accompanied by four heavily armed Chosen soldiers.

The Anointed heard John out politely.

"I take it," he said after a thoughtful pause, "that you're the military commander of your little group."

John nodded.

"Your record against the Heaveners isn't very inspiring."

"That was the first time any army I led was ever defeated in battle—I didn't think they'd have any weapons that powerful. Now I know better."

"Even so, you'll understand that I'm not about to name you as my commander in chief and give you free rein. What I *will* do is offer my men a chance to volunteer. And I think we can sell you guns and bullets cheap—maybe even make it a loan. I don't think I like these Heaveners either, you know. And with the True Worders gone, I don't need my whole army here, sitting around eating and getting fat and lazy. Ah . . . answer me truthfully, now. How many men have you got so far? I know it isn't many, or I'd have heard about it."

"I can't say, exactly," John said. "They come and go— men volunteer, others decide they made a mistake and go home. Not many, though, I'll admit that."

"Fewer than a dozen?"

Reluctantly, John said, "Yes."

"I thought so." The Anointed leaned back with a contented smile on his face. "That's all right, though; you know the enemy better than we do. I'll call for volunteers and send them along. You'll have to wait just across the border—can't have any hostile acts on Chosen land. The Heaveners might be watching, with those airships of theirs."

"I suppose they might," John agreed calmly. He forced himself to smile back.

Chapter Thirteen

*Have not I commanded thee? Be strong
and of a good courage; be not afraid, neither be thou dismayed: for the Lord thy
God is with thee whithersoever thou goest.*
—Joshua 1:9

THE Heaveners had, in a way, been very obliging in settling
in the high hills; John and his men had no trouble finding
places to hide amid the rocks and valleys surrounding the Citadel. Had the city stood on an open plain, or gently rolling
countryside like that around New Nazareth, they would have
had to find concealment within the walls, and confined themselves to sabotage and assassination instead of raiding.

John's company was a good-sized one. Eighty-five of the
Chosen had volunteered, including three officers, and every
one brought a rifle and five rounds; John guessed that that
must have virtually emptied the Anointed's arsenal. As soon
as he and the Chosen had their home camp set up and a basic
organization established, John headed for the nearest town,
intent on more recruiting; he did not like being one of only
two non-Chosen in his own army.

He quickly discovered that the handful of survivors of his
own destroyed True Worder army were still scattered about
the Citadel and a few of the surrounding towns; the Heaveners had simply turned them loose when they were sufficiently
recovered, just as they had with John himself. He had assumed previously that, as commander, he was given special

treatment, but such was not the case. Of these men, fourteen were successfully recruited; the other survivors either refused to join or were never found. John considered this a disappointingly small response; he had hoped for greater loyalty from his own men.

As word of their presence spread, though, a handful of other recruits turned up. Eight volunteers drifted in from True Worder lands, three of them soldiers in Habakkuk's army who felt guilty about turning back before the massacre, the other five civilians who had disagreed with the decision to surrender and join the protectorate, army or no army. Four other men and two women also wandered in from various places.

John was surprised that Miriam never came looking for him, to wait for a chance to watch him die, but there was no sign of her.

With over a hundred men John felt ready to begin his campaign. He had hoped for more, perhaps enough to split into several bands, but he would take what he had and use it as best he could.

The Anointed had provided tents, but John had refused to set up such ideal targets, and had used the oilcloth to roof over a washed-out gully instead, scattering dirt and various red plants across the top for camouflage. The result was a cool, dim interior, long and narrow, with steep sides and a rough, slanting uneven floor. John made his headquarters at the upper end; below that was the kitchen area, and the remainder was divided between sleeping areas wherever the ground was relatively flat and dry, and open commons wherever it was not. One walled-off corner of the lower end served as a latrine, the other as a stable.

It was rather pleasant throughout most of October, but late in the afternoon of the next to last day of the month, the twenty-third, as John sat cross-legged on a rock planning the last few details of the opening raid on the Corporate Headquarters building, scheduled for that night, the fall rains arrived, drumming heavily on the fabric roof and dripping down through the seams.

Men who had been outside for one reason or another came rushing in, hands on their heads; of the dozen who had been gathering fungus for the kitchen supplies only one kept hold of his load, the rest dropping the pasty red lumps wherever they were so as to run better. The clouds had been building for days, but had not been expected to break quite yet.

The trickle of water down the center of the gully widened perceptibly as John watched. He sighed and put down his pen and parchment. The rain would be good cover for the raid, but he was sure the men wouldn't see it that way. They would only notice that they were cold and wet.

"All right," he called over the general hubbub. "Those men going on tonight's raid, let's get moving; this weather is going to slow us down. If we want to get there and get back before dawn we'd better get started."

"But, Captain," someone called, "we can't go in the rain!"

"Why not?" John demanded.

"Won't it ruin the guns?"

"Not if you're careful. Come on, then." He clapped his own helmet on his head, slid the waxed-wool rust protector over it, then picked up his bundled supplies; his new sword, bought a week before in the protectorate village of Christ's Corner, was already on his belt, and his heavy leather jacket on his back. He had no rifle; he had never liked them.

Reluctantly, the others he had selected gathered about him: eight of the Chosen, two of his loyal True Worder soldiers, and a blacksmith from Truechurch who had resented the Heaveners' trade in plastic. All ten soldiers carried rifles, with two rounds in each; the smith carried an assortment of explosives and a good sword, but, like John himself, no firearms.

A few months earlier John would have considered twenty bullets an incredible extravagance for a single raid, but since the Heaveners had turned up with their apparently infinite supply of powder—if it was actually gunpowder they used, and not something else, as John had heard suggested—bullets were suddenly more plentiful, and had the advantage of being useful at long range. Guerrillas could not afford to get in close enough to a fortress to use blades.

Besides, the Chosen were supplying the ammunition; it cost John nothing, and the Chosen officers had assured him more would be forthcoming if he needed it.

He had no grandiose ambitions for this initial raid; it was simply to get the men doing something, rather than sitting around letting the weather deteriorate. A raid would stir things up, would encourage the men, and might even attract more recruits. John had a dozen of his most reliable and intelligent men scattered about the local markets and taverns, looking for likely candidates as well as trying to pick up useful information about Heavener activities or organization.

The men he had chosen for the raid were his second-best dozen; he looked them over as he spoke a brief invocation, carefully kept nondenominational out of respect for the doctrinal differences between True Worder, Chosen, and Truechurcher. They seemed sound enough, reassuring him of his earlier selection. He did not care to increase the risk of failure by using men who might panic and freeze or flee, and he was confident these men would not. Although they grumbled, when he announced ''In the name of the Lord, amen!'' they echoed him promptly and followed him readily enough as he led the way out into the driving rain and up the hillside toward the Citadel.

Visibility was poor; the sun was still above the horizon when John broke out the rolls of string he had brought to link the men together and prevent them from getting lost in the dark. As long as each was tied to his string, the twelve of them would stay together; if any of them got lost, they all would. He had originally chosen string because a lantern would have been too easy for the Heaveners to spot, but he blessed his choice now because he doubted a lantern would have been enough in the downpour.

They struggled on, some of them complaining loudly, the others persevering in silence that could be either determination or simply resignation, and an hour or so after sunset they spotted the lights of the Citadel ahead of them.

They were approaching from the rear, with the intention of doing what damage they could to the fortress without involving any native Godsworlders. This side was not guarded, so far as anyone knew; the cliff below the fortress was presumably thought to be guardian enough. That was a major reason John had chosen it, instead of the "airport," for the first attack.

The cliff, however, was not really that bad at all; he had investigated it himself a few days earlier. It was steep, true, far too steep for horses or vehicles, but by no means sheer, with plenty of handholds and ledges, not a very difficult climb for a healthy man.

Of course, John had not climbed it in the dark, in pouring rain. His companions balked at first when they reached its base.

"Come on!" he said. "It's easy!" He snatched a rifle from its owner. "I'll show you myself!" He began marching up the slope, using one hand to steady himself, the rifle clutched in the other.

When he was twenty feet up he heard the scrape of boots on stone and knew that his men were following him. He kept moving, and only when he was almost halfway up the hundred-and-fifty-foot climb did he glance back to be sure they were all there.

They were. "Safe-in-God's-Hands, come get your rifle," he called.

The Chosen soldier scurried up to where John was waiting and accepted the return of his weapon. The rest of the climb was made in silence.

The slope levelled off as they climbed, and they soon found themselves standing on a gently rising hilltop below the fortress wall.

The fortress loomed above them, its windows glowing golden through the gloom; the lowest were a few feet above John's head.

"All right, Safe," he said, "let's see what you can do with that gun of yours." He gestured at the windows.

Silas Safe-in-God's-Hands lifted his rifle, selected his target—they had hoped to find a Heavener to snipe at, but he saw no sign of anyone in the windows—took careful aim, and fired.

Instead of the sound of breaking glass, however, his shot was followed by the whine of a ricochet. Embarrassed, he lowered his weapon. "I must've missed, sir," he called. "But I don't see how. Must've been the rain."

John had been watching the window, and thought he had seen it shiver as if something had hit it. "You were close, anyway. Here, move right up next to one and try again."

The range had already been short, but Silas obediently took a few steps forward and aimed at one of the lowest tier. He was so close that he was thrusting the rifle up more than forward. It was absolutely not possible for him to miss at this distance; he squeezed the trigger.

Again, the bullet whimpered away as a ricochet, and the window remained intact. John stared up at it for a moment, then stepped up as close as he could and studied it intently.

There was a narrow scratch on the glass, dead center. He motioned for the men to move in.

"Here," he said, "someone lift me up and let me take a look at this."

Two men crossed arms to form a seat, and John was lifted up until his eyes were level with the bottom of the window. The scratch was definitely there. Peering in, he could see that the room was full of machinery quietly whirring about its business; he saw no sign of any human inhabitants.

He reached up and tapped the pane with one finger, then closed his fist and rapped on it with his knuckles.

"Darn!" he said. "It's not glass!"

"What is it, then?" someone called.

"I don't know—but whatever it is, it's bulletproof. Let me down."

He was lowered to the ground, where he stood staring resentfully up at the warm glow of the window.

"What do we do now?" someone whispered.

"Well," John said, "maybe we can't shoot out the windows the way we planned, or pick anyone off, but we've still got ourselves enough explosives to blow a hole in their wall, I'd say.'' He looked around for the Truechurcher black-smith.

The smith's name was Thomas Across-the-Jordan. ''Jor-dan,'' John called, ''let's see what you can do with that stuff.''

''All right, Captain, but I'm not too sure about the fuses in this rain.''

''Do your best.''

The smith set to work. While he unpacked his knapsack John announced, ''If any of you have any ideas or sugges-tions, I'd be glad to hear them; I was figuring half of us would be inside by now, not still out here in the rain.''

After a moment of uneasy silence, someone suggested, ''We could work our way around the walls and go in the front, couldn't we?''

''We'd have to go over the old town wall,'' someone else answered.

''We could head out to the airship port,'' a third voice said.

''Could we?'' John asked. He turned to look at the build-ing's corner and consider the possibilities.

''Sure! If we stay right under the walls, no one will see us coming; we can slip right in and wreck the place, maybe cut the Citadel off.''

John nodded. ''I wasn't planning to do that tonight,'' he said, ''and I'm not sure we can get past the guards without a fight, but it's as good an idea as we're going to get. Soon as Tom here blows out that wall, we'll make a run for it; the mess here should keep the Heaveners too busy to stop us.'' He glanced back at Across-the-Jordan, then at the corner. ''In fact, why wait? Tom, you can handle this by yourself, can't you?''

Across-the-Jordan looked up. ''I reckon I can, Captain,'' he said.

''Well, I'll leave two men here just in case you need them, and the rest of us will head for the airport. Silas, you've used up your bullets; you stay here and help out if you can. Si-mon,'' he said, indicating another man, ''you stay here as their lookout. Soon as that wall blows, the three of you come along after us; we shouldn't be too hard to find.''

The three men selected all nodded acknowledgment, and John led the others around the corner and onward toward the airport.

They had just reached the juncture of the Corporate Headquarters and the old town wall when the explosion roared out behind them.

"Sooner than I expected," someone remarked.

John said nothing, but he was suddenly worried. The explosion had, indeed, come sooner than expected, much sooner; he hoped nothing had gone wrong. He heard nothing after the initial blast, no sound of settling rubble; that was bad.

Then the sky lit up, greenish gold, turning the rain into a shower of glowing sparks. John looked up.

The light was coming from an airship hovering over the headquarters building; it was roughly triangular, barbed and evil-looking, and a dozen sections around its edges were ablaze with light. John estimated it to be thirty or forty feet long.

"What's that?" one of his men hissed. John shushed him. "I think we better get out of here," he said.

"Back the way we came?"

"No," John said, looking appraisingly about him, "that's where the airship will be looking for us. Down the slope right here and head for home."

"What about Silas? And Simon and that Jordan?"

"Hope for the best," John said. "I think the explosion got them; it came too soon. We can't afford to wait and see if I'm wrong." He headed straight out away from the town wall, moving at a fast walk, half-crouched.

"Hey!" an unfamiliar voice shouted; John glanced back and saw someone standing on the wall, holding a gun.

"Run!" he called, suiting his own actions to his command.

Five of the others obeyed; one had frozen, one was running back toward the site of the explosion instead, and the last raised his rifle.

The man on the wall fired first, with the rattle of a machine gun; the man with the raised rifle fell.

A guerrilla commander could not leave wounded on the battlefield; John knew that. "Get that sentry!" he called as he turned and ran back for the injured man.

Three men raised their rifles; two of them fired, the third went down in a spray of bullets. Another went down after squeezing off a shot; the third fired his second shot, then turned and ran for cover.

Someone had scored; the man on the wall also fell, and did not reappear. John thanked God for that small favor as he scooped up the man who had been first to fall.

He was unconscious, with red oozing from his scalp and running from his side. John dragged him down toward the cliff.

Beside him, the man who had managed to fire both bullets was on his feet again, struggling to lift another wounded man. The man who had frozen by the wall joined them; the other two men had already fled out of sight.

"Head for home!" John called. He lifted his burden up across his shoulders and broke into a stumbling run.

The other two unhurt guerrillas followed him closely, each with a wounded man. One was able to hobble along with minimal support; the other was dragged like a sack. John hung back and looked at the dragged man; he did not like what he saw. When they were out of sight of the wall, all panting heavily, John checked the man out.

As he had feared, the man was dead, had probably been dead when he first hit the ground, with half a dozen bullet holes in a line across his chest. The man John had carried was still breathing, though badly injured; the other had taken a bullet through the meaty part of the thigh, but was otherwise unhurt, and could hobble along, using his rifle for a cane as needed.

Leaving the corpse, they struggled onward, down the slope and heading for home, alone in the darkness and rain.

Somehow they made it eventually, all five of them, reaching the roofed-over gully late in the afternoon. The man John had carried remained unconscious for the entire journey, and the three uninjured men took turns carrying him.

The two who had disappeared into the night, ignoring John's order to turn and shoot, never turned up; John never saw either of them again, nor any of the four who had been at the back of the building. That made one dead, two wounded, six missing, out of a party of twelve men; John guessed that of the six, three were killed by the explosion, one captured, and two deserted.

It was a very bad beginning, but in the following weeks the situation only got worse.

Chapter Fourteen

If the spirit of the ruler rise up against thee, leave not thy place; for yielding pacifieth great offences.

—Ecclesiastes 10:4

AFTER that first debacle John had expected it, but it still hurt to admit it—his biggest problem was desertion. Late in the afternoon on the twentieth of November he looked down the slope at the mostly empty interior of his base and admitted to himself that the pitiful handful of men who had stayed with him, loyal as they were, would not be enough to accomplish anything during the winter. He could not expect to recruit more men while the cold lasted—it would be hard enough feeding those he had, and keeping them warm. The cloth-covered gully did not hold heat well.

It held odors, though; John himself hardly noticed the stink anymore, but the men still always complained of it whenever they returned from any trip outside. Ever since the first rain the smells of the stable and the latrine had simply accumulated, instead of blowing away. That would improve once the cold arrived—but little else would.

And would he be able to keep the horses healthy without solid walls?

He shook his head. Wintering here would not work. It would do no good; they would be unable to harass the Heaveners and then slip away once the snows came, as they would leave clear footprints—even assuming they dared to make the journey across country in the first place. With just twenty-three men and two women—women who had both shown far more determination than John had expected—left in the camp, staying here was pointless. What would they do if they were stricken with some sickness? Trapped beneath a blizzard? Washed out by spring flooding? What could they accomplish?

Nothing, that was what they could accomplish. It was time to retreat and regroup. He and his handful of loyal supporters would go underground in the surrounding towns, then return in the spring.

They had at least done a little during their stay; half a dozen raids had been made on nearby villages, though they had, as yet, not managed to do any damage at all to the Citadel itself in their four attempts. Not only was the Corporate Headquarters bulletproof and bombproof, so was every other Earther-built structure or craft; the heaviest slugs he had been able to find had simply rattled off the black-painted sides of the airship like hail—and that had been when they had finally managed to get close enough to shoot at it, which had been a major effort.

Even the Earthers themselves were partially bulletproof—John had seen one shot in the chest, at close range, who came away with only a slight bruise. He could not imagine how the thin shirts the Earthers wore could stop bullets, yet they did.

When shot in the face, of course, an Earther went down as quickly and died as messily as anybody else; John had seen that, too, when a sightseer was jumped in the village of Withered Fig that very morning. That was the first confirmed killing of an Earther, ever, anywhere on Godsworld.

One of them, out of a few hundred—and John had lost at least eleven, probably eighteen, men, not counting those known to have deserted or been captured, not counting the six thousand who died in the fusion blast, not counting those cut down by the machine gun at Marshside. Scattering his men through the towns for the winter might actually be a better idea all around—perhaps they could become assassins, picking off Earthers whenever possible, until the survivors retreated into the Citadel and stopped interfering with Gods-world. Even if the assassins were captured or killed, a one-for-one exchange would be far better than he had been doing so far.

Of course, convincing men to become assassins could be difficult; of his remaining troops he estimated that only four or five were fanatical enough for such a role.

Still, whether any assassinations were carried out or not, dispersing for the winter was undoubtedly the best thing to do.

Despite all the logic that led to the same conclusion, he hesitated. If he once broke up the little band, would he ever be able to get it back together again?

He wasn't sure.

He kicked the question about for the remainder of the evening, sitting quietly throughout a subdued supper. He had no one left that he trusted enough to confide in; Habakkuk was back in New Nazareth, Jonas had deserted weeks ago, and none of the others had spoken to him much about anything but military matters. He had to think it through himself and make the decision.

He would sleep on it, he told himself, and decide in the morning. He said his evening prayer for the little congregation, congratulated again the man who had shot the Earther, then went quietly to bed.

He woke up suddenly, unsure what had disturbed him. He listened.

Someone was moving about nearby—several someones. A bright light flashed in his face; he blinked.

"You John Mercy-of-Christ?" someone asked.

This was obviously not the belated arrival of more volunteers; the man spoke with a thick Heavener accent. John did not answer.

"It's got to be him," another voice said.

"All right, whoever you are, get up; you're coming with us." Hands reached down and grabbed his arms; reluctantly, he allowed them to pull him to his feet, wishing he had kept his sword within reach.

The light shone in his face again.

"That's him—right, Sparky?"

"Correct," an oddly neuter voice said. Remembering Cuddles, John guessed it to be a machine of some sort.

"Let's go, then."

He was dragged up out the upper end of the camp and hustled into an open doorway in a gleaming dark blue wall, a wall that had never been there before; still not fully alert, it took him a moment to recognize it as an airship, probably the one that had hovered over the Corporate Headquarters the night of the first unsuccessful attack on the Citadel.

Corporate Headquarters—his sleep-fuddled mind wondered idly why it was called corporate. Was there a Spirit Headquarters somewhere? And the Heaveners called themselves a corporation—was that like a congregation? Did they worship the body? Their lives were luxurious enough to make such an idea possible.

It didn't matter. They strapped him into a seat aboard the airship, seated themselves all around, and ignored him for the few moments it took to fly back to the Citadel and set down on the fortress roof, chatting amongst themselves in a strange tongue.

Once the airship was down again he was dragged out of the craft and across a dozen feet of open roof, through a sliding door into a small room, where his guards simply stood, as if waiting for something. A moment later he felt a sudden odd lightening and realized that the room was sinking down into the building somehow.

When the door slid open again he faced a richly upholstered chamber, only slightly larger than the movable one he was in, with a single door in its far wall. "This is as far as we go," one of his captors announced. He was unceremoniously shoved forward into the chamber; the doors of the moving room slid shut behind him, and he was alone.

He paused to straighten his rumpled clothing, wishing that he had been allowed to put on his hat and boots and maybe his jacket; with the increasing cold he had kept on his shirt and trousers, so he was not completely unsuited to seeing people, but he would have preferred something more than woolen socks on his feet. He looked about.

The chamber was carpeted in very dark red; the walls were dusky orange, and padded, the padding covered by an unfamiliar fabric. There was no furniture whatsoever. The ceiling glowed, like most of the ceilings he had seen in the Earthers' headquarters.

The inner door—which was dark red, a shade lighter than the carpet—slid open, and he faced another chamber, but the walls were an odd shade of light blue, and a row of windows made blocks of darkness along one side. This room was furnished, though he could not identify everything he saw; hanging just to one side of the room's center, for example, was a cloud of tiny glowing sparkles, arranged in a swirling helical pattern. He had no idea what they were or what they were for, or what supported them in midair. Cushions, in a dozen shades of red and dark blue, were scattered about. A single straight-backed chair, obviously made here on Godsworld, stood beside the sparkles, and facing it was a broad, gleaming reddish thing that he recognized only with effort as a desk.

The desk would have dominated the room, save for the woman sitting behind it; it was she who dominated. She was tall, even seated—and even for an Earther. Her hair was black and long, but pulled back over the top of her head in a way John had never seen before that seemed to thrust her face forward. Her eyes, too, looked black, but did not have the odd shape that so many of the Earthers' eyes had. Her nose was small and straight, her jaw set firmly. She was wearing a yellow garment that covered her decently but was cut tight, far too tight by Godsworlder standards, particularly over her breasts.

"Come in, Captain Mercy-of-Christ," she said, her voice surprisingly smooth and pleasant, and revealing only a faint trace of accent. "I'm America Dawes."

Hesitantly, John took a few steps forward into the larger room. The door slid shut behind him. "I've heard of you," he said. "Pardon me if I don't shake hands, but I reckon we're enemies. I won't make my hand a liar."

"That's fine," she said. "I'm not fond of needless ceremony myself."

"Well, that's good, then."

"Sit down; we need to talk to each other." She gestured at the Godsworlder chair. "I had that sent up, in case you don't like our unfamiliar furnishings."

Reluctantly, John seated himself.

"There are going to be two parts to this little talk, Captain. First I'm going to explain the situation and tell you what I want, and you're going to just listen; after that, I'll answer any questions you care to ask, and ask you a few in return, and maybe we can settle a few things and get to know each other a little better. Is that all right with you?"

"I reckon it is," John replied cautiously.

"All right. Now, I'm the chief executive officer of the People of Heaven, a wholly owned subsidiary of the New Bechtel-Rand Corporation; that's a company, a business, but one so big that no one person or group of partners could own it all or run it all. The New Bechtel-Rand Corporation has been given permission by the government back on Earth to trade with Godsworld and to maybe develop it a little—that is, to see if we can improve things here so as to make trade even more profitable for both sides. I know you're a soldier, not a merchant, but it's obvious that it's more profitable to sell to a rich man than a poor one, so Bechtel-Rand is trying to make Godsworld a little bit richer, so that Bechtel-Rand can be a little bit richer. You understand that?"

"No," John said truthfully.

She frowned. "All right, it doesn't matter. My point is that we aren't trying to hurt Godsworld. We won't interfere with your beliefs; we aren't going to conquer anyone. We won't take anything we haven't paid for. We aren't criminals or invaders, we're just businesspeople. All we want is to trade with you people; you have things here on Godsworld that are precious back on Earth, and we have things that are precious here. *All* we want is trade."

She paused; John said nothing, simply looked at her.

"Look, if anyone from Earth wanted to conquer Godsworld, do you think you could stop us? You've seen our weapons. But we aren't *allowed* to conquer Godsworld, or anywhere else; Earth has laws and can enforce them, and anybody who from Earth who broke those laws here on Godsworld would be punished severely. We can't do anything illegal—we don't dare. We can defend ourselves, as we did when you attacked us; but if we aren't attacked, we can't harm a single Godsworlder, or interfere with your religion, your customs, your rights in any way, or the authorities back on Earth would revoke our trade licenses and we'd be out of business. We'd have to leave Godsworld entirely, and let a competing corporation have a try at doing better. So, you see, we aren't going to harm you, any of you."

John sat, looking at her.

"Now, you and your little band of marauders have been causing us trouble. You're interfering with business. You've attacked us. It's cost us money. However, we didn't want to stir things up too much—if we fought back it might cause bad feeling among the people we came to trade with. They might see it as a big strong bunch of bullies fighting dirty, turning Earthly weapons against your brave little company. With that in mind, we preferred to just wait and see if you and your compatriots might not get tired and give up. I think in time you would have—or else your fellow Godsworlders would have taken care of you, since, after all, your more successful attacks have been against them, not us."

She paused again.

"That is, until today. This morning you killed one of our stockholders, one of the people who own a part of Bechtel-Rand. The laws back on Earth say that we have to let anyone who owns more than one percent of one percent of our company come here and roam freely—it's supposed to help keep us honest. We're required to let these people come in, at our expense, and do as they please, and we're required to protect them. We try to protect them, but we can't be everywhere they might wander, so we don't always succeed. One of your men blew the face off a stockholder this morning, down in Withered Fig, and that could mean that we're in very big trouble. I think we'll come out of it all right—this is a barbaric planet, so they'll make allowances when they investigate—but we can't let it happen again. Ever. That means that your little band of guerrillas is going to be gone by noon tomorrow, one way or another. Do you understand?''

"I'm not sure," John answered.

"I mean that at noon tomorrow, if anyone is still in that camp of yours, we're going to vaporize the entire place. We don't want to do that—particularly because we know perfectly well that you could easily put together a new group, that you have agents scattered all through the protectorate. We would much rather settle this all peacefully. Is that clear enough?''

After a long silence, John admitted, "It's clear—but how do you figure on settling it peacefully?''

"By giving you what you want, so that you don't have to fight for it—if we can. What is it that you and your men want?''

John stared at her for a long moment, wondering if she could really need to ask. "We want Godsworld back the way it was, with no trace of you people left to pollute it," he answered finally.

"Well, we can't do that. I think I've finished my explanation; it's time for some questions and answers. *Why* do you want us off Godsworld?''

"Because you're destroying it.''

"We aren't destroying anything! I told you, we aren't allowed to.''

"But you *are* destroying it! I don't mean the people or the houses—I don't care about those. You're destroying our way of life! You've brought in weapons that make wars too dangerous to fight, and all these cushions and colors everywhere make life too soft to live!'' He got to his feet, unable to contain himself, and leaned forward across the desk. "You're decadent and corrupt yourselves, like all of Earth, and you're making Godsworld decadent and corrupt, too.''

"Decadent? Soft? Because we've introduced a few little improvements?" She rose, too, and John was startled to realize that she was taller than he was. "The most luxurious life ever lived on Godsworld would be abject poverty to your ancestors back on Earth! Decadence isn't a physical thing—a few pillows and hangings aren't going to turn people decadent. It's a way of thinking—a spiritual thing, in your terms. If Godsworlders are decadent now, then they always were—they just didn't have a chance to show it before. We're not forcing these things on anybody, we're *selling* them; if they're evil, as you say, then the righteous should resist the temptation. I've read the Bible, too, you know—in my own language, not your King James version, but it can't be that different. I've also read Mark Twain, which you haven't—an ancient American philosopher who proved that it's easy, and therefore meaningless, to resist temptation when there isn't any."

"Oh, you can say anything you please—the Devil can quote Scripture, they say—but you people are foul and decadent, and we don't want you on Godsworld."

"Why are you so certain that we're foul and decadent?"

"Because I've seen it!" John shouted. "That slut who called herself Tuesday!"

"Tuesday?" Dawes' eyes widened. "Tuesday Ikeya? You ran into her?"

Taken aback by the Earther's startlement, John said, "I met a pervert who called herself Tuesday, who abused me, yes."

"That idiot! She's just a stockholder, Captain; she doesn't work for us. What did she do? Rape you, and use the empathy spike? That's her usual routine."

Bothered by hearing it said aloud, and by a woman, John had trouble answering. He nodded, once.

"No wonder you think we're decadent! Captain, she isn't one of us—she's not one of the People of Heaven. I should have kept a closer eye on her—I'll check the tapes tomorrow and see if she's done anything else harmful. We're required to let her do what she wants here, but she isn't one of ours, she's a spoiled-rotten rich nuisance. She sees the universe and everyone in it as toys to be played with. If you took her for a representative of our people, I can understand that you would be upset, but I promise you she's not."

"Oh?" John was sufficiently recovered from his shocked embarrassment to put his bitterness into words. "Are you trying to tell me she's unique, that other Earthers aren't like that?"

"Not all of us . . ."

"What about her friend Esau, who had himself pain-wired?" John demanded. "And who gave her that spike thing in the first place?"

"I didn't say she was unique; she's not. Plenty of Earthers are hedonistic monsters. But not *all* of us—not the people who work for *me*. I won't have it. I don't hire rewires or rebuilts or variants, and I insist on specifications on anyone artificial—and I wouldn't use any of them on a planet like Godsworld even if I had them. I *respect* your culture here, and I don't want to interfere with it—after all, if Godsworld were just like Earth, what sort of trade could I do?"

John had no idea what the woman was talking about. He simply stared at her across the desktop.

"You don't trust me," she said. "I suppose there's no reason you should. Still, I mean what I say; Tuesday isn't one of the People of Heaven. I wouldn't allow her kind here if I had any choice."

"And I wouldn't allow any of you here at all," John replied.

"Ah, but you don't have a choice, any more than I do! We're here to stay; if you drive us away, another group will move in. Once a colony is rediscovered, it's never allowed to slip away again."

"We're not a colony! We've been independent for three hundred years!"

"Is it *that* long by your calendar? I hadn't checked; for us it's two hundred and something. All right, not a colony, then, but a human settlement. Captain, once Earth finds a market, we never let it go."

"And I'm supposed to just accept that?"

"You *have* to accept it. It's the simple fact." She took a breath, then continued. "We aren't getting anywhere yelling at each other like this. I'm ready to make you a good offer for giving up your fight, grant any terms that won't cut seriously into my profits, but I don't know what it is you *want*. I can't put Godsworld back the way it was, and I wouldn't if I could. I don't think most of your people would want it back. Short of that, what can I offer you? Money? I can give you almost unlimited credit, make you the richest man on Godsworld. Power? I can put you in charge of the entire True Worder territory, if that's what you want. You've told me you think physical comforts are decadent—sinful, I suppose—but I can provide them, if you'd like, more than you've ever imagined." She looked at him, not pleading, as her words might have led him to expect, but measuring him carefully.

"And what would I do with this money and power? My life has been dedicated to bringing the true faith to the heathen and the heretic, with fire and sword—do you expect me to sit back and spend the rest of my days in indolence? I have a calling in this world, and I mean to pursue it!"

"Do you? I have no objection if you want to preach your gospel."

"I'm no preacher, woman, I'm a warrior!"

"War," she said, "is bad for business. It uses up money and kills off our customers. I don't think there will be many more wars on Godsworld—certainly nobody is going to fight any against the protectorate. No one will live long if they try."

"You see? You've destroyed the one true way, cut it down, stopped it from spreading the truth by destroying our army!"

"You think that the People of the True Word and Flesh had the one true religion, and all the others were false?"

"Heretical—the others had part of the truth, but had corrupted it."

"You're so very certain that yours was the true way? Then why did God allow your army to be wiped out so easily?"

That very question had troubled him greatly in the past few

weeks. "The Lord moves in mysterious ways," he said feebly.

"Captain, I've studied your religions here on Godsworld, and the records back on Earth about the expedition that brought your ancestors here—what records there were, anyway. There are two hundred faiths on Godsworld, at least, spread among two hundred tribes, and out of those two hundred *not one* is actually the same faith those original settlers brought! *No one* follows the Founders' religion—not you, not the Chosen, not the Old Churchers, none of you!"

"You're lying," John said, but without conviction.

"No, I'm not. I know I can't prove it to you—you'd accuse me of faking the records—but it's true. Your religion has changed to fit the situation here, just as religions always do."

"You're lying," John repeated. "You're an agent of Satan, trying to weaken me."

"Oh, d— No, I didn't mean to make you think that. Wait a minute." She leaned back, then slowly settled back into her red-upholstered, oddly shapeless chair. "Sit down."

John hesitated, but then sat down.

"Captain, I don't think that your faith is what's really important to you—and hear me out before you argue!" John subsided, his protest half-formed. "I think that what really interests you is power—not *having* it, but *getting* it and *using* it. It's not religious fervor that drives you into battle, it's the need to prove yourself, the challenge, the chance to face and defeat a worthy foe. You need to win, to conquer. You want to fight for something. So far you've fought for the True Word, as you call it, and you've fought with guns and swords, but I don't think that's what's really important; I think you'd be just as happy fighting for New Bechtel-Rand, using credits and trade goods as your weapons. I can't afford to let you fight against us; I want you to fight *for* us. That's what I'd like to give you in exchange for peace."

"What?"

"Captain, I'm offering you a job."

He stared at her for a long, silent moment, wondering if she might be mad. "A job?" he asked at last.

"Yes. You're determined, a good leader—oh, you haven't done very well against *us*, but no Godsworlder could. You don't have the technology. You probably thought we knew where to find your army because of hidden lookouts, or that we found your guerrilla camp by questioning your deserters, but that's not true; we used satellites in orbit around Godsworld that were able to see everything you ever did. You thought that our most advanced weapons were machine guns, because that's what you saw, but that was because we consider those so primitive that we don't mind selling them to people we think of—forgive me—as little more than savages; how could you know we had limited fusion weapons? You put up a good fight, but you never had a chance. Join us, and we'll send you back to Earth for retraining, and next time you'll have that technology fighting *for* you, not against you. We have a dozen development projects planned for Godsworld that could use a man like you in charge."

"No," he said, without thinking.

"Are you sure? You can take some time to think about it . . ."

"No," he repeated.

"Well, then, perhaps somewhere else? New Bechtel-Rand is developing fourteen rediscovered colonies at present, and any number of other projects. We can find any work you like, anywhere in human-inhabited space."

"Working for you?"

"Not me, personally—I'm only in charge of Godsworld. But for the corporation, yes." Before John could reply, she added, "If it bothers you, working for a woman—well, I hope you'll get over that, because that's one of the worst things about Godsworld, this whole sexist setup you have here, but even if you don't, at the moment a man's running Bechtel-Rand, and I'm sure we could find a position where none of your direct superiors would be female."

A few steps behind, John asked, "You said you would ship me back to Earth?"

"Yes."

"How could you do that? It's a century each way; by the time I got back here you'd be long dead—probably all Gods-world would be dead, with the sustaining faith destroyed."

"Oh, Lord, Captain, you don't think we spent a century coming out here, do you? If we were still limited by that we'd have left Godsworld alone. It's been over a hundred years since faster-than-light travel was developed. That was what brought down the United Nation and started Earth moving again! We don't really travel through space at all, we sort of . . . I can't explain it in your language, but it's only a couple of hundred *hours* of subjective time to Earth, not a hundred *years*. Earth hours, at that, which are a little shorter than yours."

"Oh."

"Captain, I can see that this has all been a great deal to absorb. I'm going to have my people fly you back to your camp now, and at noon tomorrow we're going to wipe it off the planet, whether you and your people are in it or not. You can go on fighting us, but it won't do you any good, and if any more of our people die, either employees or stockholders, we're going to start removing *your* people, one way or another. I would much rather you joined us; we aren't the monsters you think us. Very few of us are like Tuesday; I'm sure that you have your own degenerates here on Godsworld, but we don't judge you by them, and we ask that you not judge us by ours. At least think it over, and if you decide to join us, come see me—announce your name in the entrance hall and the machines will bring you here. Just think it over, Captain—that's all." She rose; John stood in response.

A section of the wall behind her slid aside, revealing gleaming golden walls; before John could see any details, she stepped through and the wall closed again. As she vanished she called, "Remember, be out by noon!"

Chapter Fifteen

When the wicked are multiplied,
transgression increaseth: but the righteous shall see their fall.

—Proverbs 29:16

FOR a moment he was alone in the room; he turned to look it over.

The door he had entered by had opened again, and the two men who had brought him were standing in the room beyond. "Whenever you're ready, Mr. Mercy-of-Christ," one of them called. "The airship's waiting on the roof."

John took a final glance around, decided that there was no point in lingering, and marched out. His escorts fell in on either side as he stepped into the open door of the moving room.

The conversation with America Dawes was roiling in his head, with first one fact or question bubbling up, then another. As he felt the floor rising beneath him he glanced up automatically, and noticed the glowing ceiling.

"Why are your lights all that awful color, and so bright?" he asked. "Can't you make them any color you like?"

"Of course we can," one of the guards replied. "That's the color of sunlight back on Earth. Earth has a yellow sun, you know, not a red one like yours. Godsworld seems pretty dim to us."

John noticed how much more respectfully he was handled now than he had been in being brought here, and guessed at the reason—before he had only been an enemy, whereas now he was a prospective member of the People of Heaven. These two were treating him with mild deference—if he accepted the offer of a job he would presumably be their superior, and that deference would be appropriate. He had no intention of working with the People of Heaven, though; if he did accept the offer of a job, it would be to attack them from within. He realized now that his enemy was not Dawes herself, but the people back on Earth who had sent her. He was still not sure exactly what a corporation was, whether a tribe, a congregation, or, as Dawes had said, merely an overgrown business, but he was sure that it was the New Bechtel-Rand Corporation that was destroying Godsworld, not any individual Earther.

And was Tuesday really not a part of the corporation? He still did not understand what a ''stockholder'' was, but whatever they were, if Dawes had not lied they were outsiders with special privileges. *Had* he been unfair in his assessment of the People of Heaven? That would bear some thought; they might not be the degenerates he had thought them. Oh, they were still his bitter enemies, there could be no doubt of that— they had destroyed Godsworld's traditional way of life, reduced the People of the True Word and Flesh to chattels and robbed them of their approaching triumph.

He needed to know more, to understand just exactly what Bechtel-Rand was. Would he have to go to Earth to destroy the corporation, or to drive it permanently off Godsworld? If so, he would probably need to accept the job offer—there was no power on Godsworld that could transport him off the planet other than Bechtel-Rand itself.

He certainly could not stay and fight as he had been fighting. He had no doubt that Dawes meant exactly what she said about destroying the camp, and he had been almost resigned to abandoning it for the winter in any case. Going underground in the towns would be difficult, all the more so now that he was being watched, and he was not sure he cared to attempt it. He had been offered a choice of death or surrender, and, as he had always told himself he would, he chose surrender.

He was not, however, willing to give up completely. He would abandon his little band of guerrillas, but not the fight against the corrupting influence of the Earthers. He remembered how he had thought men who refused to acknowledge defeat to be fools, but thrust the thought aside; he had lost a battle, but not the war. He could still fight—if he knew what he was fighting, and how to attack it.

Right now, he had no idea how to find out what he had to know, other than accepting the job. He hesitated at that thought; the prospect of actually going to Earth was simultaneously exciting and terrifying. Earth, hotbed of sin and corruption, heart of temporal evil—but the birthplace of mankind, the world where Jesus had walked! A world where the false god Progress had not been denied, where machines usurped the rights of men—and a world where a thousand green plants grew, instead of the handful on Godsworld.

Only green plants, no red ones—what did they use for nearwood? Was that why the Heaveners paid so much for it?

His two escorts seemed willing to talk; he asked, "What's Earth like?"

The guards smiled at each other. "How am I supposed to answer that?" said the one who had explained about the light. "It's an entire world! And a much more complicated one than yours, I'd say. There are nine billion people, cities, starports, mountains, oceans—what can I say?"

John skipped over the absurd population given as ordinary exaggeration. "I just meant generally—is the sky blue? The soil gray?"

"The sky is blue, but lighter than yours, and the soil comes in different colors. It's a brighter world than yours—more color, as well as the brighter sun. The air is thicker, and there's much more wind; the gravity is a little stronger, so everything's heavier. There are trees—big plants, taller than people."

"I know what trees are—they're in the Bible!"

The guard shrugged. "I've spoken to Godsworlders who

didn't know, despite what your holy book says. I don't understand why Godsworld hasn't got any trees, myself. Your ancestors should have brought some.''

"They tried, the legends say, but they wouldn't grow here.''

"Oh." The guard nodded. "Could be.''

They stepped out on the roof and boarded the airship. When they were seated, John asked, "The people you work for, the corporation—what are they like?''

The talkative guard shrugged again. "Oh, like any other big corporation, I guess—good people and bad ones. I do my job and they pay me.''

There were other corporations, then. "Is the New Bechtel-Rand Corporation one of the big ones?''

He nodded. "It sure is.''

"The biggest?''

"Oh, I don't think so—not even the biggest developer. ITD's bigger, I think.''

"Ahtadi?''

"ITD—stands for Interstellar Trade and Development Corporation.''

"Oh." He thought for a moment. "How big *is* Bechtel-Rand?''

"Last I heard, they had about a million and a half employees and were earning half a trillion credits a year.''

John balked at the numbers. "A million? Do you mean a thousand, ten times a hundred?''

"No, a million—a thousand times a thousand. A one and six zeroes.''

"And a trillion?''

"A one and twelve zeroes—a million million.''

Resentfully, John said, "If you don't want to tell me, just say so; you don't need to make stupid jokes.''

"I'm not joking!" the guard insisted, obviously offended.

"A million and a half people? There aren't that many people on all of Godsworld!''

"Oh, I'm not sure of that; Cheng, what was our census count?''

"*I* don't remember," the other guard replied. "Ask Sparky."

"Sparky? What's the population of Godsworld?" the guard said, addressing the ceiling.

"No exact count is available, sir, but the current estimate is four million, one hundred thousand," said the neuter voice of the machine.

"There, you see?" The guard was triumphant.

John subsided without further protest and sat silently for the rest of the brief flight. He had trouble imagining any reason for the Earthers to lie about such details; they could not have known in advance that he would ask the questions he had asked. Therefore, he had to assume that the numbers were reasonably accurate. That meant that if he roused the entire population of Godsworld, including every man, woman, and child, he would have the healthy, heavily armed adults of the complete Bechtel-Rand outnumbered by less than three to one, and would not have enough people to even think of challenging Earth itself. The five hundred Earthers on Godsworld were nothing, merely a figurehead. In any battle, as he was well aware, knowing the enemy's reserves and countering them was as important as defeating the frontline troops.

He needed allies; he had to turn the Earthers against each other. He had done it often enough as Armed Guardian, in dealing with small tribes—tempt one into attacking another, then move in and pick up the pieces without any real resistance. The Chosen had probably intended to do the same in the war between the Heaveners and the True Worders, but never had a chance, since the massacre had been so fast and so complete. Godsworld would never be able to destroy Earth, but, John thought, the corporations might be kept so busy fighting one another that they would have no chance to do Godsworld further damage.

Why had only one corporation come to Godsworld in the first place?

There was still too much he didn't know, and the airship was settling to the ground at the head of the gully. The first dim red light was on the eastern hills, he noticed as he emerged from the craft, and he had to get his men and as much matériel as possible out of the camp before noon; long-term plans would have to wait.

Before the door of the airship had closed behind him he was running down into camp, shouting the alert, rousing his men.

Chapter Sixteen

*A good name is better than precious oint-
ment; and the day of death than the day of
one's birth.*

—Ecclesiastes 7:1

ONCE they were all out of the gully there was no reason to
hurry; John slowed his horse to a walk and turned for a final
look at the camouflaged oilcloth. A minor pang ran through
him; he was going to miss the place, miserable as most of his
stay there had been. It had been *his,* the first place that ever
truly was. Always before, when he was in charge of a place,
he had been working for someone else—his father, his uncle,
the Elders—someone. They had all betrayed the truth and
surrendered to the enemy, though.

He had not; he would carry on fighting even now. He
glanced up at the sky, wondering whether the same airship
that had picked him up would be the one to destroy the camp.
He doubted that the Heaveners had more than a handful of
airships. He had wanted to pack up and carry as much as possible, so that it was now just about noon, and the attack was
due.

He never even saw what it was that did hit the camp; he
glimpsed a quick flicker in the air, gone before he could turn
to look at it, and a moment later the gully erupted in flames.

The fire did not last long; within ten minutes it had died
down to isolated patches of flame, leaving most of the gully
adrift with white ash.

John shook his head. Nothing on Godsworld could fight that kind of weapon; they needed outside help.

He had no illusions about what sort of help he was likely to find; whatever other corporation he could bring in, if he could do it at all, would probably be just as unchristian, just as evil, as Bechtel-Rand. He no longer cared. The old Godsworld, where the righteous stood alone and took their strength from the truth, was gone. He knew he could never eradicate the changes the Earthers had brought. Even if they were driven off Godsworld forever, all of them, things had been changed. The protectorate might survive without them; the People of the True Word and Flesh, however, would not. All the relative strengths and military balances that John had known for years had already been thrown off irretrievably. And the trade goods—dyes, fabrics, guns, ammunition—would be around for years, maybe centuries. Beliefs would change; the Apocalypsists could no longer maintain that Earth had been destroyed, and that the starships had been the new arks. Simply the knowledge that Earth was still out there, that people could travel between worlds, would change how people thought. Attempts might well be made to recover the lost arts of Earther technology, even to build new starships.

But that was all conjecture; in fact, the Earthers were not going to abandon Godsworld. All he could hope to do would be to slow, perhaps halt, their spreading contagion. If he drove away or destroyed Bechtel-Rand, another corporation would come—that was one thing Dawes had told him that he did not doubt at all.

Even a delay would be welcome, though. It would give the Godsworlders time to adjust to the changes, time to do what they could to maintain their way of life in the face of Earther encroachments. John also thought that he would prefer that Bechtel-Rand not be the group to profit from the ruin of Godsworld. If someone must, it need not be his personal enemies.

He turned away from the smoldering ashes in the gully and urged his mount to a trot; the way to the Citadel by horse was long and winding.

Beside him rode three of his last handful of men and one of the two women; in these last days the camp had kept only five horses. The rest of the band, left on foot, had scattered in all directions, with arrangements made for meetings and contacts throughout the central part of the Heavener protectorate. The resistance against the Earthers' encroachment was not done yet.

"What *was* that?" one of his companions asked.

"What was what?" John replied, startled out of his thoughts.

"That flash that burned the whole camp like that!" The speaker was Thaddeus Blood-of-the-Lamb, one of John's original True Worder soldiers—one who had joined the retreating half and thereby survived the massacre.

"I don't know; it doesn't matter. It's just another Heavener weapon. It's not the steel of the weapons that matters, Thaddeus, it's the steel in the man who uses them."

"That wasn't steel, Captain, that was hellfire," said David Beloved-of-Jesus, one of the Chosen, on his other side.

"Just steel—a machine, that's all. The Earthers are just men and women, not demons."

"They're both," David insisted, and John thought better of answering. Just machines, he told himself, designed and built by people. He wondered if his ancestors had made the right decision, abandoning most of Earth's technology.

The image of an ordinary religious war fought with Earther weapons came to him, and he decided quickly that the ancients had chosen wisely.

There were to be no more ordinary religious wars, though; the Heaveners didn't like them. The next war, John hoped, was to be between corporations. He couldn't expect that all the fighting in this new kind of war would be back on Earth; to make it worthwhile for Bechtel-Rand's opponents they would have to be invited to share in the trade on Godsworld. He hoped that if nukes and other such incredible weapons were used the targets would be chosen very, very carefully.

For a moment his determination to destroy the New Bechtel-Rand Corporation faltered; would it be worth risking the lives of the Godsworlders who would inevitably be caught in the cross fire?

Yes, he answered himself, because only their bodies would die. Saving souls was worth any risk.

The route they followed was a long and winding one; they passed through two small villages and made camp in the wilderness, and only in the early afternoon of the following day did they reach the gates of the Citadel. By the time they arrived John had evolved a plan.

He would not immediately accept the offered job; instead, he would ask that it be held open while he explored possibilities and thought it over at length. He would then try and find another way of contacting another corporation back on Earth, rather than going himself. Corporations did not appear to be all that different from tribes, and, as he well knew, any large tribe is likely to harbor spies and traitors, or simply weak-willed individuals whose loyalty and aid could be bought. If he could find those weaklings, spies, or traitors among Bechtel-Rand's people on Godsworld he would be able to contact his proposed ally indirectly.

He would talk to the Earthers, to any and all Earthers he could find, under the guise of considering the job offer—it would be only natural to find out more about his prospective employer, after all. The right questions, carefully asked, should find him what he was looking for. That corporation the guard had mentioned, ITD—that sounded very promising. If he could find no genuine spies, he would just try to hire someone to put him in touch with ITD's leaders. If ITD was bigger than Bechtel-Rand, then it should be able to destroy his enemy.

They were in the market square now. "Where are we going?" Thaddeus asked.

John glanced at him. "*I* am going to find a room at an inn; you're welcome to accompany me, but you're free to find your own place."

"I have a brother nearby," said Eleazar Freed-by-the-Truth. "We'll stay with him." His sister Esther nodded agreement.

"Abihu didn't come with us because he has a wife and two babies to look after," she said. "But he'll keep us safe."

"That's good, then; stay with him. If you want to find us, check the market around midafternoon; I'll have someone here whenever I can, to keep us all in touch. David?"

"I'll come with you."

"Thaddeus?"

"I will, too."

"Fine. Eleazar, Esther, God be with you; we'll see you again." He watched as the pair rode away down a side street.

When they were out of sight he prodded his own horse forward again, and his two remaining companions followed. After a moment's indecision they headed for the inn where John had stayed before, the Righteous House.

They reached it without difficulty; John dismounted at the front door, intending to ask what rooms were available before leaving the horses in the stable. When he turned to enter, though, a woman was standing in the doorway. He stared.

"Ms. Humble?" he asked.

"Captain John!" Miriam answered, staring back.

She wore a new dress, John noticed—dark green, of an unfamiliar fabric. She appeared confused and uncertain. Otherwise, she looked much as she had when last he saw her.

He studied her expression and could see no trace of malice. "A pleasure to see you again, Ms. Humble," he said, forcing a smile. "Allow me to present my companions, Thaddeus Blood-of-the-Lamb and David Beloved-of-Jesus."

She nodded polite acknowledgment. "I thought you were living out on the hills somewhere," she said.

"We were, but circumstances have changed. If you don't mind, Ms. Humble, we're here to find rooms for ourselves."

"Oh," she said. She stepped aside; John and Thaddeus entered the inn, leaving David to watch the horses. When John and Thaddeus had passed, Miriam turned hesitantly to follow them.

She waited and watched silently as they took two rooms

and assured the care of the horses; then, as they turned back toward the door, she said, "I want to talk to you, Captain."

He glanced at her, then back at Thaddeus. "Go on out, Thad, and help David with the horses; I'll meet you at the rooms later."

Thaddeus nodded, looking at Miriam curiously, and obeyed. When he had gone John led the way to a quiet corner table, seated them both, and asked, "What is it? Are you still trying to get me killed?"

"No—at least, I don't think so."

"Don't you know?"

"No, I don't know—not anymore."

"I reckon maybe you don't, at that; I pretty much expected you to find our camp and come out there to bother me, but you never did. When I found out that the Earthers knew where we were I thought you might have told them, but it wasn't you at all, it was one of their 'sat-alights.' I thought I'd seen the last of you."

"Well, I didn't expect to see you again, either! I thought you were so stubborn that you'd stay out there all alone after your men all deserted you, and freeze to death by Christmas!"

"I may be that stubborn, but I'm not that stupid. Suicide's a sin—besides, he who fights and runs away lives to fight another day, as the saying goes."

She stared at him, momentarily at a loss for words.

"What was it you wanted to talk to me about?" he demanded.

"Oh. I don't know how to explain, exactly. I wanted to tell you . . . no, ask . . . no, *tell* you something. About how I feel about you."

"Tell me, then." He sat back, expecting her to spout either gleeful anticipation of his impending death at the hands of the Heaveners, or a tearful forgiveness.

"I hated you, so very much—you took my home, killed my father, a dozen of your men raped me. I wanted to see you die, slowly." She paused, looking up at him across the table.

John was uneasy. This was not the raving he had anticipated. He had rarely heard anyone speak so openly and directly. He tried to answer soothingly without lying or distorting the truth. "That's natural enough," he said. "The Lord said to love your enemies and forgive the wrongs done you, but it's hard—about the hardest thing there is, I guess. I'm sorry about what my men did to you—it's the custom, in war, but that's hard, too. It was a just war, to bring people to Jesus, but I can't fault you for hating it."

"I hated *you*, though," she said. "I blamed it all on you. You had led the invaders; I heard an officer say that it was your idea to use Marshside for a base instead of attacking the Chosen directly, and I knew you'd given your men permission to pillage the town."

"It wasn't really my idea—one of the Elders—"

"That doesn't matter," she interrupted. "Let me finish. I hated you, I thought you were an inhuman monster. When you took that splinter away from me so easily I was sure of it, and when you refused to rape me because the Bible says a man should be chaste I thought it was because you weren't human enough to rape a woman. I thought you were a demon. Maybe not really, actually a demon, but not really a *man*. You were the Enemy. And my enemy's enemy is my friend, so I believed that the Heaveners were honest and good, come to help Godsworld. You understand?"

John nodded, cautiously.

"Then you told me about that woman, Tuesday—you had a reason to hate the Heaveners, after all. And you'd lost your army; you weren't unbeatable, you'd suffered. I was confused by all that, Captain. I wanted to see how much of what you said was true. So I came back here, and got a job at the inn here—I told them I was the widow of one of your men. And I went to the fortress and talked to people there, and I saw some of the records they have, and what you told me about Tuesday was true; I saw the tape of you and her together."

"What?!" John's outburst was involuntary, the result of astonishment and outrage. "What tape?"

"Oh, they tape everything there, pictures and sound—it's almost like watching through a window. Any time anyone moves, anywhere in the Corporate Headquarters, it's carefully recorded and filed away. The machines do it all. I got to know some of the Earthers pretty well in the past few weeks, and one of them let me watch the tapes of you. I watched it all half a dozen times, from different angles. You were raped, just the way I was—and you took it the same way I did, you wanted revenge. You're just human, like me; you're not a monster."

He stared at her for a long moment, unable to reply.

"I just wanted you to know that I know that now. You're just human, and you've been raped and your family killed—the army was your family, wasn't it?—and your home was destroyed, just the way it happened to me. We're even now; I can forgive you, at least partly. I still won't weep if you get killed, Captain, but I don't need to see it. I wanted to tell you that." She pushed back her chair and stood up. "That's all."

"Wait a minute!"

"Yes?"

"It was all recorded?"

"Well, not all—you can be glad of one thing." A vicious smile suddenly lit her face. "Did you know they can even record what comes over an empathy spike? Tuesday didn't do that, though—what you felt is gone forever. Thank God for the small favors, Captain!" She walked away, her hips swinging in saucy derision.

Chapter Seventeen

> And thou, even thyself, shalt discontinue
> from thine heritage that I gave thee; and
> I will cause thee to serve thine enemies in
> the land which thou knowest not: for ye
> have kindled a fire in mine anger, which
> shall burn forever.
>
> —Jeremiah 17:4

AFTER sending a message to Dawes that he needed time to consider her offer, John spent most of the next two days resting and thinking, while his few remaining followers were out in the streets and markets trying unsuccessfully to recruit new men, and making contact with their fellows, now no longer spies for an army but merely a band of saboteurs. It was the morning of the third day when John was certain of his decision; he tracked down Miriam. She worked days as a chambermaid and evenings as a waitress, rarely leaving the inn, so finding her was not difficult.

After a few stiff formalities, John said, "You told me that you knew some of the Earthers pretty well."

She looked at him warily before replying, "Mostly just one, really."

"The one who showed you those tapes."

"Yes."

"What sort of a man is he?"

"How do you mean that?"

"Well, showing you the tapes—that wasn't something he was expected to do, was it? Did his superiors approve?"

"I don't know; I didn't think about it. Why? What does it matter?"

"I want to talk to an Earther, that's all—a reasonable one, who won't turn down a proposition before he hears it."

"You want to hire a spy?"

"No, not really—just someone who will do one or two things for me, nothing dangerous."

"Kwamé might do something like that, I don't know."

"Kwamé?"

"That's his name."

"I don't like these pagan Earther names; they don't *mean* anything. It makes them hard to remember."

"His name is Kwamé Montez; he says he's from a place called Australia, back on Earth."

"I never heard of it."

"Neither did I," Miriam admitted. "This proposition you want to make—you're still trying to drive away the Earthers, aren't you?"

"I might be," John said.

"Are you?"

"Yes," he admitted.

"That's what I thought—you don't give up easily. I don't know if Kwamé will help you—he's not really dishonest, he's just . . . well, playful. He is a Heavener, a real Heavener, not a stockholder like Tuesday; he wants them to stay on Godsworld."

"I just want him to listen to my offer. I'm not trying to hurt anybody. I won't ask him to damage anything."

She looked at him carefully. They were in one of the unoccupied rooms, where she had been replacing the bedsheets. "What are you up to?"

"Nothing that will hurt you. Just introduce me to this Kwamé, that's all. I can do you a favor in exchange, or pay you a little, if you like."

"Are you going to ask him to get you something? Steal something?"

John shook his head. "Don't ask me a lot of questions."
She was uncomfortably close to what he had in mind. He had
not expected her to figure anything out, or even to try. He
hadn't thought her capable of thinking like that.

"Are you planning to buy Earther weapons and meet the
Heaveners on even terms?"

That was not exactly what he had in mind, but he could
understand how Miriam might have come up with such an
idea. For his own part, he had dismissed the idea a few weeks
earlier; open warfare with Earth weapons on both sides would
be far too destructive. Half of Godsworld might perish in the
cross fire.

"No," he said. "I don't want to fight the Heaveners
openly anymore; they can do too much damage."

After another moment's hesitation, Miriam gave in. "All
right," she said. "I'll take you to see Kwamé."

"Good," John replied. "Where and when can I meet this
mysterious person?"

"I'll take you there right now."

"Now?" John was startled and made no attempt to hide it.

"Yes, now; tell your friends you'll be back later."

"I don't—" he began.

"Come now or forget it, Captain!" she interrupted.

He gave in. "I'm coming," he said.

After a detour to the market to tell David and Thaddeus,
who were currently stationed there, that an urgent errand had
come up, John followed as Miriam led the way at a brisk pace
directly toward the Corporate Headquarters. She marched in
through the open door without hesitation, turned left, and
proceeded along one of the door-lined corridors. A right into
another corridor, then a left, and she began counting doors.
At the fifth she turned and tapped on a panel in the wall beside
it.

The door slid aside; she stepped inside, John entering close
on her heels.

He froze the moment he was inside. Despite minor rear-
rangement, he recognized the room; he had been here before.

The door had closed behind him. He was trapped. He

about the Earth government? Or other corporations? Or religions seeking converts?''

''Oh, I see what you're asking. Bechtel-Rand won the development contract when Godsworld was rediscovered. I'm not sure if the Godsworld job was a bid, a lottery, or rotation, but when they let the contract we got it.''

''When *who* let *what* contract?''

''When the Colonial Redevelopment Authority gave out the right to develop Godsworld.''

''How does that work?''

''Well, the CRA is in charge of everything concerning the old sleepership colonies, both vol and shangman—''

''What?''

''The CRA—the Colonial Redevelopment Authority— controls everything about the colonies founded by the United Nation, back before FTL was developed . . .''

''Eftial?''

''Faster-than-light.''

''Go on.''

''Right. There are a lot of colonies—the United Nation got rid of anyone who made trouble by shipping them off quick-frozen. Some were founded by volunteers, like Godsworld— people who wanted a world of their own—and others were founded by prisoners or just people off the streets who happened to get caught, who didn't want to go. The volunteers are called vol, and the others are called shangman—I'm not sure where the word came from. Anyway, it doesn't matter which they are, the CRA controls them all.''

''All right, I understand that—but then, why is Bechtel-Rand here, instead of the CRA?''

''The CRA doesn't develop planets itself; that's not their job. They're just a branch of the Interstellar Confederacy overgovernment in charge of making sure that everyone plays by the rules. One of those rules is that lost colonies need to be handled carefully and treated with respect; nobody wants to start an interstellar war. So when a colony is found, the way Godsworld was, the CRA assesses the situation and chooses one developer who is allowed to move in slowly and establish contact between the colony and Earth. They're supposed to pick the developer best suited to handle each particular situation, but sometimes nobody can decide which company that is, so they hold a lottery, or if there are one or two companies that would do equally well, whichever one didn't get the job last time gets a turn. I don't know how they decided about Godsworld, but they gave it to Bechtel-Rand.''

''Why only one?''

''Because if there were two, they would compete with each other, and that could be dangerous for the colonists. Keeping one corporation in line isn't that hard, but when there are two competing in the same market it's almost impossible, and the CRA doesn't want to try. Besides, why confuse the colonists with two developers, or three? On some worlds the developers are practically gods—and if a tribe thinks one developing corporation is the gods, then the other one must be demons. You can get some nasty little wars that way.''

John nodded. The explanation made good sense, and was in line with some of his own guesswork.

''Does that one corporation keep the contract forever?''

''Oh, no, of course not! Eventually the colony reaches the point where it can handle modern civilization, and allow in other corporations, or even build corporations of its own. There are a dozen colonies that were never handled by a single developer, and a few others that outgrew it. After all, FTL was invented by one of the colonies in the first place—Achernar Four, the home of the Interstellar Confederacy. *They* weren't going to stand for giving one company from Earth a monopoly!''

John did not entirely follow this, but did not let that distract him; he latched onto the point that concerned him. ''How do they know when a planet is ready to let other corporations in?''

''Oh, that's easy—when the people of the planet invite other corporations, they're free to come. The CRA only chooses the company that can land without an invitation. The colonists own their own planets, though, so they have the final word about who comes and goes. I suppose they could even refuse to let the CRA's developer land at all—but that's never happened, so far as I know.''

"You mean that if another corporation received an invitation from someone on Godsworld, it could move in tomorrow?''

"Worried about someone competing with you if you work for Bechtel-Rand, huh? Well, it's not quite that simple. First off, it would take more than a day for a message to reach Earth and a ship to come here. Second, the invitation has to come from someone who has the authority to issue it—the ship has to have a place to land. An innkeeper can't just invite in another company because he wants a better price on his liquor; you can't land a starship in a stableyard.''

"I suppose not.'' John looked at Kwamé thoughtfully. "How big an area *do* you need to land a starship?''

"Oh, a dozen hectares or so.''

"What's a hectare?''

Kwamé snorted. "I think Godsworld must be the only planet in the entire galaxy where people don't use the metric system! Why your ancestors decided to use the ancient American system I will never understand!''

"They were Americans,'' John said stiffly. Insulting the Founders was not something he could take lightly.

"Yes, I know, but even then America had been using metrics for a century or so!''

John had not been aware of that, but refused to be distracted. "What's a hectare?'' he repeated.

"It's . . . it's . . . I don't know your units well enough. You could land a starship in a square about a thousand feet on a side, I think.''

"A thousand-foot square? That would be twenty or thirty acres. That's not that much.''

"It's enough.''

"If I had a hundred acres of land somewhere, then, I could invite another Earth corporation to land there and trade with me and the rest of Godsworld?''

"Well, yes, I suppose you could—if you had some way of getting a message to them.''

"Ah! That, Mr. Mawn-Tess, is why I wanted to talk to you where the machines couldn't hear us. Ms. Humble tells me you don't mind bending rules a little—would you consider delivering a message to the ITD Corporation for me?"

"What?"

"You heard me."

"Are you crazy? I'd lose my job! Why would you want to do that?"

"Mr. Mawn-Tess, I don't like the New Bechtel-Rand Corporation; I don't like the way they do business. I don't think they deserve to be the only corporation on Godsworld, and I want to invite in another one to take part of the planet away from them. If you won't help me, I can find someone else who will—and if you *do* help me, I would think that the ITD Corporation might be grateful enough to give you a job if you lose your position with Bechtel-Rand."

"They might, at that." Kwamé looked at him thoughtfully. "They just might—and there could be a nice bonus in it, too."

"You see?"

"I'd need your word that you'd demand they hire me and keep me hired—after all, you'd be issuing the invitation, so you'd be the one with some say."

"I'd be glad to do that, Mr. Mawn-Tess."

"You'll need that landing site—thirty heckus, or whatever you said, of flat, clear ground."

"Acres—thirty acres. That won't be a problem."

"In that case, Captain Mercy-of-Christ, you've got a deal." He stuck out his hand. This time John's shake was more enthusiastic.

Chapter Eighteen

Where the word of a king is, there is power: and who may say unto him, What doest thou?

—Ecclesiastes 8:4

It had been easy to say that finding thirty acres he could use for a landing site would be no problem—easy to say, but not necessarily true. Certainly Godsworld had no shortage of empty land, but John did not happen to hold title to any of it, nor did he have any clear idea of how to remedy that lack. He did not have any significant amount of money; what had come in in donations to his guerrilla army had gone out to buy supplies of food and ammunition. He had never bothered to save his own money when he had been Armed Guardian of the True Word and Flesh; he had assumed that if he lived long enough to need it he would either be granted a pension or made an Elder. His family lands had gone to his uncle Lazarus, at John's own request—he had never wanted to be a farmer.

Furthermore, Kwamé pointed out that it would be better if the invitation came from a government of some sort rather than an individual. That made sense, John had to admit, but he no longer represented a government. The Anointed had, after supplying his initial wants, not bothered to stay in contact; still, he was the closest thing to an ally that John had. The Chosen had plenty of land—more of it than anyone else on Godsworld except the Heavener protectorate, now that the

True Worders were out of the running. An invitation from the Chosen to ITD would be ideal.

For one thing, if the Chosen issued the invitation and events then devolved into open warfare, the brunt of it would fall on the Heaveners and the Chosen, and John still did not find himself in sympathy with either group. The Anointed had helped him, but only out of the basest of motives, and never as openly or effectively as John might have liked.

All he had to do was convince the Chosen to issue the invitation. For something this important John decided not to rely on messengers, but to go himself.

As escort—as commander, he could scarcely go alone—he chose David Beloved-of-Jesus, himself one of the Anointed's men, and Thaddeus Blood-of-the-Lamb. The pair had been decent companions, and having one of the Chosen and one of his own men seemed like a good distribution. He expected Miriam to insist on tagging along, but she surprised him by announcing her intention to stay at the inn. Kwamé, of course, could not leave his job in the fortress without raising suspicion.

That settled, the threesome set out at dawn on the second of December, on horseback—John had become quite familiar with the roads and countryside in the area during his time there, and although taking an airship to one of the outlying towns to the northwest would have saved a considerable amount of time, John thought it would also be far more likely to attract the attention of people at Bechtel-Rand whose attention he preferred to avoid.

The first day was quiet and uneventful. The second was marred by a long, loud theological argument between David and Thaddeus; David maintained that all men were damned unless they served the Lord's Anointed, while Thaddeus insisted that, quite aside from any spurious claims to divine authority made by mere mortals, God was sufficiently merciful to allow a second chance for any who lived out their lives without ever hearing the Word of God—such would be reborn to live new lives, again and again, until they got it right. Neither side sounded exactly right to John; Thaddeus' version was not quite in accord with his own understanding of True Worder doctrine. He declined to intervene, however; since the defeat of the People of the True Word and Flesh John was no longer certain that he considered their doctrines to be absolute truth, and furthermore, for a commander to take sides in such a dispute between two of his men would be extremely foolish. He ignored the entire discussion and simply refused to hear questions or demands for intercession directed at him.

Other arguments sprang up, but none developed into anything worse than a moment's shouting, and the three men reached Spiritus Sancti without coming to blows, either amongst themselves or with the four soldiers who formed their escort for the last leg of the journey.

Once in the Chosen capital, however, events did not proceed as smoothly as John had hoped. Unlike his previous visits, he was kept waiting in the courtyard for virtually an entire afternoon; his men were not permitted to accompany him. Finally, only a few minutes before sundown, the great nearwood doors swung open and four men surrounded him.

He had the distinct impression that had he not stepped eagerly forward he would have been dragged, willing or not, into the audience chamber. One of the men kept a spear levelled at him the entire time he was in the chamber, and another had a hand on his sword hilt; this was obviously no ceremonial honor guard.

He walked up the center aisle, as before, but upon seeing the Anointed's expression of extreme displeasure he stopped a few paces further back than he had previously.

Before he could decide what to say, the Anointed himself spoke.

"So, John Mercy-of-Christ, you're back—what do you want *this* time?"

John decided against any preliminary rigmarole. *"J'sevyu,* sir; I have only a small favor to ask," he said, "requiring simply the use of your name on an invitation and a few acres of barren land . . ."

"Oh? No more men to be killed or to desert their loyalties?"

"No, Reverend Sir . . ."

"Has it occurred to you that your schemes have not been very successful, Mercy-of-Christ? You've lost two entire armies now, one in the field and one of guerrillas."

"No, sir, I have not; I did not lose my guerrillas! They're in hiding in the protectorate!"

"Oh? Of the eighty-five men I gave you, ten are known dead and twenty-eight have returned here after leaving your service."

"I admit I've lost men—that happens in any war! And desertions have been a problem because we're facing a powerful enemy, and with little support!"

The Anointed glared at him for a few seconds of tense silence, then calmed somewhat, waved a hand in dismissal, and said, "All right, then, what's this new idea of yours?"

John spoke slowly, trying to choose his words carefully. "I have discovered that the People of Heaven are more powerful than I had thought. I don't think that any army on Godsworld can succeed against them—I don't think all of Godsworld put together could defeat them. However, that doesn't mean that they can't be stopped. I propose to invite one of their enemies to come in and oppose them, with our help. They're known back on Earth as a corporation, the New Bechtel-Rand Corporation—it's something like a tribe or congregation. Theirs is the second largest, second most powerful of all the corporations that 'develop' worlds like Godsworld. I want to invite the largest, ITD Corporation, to come to Godsworld and compete against them, destroy them if possible."

There was absolute silence for a long moment. Finally, the Anointed asked, "Are you crazy?"

John did not answer.

"Isn't one of these what-do-you-call-its bad enough? You want to invite *another* one?"

"That's right; the two of them should slow each other down, maybe destroy each other."

"That's crazy!" The Anointed stared at him for several seconds; John stared back.

At last, the Anointed sighed. "All right, then, why do you need us? If you have some way of inviting in this other 'corporation,' why don't you just do it?"

"I can't," John said. "These people are bound by a sort of covenant—only one is permitted onto each world unless others are invited. The invitation has to come from someone in a position of authority, who controls a piece of land big enough for their ships to land on—my informant said that thirty acres of reasonably flat country would be about right. I need your name on the invitation, and the use of thirty acres for the landing field."

"I see. And if I agree to this, what happens next?"

"Well, in a few weeks their first ship would arrive, and they would negotiate a trade agreement, just as the Bechtel-Rand people did with the old People of Heaven. They would sell you weapons, I assume, and set up a base here, and whenever the People of Heaven or any of their client states gave you any trouble after that you could ask for help."

"Why shouldn't I just join the protectorate, then, if I'm to give up my freedom?"

"You wouldn't be giving up your freedom! ITD would be here at your invitation; you would have complete say over what they do here on Godsworld!"

"Oh? Why would they do that? What's to stop them from simply taking over the entire realm of the Chosen?"

"They have laws—"

"Laws! What good are laws, when these people aren't even true Christians? What can bind men who don't honor the word of God? Do you know what happened to Stephen Christ-Is-Risen, the Shepherd of the People of Heaven, when the Earthers arrived in the Citadel?"

"Uh . . ."

"It was one of your own men that told me, Mercy-of-Christ—one who deserted your camp to return home to his wife and children. He heard it from one of your spies in the

Citadel, who never told you because you never bothered to ask about what happened to the rightful rulers of the place!''

It was true that John had never troubled himself with learning the details of the Earther takeover of the People of Heaven; he had simply accepted it as an accomplished fact. It had not even occurred to him that there might have been resistance, and he had never before heard either the name or the title of Stephen Christ-Is-Risen, Shepherd of the People of Heaven.

''Well?'' the Anointed demanded.

''I don't know,'' John admitted, imagining assorted horrors—involuntary painwiring, perhaps, or some other even more perverse punishment.

''He agreed to let them trade, allowed them to build their headquarters and their airport—and then disappeared! He went into their headquarters one day and never came out, and all the Earthers would tell anybody was that he'd gone off somewhere! By then the Heaveners were too far gone to care, though—they never argued, just took orders from the Earthers as if their Shepherd had told them to. They didn't *care!*''

John was startled by the Anointed's vehemence.

''Do you think that I'm going to let some ship land here and entice my people to sin, so that when these invaders get tired of me *I* could simply vanish without anyone even paying any attention?''

John suddenly understood. The Anointed had not brought up Stephen Christ-Is-Risen as another example of the untrustworthiness or evil of the Earthers, but because he feared the same fate—whatever it was—himself. He was jealous of his own power and prestige.

''Oh,'' John said. ''No, I reckon you won't.'' Further argument was obviously not going to accomplish much.

The rest of the audience was trivial; the Anointed asked for an accounting of the men and supplies he had provided, which John did his best to supply. It was agreed that any of the Chosen John could contact were to be ordered home to Spiritus Sancti; John refrained from voicing his suspicion that many of them would not obey such an order. There were no supplies left to return, as John told it; he had no intention of giving up the few remaining arms he had salvaged from the destruction of his camp. Throughout the remaining conversation the Anointed was visibly tired and irritable, while John was simply impatient to be done and leave. He was quite certain that, barring the overthrow of the Anointed, he would not be getting any further help from the Chosen of the Holy Ghost; that meant that any more time spent in Spiritus Sancti would simply be wasted. He was eager to move on and find a tribe that would issue the invitation to ITD; surely, among the dozens of smaller tribes in the hills of Issachar and Gad, there would be one or more eager for a chance to become a rich and powerful nation, even at the cost of independence.

As he talked about missing men and squandered ammunition he ran through the possibilities in his head. He would need a tribe where the government was not as jealous of its power as the Anointed of the Chosen.

That limited the field considerably. He thought over what he knew of the politics of the region, and was surprised to realize that most of the tribes he was familiar with were out-and-out dictatorships of one sort or another, ruled by prophets, military men, or hereditary monarchs. That was hardly in keeping with his own beliefs—hadn't Christ taught that all men are worthy? The ancient Americans had had a republic, and the original plan among the Godsworlders was for a democracy, with all laws set by referendum, but little seemed to remain of that; each group that had split off from the founding colony at New Jerusalem had followed its own leaders and set its own precedents, and New Jerusalem itself had elected the first Lion of Judah as its absolute ruler within a century of the Crossing—not that it mattered, since the city had been sacked by the Children of the New Israel long ago, and never rebuilt.

The People of the True Word and Flesh were not a dictatorship, of course—or at least they weren't before joining the protectorate—but they hadn't been a democracy, either. They were ruled by the Elders, who served for life, with death-created vacancies filled by vote of the eleven survivors. Such a council, made up of those who guarded the true faith, might be jealous of its prerogatives, too. John tried to imagine what the Elders would have said if he had asked them to issue the invitation, but could not decide.

That didn't matter, he told himself; his own people were part of the protectorate now, and therefore in no position to invite ITD.

He would surely be able to find a tribe somewhere that would do, he told himself. After all, even if he could only find dictatorships and oligarchies, he would not point out Stephen Christ-Is-Risen's disappearance, and he might well turn up a dictator whose greed outweighed his caution.

When the Anointed finally dismissed him it was full dark; he returned to the room he had been provided, impatient for morning, when he could begin his search. He ate his dinner without tasting it, and slept hardly at all as he ran through everything he knew of the tribes not yet committed to either protectorate or Chosen. He hardly noticed when an officer came and escorted David Beloved-of-Jesus to the barracks to return him to regular service.

He was up at dawn, saddling his horse before the sun cleared the horizon, ready to ride for Issachar. He had three tribes in mind already. Thaddeus was barely able to keep up, but, unwilling to be left alone in a strange and hostile city, he did his best. It was not until they stopped for lunch that he was able to ask John where they were going.

Chapter Nineteen

And if a stranger sojourn with thee in your land, ye shall not vex him.

—Leviticus 19:33

THE Followers of God had listened politely to the proposal, debated it for a day and a night, then declared John an agent of the Antichrist; he fled before they could lay their hands on him.

The People of Christ's Blood had listened only after much argument, and dismissed the entire matter the moment John mentioned trade; they felt ordinary business and commerce unworthy of their attention, and tossed John and Thaddeus on a dungheap.

Despite their disdain of material possessions they kept the horses, so that the two men had to walk over the hill to the village of Savior's Grace, whose people had no established name for themselves. They came across no streams, and at Thaddeus' insistence did not take time to rest, so that they limped into the village stinking and filthy and exhausted.

There was no inn, but the minister, Seth Bound-for-Glory by name, brought them to the rectory, where his children took over; the three daughters washed the soiled clothes while the two sons heated and hauled water for long, luxurious baths; they also provided a few small cakes to ease growling stomachs. The minister's wife saw to preparing a suitable dinner a little later in the evening.

It was only after dinner, feeling greatly refreshed and relieved, that John and Thaddeus explained their mission.

"Have you heard about the People of Heaven?" John asked, to begin the conversation.

"Is that the protectorate that's been developing of late?" the minister asked.

"Yes, it is," John said.

"A man of theirs came by a few weeks ago, with samples of their goods and a smooth line of talk; we've been considering the offer, but haven't decided as yet. They set no deadline, so we're not in any hurry. It sounds good, but fair speeches aren't always the truth."

John nodded. "I might as well admit, right up front," he said, "that I'm an enemy of the protectorate. They destroyed my own tribe's army."

"You're a True Worder? That fellow boasted about defeating those folks."

John nodded again. "We're both True Worders."

"Ah!"

John had hoped for a more informative response; he glanced at Thaddeus, who shrugged slightly.

"We came looking for someone who would like to stop the spread of the People of Heaven." He held his hand up quickly to forestall any protests. "Not by open warfare—I'm not looking for allies for another war. I want to defeat the Heaveners at their own game—trade and negotiation. I don't have the means to do it myself, but I know how it can be done making the doer rich in the process; all I need is the cooperation of a government with thirty acres of empty land to spare, and a willingness to work with strangers."

He tensed, watching the minister's reaction.

"That sounds right interesting," Bound-for-Glory said. "Tell me more."

John smiled his relief and explained.

When he had finished there was a long moment of silence; finally, Bound-for-Glory said, "We'll need to talk it over."

"We?"

"The folks here; I'm not the boss, just the spokesman. Everybody has a say in what we do."

John smiled again. That was exactly the situation he was hoping for.

"I'll say right now, though," Bound-for-Glory added, "that we'll probably do it. I'd reckon that sooner or later somebody's going to, and that someone's going to get rich off it. Might as well be us, then—I figure I'd like being rich." He smiled back.

John and Thaddeus were lodged in a spare room in a neighbor's house while the villagers jammed into the minister's house for the discussion. Assuming the debate would last a few days, John quickly settled in to sleep, intending to rest after his recent efforts and be ready to start back toward the Citadel as soon as the decision came. He was startled by his awakening after what seemed like mere minutes; a glance at the window assured him that it was still dark out. He looked up at the unfamiliar form looming over him, the features hidden by shadow, as the room's only lamp was on a bracket beside the door, behind whoever it was.

"Mr. Mercy," the figure said, "we've decided. I won't keep you in suspense; we'll make the invitation."

"Oh," John said, "good. What time is it?"

"Around midnight; we figured we'd let you know now so you wouldn't have a chance to slip away in the morning before we could talk to you."

"Why would I want to do that?"

"Oh, I don't know—we've had a swindler or two come through here. And, Mr. Mercy, if you're one of them, if you've lied or deceived us about this, I just want you to know that around here we skin our enemies alive." Before John could reply, the figure retreated back through the doorway and out of sight.

John stared after him. He had thought that the people of Savior's Grace were some of the calmest, friendliest, most sensible folk he had yet encountered, but this midnight visitation disproved that. Some of them, at any rate, were just as unpleasant as people anywhere else, and their behavior just as unpredictable. He hoped that nothing would be done that might disrupt his plans.

He worried for perhaps five minutes before falling asleep again.

In the morning, when he had arisen, washed, and dressed, he met with a deputation of the townsfolk, who confirmed what his midnight visitor had said, even providing a written document to that effect. That done, Seth Bound-for-Glory apologized for the nocturnal intrusion.

"Don't pay old Hezekiah any mind," he said. "He's impatient and mistrustful, that's all. You just go tell your corporation that the Free People of Savior's Grace want them to come here and talk to us, and that they can use that flat piece of pastureland at the foot of the hill here for their ships."

John nodded. "Thank you; I'll get moving just as soon as I can. If anyone could lend me a horse, or better still two, for me and my comrade here, we'd make better time . . ." He stopped upon seeing the expressions of the half-dozen men facing him go hard.

"Mr. Mercy, it's not that we don't trust you," Bound-for-Glory said, "but all we have is your word, and you haven't shown us a dime. This *could* all be just a way of talking us out of two horses, you see. I don't reckon we can spare any."

John looked around, then nodded. "I understand. God be with you, then—I'll be back as soon as I can." His meager supplies were already packed; he slung the sack on his shoulder and marched out of the village without further conversation, Thaddeus close behind. He had no money for horses or airship fare; even when they reached the protectorate they would still have to walk the entire way, unless someone took pity on them. John knew that was unlikely.

They were perhaps halfway to the Citadel when the first snows began, and the going got steadily rougher; John doubted whether he would make it before Anno Domini 2593 gave way to Anno Domini 2594, but on December 22 he looked up at an unfamiliar sound and saw a gleaming metal something rising straight up into the sky. After a moment's astonishment he recognized it as one of the ships that came and went from the field beside the Corporate Headquarters of the People of Heaven, and that meant that he was almost to the Citadel.

He had never seen one of the starships flying in daylight before; they had always taken off and landed under cover of darkness, showing no lights.

It flashed in the sun's ruddy glow, dwindled, and vanished; John stood for a moment staring after it. It was a beautiful thing, he admitted that readily, despite his hatred of what it represented.

They reached the Citadel in the midst of a blizzard on the twenty-third, and after making their way through the empty streets found Miriam waiting at the Righteous House. She hurried them to a table, wrapped blankets about their shoulders, and supplied them with hot beef stew and herbal brew.

When he had recovered sufficiently to speak, Thaddeus announced, "Captain, I've had all I can take. I wish you luck, but I'm not going back to Savior's Grace with you; I'm going home as soon as I can raise the fare for an airship ride to New Nazareth."

John nodded. "I don't blame you," he said. "Go with my blessing."

They sat for a moment in silence, warming their bones.

Miriam sat down at the table and said, "Kwamé told me you were coming; he's been watching you when he could."

John looked at her. "Watching us how?"

"By satellite, mostly."

"Those things again." He shook his head, then looked up at her. "Do you mean that the Heaveners have known where we were every step of the way?"

"Oh, I don't think so—Kwamé was keeping track of you, but I don't think anyone else was. The rumor seemed to be that you'd gone underground again, and no one was very concerned about it."

"They weren't?"

"I don't think so; I'm not really sure."

"They should have been. We found what we wanted." He sipped his brew.

"Kwamé thought you had; he's been thinking about going out in one of the airships to get you, but he decided not to risk it—at least, until this blizzard hit. If you hadn't made it when you did he'd have come after you."

John did not find that reassuring, somehow; he suspected that Kwamé might well have waited just a little too long, thereby keeping a clear conscience while ridding himself of potential trouble—and, of course, potential profit as well. Before he could think of anything appropriate to say, the door of the inn slammed open, caught by the wind, and Kwamé himself stepped in, wrapped in a dull gray cloak.

John noted that somehow none of the wet, driven snow had stuck to the garment; Kwamé was able to take it off and fold it up without shaking it out. Not only was there no snow adhering to it, it looked dry. Another bit of Earther technology, John thought with resignation. Even miracles could lose their savor when they came too often, and the Earthers seemed to produce one minor miracle after another, without letup.

"You made it," Kwamé said as he sank into the table's only remaining vacant chair.

John nodded. "So we did," he said.

The Earther seemed uncertain of what to say next, so John went on. "We got the invitation, from a village called Savior's Grace up in Issachar—they call themselves the Free People, but so do a lot of independent villages. There's a big meadow at the foot of the hillside they're on that should be just about large enough for the landing site." He pulled out the document Bound-for-Glory had given him.

Kwamé accepted it, unrolled it, and began reading. John interrupted to ask, "What happened to Stephen Christ-Is-Risen?"

Kwamé looked up. "Who?"

"Stephen Christ-Is-Risen, Shepherd of the People of Heaven."

"Oh, you mean the preacher here? He's out on Fomalhaut

Two, I think—wanted to preach the word to the heathen, I suppose.''

"He's alive?"

Kwamé lowered the document. "Of course he's alive! Why wouldn't he be?"

"The rumor in Spiritus Sancti is that you people murdered him when he got in your way."

"Oh, no! We couldn't get away with that. He just felt useless after we started running everything; his last few meetings didn't get more than a dozen people. When he complained, Ricky Dawes offered him free transportation anywhere in the confederacy, and he took it."

"He did?"

"Sure, why not? What is there here on Godsworld for him?"

"It's his home."

"So what? He's a preacher—he wanted people to preach to, and the people here weren't interested anymore. They have plenty of preachers. Out on Fomalhaut Two organized religion was outlawed for a couple of centuries, so the miners are eager for interesting preachers."

"Oh." John found it impossible to answer intelligently. Kwamé and the other Earthers knew so much more than he did, about the universe and everything in it, that he often found himself feeling like a stupid child when talking with them. Changing the subject, he tapped the document. "How do you like your Christmas present?"

"Christmas?" He looked down at the paper, then up at John. "Oh, Christmas! I see. I like it fine!"

"Don't they still celebrate Christmas back on Earth? I know true Christianity is dead, but I thought the trappings still lingered."

"Oh, we do! But we call it Exmas, and Earth's on a different calendar from Godsworld; it's only October to me. I haven't adjusted to the change yet."

"Oh; here, tomorrow is Christmas Eve, the day after that is Christmas, and the day after that is New Year's Day, the start of Anno Domini two thousand five hundred and ninety-four—that means 'the year of the Lord.' "

"I know that, I'd just forgotten for a moment. On Earth it's October, twenty-five forty-three, Standard Reckoning."

John nodded. "What do they reckon from?"

"The same thing you do, except that your years are shorter. That's not important. John, this invitation doesn't mention *you* anywhere."

"Oh?"

"Don't you want to have some say in what happens? *I* want you to—*you* promised me a job with ITD, but this Seth Bound-for-Glory never did."

John shrugged. "I'd like to help run things, but I won't insist. If you're worried about your own job, just demand they hire you before you give them the invitation—or at least before you tell them where Savior's Grace is. You just get them to come here, and I'll take care of myself."

"All right," Kwamé said. "There's a ship going out tomorrow morning; I'll see if I can get on that. I'm due for some vacation time."

That reminded John of something. "Why are they flying their starships by daylight now?" he asked.

"Oh, that's your doing! You made such a big point of telling everyone that we're from Earth that there didn't seem to be any reason to hide it anymore; they've been flying in daylight since four days after you left." He rolled up the invitation and stood. "I should get going; I'll be lucky to get on this flight as it is." He paused. "I'm not sure whether I should thank you or not."

"Don't worry about it," John said. "We'll see how things turn out."

"Right. I'll probably be coming back on an ITD ship and landing directly at Savior's Grace, I guess."

"I'll be there waiting for you," John said; he reached out and shook Kwamé's hand in farewell.

The Earther flung his cloak about his shoulders and marched out into the snow.

Chapter Twenty

Withdraw thy foot from thy neighbour's house; lest he be weary of thee, and so hate thee.

—Proverbs 25:17

DESPITE his attempts to earn his keep by shovelling snow, carving nearwood, and breaking up ice for drinking water, it was obvious to John that he was wearing out his welcome in Savior's Grace. Although few said so openly, he doubted that more than a handful of the villagers still believed an ITD ship was coming.

John was not entirely sure he believed it himself. He had hurried back to Issachar, unsure whether the ship might come before he could reach Savior's Grace, but his haste turned out to be completely unnecessary. January and February passed without any sign of a ship, and with the first week of March and the spring thaw he began to wonder if something had gone wrong. Had Bechtel-Rand discovered what Kwamé had in mind, and somehow stopped him? Had ITD refused to co-operate for some reason? Had they thought it was a trick, or dismissed Godsworld as not worth fighting over? Had Bechtel-Rand shot down the ITD ship?

Late in the afternoon of the eighth of March he was working in a nearwood field, carving away the soft red pulp from an unusually large, fine mass, when he glanced at the sky for the thousandth time and saw a distant glittering.

He froze, the machete half-raised, and stared.

The glittering grew brighter; something shiny was falling out of the sky.

He dropped the machete and ran for the meadow, shouting, "The ship! The ship's coming! Clear the field!"

Around him his fellow workers stopped and stared. "Get back here!" the nearwood field's owner called; John ignored him and kept running.

By the time he was past the stone fence he could make out the ship's general contours; it was roughly cylindrical, with several odd lumps and bulges. It was descending rapidly; John had no way of judging its size, but it was obviously enormous.

He charged full tilt down the hillside toward the meadow chosen for the landing, just barely managing to slow down in time to avoid colliding with the wire surrounding it. The ship, too, slowed as it neared the meadow; its shadow spread across the field.

Others had seen the immense vessel's approach now, and were trickling down toward the fence in twos and threes. Following John's example, none stepped over into the meadow.

The ship was now dropping so slowly that it scarcely seemed to be moving at all, and that, combined with the utter silence of its descent, gave the scene an air of unreality. John wondered for a moment if its arrival were all just a wish-fulfilling dream. He stared up at the ship, now only a few hundred feet from the ground as best he could estimate.

He tried to guess its size, comparing its shadow to the length of the meadow and the villagers who were now crowding the uphill side of the fence, and came up with a diameter of two hundred feet. That seemed unreasonably large—it was certainly far bigger than the ships he had seen in the Citadel of Heaven—but within the bounds of possibility.

The ship seemed to suddenly accelerate, as if it were simply falling the last few yards, and there was a sudden roar of wind accompanying it, followed by an earthshaking boom as it struck the ground.

That was followed by a long moment of silence as the thing

settled into the soil. No one in the watching crowd spoke; all just stared in silent amazement.

Now that the thing was done, John revised his earlier estimate. It was over a hundred feet in diameter, but well short of two hundred. It stood upright on one flat end, and he judged the height at roughly five or six hundred feet. Not the monster he had first thought it, but quite big enough. The sides were gleaming silvery metal, for the most part, with red and white patterning; in addition to the bulges he had seen during the descent he could now make out odd bits of piping, hatchways, and printed messages. The only one large enough for him to read at this distance was also the only one that was neither red nor white; halfway up the side facing him were three immense blue letters, with narrow horizontal yellow stripes across them.

The letters were ITD, removing any possible doubt about the ship's origin.

He glanced away from it at the villagers; it appeared that the entire population of Savior's Grace was lined up along the fence, staring at the cylinder. This was the ideal opportunity to impress them, to convince them once and for all that he was a man due their respect, not just a swindler. He climbed up on the stone baseline and lifted one leg over the wire.

Before he could put his foot down on the other side and swing himself completely over there was a sudden change in the crowd's silence, as if everyone had caught his or her breath at the same instant. John looked over the line of faces, but saw no explanation there; he turned, still straddling the wire, and looked up at the ship.

A hatchway had opened, some fifty feet off the ground, effectively stealing his thunder. Hurriedly he finished crossing the fence and stepped down into the meadow, a hundred yards from the towering vessel's side.

A man was standing in the open hatchway. John looked up and waved.

The man leaned forward, and called, "*Hlo*, John, is that you? We made it!"

John smiled, and shouted back, "*J'sevyu*, Kwamé! Welcome to Savior's Grace!'' His importance had been neatly established, right at the start.

"I'll be right down!" Kwamé answered. He stepped back inside, and the hatch closed again.

The silence around the field was broken, and a babble of voices poured from the line of villagers. John stood, arms folded, waiting for Kwamé to reappear.

A moment later another hatchway opened, this one only about eight feet above the ground; a ladder appeared from the side of the ship, though John was not quite sure exactly where it emerged. Kwamé stepped out and carefully descended the ladder. When he was safely on the ground he turned and waved.

John walked slowly toward him, hand upraised in formal greeting. Kwamé picked up his cue, and began walking toward John, hand up. When they reached the midpoint they shook hands.

"I was beginning to wonder what was keeping you," John said.

"Oh, you know bureaucracy; the executives spent a couple of weeks arguing. I don't think there was ever any real doubt they'd accept the invitation, but they had to make it look good. Besides, it takes a while to put together a big expedition, even for a company like ITD. Sorry if you were worried."

John shrugged it off. "It doesn't matter now that they're here." He paused. "Now what?" he asked.

"Now ITD's chief negotiator talks to the village elders, or whoever's in charge here."

John looked around at the spectators. "Savior's Grace is pretty loosely run; that invitation came from a vote of the entire adult population. I reckon the minister, Seth Bound-for-Glory, would do as a spokesman." He pointed. "That's him yonder, in the brown jacket and black hat."

Kwamé nodded. "I take it you're not in a position of authority yourself."

"Me?" John snorted. "I was lucky they didn't chase me away weeks ago! If they hadn't had a good crop of nearwood to cut they would have."

"As bad as that?"

"Just about." He did not offer any details, preferring not to admit that he had been found, by the villagers and by himself, to be amazingly inept at ordinary labor. He had the necessary strength, dexterity, and intelligence, but had simply never acquired any of the skills.

Kwamé shook his head. "Then it's just as well I anticipated that. I've got a job lined up for you if you want it, as an on-site consultant."

"A what?" Anything that required no heavy physical work would sound good.

"A consultant—an advisor. You'd be at the side of the planetary administrator—that's the person in charge of the operation, the way Ricky Dawes is at the Citadel. Different companies, different names, but the same work. Your job would be to answer questions about how the people of Godsworld think or anything else about the world that the administrator might want to know, and to make suggestions and comment on any plans. It pays well, and it's good work—productive, but it won't kill you. There's room for advancement, too; you'll be learning how the company works at the same time you'll be teaching the company about Godsworld, and if the planetary administrator gets promoted off planet you'll have a good shot at replacing him." He coughed. "*I* think it's a good job, anyway; they've budgeted two on-site consultants for this post, and I'm the other one."

"I'll need to think it over," John replied. "Right now there are other matters to settle."

"Yes, I suppose there are. I came out first so that you'd see a familiar face, and so the people here could see us talking like old friends, but I don't really have any authority yet—my job's contingent on setting up a post here. It's the PA—the planetary administrator—who'll have to do the actual negotiating. It's his show; he says he wants to do his own talking, doesn't trust anyone else to do it. I'll go get him down here if you'll go get this Bound-for-Glory person—have I ever mentioned how much I like your family names here on Godsworld?"

"Not that I recall; have I ever mentioned how much I *dis-*

like all the pagan, meaningless, apocryphal names you Earthers use?''

"Not in my hearing. You may like our PA, then—his name is Gamaliel Blessing. I think that may be what got him this job; it certainly wasn't his looks.''

"What do you mean by that?'' John asked, suddenly worried.

"Oh, you'll see. I'll go get him; you get the minister.''

Kwamé turned and strode back toward the ship while John turned and headed for the spot along the fence where he had seen Seth Bound-for-Glory. He wondered what Kwamé's remark about the administrator's looks could mean; he had distinctly called this person "him," so John was sure that it was not a woman, as he might otherwise have feared.

The minister saw him coming, and clambered awkwardly up over the wire. "You want me, John?'' he called.

"Yes, Reverend, I do; can you act as spokesman for your people here? The Earther commander wants to do some negotiating.''

Bound-for-Glory was visibly nervous. "Seems to me you're doing fine," he said.

"Oh, no, Reverend,'' John replied, suppressing a grin. "You've got it all wrong. I'm not one of the Free People at all, now, am I? You folks have made that plain these past months. I work for *them,* not for you!'' He waved a hand at the towering starship, gleaming golden-red in the sun. He had not actually decided whether to accept the job he had been offered—he had strong reservations, not entirely clear even to himself, about working for *any* offworlder—but he saw no point in admitting that to the minister.

"Oh,'' Bound-for-Glory replied. "Well, then, I can just talk to you, can't I?''

"Well, now, the commander wanted to speak for himself. Come on, now; he's just a man.'' He glanced back at the ship and waved toward the hatch.

A figure was emerging—not Kwamé, but someone much larger.

"There he is now," John said, turning around for a good look at the administrator.

As he stepped out of the shadowy hatchway the explanation of Kwamé's remark was suddenly obvious.

Gamaliel Blessing stood more than seven feet tall, John was sure, certainly taller than any other Earther John had ever seen, let alone any Godsworlders. He was heavily built, too, not the tall and slender sort. He wore tight black trousers—not jeans—gleaming black boots, a loose, open yellow vest, and a great deal of metal apparatus; no shirt, no jacket, no hat, despite the lingering winter chill. His skin was a deep brown, almost black; his hair was black and curly, and his eyes glowed—literally glowed—a peculiar milky white. His metal trappings were not mere ornaments hung on his limbs, but were set into his flesh; some sparkled and flickered with unnatural lights and colors. A silvery band ran around his head, with several oddly shaped protrusions; metal blocks jutted from his chest; wires were woven through his arms.

Perhaps worst of all, three more irregular metal blocks hung in the air behind him, following along just above his shoulders.

John heard Bound-for-Glory whisper, "Oh, my good Lord in Heaven! What is it?" He said nothing himself, but his feelings were similar.

The hideous apparition turned and climbed down the ladder; Kwamé emerged right behind him and also descended, again moving very cautiously down the metal rungs. At the bottom of the ladder the brown-skinned man-thing turned and looked over the villagers who still lined the fence. The three metal things drifting in the air suddenly fanned out across the meadow, spacing themselves along a line parallel to the fence, but a hundred feet in, and hanging about eight feet off the ground. Several villagers started back in alarm.

"*Hlo!*" boomed a voice, coming simultaneously from the three flying contraptions and the huge Earther. "I'm Gamaliel Blessing, representing the Interstellar Trade and Development Corporation!" It spoke with a thick Earther accent.

Kwamé tugged at Blessing's arm, and led him to meet John and the minister.

John stepped forward readily to shake the monster's hand, trying to hard to hide his dismay at Blessing's appearance and to resist the temptation to stare rudely at the opalescent artificial eyes. Kwamé introduced him. "Mr. Blessing, this is Captain John Mercy-of-Christ, formerly the Armed Guardian of the True Word and Flesh, currently under consideration to be your on-site consultant. John, Gameliel Blessing, planetary administrator for ITD."

"Captain Mercy-of-Christ, a pleasure to meet you."

John winced at the incorrect form of address. He wanted the Earther to come across well, and silly little mistakes in form would not help at all. "*J'sevyu*, Mr. Blessing; this here is the Reverend Seth Bound-for-Glory, spokesman for the Free People of Savior's Grace and pastor of the Savior's Grace Church of Christ."

Blessing stuck out a hand; Bound-for-Glory took it reluctantly, apparently surprised to find it felt like any other man's hand. "Reverend," Blessing said, "I hope we can do business together. I understand Godsworld is short of plastics; would ITD be able to lease this meadow with plastics, or is there something else you'd prefer? I don't suppose that you have much use for Terran credit out here."

"Plastic?" The minister's face lit up. "I think we can make a deal, Mr. Blessing."

From that point on it was easy. The villagers quickly forgot Blessing's mechanized body and dark skin when other crew members, almost all of them completely human in appearance despite a wide range of skin colors, began bringing out crates of guns, ammunition, plastic sheeting, and other trade goods.

John followed the negotiations with interest, and found himself, without really meaning to, giving both sides advice on how to deal with the other, correcting misunderstandings, explaining obscure references, and interpreting phrases that one or the other did not understand. By noon the next day he had formally accepted Kwamé's offer and signed on as an ITD employee.

Chapter Twenty-one

*For what hath man of all his labour, and
of the vexation of his heart, wherein he
hath laboured under the sun?*
—Ecclesiastes 2:22

JOHN glanced impatiently at the cabin door. "I don't understand how ITD could be so stupid," he said. "How could they send a rebuilt black man to run their operation on an all-white world where cyborgs are traditionally considered the work of the Devil?"

"John," Kwamé said patiently, "ITD is an equal opportunity employer. They hire the most qualified people without worrying about their skin color or how many gadgets have been built into them. Hell, at least he's human! They could have sent an arty or a sport model or something. Black skin isn't so bad when you consider the other possibilities."

"What other possibilities?"

"Green and scaly, say."

"You mean they've found intelligent beings out there besides humans?"

"No, they built them. Maybe they've found some, too—there were rumors when we left."

"Oh." John shook his head. "It still seems wrong, somehow, messing around with God's image."

"God's image?"

"Man was created in God's image—the Bible says so."

"Which man? Is God white?"

John looked down at the table for a moment, then looked up again. "I don't know," he said. "A year ago I probably would have said yes, but now I don't know. I do know He isn't green and scaly."

Kwamé shrugged. "That's more than *I* know about Him; I'm not even sure He exists!"

"Well, you're not a Godsworlder—and Gamaliel Blessing isn't even close. Couldn't they have found someone who would be more . . . who would fit in better?"

"John, they didn't even try. I don't think you really understand the situation. You invited ITD to come here; that's supposed to mean that you're ready to deal with the people of the Interstellar Confederacy, that you and these other Godsworlders are reasonably sane and civilized now. To anyone out there in the Confederacy, that means you're supposed to be able to accept people as people, however they may vary; that's just about the most basic rule our civilization has. Gamaliel Blessing is a person, even if he has had half his nervous system rewired and any number of things added; Godsworld is going to have to accept that if they're going to deal with civilized people. Now, you know and I know that ITD was invited in here because you feel Bechtel-Rand wronged you, not because Godsworld is actually ready for open trade; you know and I know that Savior's Grace issued the invitation and ITD accepted it because they both smelled a profit; but ITD can't *admit* that, because the CRA wouldn't allow them to trade here if they did. They have to behave as if Godsworld really were civilized."

"It *is* civilized! More civilized than Earth!"

"Oh, come on, you know better than that!"

"We have the perfect way of life here, following the Word of God! How can anything be more civilized than that?"

"The perfect way of life? Living on the edge of starvation, fighting petty little wars over whether to use wine or grape juice to simulate human blood?"

"That war was over centuries ago! The prohibitionist heretics were wiped out!"

"That's civilized?"

"Yes!"

"I think we may have a problem in translation here; you may have noticed that those pop up, where words have changed their meanings over time. Godsworlder English isn't *exactly* like the evolved Old American that the machines taught us before we came here. Just what do *you* mean by 'civilized'?"

John opened his mouth, then closed it again. "I don't know," he admitted.

"That's what I thought."

"It seems to me, though, that a guest should respect a host's customs, and we don't allow mixing men and machines here."

Kwamé shrugged. "Get used to it," he said.

"We also try and keep our appointments; when is this strategy session going to start?"

"When Blessing gets here. That idiot minister of yours is probably arguing about some stupid detail."

"He's not *my* minister. And I still think picking a black *and* a cyborg was . . . inconsiderate."

"Oh, I don't know," Blessing said from the doorway. "I think they wanted someone *impressive*. And you must admit, Captain, that to your little pale people here, I *am* impressive.*"

"I didn't hear you come in," Kwamé said.

"I didn't want you to," Blessing replied.

Impatiently, John said, "Forget that. Sit down, Mr. Blessing, and let's talk."

"Gladly." He sank into one of the cushions; it billowed up around him, supporting his weight and pillowing him on all sides. "The robots have started digging our headquarters. I hope, Captain, that Godsworld has no taboos about building underground? Mr. Bound-for-Glory made no objection, but he might have been constrained from speaking by some custom of which I am unaware. He did not appear happy, however."

John stared at him. "You can't build underground on Godsworld; the soil's only a few feet deep. You'd need to blast out rock. We don't have any laws against it—I don't know what you mean by 'taboo'—because we never needed any.''

"Oh, we can go through rock; that's no problem. It explains our host's misgivings, though. ITD learned its trade on planets where the atmosphere was not breathable, Captain; we always build underground unless local custom forbids it. It would be a shame to disturb the fields here, wouldn't it?''

John accepted another amazing accomplishment of Earther technology without further argument. "Oh," he said. "Well, there's no graveyard here; if there were there would be headstones.''

"Ah. Good. That makes it easy." He nodded. "Then the robots should have the basic rooms ready in a few hundred hours. Already we have arranged to purchase a few tons of this fungoid you call nearwood from the village here, in exchange for firearms, in addition to leasing our headquarters site for a few tons of cheap styrene.''

"Firearms? You mean guns?''

"Yes, guns. Your people seem very fond of them.''

"These aren't my people; I'm a True Worder, not from Savior's Grace.''

"All Godsworlders, Captain; I meant no offense. At any rate, they seem pleased to have us here. We should be able to make quick progress.''

"Do you expect the People of Heaven to try and stop you? Are you putting your headquarters underground for defensive reasons?'' John asked.

"No, no, Captain; I told you why we build underground. The People of Heaven certainly know we're here, and will undoubtedly try to prevent us from establishing ourselves on Godsworld; I expect them to cut their prices and aggressively expand their trading.''

"Cut prices?'' John sat stunned for a moment as vague misgivings that had been mounting since the ship landed suddenly crystallized. Blessing and Kwamé did not notice; Blessing was inquiring what Bechtel-Rand's former employee thought would be the best-selling products on Godsworld.

John was realizing clearly for the first time that ITD and

Bechtel-Rand were not immediately going to start shooting at each other. America Dawes and Gamaliel Blessing were merchants, not warriors.

They would not kill each other off.

He had made a mistake, a disastrous and irreversible mistake. ITD and Bechtel-Rand were not going to drive each other off Godsworld. They would split the planet between them.

He might still be able to salvage something from the situation, he told himself. The two were competitors. If he could keep them nibbling away at each other they might yet leave the rest of Godsworld alone.

And at the very least, Godsworlders would now have the choice of *two* Satanic organizations to surrender to, instead of only one. Somehow, John did not find that thought comforting.

He returned his attention to the meeting, and found that one of Blessing's remote floaters was projecting an incredibly detailed topographic map of Godsworld on a nearby cream-colored bulkhead.

"We're here," Blessing said, pointing to a spot in the northeast of Issachar, "and Bechtel-Rand's base of operations is here, in the Hills of Judah, far more centrally located. Of course, with the opening contract and development license, they were able to pick any spot on the planet. Now, where would you two suggest we send our first batch of envoys?"

Kwamé shrugged. "That's not my field," he said.

John looked at the map carefully, trying to match it up with the distorted and crudely drawn maps he was familiar with. "Would this be the Little New Jordan River, here?" He pointed.

"Yes," Blessing said after an instant's hesitation, "that's what the ship's records call it."

"Then this must be the marshes; there's a village there that I don't see on here."

"Oh, we can't show every single village on that map! If you like we can have it enlarged until the village does show. Why? What did you have in mind?"

"Oh, I'm just trying to get oriented. I was thinking you

might try Little St. Peter. I have three men there loyal to me who might be able to sabotage the defenses.''

"Captain, we aren't trying to capture towns from Bechtel-Rand's net quite yet; first we need to establish ourselves. We'll be cutting into their markets soon enough, but for now we need to turn a profit quickly to convince the home office it's worth investing further, and to do that we want previously untapped markets, where we can set our own prices. Once we have more funds available we can start picking at the edges of Bechtel-Rand's little empire.''

"Oh.'' That was just good military sense, of course; build a base first, exploit that to support your attack . . .

But there wouldn't be any attack. ITD was not interested in killing or converting the people of Godsworld, but only in buying and selling. Odd, John thought, how very similar the strategies might be.

"What about the other villages in these hills around us—Issachar, they're called?'' Blessing asked.

"Yes, Issachar. Probably not worth bothering with, actually,'' John said without thinking. "Too many of them, too small, all independent of each other. It would take years to pick them all up piecemeal. That's why nobody ever conquered them—too much time and trouble for little gain.''

"Ah. Small markets, then. We'll send out a few people to see what they have to offer, but I'd prefer something larger for our major campaign. What about this city-state here—doesn't it have something of an empire of its own? And trade, as well?'' He pointed to a dot that John realized must represent Spiritus Sancti.

"That's the realm of the Chosen of the Holy Ghost,'' John said. "They're big and rich, all right, with a good location—protected on two sides but open to the western plain—but I don't think you'll be able to trade with them.''

"Why not?''

"Because it's ruled by a man called the Anointed of God who doesn't trust Earthers. I tried to get him to invite you here, but he threw me out, and I wound up in Savior's Grace instead.''

"Oh." Blessing looked at the map. "It's too good to pass up, though. We'll have to offer this Anointed of God a deal he can't refuse. Either that, or depose him somehow." He gazed thoughtfully at the map.

John, too, stared at it. Depose the Anointed? These Earthers might be merchants, not killers, but they had possibilities after all. Blessing was a pervert, by Godsworld standards, corrupting his own flesh with steel, but he had drive and intelligence; he was not wholly decadent, not a simple thrill seeker like Tuesday Ikeya.

John wondered for a moment whether his rewiring included an empathy spike, but thrust the question aside as irrelevant.

This campaign, he thought, was going to be interesting. "How would you do that?" he asked.

"Oh, there are ways—but let's hope it doesn't come to that. Why doesn't this Anointed person like Terrans? I mean, Earthers?"

John described his last meeting with the Anointed, and told the story of Stephen Christ-Is-Risen as he understood it.

Blessing frowned as he listened; when John had finished he thought silently for a moment. "This Stephen Christ-Is-Risen," he asked finally, "do you think Bechtel-Rand really sent him off planet?"

John floundered for a moment, then looked at Kwamé.

"I think they did," Kwamé said.

"Then I don't think we need to worry about protests to the CRA if we depose the Anointed," Blessing said, "though I still hope it won't come to that. We can make anything *we* do to the Anointed look like what *they* did to Christ-Is-Risen. I like that." He paused. "It shouldn't be necessary, though. John, you've talked with this person, so I'll be sending you along, but you won't be speaking on our behalf—if anyone asks you're just along as a guide. I know just the person to send to talk to this Anointed." He smiled, and one of his three floaters did a slow roll in midair.

Chapter Twenty-two

And the maiden pleased him, and she obtained kindness of him . . .

—Esther 2:9

THE woman let out another little startled yip, and again John glanced sideways at her in disbelief. Even riding astride at a slow walk she was obviously having trouble staying in the saddle. John knew perfectly well that horses were extinct back on Earth—or nearly so, anyway—but he had not realized anyone, even a woman who had never seen a horse before, could have quite so much trouble riding one.

This woman, however, was doing just that. Three times now the entire expedition—John, the woman, and an escort of four of the Free People and two ITD employees—had come to a halt while John adjusted her saddle and boosted her up until she was reasonably steady once more. The stirrups had been shortened almost as far as they would go, the cinch strap pulled so tight the horse was visibly uncomfortable; fortunately, the beast found for her was so placid it made no protest, but merely walked all the more slowly and gingerly.

John had great difficulty in believing that this tiny, frail, clumsy woman was Premosila Kim, the incredible salesperson that Gamaliel Blessing had been so proud of. She was less than five feet tall—a meter and a half, she said—by far the shortest Earther John had yet encountered, with black curling hair and big dark eyes, but flat-chested and scrawny. She did, he had to admit, have a delightful smile—she had used it on him when they were introduced—but it would take more than a smile to win over the Anointed.

She gasped suddenly as she slipped sideways; she caught herself with both hands grabbing the pommel, but her riding skirt fell away.

After spending as much time as he had among Earthers John was no longer shocked or intrigued by the sight of a woman's legs, particularly legs as thin as these; he simply reined in his mount, slid to the ground, and walked back to recover the skirt. It would not do to let her be seen bare-legged by any of the Chosen.

Two of the men from Savior's Grace were staring, while the other two averted their eyes; John shook his head in disgust. Their reactions would be different a year from now, he told himself, when the Earthers had been around their village for a while. The two ITD people were not staring, but simply watching calmly and casually—but then, one of them was a woman herself. The other claimed to be from someplace called Groombridgiana, which he insisted was not on Earth at all, and for all John knew the women in Groombridgiana ran around stark naked.

He threw the skirt across the horse's back behind her, and stood by as she tugged it into place again.

"Thank you," she said, smiling at him for the second time.

He smiled back without meaning to, then remounted and spurred his horse forward again. A pretty smile would not be enough to win over the Anointed—but it might help.

That was the last time she slipped; somehow she seemed to suddenly get the hang of riding after that, and by the time they reached the border of the Chosen empire the party was moving at a decent pace and able to converse with one another.

John knew that long before they reached Spiritus Sancti, word of their coming would reach the army and an escort would meet them; that meant that this was his last opportunity to talk with Kim where there was no chance of being overheard by unfriendly ears. He had held his peace through all the long ride through the hills and while they wandered along the Upper New Jordan searching for a ford, but he could resist no longer.

"Are you sure you want to do this?" he asked her at a moment when they happened to be out of easy earshot of the others.

"Do what?" She looked honestly puzzled.

"Talk to the Anointed. He hates Earthers; it's entirely possible he'll have you imprisoned or even killed."

"Oh, I don't think he'll do that."

"I'll do the talking, if you like."

"No, no; it's my job."

"But it's dangerous!"

"Captain, it's my *job*. I don't think you understand."

John was getting tired of being told that he didn't understand things, but he knew that it had usually been true when one of the Earthers had said that. "Oh?" he replied.

"Be honest, now; you've negotiated with this person three times so far. Have you ever gotten what you wanted?"

John had to admit that he had not gotten the alliance he had asked for, nor permission to land the ITD ship on the Anointed's land, but he insisted, "I got my guerrillas!"

"Yes, given grudgingly and undersupplied, and taken back again later!"

John had no answer to that.

"Besides, how can you speak for ITD, when he knows you as a True Worder? He won't really accept what you say. *I* know you work for ITD and hold a responsible position, but *he* won't believe it. He thinks of you as a Godsworlder and ITD as Earther, and if he's as rigid in his thinking as you've led me to believe he won't accept any crossovers."

"Not me, then, but you need a strong negotiator, someone he'll respect . . ."

"No, you don't. You're thinking in military terms again, Captain, where the object is to scare your enemy. We're not an army. We want to look just as harmless and weak as we can, don't you see that? We want him to believe that he has nothing to fear from us, that he can allow us the free run of his whole empire without worrying about his security. And if he's like other primitives—forgive me, Captain, but that's what Godsworlders seem to us—then he'll equate physical size with power. If he sees me as the representative of ITD— as their spokesman and as their symbol both—then he'll think he's safe, that we're weak and harmless. He'll agree to terms that he would not risk granting to a big strong male like yourself."

"Oh." John saw the logic to what she said, although it still went against his accustomed beliefs. After a moment of silence, he asked, "But aren't you really just as weak as he sees you to be? You don't have your ship here, or any of your machines . . ."

Kim sighed. "Take my word for it, Captain, I can handle it."

"But . . ."

She urged her horse forward before he could finish his question, putting an end to the conversation, and twenty minutes later their escort appeared.

In Spiritus Sancti they were met by two of the Anointed's advisors, both small, delicate men, who interrogated them politely in a small office; John noticed for the first time, now that Kim had brought it to his attention, that none of the government officials among the Chosen, and none of the higher-ranking officers, were really very large. John guessed that the Anointed did, indeed, equate physical strength with ambition and power, and allowed no big strong men into positions of power lest they one day overthrow him. That seemed odd, since the Anointed himself was so grotesquely fat that the effort of hauling his own weight around left him with little strength for anything else.

Or perhaps it was not so odd, at that. John thought of the Anointed as a man of great power, certainly, since he commanded an empire, but perhaps *he* saw himself as a weakling. His fear of being subverted by the Earthers certainly said little for his self-confidence.

At Kim's insistence John did not speak to the advisors during the questioning, but stood silently with the four men from Savior's Grace as the three offworlders were interviewed. He made no protest when the advisors recognized him and demanded to know why he was there, and were told that he had been hired simply as a guide. He understood that admitting a connection between himself and ITD might harm the negotiating; he also knew that with their mysteriously perfect maps—he was still unclear on what a ''satellite'' was, though he had learned to spell and pronounce the word—the Earthers had no need of guides in the usual sense.

Kim did virtually all the talking for the Earthers, despite the attempts of the advisors to draw her male companion into the conversation. The Groombridgian was adept at finding various ways of saying, ''That's not my field; you'll have to ask my superior, Ms. Kim.''

Something about Kim seemed to make the two Chosen uneasy, although John could not see what it could be; she was being the very picture of deference, smiling, nodding, apologizing, and speaking in simple, sometimes broken sentences, as if she were not fluent in English—or rather, Godsworlder English, as the Earthers called it. Apparently it differed greatly from the dead language known as English back on Earth.

It was only as the conversation was nearing its end that John realized the Chosen were having trouble dealing with her because she was a woman. He had been associating so much with Earthers that he had forgotten how thoroughly the Chosen despised women, the heirs of sinful Eve. The People of the True Word and Flesh had relegated women to secondary roles, as did every Godsworld society, but the Chosen carried it to an extreme—while the Earthers at times seemed totally oblivious of any difference between the sexes. Perhaps that was another reason that the Anointed had wanted nothing to do with them.

And not only was Kim female, but John realized when they all stood again that she had managed to loosen the collar of her blouse, as if by accident. Throughout the interrogation the Anointed's advisors had been staring down her neckline, too polite to mention her apparent disarray; a Godsworlder woman would have noticed their stares and fixed the collar.

She certainly knew the difference between the sexes, and was willing to exploit it. That was nothing new on either planet, John was sure.

It was decided that Kim, the man from Groombridgiana, and the senior of the men from Savior's Grace would be permitted to discuss the possibility of trade with the Anointed the following morning. The entire party was escorted to rooms up the street, which John remembered well.

When they were gathered in their two rooms, John remarked quietly to Kim, "I'm impressed, I think—you probably convinced those advisors you're a harlot, and not a very bright one at that."

"Do you think so?"

"Yes."

"Oh, good! I was hoping that was their impression, but I wasn't sure how far to go to convince them without being blatant."

"Oh? You planned on being taken for a whore?"

"Certainly! Is there anyone more despised and harmless in your culture? They probably think I'm Blessing's woman of the moment, and the fact that he sent me on a delicate mission should convince them he's either an idiot, drastically shorthanded, or both. How much of a threat can his organization be, then? You see? *You* couldn't have done that—no man could."

John shook his head in admiration. "You Earthers may not all be Satanists—I haven't decided that one yet—but you're tricky enough."

Kim shrugged. "Just psychology."

"I still don't think he'll let you open a trading post here, though."

At that, Kim just smiled.

John had underestimated the Earther salespeople and the Anointed's greed; Kim returned from her first audience with a signed agreement allowing ITD traders freedom to cross the borders at will until further notice. She was also bubbling with suppressed laughter at the Anointed's ludicrous attempts to seduce her.

Within a fortnight the Chosen of the Holy Ghost had not merely agreed to the establishment of a trading mission, but had joined the Free Trade Federation, ITD's puppet organization intended to counter the Protectorate of Heaven, outright, signing exclusive contracts stating that ITD was to supply all new weapons for their army.

Once the Anointed had signed the contract and joined the Federation the two corporate powers shared a border—the border between the Chosen and the True Worders, the site of conflict for as far back as John could recall. Upon his return to Savior's Grace John spent an hour or so pondering this on the incredible maps ITD's ship generated upon request, and brought up the subject at the next strategy session.

"You know, if the Chosen were to march south across the Little New Jordan, then swing west, they could cut the True Worders off from the rest of the protectorate and probably march right into New Nazareth unopposed. The True Worders don't have much of an army; they lost it fighting the Heaveners."

Kwamé stared at him. "They lost it under your command."

"I'm well aware of that!" John snapped.

"Are you suggesting, Captain," Blessing said, casually flicking at a wire that protruded, at the moment, from one of his fingertips, "that we arm the Chosen and prod them into conquering your own native land?"

"Not conquering; recapturing!"

"It looks very much like conquest to me," Blessing replied. He folded the wire down; it vanished into his finger. "Weren't you leading an army against the Chosen a year ago?"

"Yes, I was."

"It seems you've changed sides."

"No, I haven't—everyone else has! My people surrendered to the Heaveners, and the Chosen surrendered to us."

"There would be a bloodbath, you know; we've armed the

Chosen with light machine guns and armor-piercing bullets, and I'm sure Bechtel-Rand has equipped the True Worders with equally formidable weapons. Casualties would be enormous. Even if the True Worder army was destroyed, surely they have some sort of militia, and you yourself told us that they joined the protectorate in order to acquire the means to defend themselves. And furthermore, Captain, as its name implies, wouldn't the protectorate be obligated to come to their aid? True, the Chosen could cut them off on the ground, but Bechtel-Rand has enough aircraft to keep True Worder resistance well supplied for months, even if they don't decide to use their starships, as they well might.''

John stared at the map. Blessing was right, he knew. He had still been thinking in the terms of old Godsworld, where wars could be fought without interference, and where trained men, horses, and steel blades decided battles. He had not considered either the heightened firepower or the presence of aircraft.

"Besides," Kwamé said, "what's the point in killing potential customers?''

Reluctantly, John pulled his eyes away from the map and nodded.

"However," Blessing said, "I think you may be right in choosing our next target. The agreement that your former people signed upon joining the protectorate—was it an exclusive contract?''

"I don't know," John admitted. "I never thought about it.''

"Well, Captain, if you're to go on working for ITD you need to think of such things. Just because Bechtel-Rand has trading rights in New Nazareth and holds the contract to defend the tribe, doesn't mean that we can't trade with them *as well.* ''

John stared at him.

"In fact, Captain, I think that tomorrow morning you'll be leaving for New Nazareth, to see if you can't open trade there.''

Chapter Twenty-three

*Though he slay me, yet will I trust in him;
but I will maintain mine own ways before
him.*

—Job 13:15

THE airship dropped him and his party at the border; he and Blessing had decided that it would be unwise to fly directly into New Nazareth until they had a better idea how matters stood there. John had a small metal device that was supposed to signal the airship to come and get him, wherever he might be at the time, when he was ready to leave and return to Savior's Grace.

He had wanted Kwamé along on this expedition, but the Australian had refused; in fact, John noticed that he no longer left the ITD headquarters except to go aboard the ship for one reason or another. He had obviously lost interest in Godsworld.

Besides, as Blessing pointed out, it was reckless and wasteful to send both of his local experts—only Kwamé used the official term, "on-site consultants"—on a single expedition.

Premosila Kim, however, was available; once the opening rounds of negotiation were out of the way Blessing had replaced her in Spiritus Sancti with a man, someone that the Chosen could deal with more comfortably.

John found himself thinking the worse of the Chosen for their prejudice against women, even while he realized that he himself had not been much better for most of his life. He was still not ready to concede women full equality with men, as the

196

Earthers did, but he certainly respected some of the Earther women far more than he ever had any Godsworlder women.

For one, he respected Kim, despite her occasional awkwardness with the details of everyday life on Godsworld; he accepted her inclusion gladly.

He also took along a deacon from Savior's Grace, to lend the group some official status by Godsworlder tribal standards, and a young male Earther in case the True Worders refused to deal with Kim.

The four of them walked from the border as far as the outskirts of New Nazareth, a journey lasting about a day and a half, before anyone stopped them or asked their business. Finally, out a hundred yards from the city's open gates, a patrol marched out to meet them, apparently alerted by a lookout somewhere.

John introduced himself by name only, since his titles had been revoked, and explained that he had come to speak to the Elders on behalf of himself and his companions. He did not offer any explanation of who his companions were.

Two of the six men in the patrol obviously recognized him immediately; he was unsure of the others, and did not himself recognize any of them well enough to call by name.

"Captain John," the patrol leader said, "we thought you were dead."

He felt an unreasonable warmth at simply being addressed by his old familiar title, rather than just "Captain," as the Earthers called him, or by a civilian name, as the Chosen did now that he no longer had an army.

"No," he said. "I came close once or twice, but God's not ready for me yet."

"Either that, or the Devil thinks you're more use here than there!" The patrol leader smiled, but John did not laugh at the jibe; he was too uncertain of his reception among his own people.

"I need to talk to the Elders," he said. "Can that be arranged?"

"I reckon we might get a couple of them to see you," the

soldier answered. "Old Captain Habakkuk's an Elder now, and I'm sure he'll be eager to see you again, sir!"

John smiled. "I hope so."

"He's up at the garrison, sir; would it be all right if I brought you and these others there?"

John nodded. "It'd be fine with me—you know what your orders are better than I do now. Don't break them just because it's me."

"Oh, they don't get very specific about it, sir; we're to use our own judgment, so I'll take you to Captain-Elder Habakkuk."

"Good," John answered. "We'd like that."

In practice, however, they were not taken directly to Habakkuk, but rather to one of his aides, in a small, cluttered office at one end of the garrison barracks. There they were kept waiting at swordpoint—John noticed that all six soldiers carried revolvers on their belts, but two swords were the only weapons drawn to guard the foursome—while the aide went to consult with his commander.

They sat on the floor for almost an hour before the aide finally returned.

"Mr. Mercy," he said, "the Captain-Elder will see you now."

The civilian address struck John as a bad sign as he got to his feet. He said nothing, but followed the aide up a flight of stairs to Habakkuk's office—an office which had once been his own.

It had changed very little, he saw when the door swung open. Habakkuk, too, had changed very little—except he did not stand up when John entered the room. That was a mark of respect to a superior officer; whatever form of address the patrol leader might have used, Habakkuk obviously no longer saw John as his commander. He sat behind his desk, his heavy body squeezed into the familiar chair, his square face expressionless, and said nothing. The initial warmth John felt at the sight of his old comrade quickly faded before that lack of response.

They stared at each other for a long moment.

"*J'sevyu,* Captain-Elder," John said at last.

"*J'sevyu*, John," Habakkuk replied. "I never expected to see you again."

John nodded and was about to say something when Habakkuk added, "I never *wanted* to see you again."

John's mouth, opening in preparation for speech, continued to open, but no sound came out for the first few seconds. "What?" he managed at last.

"You heard me."

"Yes, I heard you, but I don't understand you. I thought we were friends."

"Maybe we were once, but we aren't now. You betrayed your own people; how can I be friend to a traitor?"

"I'm no traitor!"

"No? You prevented our people from conquering the Chosen when we had the chance; you led our army into a trap and saw it destroyed instead. When we had found an ally in the People of Heaven to protect us from the Chosen, you waged a guerrilla war against them. Now you've come here openly as an agent of the Chosen. What did they pay you for all this, John? Was it worth it?" John could hear the bitterness in Habakkuk's voice.

"Nobody paid me!" he replied. "And I'm not here as an agent of the Chosen!"

"You aren't under the Anointed's protection?"

"No!"

"I didn't think you'd be stupid enough to come back here any other way. If you're not here as a foreign agent, then you're still a True Worder, and a traitor. Will you insist on a trial, or can we just get right on with the hanging?"

"Darn it, I'm not a traitor!"

"Oh, come on, John!"

"I'm not! I made mistakes—bad mistakes—but I'm not a traitor!"

The two men stared at one another for a long moment; then Habakkuk demanded, "Well, if you aren't here as an envoy for the Chosen, why *are* you here? Were you just coming home?"

"No," John admitted. "I *am* an envoy, but not for the Chosen."

"Who, then?"

"The Free Trade Federation."

Habakkuk looked utterly blank. "Who?"

"The Free Trade Federation," John insisted. "It's . . . well, an alliance. Intended to counter the Heavener protectorate. Our base is in Savior's Grace, up in Issachar."

"I never heard of it."

"We're still pretty new, but we've signed up the Chosen—"

"I knew it!"

"Wait . . ."

"I *knew* you were working for the Chosen!"

"Darn it, I am *not!*" John was infuriated. Habakkuk had always had a tendency to hang onto ideas that had outlived their usefulness; John had tolerated it before, but never before had one of those ideas been directed against him. "I'm working for ITD!"

Habakkuk stared at him for a moment. "Get your story straight, John," he said at last. "Who's Ahtedeh? And you said you worked for this federation."

"I said I was here on their behalf, not that I worked for them."

"Not much of a difference from where I sit."

"There is, though. I work for the Interstellar Trade and Development Corporation; it's an organization that competes with the People of Heaven back on Earth. I brought some of them to Godsworld to give the Heaveners a little of their own medicine. The corporation is called ITD for short, and ITD runs the Free Trade Federation, which is based in Savior's Grace, and which has signed up the Chosen as a client state, just the way the Heaveners signed up you folks."

"You work for Earthers?"

"Yes—Earthers, but not the Heaveners."

"Earthers are Earthers, John; I thought you hated them all for the pagans they are."

"I hate the Heaveners for coming in here and destroying what we had on Godsworld, corrupting the people and usurping power and destroying my homeland. If I have to work with Earthers to fight them, I will.''

''How long have you been working for the Earthers? Were they the ones who paid you to attack the Heaveners instead of the Chosen?''

''*Nobody* paid me to do that, Hab! It was a mistake!''

Habakkuk stared at him.

''Look, I've been working for ITD for about a month now—that's all.''

Habakkuk stared for a moment longer, leaning back in his chair. Then, abruptly, he leaned forward across the desk.

''You swear you weren't paid to betray us?''

''I swear it, by God and Jesus.''

''All right, then, I believe you—I think. What did you come here for?''

''To trade—the Free Trade Federation wants to trade with you.''

''We're part of the Heavener protectorate, you know.''

''Yes, of course I know that, but you can still *trade* with us, can't you? Anything the Heaveners can sell you, we can sell you—and probably at a better price.''

''I'm no trader.''

''I know that—but you're an Elder.''

''True enough. All right, keep talking.''

''Let me get my assistant up here; she's the expert.''

''*She?* You mean that woman isn't just baggage?''

''That's Premosila Kim, our top salesperson,'' John said proudly.

Habakkuk sat back and stared in astonishment.

It took four days of haggling to arrange for a caravan's reception; John stayed quietly in the background while his companions handled the details.

After the initial explanations were made, Habakkuk, too, stayed in the background, letting the other Elders handle things; his specialty was the military, and he left other matters to other people. Once, on the second day, he came and sat beside John throughout a long debate, but did not speak; the coldness between the two men had not been completely dispelled.

On the third day he did speak, remarking casually, "That woman's quite a talker; when you brought her here I thought you'd gone mad, putting so much faith in a woman."

John nodded. "She's smart, all right."

"She says you're second-in-command of ITD's entire force on Godsworld," Habakkuk continued.

"I thought I was third," John replied truthfully, "but I reckon I might be wrong." He had never inquired as to how he stood relative to Kwamé.

Habakkuk nodded silently, accepting the information. After a long pause he said, "Then I don't guess you plan to come back here again."

John thought long and hard before finally replying, "No, I guess I don't."

He had never thought about that, never planned that far ahead. He had only been concerned with opposing the Heaveners, never worrying about what he, personally, would do when he no longer had a part to play in that opposition. Now that he did think about it, though, he knew he would never be happy returning to the People of the True Word and Flesh. They would never again wage war upon their neighbors, he was certain; the spirit had been destroyed, the steel stripped from their souls, by their crushing defeat at the hands of the People of Heaven. Their empire had been swallowed up by the protectorate, and John could not believe that it would ever again be the proud and independent power it had once been.

That was no place for a man like himself.

"Reckon it's just as well," Habakkuk said. "You aren't real popular around here, traitor or not."

John nodded. That, too, was true.

When the negotiations were finished he signalled the airship, eager to return home—home to the ITD headquarters in Savior's Grace.

Chapter Twenty-four

*My lips shall not speak wickedness, nor
my tongue utter deceit.*

—Job 27:4

AFTER the Chosen and the True Worders, John spent several
weeks visiting various old allies, accompanied by ITD salespeople, stopping back at Savior's Grace every so often for
more supplies and to report back to Blessing. Several tribes
had agreed to open trade with ITD, which was, for once, all
John was asking for—no military commitments or exclusive
contracts.

He had made a good trip through eastern Reuben and was
just off the airship, bound for Blessing's office, when someone called to him from across the landing field.

He stopped and looked; a woman was waving at him from
beyond the fence.

"John! Over here!" she called.

Puzzled, John turned aside, motioning to the two sales
representatives who had left the airship with him to go on
without him. He strode quickly to the fence.

The voice and figure had been familiar; the woman was
Miriam Humble-Before-God.

"What are *you* doing here?" he asked.

"I came to see you," she answered. "And maybe
Kwamé."

"Why?" John could guess why; she was probably renewing her drive for vengeance against him, and hoping to revive her friendship—if that was what it had been—with Kwamé.

"Ms. Dawes sent me."

He had not expected that. "Oh?" he said.

"Yes. Can we go somewhere else, somewhere more comfortable?"

"I have an office in the headquarters here."

"No, somewhere we can't be watched."

He glanced at her curiously. He had never asked Blessing whether his office was monitored, but in all probability it was; that was standard for all rooms in Earther buildings, even the lavatories. He had become accustomed to the idea—just as he had become accustomed to Earther lavatories and the incredible amounts of water they used. Kwamé had assured him that all the water was purified and reused, not simply wasted, but it had still taken him weeks to adjust to the idea of intentionally polluting water with his own wastes.

He had adjusted, though, and now he was bothered by the smell whenever he had to use Godsworlder facilities, and annoyed by the inconvenience of carrying a communicator with him when outside headquarters, rather than being able to talk to anyone he chose simply by addressing the ceiling.

Miriam said she was working for Dawes, and wanted complete privacy; it was easy to guess that whatever was to be said to him was something Bechtel-Rand did not want ITD to hear. That might be interesting; it might well be something he could use against Bechtel-Rand.

"All right," he said. "I know a hollow over in the rocks." He pointed with one hand and slipped the other into his pocket, checking the settings on his communicator and trying to decide whether or not to use it to record the conversation.

Miriam nodded, and he led the way up to where a rocky shelf jutted out from the hillside. A piece had broken off and slid down the slope a few yards, leaving a gap where they would be sheltered on three sides.

When they reached the spot, John turned expectantly to Miriam.

"What is it?" he asked.

"What's in your pocket?" she demanded.

"What?"

"You shouldn't wear your jeans tight, like the Earthers, if you want to hide things in the pockets—I can see you've got something there. What is it?"

Reluctantly, he pulled out the communicator. She snatched it away and tossed it down the hillside.

"You can fetch it back later, if you want," she told him.

"All right, then," he said, "you've got your privacy, Ms. Humble; what is it you wanted to tell me?"

"The People of Heaven hired me to come and talk with you because they were pretty sure you'd talk to me, where you might not talk to one of their own people. I'm not saying I like what they're doing, but they're paying me enough to buy my *own* inn, if I want, so here I am."

"What is it?"

"I just want you to understand I'm not here on my own— I'd given up my revenge. I think you deserve this, but it's not my doing."

"*What* isn't your doing? Darn it, woman, will you get to the point?"

"They don't want you working for ITD anymore; they want you to break up this Free Trade Federation if you can, but whether you do that or not, they want you to go away from here. They don't like having a native Godsworlder running things for ITD here—it's making ITD look good and the Heaveners look bad, especially when it's you, the man who fought the Earthers for so long. It makes it look like ITD belongs on Godsworld more than the Heaveners do."

"Maybe it does."

"I don't know, maybe it does—but that's not the point. Ms. Dawes wants you to stop working for ITD. She doesn't care what you do after that—her job offer is still open, she says, or you can just go home, or whatever, just stay away from ITD."

"Why should I? I don't owe her any favors!"

"She'll pay you."

"ITD is paying me, and they can match anything she can offer."

"All right, then; I was hoping it wouldn't go this far. Do you know what a videodrome is?"

"Of course—Mr. Blessing is thinking of building one here."

"Ms. Dawes *has* built one in the Citadel, and she's going to open it to the public tomorrow, free of charge. And if you're still in Savior's Grace, the first tape she'll have shown is the one of you and Tuesday Ikeya; she's had copies made, and one will go to every town in the protectorate. You'll be a laughingstock."

John stared at her silently for a long moment. "You think so?" he said at last.

"Of course! The great warrior, humbled by a mere woman!"

"I don't think that's how it'll look, Miriam. I think that if you hadn't seen that tape while you still hated me you'd know that."

Suddenly uncertain, Miriam asked, "What do you mean?"

"Think about it. The Earthers are planning to show Godsworlders an obscene tape—first off, how many do you think will actually watch it? How many of them will dare admit they watched it? Most places on Godsworld strong men still blanch when one of our saleswomen adjusts her collar; do you think they'll watch a tape of a perverted rape? And you think that if they do, after watching me and this naked slut of an Earthwoman, they'll think the worse of *me* but not of her?"

"No, but Tuesday isn't here anymore; she doesn't matter."

"Doesn't she? Do you think that your ordinary Godsworlder will think that? He'll see an Earthwoman wallowing in decadent lust. Do you think he'll say, 'Oh, that's just this one pervert'? No, he'll say, 'I knew those Earthers were bad!' "

"But, John, they'll see you naked!"

"No, they won't; she didn't get my clothes off."

"No, I mean they'll see . . . see *you!*"

"They'll see a lot more of her, as I remember it."

She stared at him. "What kind of man are you? You can stop the tape from being shown, and you won't? You don't *care* if half the population of the world watches you rutting like an animal?"

"No, actually—I *don't* care. I suppose I should, but it hardly even seems as if I'm the same person I was then. I was naive and ignorant, like most Godsworlders; I'm not anymore."

"You're still a Godsworlder."

"Am I? I haven't attended services in months; the minister here doesn't like me, and I don't like him. I'm not a member of any tribe; the True Worders have disowned me. I live here in the Earther headquarters, like an Earther myself—I eat their foods and I use their furniture."

"You're still a Christian, with morals . . ."

"Am I? I'm not sure about that. Look, I followed the rules in my tribe for all my life; I thought we had the one true path, God's intended way, and that anyone who lived differently was wrong, evil, lost—and that all those people would have to be miserable, suffering for their sins, that the only joy was to be found in Christ. Isn't that what you were taught?"

"Yes, of course!"

"Well, it's not true. The Earthers live just as they please, and they don't suffer for it. God doesn't punish them. They don't know Christ, but they're happy, happier than anyone I ever knew before they came. They're comfortable—not just physically, either, they're comfortable with each other and with themselves, most of them. They don't worry about sin. Maybe they'll all burn in Hell, I don't know, but in *this* life they're better off than Godsworlders, and a lot of it is because they don't worry about things like sin and righteousness. I'm not going to worry about strangers watching that tape—if I ever had any reputation for chastity or dignity it doesn't matter anymore. I *am* going to worry about going on with my work. I don't like Bechtel-Rand, and I don't like America

Dawes. Let her show the tape; if things get too rough for me here on Godsworld I'll leave.''

''What?''

''You heard me; if Bechtel-Rand makes me unwelcome on Godsworld there are plenty of other worlds out there.''

''You mean leave Godsworld? But you *can't!* This is your *home!*''

''Is it? I don't think I have a home anymore. Stephen Christ-Is-Risen went somewhere else when the Heaveners ruined his home; I can do the same. Listen, Miriam—you tell America Dawes that she can run that tape if she wants, but I'm not leaving ITD, and it'll hurt her business more than it'll hurt mine. She must know that.'' To himself, he added silently that Dawes must be desperate to make such a foolish attempt at blackmail.

Miriam stared at him. ''They've corrupted you. I thought you were the great fighter who would never give in!''

John shrugged. ''I'm still fighting—but for money, not for God.''

''That's disgusting!''

''Is it? Look at this way, Miriam. I haven't killed anybody since I left the Citadel, haven't ordered anyone to his death. No one from ITD ever raped anybody—except financially. Our conquests don't leave widows and orphans and burned villages; they leave a more comfortable life.''

''A year ago you heard those same arguments and denounced them.''

John shrugged. ''I was wrong,'' he said.

When Miriam had gone he sat in the rocky hollow for a moment staring at the sky and thinking.

Miriam was quite right; a year earlier he had been determined to wipe every trace of the Earthers off Godsworld, and now he was working with them, doing the best he could to expand ITD's influence, yet he wasn't aware of any great change in his thinking.

A year ago he had thought Tuesday Ikeya's empathy spike an unspeakable abomination; now he was working for a man equipped with an identical one, and other rewirings as well, and was not troubled by it.

Of course, Blessing never raped anyone, so far as he knew, but still, his own attitude had changed.

The change, he decided, had been a gradual thing, the result of working, first as a common laborer in Savior's Grace, then as ITD's local expert. He had never done common labor before that; his family had always been wealthy, by Godsworld standards, and he had entered the army as a boy of fourteen. That had been dangerous, but always exciting. He had never really seen the grinding boredom and exhaustion most people lived with. His stay in Savior's Grace had destroyed any ideas he had still held about the nobility of ordinary life on the old Godsworld. That old life was simple misery for most people, unending drudgery just to stay alive. His ancestors had been fools to give up Earther technology— even the less sophisticated technology of their time.

And working for ITD he had found the excitement of the military back in a new guise. Dawes had told him, when she spoke to him in her office those months ago, that he was not really interested in beliefs, but in using and expanding power, and she had been, he had to admit, quite right. He had hated the Heaveners for ruining his old life, destroying his position of power and privilege—but Earth had provided a replacement. He had refused the first one offered, by the Heaveners themselves, like a petulant child refusing a new puppy and demanding a dead one be brought back somehow—but he had brought ITD to Godsworld to punish Bechtel-Rand, and, worn down by his "puppyless" stay in Savior's Grace, he had taken what was offered.

He did not regret it at all.

Chapter Twenty-five

So I was great, and increased more than all that were before me in Jerusalem: also my wisdom remained with me.

—Ecclesiastes 2:9

By the local calendar it was Christmas Day, Anno Domini 2596, when the ship bearing news of Gamaliel Blessing's promotion set down at Savior's Grace. John watched the landing through his office window; he had been the first to lay claim to a window when the aboveground addition to ITD's headquarters was built, and had made sure he had a good view of the spaceport.

He already knew about the promotion; the ship had transmitted the news from orbit. What had not yet been mentioned was the name of the new planetary administrator. There were three possibilities, as he saw it: himself, currently the director of planning for all Godsworld; Premosila Kim, director of sales; or someone aboard the ship, sent from Earth to take over.

He wanted the job badly. Premosila was very good at what she did, certainly, and had perhaps the best intuitive grasp of practical psychology he had ever seen, but he had doubts about her ability to handle the job's other aspects. And a stranger from Earth would not know Godsworld the way he did. He had done a good job, he knew, helping ITD fit into Godsworld better than Bechtel-Rand ever did—the old protectorate had added no clients for two years now, while the

Free Trade Federation was everywhere on the planet. He deserved recognition for his work.

Besides, it was the only promotion open to him, and he had always wanted to be at the top of his profession.

He watched the freighter settling onto the concrete pavement—the old-line folks in Savior's Grace had put up a fuss about that pavement, but it allowed larger ships to land safely, and when it was explained that that meant lower prices, the old-line folks had been decisively outvoted.

He could stand the suspense no longer. "Get me a line to the ship," he told the wall.

"ITD vessel *Clydesdale,*" a woman's voice answered.

"This is John Mercy; can you tell me whether Mr. Blessing's replacement is aboard?"

There was a moment's hesitation before the woman answered, "Mr. Mercy, I'm just the pilot; they don't tell me what's going on, they just tell me where to put the ship. We have a company executive aboard, but I have no idea whether he's anybody's replacement."

"Oh."

"He'll be debarking in a minute; why don't you come ask him in person?"

"Thanks, I'll do that."

His duties did not ordinarily include meeting new arrivals, but this was a special case; he stood, slapped his belt to be sure his communicator was working, and headed for the field.

By the time he stepped out onto the concrete, crates were unloading themselves, sliding out through the upper hatchways and neatly stacking themselves on the waiting cargo platform. Most of the goods would have to be transferred to other containers before sale—Godsworlders were still uncomfortable around machinery that needed no human direction, and besides, the crates' brains were worth reusing.

The lower passenger hatchway was open, and three people had emerged. Two of them were ordinary ship's personnel, come aground on their own business; the third was a silver-haired man in a bizarre dark gray jacket and matching pants of a cut John had never seen before.

"Hlo and *j'sevyu,"* John said, extending a hand. "Welcome to Godsworld."

"Hlo," the stranger replied. "I'm Colin Szebenyi."

"John Mercy, director of planning."

"Ah! Good, good—glad to meet you."

"Mr. Seven-Ye . . ."

"Szebenyi."

"Szebenyi, yes. Mr. Szebenyi, I won't waste any time; why are you here? Are you Mr. Blessing's replacement?"

"Direct, aren't you? Is that the local custom, or is it just you?"

"A little of both." John noticed that Szebenyi had not answered the question.

"Ah. Well, yes. I'm here to evaluate the situation; the development committee has given me free rein. If I think it's necessary, I have the authority to take over here and run things myself, but I don't plan to—and I don't want to, either. Does that ease your mind?"

John smiled. "Yes, it does. What can I do for you?"

"Take me to Blessing, first off."

Three hours later, as Christmas Day was fading with the setting of the sun into New Year's Eve, John, Blessing, Szebenyi, Premosila, and Kwamé were gathered around the table in Blessing's office.

"It looks good," Szebenyi said.

"Thank you, sir," Blessing replied.

"You've got an outlet within ten kilometers of every village on the planet that's not exclusive to Bechtel-Rand, is that right?"

"Yes, sir."

"You've got regular airfreight running?"

"Yes."

"Stable currency?"

"Yes."

"You're buying foodstuffs, leather, this weird nearwood fungus, and plenty of handicrafts—anything else?"

"Not really, sir—Godsworld has no fossil fuels at all, since it's never had dense enough carboniferous life and has been geologically stable since before life really even got established. It's extremely poor in heavy metals and even some of the lighter ones. There's no established industry at all—the original colonists were mildly BTN, and with so little to work with—''

John interrupted. "What's BTN? I never heard that term."

" 'Back-to-Nature,' " Kwamé explained. "Antitechnology. It's a recurring problem on colony planets."

"Aren't any of the other native life-forms useful?"

"Not that we know of; there *are* no native fauna, only the fungoids—red plants, the locals call them. They aren't really fungi at all, they're a whole new category—but not a very useful one, except for nearwood. They're not biologically interactive with any terrestrial life, though in an emergency they can be eaten without ill effect. The nutritional value of the best of them is low, and the taste is like eating dirt."

John did not consider fungusmeat to be as bad as that, but said nothing.

"We'll want to put a biochemical research team on that all the same," Szebenyi said. "Let's see . . . any chance of tourism?"

"I don't think so, sir—the native culture is pretty drab." Blessing glanced at John, who made no objection. "About the only thing they ever did with real style was fight wars, and of course we put an end to that. They do have some very complex theology, which has produced interesting rituals—but interesting to anthropologists, not tourists. And really, sir, it's a pretty ugly planet. No trees, no real mountains, no beaches worth mentioning. We've had a few stockholders come around to look the place over, and every one of them got bored and left on the next ship out, so I don't think the place has any overwhelming attraction."

"All right," Szebenyi said. "That's what I'd heard from the computers. Blessing, we've got a new post for you—ITD just got the contract to open Harwood's World, and you've been named as supervisor—assuming you want the job."

Blessing nodded, smiling.

"For the rest of you, after looking things over here, I've

decided to cut back operations on Godsworld. This place is a backwater—it's always going to *be* a backwater. We'll keep up what we've got, but any expansion would be a waste of money; we're already at the point of diminishing return on our investment, because there just isn't anything here.'' He glanced at John, the only native Godsworlder in the room, but John simply stared back silently. He had long suspected that the profits to be made on Godsworld were limited. Even ITD couldn't make money from nothing.

''Mercy, you'll be taking over for Blessing for now; Kim, you'll be coming back to Earth as soon as you can get your operation here set up to run without you. Montez, you'll be taking over as second-in-command—use whatever title you like, we'll pay you the same in any case.'' He stood up. ''Any objections?''

No one spoke.

''Good. Mercy, I want to talk to you alone for a moment about what you'll be doing.'' He motioned for John to follow.

John obeyed, and the two men left the room; they strode side by side down the upholstered hallway, neither one speaking.

Szebenyi led the way to John's office; by unspoken agreement neither man sat behind the desk, but instead each took one of the crude Godsworlder chairs John kept handy for visiting locals.

When both were settled, Szebenyi said, ''Mercy, you've done good work here, despite your background.''

John nodded. ''Thank you,'' he said.

''Of course, it's your home planet, and that gives you an advantage.''

John nodded again.

''Have you ever considered moving on?''

John leaned back thoughtfully. ''Can't say,'' he said.

He had thought about leaving Godsworld, of course—particularly in those uncertain weeks when he still thought America Dawes might carry out her threat to show the tapes of Tuesday and himself publicly—but never very seriously.